GRIM DISCOVERY

Chapa forced the door open as wide as it would go. An instant later, the sun reached inside the structure again, just enough to reveal a pair of legs sprawled across the dirty concrete floor.

The victim was sitting up, but in an unnatural way, folded not at the waist, but higher up, around his rib cage. Chapa rushed inside. He squatted next to the body, grabbed the man's stiff shoulders and gently shook him.

The man's head swung from side to side like a broken toy.

Then Chapa saw the blood, caked on the white starched collar, coloring his shirt. Chapa recoiled when he spotted the gash across the victim's neck, so long and wide it looked like a grisly smile.

The blood appeared slick, which meant it was still fresh. Though Chapa figured the man's heart had stopped pumping it ten, maybe fifteen minutes ago, tops. It was an educated guess, based on years of reading coroners' reports and attending more autopsies than he wanted to remember.

The dead man could just as easily have been killed ten minutes after Chapa spoke with him, or ten minutes ago. And that's when Chapa felt a cold chill surge through his body and into his mind.

The killer might still be in here.

MOURN
THE
LIVING

HENRY
PEREZ

PINNACLE BOOKS
KENSINGTON PUBLISHING CORP.
www.kensingtonbooks.com

PINNACLE BOOKS are published by

Kensington Publishing Corp.
119 West 40th Street
New York, NY 10018

All Kensington titles, imprints, and distributed lines are available at special quantity discounts for bulk purchases for sales promotions, premiums, fund-raising, educational, or institutional use. Special book excerpts or customized printings can also be created to fit specific needs. For details, write or phone the office of the Kensington special sales manager: Kensington Publishing Corp., 119 West 40th Street, New York, NY 10018, attn: Special Sales Department; phone 1-800-221-2647.

This book is a work of fiction. Names, characters, businesses, organizations, places, events, and incidents either are the product of the author's imagination or are used fictitiously. Any resemblance to actual persons, living or dead, events, or locales is entirely coincidental.

PINNACLE BOOKS and the Pinnacle logo are Reg. U.S. Pat. & TM Off.

ISBN-13: 978-0-7860-2033-1
ISBN-10: 0-7860-2033-4

First printing: August 2010

10 9 8 7 6 5 4 3 2 1

Printed in the United States of America

For Cheri, who has been there through the good times and the not so.

Chapter 1

Baltimore, Maryland, 2005

The victim had died with money in his wallet, a loaded .22 in his jacket, and a strip of condoms in his right front pants pocket. One way or another, he'd been headed for a big night.

There had been a struggle, though not much of one. The kill had been as quick as it was decisive. A swift and determined swipe of blade across the sandy-colored skin of his neck, severing the head of the cobra tattoo that led from his chest up to his chin. A prime piece of prison ink, ruined.

The body was found alongside a nameless, moss-covered pond in McClain Park, stretched out between a cluster of trees and a large rust-bitten waste can. An early morning jogger, still working on breaking that day's first sweat, mistook the mound of humanity for some homeless guy passed out by the water—a rare sight in this part of town. Then he saw the blood, and started sweating.

Baltimore had become known for its violent crime in recent years. Turf wars and careless tourists routinely led to dead gangbangers who hadn't seen it coming and battered out-of-towners who never imagined it could happen to them.

But this one was different. This corpse didn't belong here, not in this quiet residential part of town where every house was equipped with a security system because the home-owner could afford the tab.

That was one reason the cops had arrived so quickly, even before the onlookers, though they too were there now. Two dozen or more spread out unevenly behind the police barrier. Housewives on their way back from dropping their kids off at school, men and women dressed for business, some al-ready late for work, joined by the usual array of folks who appear to have nowhere else to be.

All of them observing the lead detectives examine the body and its immediate surroundings, while a forensics team methodically set up to do its thing. A mass of curious people all watching the same thing, and generating a barely audible buzz, as though conversing any louder might wake the dead.

But not everyone is there for the same reason. One man in particular is more invested in this scene than the others. He hasn't slept, he never does before or after a killing. But no one would know from looking at him.

He is of average height, average weight, and his face is as common and forgettable as dust. The way he's dressed, this man could be mistaken for the guy in the third cubicle down the hall in any office. White shirt, blue tie, department store windbreaker, twenty-dollar haircut. Just another middle manager who hates what he does and counts the years to re-tirement.

Except this man is no middle manager, and he enjoys what he does. It's the thing that keeps him going. Someone in the crowd sees that the victim's neck has been cut from ear to ear, and whispers to no one in particular, "This makes seven—no, eight."

Staring back at a plainclothes cop who is scanning the crowd, the man thinks, *This makes nine.*

* * *

As his eyes made their second pass across the crowd, Detective Conyers realized how after a while all crowds look the same. Eighteen years on the force, the last seven as a homicide detective, had made it difficult for him to separate the faces that always seemed to be part of these scenes.

He imagined how Roman gladiators in the Coliseum might have regarded ancient spectators in the same way. Blank faces gazing at a scene that offers them only violence, death, and nothing of real value. Vain attempts to sneak a look at something they don't truly want to see.

The odor of death blended with the delicate scent of a newborn day in a way that was both perverse and familiar to Conyers. He wondered if any of the onlookers noticed it, if it made them want to turn away or just get on with their lives. Conyers doubted it.

No one stood out from the rest of the crowd. Though he'd been trained to look for anyone with a motive beyond morbid curiosity, he had never succeeded in picking out a potential suspect. Not even once, not even close. After another pass revealed nothing new or useful, Conyers gave up and glanced over at Murphy, his partner, who was dictating the details into a tape recorder as though he was ordering the usual at the corner diner.

"The vic is Hispanic. According to his I.D., he just turned twenty-four, and he definitely won't see the quarter-century mark. His name was Orlando Corpas."

Conyers interrupted, "He went by, 'Orlo.' I knew him when I was working a beat."

Murphy nodded, then went back to recording his observations.

"Orlando," he started, then looked up at Conyers, "a.k.a. 'Orlo' Corpas is now Corpas the Corpse on account of the ten-inch-long, quarter-inch-wide groove that someone opened in his neck. There are no signs of robbery."

That triggered a memory for Conyers. Turning his attention away from his partner's routine breakdown of the particulars, he began surveying the scene like someone playing that kids' search game where valuable objects are hidden within a crowded picture. Conyers knew exactly what he was looking for, but not where to find it.

He walked around the large trash can and examined it carefully, not too concerned about getting some of the grime on his street-worn brown leather coat. He glanced back at his partner, who looked up from the body, saw what Conyers was doing, and shook his head then went back to recording his findings.

Conyers next searched the paved biking and running trail. He walked thirty feet away from the body, no need to go any farther if the previous crime scenes were any indication.

Conyers knew he resembled a shabby bloodhound as he glanced down and from side to side with each measured step.

He heard one onlooker ask another, "What do you think he's looking for? A weapon? Blood splatters? Fibers?"

But Conyers wasn't searching for anything like that, the sort of evidence that too often cracks fictional TV cases wide open. He walked back toward the body, then continued down the path in the opposite direction. Again, he covered the area a few feet at a time. Again, he came up empty.

He looked back at the crime scene and saw that Murphy had finished and was now talking to Bulling, the lead forensics officer. The small grove of recently planted poplar trees stood about midway between Conyers and the body. His black leather shoes sank a little into the moist ground as he walked toward the trees, and he felt the chill on the soles of his feet.

Though spring had started to arrive on the eastern seaboard, it had thus far produced only a smattering of leaves on the trees. They provided a splash of color, which seemed out of place at that moment, under these circumstances. But there weren't enough of them to obscure much of the bark.

Conyers examined each tree from its base up to the low-hanging branches, but found nothing that shouldn't have been there. Maybe this killing was different from the others. He would check out the shoreline, but already knew that would be a waste of time. He had walked it searching for evidence when they first arrived.

Then, as he turned back to where Murphy and Bulling were still talking, Conyers noticed a lighter piece of bark along the bottom of a thick branch. He'd been so focused on the tree trunks that he'd missed this before.

Conyers squatted under the branch and looked up. There it was. If it had eyes, they would've been staring down at him.

"Bulling, come here right now."

Behind him, Conyers heard the large man moving in his direction, but he did not turn away from the branch.

"Yes, Detective?" Bulling asked, winded.

"We're going to need a photo of that."

Bulling carefully squatted and saw what Conyers was pointing at. A stick figure, comprised of an empty circular head, a torso, two short arms, and two legs had been carefully carved into the wood.

"Probably done by some kid, or a smartass with a pocket knife," Bulling said.

Conyers shook his head.

"I don't think so. In fact, I want you to cut this branch off at its base and take it back to the lab. I have a feeling you're going to find traces of the vic's blood in the grooves of that carving."

Murphy walked up as Bulling wandered off to find a camera, some tools, and an assistant to do the difficult work.

"Check this out," Conyers said, and Murphy bent down to get a look under the branch.

"A stick figure, big deal."

"Yeah, like the one we found two weeks ago, painted on a bench near that pimp's body. And remember last month's—"

Murphy cut him off.

"Con, you know what I see? I see a dead piece of shit over there by the water. I see a useless slab of meat that might've killed a kid in a drive-by a few days from now, or would've taken a shot at you, me, or one of our guys at some point down the line."

Conyers listened. He understood what Murphy was getting at, even shared many of his partner's views. But still . . .

"Listen, Murph, there's something going on here, something bigger than some bullshit turf war, and it has to end."

The man blends into the crowd that has been watching the two detectives. He understands what is happening, and knows what will happen next. The police commissioner, maybe even the mayor, will hold a press conference to reassure the public. They'll claim that two rival gangs are responsible for the recent deaths.

But something else will be going on behind the scenes. The cop in the brown leather coat is going to kick up some dust. His partner will have to go along. There will be an investigation—quiet, but thorough. In time, they will connect the killings. And maybe they won't stop there. They might start digging further back, expanding their scope.

That would be bad. And the thought of that possibility gives the man a bone-deep chill, makes his muscles tighten so much he worries someone will notice.

The man has been through this before. Three years earlier in Pittsburgh, and in Cleveland before, and in St. Louis before that. These people, like the ones in those other crime-infested places, fail to appreciate what he can do for their community. What he has been doing for them and their kids.

As far as the man is concerned, Orlo Corpas had sensed his own purpose and destiny. Orlo had helped the man, leading him to other area scum, helping him gain access to some of the worst this town had ever coughed up. Orlo had been paid for his services, and now he had paid for his crimes.

Maybe the man needs to teach Detective Conyers a few things about the value of appreciation. He'll do that, and then leave Baltimore. Walk away from a successful business, and never look back.

The man will find a new place to live—again. Change his name and appearance—again.

Things will be different next time. He'll find a town where the people appreciate his unique ability to eliminate the pimps, gangbangers, and junkies. The human trash that has polluted every place he's ever lived. And he's lived in a lot of different places, and been known by a lot of different names.

He has already chosen his next destination. A week ago the man saw a face staring back at him from pages of a trade magazine. A real success story, the guy in the photo. The self-made type. One of the Chicago area's bright new stars.

The man in the crowd knows otherwise.

He pulls the photo out of his wallet. The uneven edges of the thin paper are frayed and slightly curled. Taking his eyes off the crime scene, the man examines the black-and-white photo, just like he did earlier that morning, and the night before as he waited for Orlo to show up.

The smiling face looks up at him. Mocks him. The name is different, the hair too, but the man knows that face.

The man slips the photo back into his wallet as a feeling of absolute purpose rolls over him.

Yes, there's more work to do. Important work. Something he's been building up to for thirty years.

Chapter 2

Oakton, Illinois, present day

The next newspaper story bearing Jim Chakowski's by-line would be the biggest of his long and successful career. All Chakowski had to do now was live long enough to write it.

Chakowski knew he could not let his guard down, not for an instant. Right now his life depended on his ability to stay cool, focused, and aware. He was good on two of those three—his cool had checked out a few days ago.

Navigating through the crowded downtown street festival, Chakowski did his best to avoid eye contact, while still remaining fully in touch with his surroundings. A thousand or more people had gathered along three city blocks to listen to the REO Speedwagon cover band, drink beer, and just hang out.

Though Chakowski had grown up in Oakton—one of Chicago's largest suburbs—worked here his entire adult life, made the place his own, it all felt foreign to him now on an otherwise pleasant October evening. He'd spent more than two decades writing Oakton's story, chronicling the lives of its people—the powerful and the not so. But now he felt like a virus the city was determined to purge.

Like a familiar stranger, he sensed the edgy glances and heard the whispers, real or imagined, as he weaved past people who were too tuned in to the music, or engaged in their own conversations to know what was going on. The size and density of the crowd was preventing Chakowski from doing what he desperately wanted to do—run to his car, lock the doors, and drive away as fast as he could.

The sound of drumbeats and electric chords bounced off Oakton's century-old downtown buildings along Clinton Avenue and conspired with smoke from grills to make Chakowski's head pound and his stomach churn. He couldn't remember the last time he'd eaten, but this was no time for small concerns.

He glanced back after every few steps. Was that guy, the one in the St. Louis Cardinals cap, following him? What about that other one, over by the beer stand? Did Chakowski recognize him?

Once most of the crowd was behind him, Chakowski started walking faster, almost running, cutting down a side street, then another. The music and crowd noises fading away into the night, he rushed to his five-year-old metallic green Elantra, scanning the dark street from one end to the other before getting in.

As he emerged from his parking space, Chakowski noticed someone standing in the shadow of an alley. He thought about driving straight to the offices of the *Chicago Record*, his professional home for more than a quarter century, the only place he'd ever worked since graduating from journalism school. But he was much closer to his home, five minutes away or so, and the road didn't feel safe right now.

Chakowski would write the story at home, give it a quick revision, and email it in. Then he would drive to his office at the *Record*, and guide it through the editorial and layout process.

He kept his eyes on the sideview mirror. As he watched the orange glow of downtown Oakton being swallowed up by darkness, Chakowski estimated it would take him no more than a couple of hours to bang out a story that would change his hometown forever.

The business district now in the far distance, Chakowski noticed a set of headlights some thirty yards back. *Lots of people in Oakton,* he thought. *Even more on a night like this one, when the town throws a party. That's probably a family of four back there. Kids already asleep in the backseat.*

The headlights were still there four blocks later, then six. Right turn—still there. Chakowski's heart was trying to punch its way out of his chest. Sweat, cold and thick, gathered along his brow and washed down the middle of his back.

Chakowski gripped the wheel like it was a lifeline. No longer worried about taking the shortest way home, he turned left, sped up, then left again a block later, and fixed his eyes on the mirror.

No lights, now. The road was his, and for a moment Chakowski remembered why he loved this town.

Over the years he had turned down offers to work at bigger papers in cities that made national news much more often. He had instead dedicated himself to becoming a big frog in a midsized pond. He'd gotten to know all of the players in the city's government and business, and in the process became something of a player himself. But the ground had shifted under him over the past year, and now he finally understood why.

He leaned on the gas and kept the car moving just a bit over the speed limit. Driving down one of Oakton's wide, quiet streets, his pulse retreating toward normal, Chakowski began to wonder how much of this fear was the product of his writer's imagination.

Then Chakowski realized he had become disoriented, lost track of where he was. He turned north—no wait, west. Finally, he gave in just a little and pulled over. Peeling his hands off the wheel, Chakowski wiped the sweat from his forehead and neck, and leaned back in the driver's seat until his breathing found its natural rhythm.

As he drove off a minute later, Chakowski spotted a mailbox at the next corner. That triggered something in his mind. He pulled up next to it, popped open the glove compartment, and withdrew an envelope.

He wondered whether there was any real reason to mail it, or if the information he'd hastily cobbled together and shoved into the envelope would make any sense to anyone else. This seemed so much more important an hour ago, when Chakowski's thoughts were rabid with fear.

But Chakowski knew his concerns were real and well justified, and the reasons behind them had not changed. He stepped out of the car, peering in all four directions down the murky streets before dropping the letter into the box and hurrying back to his car.

After finding his way to a major street, Chakowski had his bearings again. He decided it was time to go home.

His house was in one of Oakton's older neighborhoods. An area that had undergone a transformation over the past decade as young couples, many with small children, had replaced the older ones. Chakowski didn't have children, and it had been some time since he'd been half of a couple. He'd lived alone all of his adult life, and now that he was in his mid-fifties, Chakowski understood it would be like that the rest of the way. He'd planned on marrying, once upon a time, starting a family, all of it, but the job always seemed to get in the way.

No, it hadn't *gotten* in the way. The job had been the way.

"You're either a good reporter or a good family man," Chakowski had once explained to his father. "Being both would require two lifetimes."

His well-maintained two-story colonial near the end of a long street of nice homes with large yards had been there for more than sixty years. Chakowski slowed to a deliberate cruise as he turned onto Dwight Street. He stared into the vague shadows that gathered around large trees and near the far end of long driveways.

Slowing down to just above a crawl, Chakowski drove past his house. Then he repeated the exercise, approaching from the opposite direction. He'd never before realized just how many hiding places his neighborhood could provide to anyone wanting to do some harm.

After the third pass, Chakowski was as convinced as he could be that no one was waiting for him in the dark. He swung the Hyundai into his driveway, then sat for a moment, letting the headlights bathe the front of his garage. Everything appeared exactly as it should.

But as he stepped out of his car Chakowski heard a jingling sound from somewhere nearby—right behind him. He ducked by the rear driver's side door, then inched toward the back of the car to get a look. Peering around the trunk of his Elantra, Chakowski saw the next door neighbor's teenaged son getting into a beater that was parked on the street. Chakowski felt foolish, and even more certain that he just needed to get this over with. Get the story written, buckle in for the fallout, then go on from there.

The only other car parked on the street was a widow neighbor's white Cadillac, right where the old woman began leaving it some years ago when backing out of her driveway started to become a challenge. The more Chakowski surveyed his surroundings, the more it looked like just another night in Oakton.

Nothing out of the ordinary. Nothing out of place. Nothing to worry about.

The house was dark, just as he'd left it. No reason to leave security lights on in this neighborhood. He wanted to approach his house as he would on any other night when he came home from work at 1 A.M., or later if he stopped to grab a drink with his colleagues. Instead, Chakowski walked to his front door the same way he'd approached his car—aware and alert, searching for any movement in the dark.

But the only moving shadow was his own, spreading across the front lawn, then climbing up the thick old ivy that clung to the façade of his house. He made a final, careful scan of his front yard and the street beyond, then keyed the lock, turned the knob, stepped inside, and quickly closed the door.

Chakowski did not turn on the lights right away, choosing instead to wait for a moment in the dark, his back pressed against the front door. Gradually, Chakowski's eyes adjusted to the darkness, and all seemed right in what he could see of his living room.

He listened for the sound of movement in his home's creaky wood floor, but heard none. Then he recognized the low-pitched buzz of the humidifier coming from his bedroom upstairs. And the hum of the refrigerator in the kitchen. He waited another minute, then two, but heard nothing else.

I'm acting like a frightened fool, he thought.

That was something Jim Chakowski had never been, and he decided right then, at that moment, that he'd filed too many hard-earned stories, tangled with far too many would-be tough guys, to start acting like a child now. Lose your nerve and it's gone forever.

This was his town, the one he'd written about and helped to define in the minds of his readers, for more than twenty-five years. And it was his life, the one he'd sacrificed to build, one byline at a time. He would not let fear enter into the equation.

Chakowski pulled back the curtain, and took a defiant look through the window at the dark, empty street beyond. Then he dropped his keys on the side table by the door and flipped the light switch. Nothing happened.

He turned back toward his living room. The light from a lamppost across the street spilled in through the window, past the curtain that he'd drawn, and reached to the far end of the room, well beyond what he could've seen before in the dark. But Chakowski didn't recognize what he saw. There were papers littered across the beige carpeting, a table was turned over, and his bookshelves had been emptied, their contents thrown to the floor.

Chakowski didn't know what to make of the sizzling sound that seemed to be moving through the walls. Then he heard a muted *pop* coming from somewhere in the basement.

But only his neighbors heard the explosion, an instant later.

Chapter 3

Interstate 80 connects New York to San Francisco, waving hello and then goodbye to several Midwestern cities along the way. But this particular westbound stretch between Toledo, Ohio, and the Indiana-Illinois border offered little of interest.

Alex Chapa watched the speedometer climb past seventy, then thought better of it, remembering that he was transporting precious cargo, and eased off the accelerator. He was about to sneak another glance at the backseat when his cell phone began playing "Daydream Believer." Until recently its ringtone had been set to "Guantanamera," the classic Cuban tune that his aunt Caridad once claimed was her signature song back when she performed at the Tropicana—*before "The Beard" ruined paradise.*

Chapa checked to see who it was, and saw *Chicago Record* on the caller I.D. He had taken two weeks off from the paper, which meant he wasn't required to give a damn about the call. It was the first time he'd been away from his job for that length of time since the birth of his daughter, more than ten years earlier.

He chose to ignore it, wondering what could be so important that someone would bother him with it during a rare off-time. There were other writers at the paper. Few with more experience, perhaps none as accomplished, but so what? He was off the clock.

Chapa let it go, and turned his attention back to the countryside racing past in dying shades of red and brown. His thoughts melting into the lonesome notes that were cascading out of a long lost saxophone and pouring in through his car speakers, Chapa focused on the road ahead, and the unique opportunities the next few days would offer.

Again, the speedometer in his late 90s Corolla slipped into the red, a fact that Chapa was alerted to by the rattling of his driver's side door handle. He eased off the gas, again. The car ran just fine at speeds beyond the legal limit, something Chapa tested on a regular basis. Despite its age, the Corolla didn't have any rust on its aqua-green exterior, the air conditioning worked most of the time, and the heater always blew hot, especially in July when the car sometimes confused the two.

But on this trip, Chapa had far more important concerns than the condition of his vehicle. For that matter, Chapa didn't much care whether he pulled into his driveway an hour early or two hours late. His priorities had shifted in a different and welcome direction.

Stan Getz was cruising through "Misty" when the phone interrupted again. Apparently, someone at the assignment desk hadn't gotten the message that Alex Chapa was not available. But it was strange that they would call twice. One call could have been an oversight, but two suggested intent. He decided to check his messages, something he hadn't done since stopping for breakfast that morning just outside of Erie, Pennsylvania.

Chapa immediately recognized a harried voice belonging to Matt Sullivan, the news editor at the *Record*.

Alex, I know you're taking some vacation time, but I could really use you back at the paper. Something

*terrible happened last night to Jim Chakowski, and
with everything that's going on right now, I need you
to step in for him as soon as you can.*

Chapa listened to the message twice. Matt Sullivan wasn't
prone to wild exaggeration or quick to panic. Chakowski
had been the paper's chief political reporter since before
Chapa started there fifteen years earlier. The veteran newsman had taken Chapa under his wing and guided him through
some difficult times.

What could've happened? Chapa wondered. *Something
terrible?* If it had been a heart attack or car accident Sullivan
would've said so. Concerned for his friend, he tried to think
of a way to find out without calling the paper. When he came
up dry, Chapa let out a long breath, and phoned his editor.

"It's awful, Alex. They're blaming it on a gas leak, maybe
some bad electrical wiring, or a combination of the two."

"How did it happen?"

"Damned if I know. But it was an old house, and it had
old wiring and probably even older pipes." It sounded like
Sullivan was making no effort to hide the tension in his
voice. "You're heading back, right? On your way home?"

"That's right. What was Jim working on?"

Chapa felt himself slipping back into investigative reporter mode. His instincts muscling out everything else.

"The usual, local business news, some politics. I'm sure
there was a pet story or two that he was tracking. But Chakowski is like you."

Chapa noticed Sullivan's use of present tense—Chakowski *is* like you. It would take a while for a lot of folks to
get used to the idea that someone as vital as Jim Chakowski
was gone, just like that.

"I take that as a compliment, Matt. But like me, how?"

"You both have a habit of telling me what you're up to on
a need-to-know basis. As a result, your editor sometimes
doesn't know much."

Chapa liked Sullivan. The guy didn't always hold his own against the brass, but he was one of the good guys and very good at his job.

"Look, Matt, I'd love to help out, I think you know how I feel about Jim, but I don't know squat about his beat," Sullivan was trying to sneak in a word or two, but Chapa didn't let him. "And even if I did, I've got other plans for the next several days."

"I know you do, and I respect that, but it wouldn't take much time, not really. Jim already had a couple of stories in the pipeline, and I could scale back the number of column inches you'd have to fill."

Chapa wanted to think about this situation, and told Sullivan that, then signed off before his editor could pitch it to him again. Part of him felt he owed it to Chakowski. Who else could take over? No one. Then there was the issue of job security, or rather the lack of it. Sullivan had been decent enough to avoid bringing that up. But Chapa, like most other newspaper reporters in the twenty-first century, had no guarantee of still having a job next month, or even next week.

Those were the simple realities of working in an outdated industry, and several years of falling revenues and budget cuts had left him vulnerable to the next wave of layoffs. He was well paid and a columnist, both of which made him expendable. Taking over an existing beat could buy Chapa an extra week on the job, and maybe that could lead to an extra month, perhaps longer.

He took his eyes off the road long enough to sneak a glance in the direction of the backseat, and reasoned that doing what his editor was asking would only take him away for three or four hours a day, tops. When Sullivan called back a short while later, Chapa didn't hesitate.

"I'll do it, Matt, but I get overtime for the next two weeks."

"I can do that."

"And none of this counts as vacation time."

"A little tougher to pull off, but consider it done."

"Give me the address."

"806 Dwight Street, it's over by—"

"I know where it is, I've lived in Oakton for a long time. I'll be there in less than two hours."

As Chapa put the phone back into a cup holder that was still sticky from a minor coffee spill a week earlier, he heard his traveling companion stirring in the backseat. He took a look in his rearview and saw her eyes open.

"Hi Daddy," Nikki said in a voice that was still more asleep than awake. "Did I hear my favorite song playing on your cell phone?"

Chapter 4

Three days earlier

Chapa stood in the middle of what he now understood to be the living room, though it was at least four times the size of an apartment he'd once rented. Unlike the other three large rooms he'd been led through on his way there, this one was two stories in height.

Carla was looking down at him from a balcony on the second floor. She smiled, nodded, turned then vanished, only to reappear across the room from him a minute later.

"You look good, Alex."

Carla looked better. She always had. Chapa wondered if his ex-wife had some work done, but he knew she didn't need any. Carla's high cheekbones, like her light blue eyes and thick blond hair, all came naturally.

She walked toward Chapa, then stopped just a couple of feet from him, like she wasn't sure whether to hug him, offer a handshake, or do nothing at all. Chapa didn't move, and he wasn't interested in any niceties, let alone physical contact. The smell of her fragrance, deceptively gentle, encircled him like a coy predator.

"You could've called, let us know you were coming, Alex."

Chapa shrugged. "I was in the neighborhood. The court order says our time together begins today. Would you like to read it again?" he started to reach inside his jacket.

Carla shook her head and turned away.

This was Chapa's first trip to Boston. The first time he'd been to the house his daughter had moved to with her mother and stepfather. Several years of court battles had seen his ability to have some say over his child's life dwindle down to an afterthought.

Chapa hadn't spoken with Nikki for more than two weeks, and had not seen the ten-year-old in nearly six months. When Carla began making some noise about her husband Stephen adopting Nikki, Chapa fired his attorney and replaced him with a far more aggressive one. Though he was still trying to figure out how he would manage to afford the guy, his new lawyer wasted no time in shutting down any talk of an adoption and doing what he could to make certain Chapa's rights as a father were protected.

"Where's Nikki?"

"She'll be home in a short while. We're part of a carpool, and today it's one of the other moms' turn to bring her home."

"If I'd known that I would've picked her up from school."

"No need. She'll be home soon."

Chapa nodded, then continued to take in his surroundings. Lush carpeting gave way to tiles that disappeared down each of the four hallways leading to the rest of the house. Various tchotchkes, which Chapa assumed had come from other countries the couple had visited, rested on tables and otherwise useless pedestals. A mirror that had been placed far too high on a wall for anyone to look into, reflected the elaborate light fixture hanging from the middle of the ceiling.

"Alex, are you sure you can take care of her?"

"She's my daughter. I took care of her for six years. I'm not new at this."

Chapa saw the concern on his ex's face. No matter his problems with Carla, and they were great in both number and scope, he knew she had worked to be a good mother from the moment Nikki was born. Though Chapa also understood it wasn't something that came naturally to her.

Some of the choices she'd made for their daughter troubled him. He had objected to the way Carla's new husband had been brought into his daughter's world. There had been very little time for Nikki to adjust to a major change in her young life.

So many changes in such a short time.

"She's a small child, she'll adapt," was how Carla had defended her decision.

He had fought the decision to move to Stephen's hometown of Boston, where his family had established a name for itself five generations ago and spent the last hundred years building a series of successful businesses.

But none of Chapa's objections had ever made much of an impression on Carla. Until now.

Standing in the middle of the multi-million dollar home in one of Boston's most exclusive neighborhoods, he knew the polite thing to do was ask how things were going, and about her legal career and her husband's various real estate deals. But Chapa was never much into small talk. And he knew he'd never get over the fact that Carla had taken his daughter from him, then done everything in her power to keep them apart.

"Nikki's homework?" Chapa asked, breaking through the heavy silence.

"Will be waiting for her every morning, along with her assignments. She just has to log on to the school's site and put in her password. Have you been able to afford a computer?"

Chapa was poised to deliver a response he might later regret, when the sound of a door closing stopped him. He turned and saw Stephen put down a briefcase and start walking toward them. Carla's husband was wearing a beige suit that clung to his sides as his brown loafers clacked across the floor. There was some sort of a bright green shirt under his sport coat that maybe harkened back to his preppier, Reagan-worshiping days. He forced a smile across his face as he extended a hand in Chapa's direction.

Chapa didn't take him up on the offer, instead he simply stared at the Boston Celtics polo shirt inside the thousand-dollar suit.

"I know, kind of loco," Stephen said without prompting. "It was a casual day, and we decided to take a golf meeting. A conference on the fairway, if you will."

Chapa had never liked Stephen, and it wasn't just that he'd married his ex-wife, and conspired to take his daughter from him, though that would be more than enough. Stephen was decent, more or less, and very successful, but also something of a schmuck. He just didn't come across as a regular guy. Chapa didn't like the way Stephen wouldn't look him in the eye, his gratuitous use of foreign words and phrases, and his chronically soggy handshake. The fact that he was a Celtics fan made Chapa dislike him all the more.

Chapa looked at his watch, then back at Carla.

"Any minute, Alex," she said. "But she doesn't even know you're here. None of us knew you were coming. Maybe we should all ease into—"

"I have twelve days with my daughter. It's not much, but it's the most time I've had with her in two years. I'm not going to wait until you've decided we've *eased* into it enough."

"Let's turn down the heat a little, why don't we, no need for agita," Stephen said, then smiled wide, exposing dueling rows of unnaturally white teeth. "If there's anything I can do to make all of this run smoothly, just ask. That's how I roll."

Then Stephen affected what Chapa assumed was supposed to be a look of empathy. "Alex, just like you, our first concern is what's best for our Nikki."

Chapa nodded as he let all of it sink in. Cocking his head away from Carla, he said, "Can we have a word, just you and me?"

"Sure, which room would you prefer, mon ami?"

"Like I give a shit," Chapa said, then noticed how the expressions on their faces suggested this house was at the epicenter of a *No Swear Zone.*

Chapa pointed to a door in the next room. Stephen nodded his approval and asked him to lead the way. They walked into a home office any Manhattan CEO would be proud to call his own. One wall was lined with bookshelves, another with framed photos of Stephen with various celebrities and politicians. A large window behind an oak desk looked out over lush green grounds that were neatly landscaped. But there wasn't a hint of playground equipment or any sign that a child had ever set foot on the evenly trimmed grass.

"Would you like a drink, Alex, there's probably a lot you and I—"

Chapa interrupted him by invading his personal space, close enough that he could smell how Stephen's expensive cologne was competing with his overpriced aftershave. Chapa wasn't wearing either.

"If you ever try to take my child from me again—"

"Alex, I wouldn't—" Stephen started, but Chapa stopped him by raising a single finger.

"If you ever try to take my child from me again, I will punch those veneers through the back of your fucking throat. Do you understand me?"

"Of course."

"Good. That's how I roll," Chapa said, then smirked, and added, "Capiche?"

Chapa heard the front door open. He hurried past Stephen, who started to say something, and stepped out into the hallway. Nikki was wiping her feet on the mat, a bulging back-pack draped over one shoulder.

She looked up, and her face was overtaken by a sponta-neous smile.

"Daddy!"

Nikki broke into a full sprint as Chapa knelt down and extended his arms in anticipation of the massive hug that was rushing toward him.

Chapter 5

In the two days since he'd left Boston, Chapa had formed a mental checklist of all the things he and Nikki were going to do. He had figured out how to cram a year's worth of bonding into a single week. But now things had become a bit more complicated.

Just past Hammond, Indiana, a few traffic-heavy miles shy of the Illinois border, Chapa pulled over at a rest stop. While Nikki stretched her legs and used the bathroom, Chapa made a call. Erin Sinclair had never met Nikki. The six months that she and Chapa had been dating coincided with his time away from his child.

"How soon will you two be here? I can't wait."

"It might be a little longer than I had planned."

He explained about Chakowski and his new assignment, worried that she might think he was a jerk for splitting some of the time he had planed to spend with Nikki.

"What if I take some vacation time?" Erin asked without hesitation or prompting. "That way Nikki can spend a few hours at my house each day and do her homework."

Chapa had thought about asking her for help, but dismissed it as being too much to ask. That's just how Erin was, though. Generous, kind, and nothing like Carla. One of these days maybe Chapa would even get around to telling Erin how he felt about her.

"You truly are wonderful," he said.

"How wonderful?"

"Really, really wonderful."

"Thank you, Mr. Articulate. So you write for a living, huh?"

Chapa laughed. Erin had a way of making him do that. Their relationship was an easy one. Short on conflict, full of good times.

"Mike is so looking forward to meeting her," Erin said. "This will give him someone to play with during the day, despite their age difference."

Chapa had wondered about how Nikki would get along with Erin's five-year-old son. Neither child had grown up with siblings, or a father around the house.

While he fought to block out the roar of passing semis and listened to Erin lay out her plans for the next few days, Chapa watched a small girl, just a couple of years younger than his own, struggling to do a cartwheel in the grass along the side of the rest stop. The child's father was too busy doing something on his handheld to notice how determined the girl was to get just one right. He didn't see her smile like she owned the world every time she came close to completing a circle and landing on her feet. Or the way she kept looking at him to see if he was watching her.

Having grown up without a father, Chapa knew how much a flash of approval from a parent, or the lack of it, could mean to a child, and couldn't understand how this man could be so detached from his daughter. Chapa never wanted to be that guy, but a part of him wondered if Nikki already thought he was.

Chapter 6

Chapa reached into the inside pocket of his black leather coat and pulled out his press pass. He draped the lanyard around his neck as he approached the police barrier that had been established half a block from what was left of Jim Chakowski's house.

The smell of burnt wood and wet leaves punctuated the air in a way that reminded Chapa of every other autumn he'd spent in the Midwest. But in this case, the sharp scent of ashes that pierced his senses was not from discarded brush.

Under normal circumstances, Chapa would have waited for the right moment, ducked under the yellow tape, and walked toward the house like it was the most natural thing he could do. But having his ten-year-old daughter at his side made these circumstances anything but normal.

"That's as close to the scene as you're gonna get."

Chapa turned and saw Sean Moriarity, a reporter for the rival *Fox Valley Times*, walking toward him. Moriarity was a few years younger than Chapa, but his reddish nose and last call eyes made him look much older.

"I see you have a sidekick," Moriarity said, looking down at Nikki. "Has the *Record* relaxed its age requirements for interns?"

"This is my daughter."

Nikki took that as a cue. She stepped forward and extended her hand to Moriarity, who responded by rubbing the top of her head.

"Tough break about Chakowski."

Chapa nodded.

"Have you heard anything new while you've been here?" Chapa asked as he scanned the crowd.

A few of the faces seemed vaguely familiar, but after working as a reporter in the Oakton area for nearly two decades, seeing faces that he maybe recognized had become an everyday thing for him.

"No, Chapa, not this time."

"*Not this time*, what?"

"You're not going to milk me for info, give nothing in return, then scoop me," Moriarity said, then leaned in close and pointed a finger at Chapa. "Not this time."

Chapa grabbed Moriarity by the elbow and pulled him away from some of the folks who were trying to sneak a look at the action beyond the barrier.

"Do you really think this is about me beating you to a story?" Chapa said in a low, steady voice. "I thought you understood me better than that, Sean. Jim's dead. He was a good man. He was one of us."

Moriarity was looking down at his shoes.

"That's what this is about, Sean."

In any other situation, Chapa might've been delivering a line, just his way of playing the competition. He'd worked Moriarity for crucial details more than once before, but it wasn't like that this time. He meant every word.

"The official story is that faulty wiring set off the blast," Moriarity said, flipping through his palm-sized notepad.

"That must have been some blast."

"Much of the electrical in the house was old, most of it original. As best as they can figure, there was a spark near the furnace, and that's what blew."

Chapa had already assumed much of this. Chakowski's house, like the others in the neighborhood, dated back to the 1940s. Chapa had lived in a house like that once and knew how the various wiring, heating, and plumbing systems seemed to conspire and take turns breaking down.

"There's something else." Moriarity sighed. "One of the neighbors, a middle-aged woman named Laura Simpson, said she saw a guy who looked like a repairman walking around Chakowski's house yesterday afternoon."

"Did she give you a description?"

"He was dressed like a repairman."

Over the years Chapa had often noticed that Moriarity wasn't big on details, and even the standard Who, What, Where, When, Why, and How of a story seemed to elude him sometimes.

"Is she still around?"

Moriarity hastily scanned the crowd.

"No. She's slim, has light-brownish hair."

"Did you get her address or phone number?"

"Why would I need those?"

Nikki walked over to them. Chapa was pleased with the way his daughter had quietly waited while he talked to Moriarity, though he sensed she'd been listening to them the entire time.

"Hey, Daddy, didn't you say we were going to go back to the police command center that we passed when we were driving in here?"

"Command center? They've set up a command center, and you didn't tell me, Alex?" Moriarity said before Chapa could ask his daughter what we she was talking about.

Moriarity glared at Chapa, who was too bewildered to do anything but shrug, then he squatted down to Nikki's level.

"Okay, little girl—"

"Nikki."

"Right. Do you remember what direction you and your daddy came from?"

"Oh, you want to find the command center."

Moriarity nodded, as his face produced something resembling a smile.

"You just go back down this street," she said, pointing away from the crime scene. "Turn left, then I think you turn right, like a block or two later, and you can't miss it. Right, Daddy?"

Chapa stood silent, mouth open wide, as he slowly and involuntarily shook his head in a neutral direction that suggested neither *yes* nor *no*.

"You're a real piece of work, you know that, Alex?" Moriarity said, and started to walk away, then stopped. "Chapa, you are dirty people."

With that, Moriarity disappeared into the crowd. Chapa turned to Nikki, who responded with a wide smile.

"We don't tell lies, Nik."

Her smile vanished.

"I'm sorry. I knew that you wanted to sneak past the policemen and you wouldn't be able to do that as long as that other newspaper man was around."

Chapa had imagined that their short time together would be filled with fun, bonding activities, the sort that would create new memories for Nikki to take back with her to Boston. Having to act as a disciplinarian had not been on his to-do list.

"We're going to talk about this later."

"Okay, Daddy. But in the meantime, it looks like the policemen have wandered off."

Chapa looked back toward the barrier and saw that she was right. The nearest uniform was at least twenty yards away.

"Nikki, listen to me. Stay right here by the tape, and don't talk to anyone."

She nodded. "Stay here. Got it."

Chapa took one last look around, zipped his well-aged black leather jacket up over his press pass, then ducked under the tape and started walking in the direction of Chakowski's house as though he belonged there.

Chapter 7

Scraps from what had been the front of Jim Chakowski's home just twenty-four hours earlier littered the street, sidewalks, and yards. The structure resembled a madman's idea of a playhouse. Most of the first level was now exposed, and the upper floor threatened to come crashing down at any moment.

Except for the debris dotting the lawns, the neighboring homes appeared unaffected, but Chapa assumed some had been evacuated as a precaution. He didn't have to write down any notes, Chapa knew the moment he saw it this was one image that would linger.

Still, he knew what Matt Sullivan would want from the only journalist to make it to the business side of the police line, so he flipped on his camera phone. Chapa had just about framed the shot when he felt a hand on his shoulder, then got spun around before he could do anything about it.

"Goddamn it, Chapa."

Tom Jackson, an officer with the Oakton force for twenty-two years, was not happy. In his wrinkled overcoat, a detective's notepad in one hand, Jackson looked like he'd just walked off the cover of an old pulp crime novel.

"We set up that barrier for a reason."

"I assumed it was for the safety of others and to aid me in my pursuit of an exclusive."

Jackson was a lifelong resident of the city he now worked to protect. Tall, built solid, with dark black hair, deep brown eyes, and simple features, he looked younger than he actually was. A former starting tight end in college who'd been known more for his blocking skills than his pass-catching, the detective looked like he could still line up across from the best defensive linemen, and maybe even teach them a few things.

Chapa got on well with Jackson, who had been a valuable source of information on more than one story. But things had changed in the past couple of years. A new administration in City Hall had brought a heightened sense of paranoia among all government employees. That, in turn, had led to a much greater level of secrecy at every level and in each department. This was especially true among the city's police.

Cops, some in uniform some not, and various official people in suits moved around the scene like scattered ants. Chapa made a mental note of how many there were and what they appeared to be doing.

"Alex, I'm already having to deal with every big shot in town worming their way past the barrier. Now if you would please, get the hell—" Jackson stopped, his eyes fixed on something beyond Chapa.

Chapa turned, expecting to confront one of Jackson's superiors, but instead saw Nikki walking toward him. If Chapa didn't know better he might have assumed she belonged there.

"What is that child doing out here?" Jackson asked everyone and no one in particular.

"She's my daughter," Chapa said, then turned to Nikki. "And she and I are going to have a lot to talk about."

"What is this, Chapa? You know better than to bring a child to a crime scene."

Nikki mouthed *I'm sorry* as she moved to her father's side.

"I asked her to stay behind the line, Tom. I apologize."

Jackson waved off two uniforms who were on their way over to help.

"It's just as the initial reports stated, Alex. An explosion due to old wiring gone bad."

One of the city workers, a bearded man with a bowler's physique, tossed a large slab of wall on top of another, making a loud noise that caused Nikki to flinch. Chapa put his arm around her shoulders, and pulled her close against his side.

"Was there anyone else in the house at the time?"

"No."

"Did you find anything unusual, out of the ordinary?"

"You mean besides the fact that half the house isn't there anymore? No."

"What about that repairman Laura Simpson saw walking around the house?"

"No. Wait, what? Who?"

"Laura Simpson, a neighbor, said she saw a suspicious man dressed in service clothes stalking the house earlier in the day."

Jackson signaled to a younger man, mid-twenties, neatly overdressed the way upstarts and wannabes often are. A moment later, Jackson was holding a clipboard with the names and addresses of each of the neighbors.

"Okay, yeah, she lives at that one," Jackson said, pointing to a brick ranch across the street and one house down from Chakowski's. "She probably saw nothing that seemed unusual until after the fact. Happens all the time."

Chapa heard a five-man crew of engineers debating how to best secure the ruins and keep the rest of the house from collapsing into an enormous pile of rubbish.

"She seemed pretty credible to me, Tom."

"I'll talk to her. Now will you get out of here."

"And you'll let me know if she has any new info?"

"No, I won't, not after this stunt of yours."

"Fine, then I'll call you," Chapa said as he took another look around. He was trying to figure out how to sneak a photo when he saw that Nikki was staring at a piece of wall, about six feet in length, at the end of the driveway.

"She needs to get away from that, Alex, now."

Chapa called to Nikki, but she continued to drift toward the jagged slab of plaster. He hadn't noticed when she wandered off, and now wished that both of them had stayed behind the barrier.

Nikki was standing over the battered remains from Chakowski's living room when Chapa reached her. It looked like a piece of wall neatly covered in beige wallpaper, except for the splash of dried blood and organic matter along one side.

Chapa's first instinct was to lie to her about what it was. But he realized there was no point in doing that. Nikki knew exactly what she was looking at.

He wrapped his arms around his daughter and turned her away from the carnage.

"Sorry about that, Alex," Jackson said, with a look of honest concern. "The techs didn't want to clear these pieces away just yet, part of figuring out exactly where the victim was when it happened."

"Jim Chakowski."

"What?"

"The *victim* had a name."

"Right, he was one of yours."

Chapa felt Nikki hug him tighter as they started to walk back toward the barrier.

"I'll call you, Alex."

This didn't bring Chapa as much comfort as it normally would, as it might have a minute ago. With his arm curled snugly around Nikki's shoulders, as he calmly walked her away from the crime scene, Chapa wondered what would be the right balance between scolding his daughter for first lying, then not listening to him, while also comforting her. This was not how the week was supposed to unfold.

"What you saw back there—"

"I know, Dad, it was some sort of an accident that happened to a friend of yours." She smiled up at him.

"We'll talk more, later."

"It's okay, really."

Should he say more about it now? Chapa did not know what to do, and didn't like that feeling. He thought about calling Erin and telling her what happened, but that didn't seem right, either.

Then Chapa saw a woman standing in the front yard of the house Jackson had said belonged to Laura Simpson. She was wearing a light blue denim shirt, a pair of jeans, and casually watching the goings on. Her light brown hair, streaked with gray or maybe it was the other way around, was pulled back away from her soft face. She was wearing makeup, but not too much, just enough to tell herself it was okay to go out in public. Chapa recalled Moriarity's thin description, and decided this woman matched it, more or less.

Chapa looked back to where Jackson had been a moment earlier, and saw him standing near the house, talking to a man who was wearing a hard hat and a tool belt. Jackson seemed to be listening intently as the guy pointed toward the sagging ceiling.

"Nikki, I need to talk to this lady over here. Stay with me and don't say anything."

She replied with a nod and a smile, which made Chapa a bit uneasy.

Chapter 8

The man goes about the task of surveying the wreckage where a house had been just a day earlier. He's there on official business. He's not an engineer, cop, or safety inspector, more of an interested party. Why wouldn't he be?

No one stopped him when he casually walked around the police barricade. In fact, he was greeted with respectful nods, and friendly handshakes. The way important men should be treated.

The damage from the explosion is worse than he'd expected, but its result was exactly what was intended. Still, he gets no joy from seeing the scattered remains of a perfectly fine house or those of its owner. And the man wishes that Jim Chakowski had been able to understand—no, more than understand—*appreciate*, his work.

He scans the area, looking for familiar faces, and sees more than a dozen people who know him by his current name, and that makes him feel good. That makes the man feel like a vital member of the community. He's building something here in this town. And he's also being more careful about his work. Only one other person knows what actually happened here in this peaceful section of Oakton, and he's not going to be talking to anybody.

There's a new person on the scene, now. Someone whom the man recognizes as Alex Chapa, a reporter from the same newspaper as the deceased. Is he here to pay his respects, or just after the story? The man doesn't know much about Chapa, they've never met.

But the man does know about Chapa's reputation for breaking big stories. And he's heard that Chapa is popular with readers, but less so downtown, or with members of the police department.

Chapa is talking to that cop Jackson. They don't appear to agree on much, which means the reporter is here for the story, not for his colleague. The man watches as a child wanders into the area. This is no place for a little girl. She appears to belong to Chapa, but why doesn't he stop what he's doing and get her out of here right now?

The man doesn't like what he sees. He pretends to go about his business, but keeps an eye on Chapa and the child, watches the little girl wander off, sees her frail body tighten as she approaches the bloodstained piece of wall. The man fights the urge to run over and pull her away. There are certain things no child should ever be exposed to. Every parent should know that. Chapa should know that. There's something very wrong with Alex Chapa and the way he cares for his child.

Maybe this was just a lapse in judgment for Chapa. Or maybe it's something worse. The man closes his eyes, so tightly that his entire face aches, and drives away his thoughts about Alex Chapa and his daughter.

There's no room for that now. He must stay focused on the task at hand. Looking back at the house, the man smiles, knowing that another obstacle is gone, and he can go on with his work. He's so close now. Just five more days. A few more tracks to cover.

He sees Chapa and the little girl walking away, heading back to safety. But then Chapa walks over to that woman across the street and starts talking to her. Still on the job. The man decides that Chapa is not just clueless, he's irresponsible, and probably unfit.

The man knows how to deal with the unfit. They're just stick figures pretending to have a mind, a heart, a soul—nothing more. They are less than human. He'll deal with Chapa, in time, but first he has a more immediate, a more *personal* goal to achieve. One that he has been chasing for most of his life.

Chapter 9

Laura Simpson didn't add much to what she had already told Moriarity, though it wasn't for a lack of trying. She'd seen a man in service clothes around Chakowski's house the morning before the explosion.

He was tall, no wait, maybe that was just the way he looked because of the shadows. There may have been two of them, but probably not. Must've been the same man, but he'd been there for a while so she could've assumed there were two. She was sure of that, just about.

After ten minutes of this, Chapa became certain that given enough time Laura Simpson would've eventually identified the man she saw as Sasquatch, the Jersey Devil, and Elvis, maybe.

"I probably should've been more suspicious," Laura Simpson had said.

"Why would you have been? It's a nice neighborhood, doesn't look like anything bad ever happened around here until now. You couldn't have known."

Chapa had spent two decades interviewing witnesses, and this sort of thing was nothing new to him. People's recollections are tricky, elusive. They can be easily led astray by their own expectations or that of others. This is especially true when the person does not realize in the moment that they're witnessing something that could be important later on. But the one thing her general confusion couldn't override was the fact that someone had been at Chakowski's house just hours before the place blew.

Still, Chapa concluded that there was nothing unusual about the man Laura Simpson had seen. If he had not been wearing work clothes, that might've been different. But as it stood, the most likely explanation was that the guy was reading a meter, or there on Chakowski's request. Chapa felt confident the police would reach the same conclusion.

Chapa was driving over the Mike Ditka Bridge on his way to the part of Oakton where he had grown up, when Nikki started asking questions.

"So do you do a lot of investigating when you write a story? Do you work with the police? Why do other reporters not like you too much?"

"Other reporters tend to like me just fine as long as I don't lie to them. Where did you come up with a term like 'command center'?"

"I watch a lot of sci-fi, especially space travel and old alien invasion movies and TV shows. There's usually a command center."

He gently, yet forcefully, scolded her about lying and butting in when he was working.

"I'm sorry, Daddy. I just wanted to help. I wanted to be a part of it."

"I understand. But the next time you want to help out, check with me first."

Downtown Oakton had undergone a transformation over the past four years. The sort of revival that many towns in the Chicago area had spent a decade or more using their resources to achieve. Rundown buildings, empty storefronts, and crumbling streets had given way to new shopping strips and businesses.

There had been claims of corruption and sweetheart deals

as an epidemic of cronyism had swept through the area. But most folks in town didn't seem to care much about that sort of thing as long as there were places they wanted to go and somewhere to park once they got there.

As they cruised past various landmarks of Chapa's youth, he wondered what a drive like this with his own father might've been like. Francisco Chapa was just shy of thirty, a dozen years younger than his son was now, when he went missing in Havana.

Francisco had said he was going for a walk and left their home in the city's Vedado neighborhood around midnight, having stopped by his young son's room to kiss the sleeping child on the forehead. Alex would later say he had dreamt that this father had told him to look out for his mother. This was one in a series of unusual details surrounding Francisco's actions that night, which, over time, had led Chapa to believe his father knew something bad was going down soon.

But most of Chapa's recollections and images of his father were second and third hand. The sort of information that, as a veteran reporter, he'd long ago learned to distrust. His own memories were no more reliable. They were as two dimensional and black-and-white as the photos in his mother's albums. Chapa had tried to color them in from time to time, adding shades and hues to the people and places that filled the four years he spent in Cuba. But Chapa knew he was just guessing. No more certain than an artist who tints a decades-old photo.

A friend of the family told them that he'd seen Francisco in the company of four official-looking men about two hours after he'd left home. Three days later, a member of Castro's government, a bony man decked out in military fatigues that were at least two sizes too big, showed up at their house. Chapa remembered hearing the knock and rushing to the door, certain that his father was on the other side. But another thought crossed his mind as he began to open the door—*Why didn't my dad use his key to get in?*

The man who stood in the doorway was wearing the uniform that had become familiar to all Cubans since the communist takeover. As was the norm with Castro's henchmen, he had a thick beard, and young Alex had been taught what that meant.

"Alejandro, you see those men standing on the corners with their guns?" Francisco Chapa asked his son one day as they drove back from the market with less than half of what they'd been promised and only a fraction of what they'd need just to get by.

"You mean the soldiers?"

"No. Soldiers shoot foreign enemies, not their own people. Those are not soldiers. Soldiers don't have beards. Whenever you see American war movies, the soldiers never have beards. John Wayne could not have captured Iwo Jima if he'd had a beard."

Francisco pointed at a trio of bearded revolutionaries, rifles strapped over their shoulders, smoking cigarettes and harassing a pair of teenaged girls.

"Those are H-D-Ps."

"H-D-Ps?"

"Yes, and you do not want to grow up to be one."

A month later, Alex and his father were on a bus headed for the beach when a revolutionary got on. He was dressed in fatigues that smelled like they hadn't been washed in weeks, lunch pail in hand, apparently on his way to work.

The boy stared at the man for a moment, noticing how odd his uniform seemed mixed in with a busload of civilians, then elbowed his father, pointed at the bearded passenger and said, "Look, Dad, it's an H-D-P!"

Several folks sitting nearby pivoted to see who had said that. An old man ignored it, as his wife fought to suppress a laugh. Francisco immediately covered his son's mouth, and turned the boy's head so that it appeared like he had seen something or someone outside the window.

Francisco quietly scolded his confused son, who did not yet understand that *H-D-P* was short for *Hijo de Puta*, or *Son of a Bitch*. Alex Chapa had been told that story many times by his mother as well as several other relatives. It was a favorite of his, and at times he believed he actually remembered the event. But he'd never be entirely sure.

One thing he was certain of. If he'd known at age four what H-D-P meant, he would've yelled the insult even louder. *Especially* if he'd known what it meant.

Chapa wondered now, as he drove past his old high school and pointed out the place where the engine of his first car had caught fire, what impact the memories from this week would have on Nikki. He'd seen so little of her over the past year, and feared that the next decade might hold more of the same.

It was just past five when they pulled into the parking lot of the *Chicago Record*. Despite its name, the newspaper was headquartered in a quiet suburb, roughly thirty miles west of the city. The *Record*'s coverage area extended from the Loop and all parts of the city, to its suburbs, some more than fifty miles from Lake Michigan.

The day staff was still knocking around as Chapa and Nikki made their way through the newsroom. Duane Wormley leaned out of his cubicle, and appeared ready to greet Chapa with one of his half-assed barbs, when his attention was diverted by the sight of a child.

Wormley was one of the *Record*'s most widely read writers. Though as far as Chapa was concerned the man had never filed a single hard news story, wouldn't know how to write one even if his life depended on it.

"Hey Duane, working on something big, no doubt. Let me guess, a pull-no-punches expose on the seedy side of candle parties?"

"Is this Take Your Child to Work Day? I don't think it is. I don't think it's Take Your Child to Work Day, Alex."

"You know darn well it's not, Duane. Otherwise you'd be at your mom's place of employment."

"My mother doesn't work, and that wasn't very nice, Alex."

"Okay, then you'd be with your mom picking up her unemployment check."

"Daddy, that was even less nice," Nikki said with a smile that reminded Chapa of the young face he'd seen in his mother's photos of himself.

Matt Sullivan emerged from his office. Sullivan looked as he always did, like he was wearing someone else's discarded clothes. The bottom of his white shirt had been recently and hastily shoved into his dark brown pants. Sullivan's worn black leather belt was narrower in those places where his gut had pressed against it, week after week, month after month. Chapa was surprised that he was still wearing his tie, though the shirt collar was open, and the knot was a good four inches below Sullivan's second chin.

"Alex, I'm glad you're here. We gotta—" he stopped and pointed at Nikki. "Um, what—"

"She is what we call a child, Matt. This one happens to be my daughter."

He could almost see the light go on in his editor's head as Sullivan remembered that Chapa had plans before he got the phone call. Sullivan's demeanor changed in an instant as he introduced himself and explained to Nikki that her father was a very important reporter.

"I know," she said, no hesitation. "I wouldn't have it any other way."

Sullivan smiled. "Yeah, she's your kid all right. We need to talk, Alex."

"Give me a second," Chapa said, and led Nikki over to a cubicle where a man in his early twenties wearing a black

Nine Inch Nails T-shirt under a plaid long sleeve button-up was pounding away at a keyboard.

"This is Zach, he's an intern, but we don't hold that against him."

The young man swiveled around to face them. If the T-shirt didn't already constitute a clear dress code violation, the Kane County Cougars cap he was wearing backwards sealed the deal.

"Alex Chapa, journalistic rock star," Zach said.

Four cubicles away, Duane Wormley chortled loudly enough for everyone to hear.

"Zach is a good guy, a terrific writer, and best of all, he plays cool computer games when no one is looking."

Zach smiled and offered Nikki a fist bump.

"Are you going to be a famous journalist too?" Nikki asked.

"No," Zach said, then clicked on an icon and a colorful game filled the screen. "I'm destined to be the newspaper industry's last intern."

Chapter 10

Alex Chapa watched as his boss struggled to find comfort in a chair that should have been replaced years ago. Chapa was one of only four reporters at the *Record* who still had an office. So, as he explained to Sullivan, they may as well use it. There was also a bit of a power play involved. It's always best to meet with a superior on your turf, even if that turf is slowly being taken away and constantly threatened.

"Do you understand what I need you to do in your current assignment?"

Chapa leaned back in his dark brown chair and took in the comforting smell of old leather.

"Figure out what Jim was working on, connect the dots, cover the same ground he would be covering, keep my job."

Sullivan let out a sigh that was big enough to inflate four tires plus the spare.

"That last part—"

"My job?"

"Yeah, that's why I wanted to talk. That may present the biggest challenge."

Chapa already knew that. The *Chicago Record* had once racked up awards so routinely that at times it seemed like some were being invented just for that purpose. Was it really only four years ago that the *Record* had been named one of the nation's top twenty dailies? To Chapa, it seemed like a lot more time had slipped past, during which countless column inches had been sacrificed to the sort of fluff and nonsense Wormley wallowed in.

Chapa had no patience for shallow human interest stories, empty feel-good pieces, and especially entertainment news, which he considered a complete waste. He wondered how so many folks could care so much about celebrities whose only similarity to real people was their dependence on oxygen. Chapa also saw little of value in the Neighborhoods section and its twelve-inch stories about folks like Floyd down the street who won a prize at the fair for growing the biggest tomato.

When it came to his views on journalism, Chapa wasn't just old school. He might as well have helped pour the cement for the building's foundation.

While Chapa thrived on stories about regular people, he believed that most journalists focused on the trivial, instead of burrowing inside to find out what made the person do whatever it was they did. Not just how Floyd grew that tomato, but what had he sacrificed to do so, and why. Was his wife really all that proud of him? Were his kids embarrassed? Was he okay with that? What was Floyd trying to prove, and to whom? And most important of all, why should anyone else give a damn?

That took work, and an ability to ask the right questions. Those were the qualities that separated him from most of the other reporters at the *Record*, and distinguished him from someone like Duane Wormley. But they were also what made him something of a dinosaur, and expendable in the eyes of some of his superiors. That, and the fact that he was one of the Chicago area's highest paid newspapermen.

"Yes, Alex, connect the dots, and I might be able to talk you-know-who into having you replace Chakowski on a more permanent basis."

"You mean Macklin?"

"Yes, of course, Mr. Macklin."

"He's an ignorant prick from way back."

"Who happens to own the paper."

"Daddy owns the paper. He just chose the runt of the litter to run it."

Another sigh from Sullivan.

"Okay, do you want to keep your job or not?"

Chapa perched his feet on the edge of the desk and looked up as though he were considering Sullivan's question. A crack ran the length of the ceiling and several inches down a wall. Chapa stared at it and wondered if he'd ever noticed it before.

When enough time had passed that Sullivan seemed to be getting nervous, Chapa said, "I'll see what I can do."

"Yes, please. You know I think very highly of you."

Chapa liked his editor, though he'd only worked with him for a couple of months. What he didn't like, however, was the way he'd flipped like a pancake every time Carston Macklin had changed the direction and priorities of the *Record*'s news division. He usually got on well with Sullivan, but wished that just once the man would find the cojones to tell Macklin to fuck off.

"I need to get into Chakowski's office, check out his files and notes."

Sullivan nodded, then reached into his pocket and pulled out a handful of keys. He sifted through them, selected a narrow office key that resembled Chapa's, and tossed it on the desk.

"Just connect the dots, Alex, that's all you've got to do, the way Jim Chakowski would have. No need to go excavating any new ones."

Chapa responded with a sparse smile, and watched Sullivan attempt to decipher what it meant, give up trying, then work himself out of the chair.

"Good luck, Alex," Sullivan said as he left the office.

Chapa heard him let out another massive sigh as he walked away.

Chapter 11

Nikki was locked into a game of Peggle on Zach's computer when Chapa walked over to let her know it would be just a few more minutes.

"Uh huh, okay, that's fine, Daddy," she said without turning away from the monitor.

Chapa rubbed her head, sending strands of blond hair swaying in every direction.

"Dad," she exclaimed and squirmed away.

"I'll be in Chakowski's office in case you need me for anything," Chapa told Zach.

Chakowski's door was just down the hall. As he walked in that direction, Chapa tried to recall how often he'd been in the senior reporter's office. Not much at all, he realized for the first time. That surprised him somewhat. They'd never truly been friends in the traditional sense, but they were friendly in the way that colleagues in any profession can be.

But there was more to it. Newspaper reporters were not typical office workers. It was a unique line of work, one that led to unusual and often fractured lives. The hours were odd, and the job often followed you home, then became a squatter in your everyday.

Like athletes and cops, reporters were often most comfortable talking to others who understood how different their day-to-day lives were. But as Chapa opened the door and walked into Chakowski's office, he thought about how private the man had been, and wondered why he hadn't noticed that before.

As he stood in the doorway and looked around, Chapa realized that he'd have to come back when he had more time, and when Nikki was not with him. The cramped room was dark except for the few threads of sunlight fighting their way in through closed blinds.

Chapa surveyed the area for a moment, then flipped on the light switch. A throw blanket rested on a well-worn couch in the corner, suggesting that Chakowski slept there from time to time. That didn't come as much of a surprise. He'd heard others say that Chakowski lived at the office, maybe that was more true than anyone realized.

Unlike Chapa's office, which was full of books, CDs, and photos, this one was crowded with old newspapers stuffed into a bookcase lining one wall, and file boxes on another. Chapa understood why light from outside couldn't get in, the window was half blocked by a large wooden shelving unit that was stuffed with LPs. The place smelled like old paper.

Out of curiosity, Chapa walked over to the shelves of records and checked out some of the artists and titles. Van Morrison, Bob Dylan, Carole King, Nilsson, the Grateful Dead, a mix of late 60s and early 70s pop. What a thirty-year-old grad student Chapa knew back in college called, "The good stuff."

Chapa was reminded of how much a music collection can reveal about a person. This one told him exactly when Jim Chakowski became the man he became.

He pushed aside a set of headphones that was sitting on top of the desk, and began looking through a stack of papers and manila folders. The desk drawers offered little in the way of useful materials, but Chapa looked through them long enough to find a do-it-yourself will kit. Odd, but Chakowski was getting up there in years, never married, and had no children, as far as Chapa knew. He hoped to find some notes that might indicate what Chakowski was working on, but gave up after a few minutes, and made a call over to Sullivan's office.

"I'm going to write Jim's obit for tomorrow's paper."

"That's fine, it will be one of several that we're going to run. Give yours a more personal slant."

That approach wouldn't have been his first choice, but Chapa agreed to give it a shot.

"Then you'll be covering the Business Council meeting tomorrow at City Hall?"

"And why would I do that?"

"Because that's what Jim would've been doing. Because that's the job, Alex."

Chapa did not answer right away as he made a mental note to double-check how much he still had left in his 401(K). He knew it wouldn't be anywhere near enough to retire, but he now sensed that he might be tapping into it soon.

Chapter 12

Chapa had his colleague's obituary finished in just under an hour. The story about the explosion, including the official police version along with quotes from the female neighbor took a little longer. There just wasn't much meat on that bone.

Every few minutes he would look around the corner and make sure Nikki was okay and that Zach's babysitting skills were holding up. After he'd milked every possible detail and cruised up one side and down the other of the story's angles, Chapa put it together as best as he could.

Nikki gently complained when he scooped her up and told her it was time to go. But there was no time for debate, they were already late for dinner.

He thanked Zach, "I owe you lunch sometime this week." Then headed out the door before Wormley said something stupid or Sullivan lured him into another hand-rubbing conversation.

Erin and Mike, her five-year-old son, were already at Barnaby's Grill when Chapa and Nikki got there, nearly forty minutes late. Chapa watched as Erin got up from where they were seated at a table by the front windows, and introduced herself to Nikki. He marveled at how natural this all seemed for her.

Chapa and Erin had met under circumstances that were less than romantic. He'd walked into her bank, the one where she still worked as a vice president, hoping to clear up the finances of his married past. They hit it off in every way, and by the end of their first month together they were seeing each other several times a week, and spending hours on the phone on nights when they were apart.

Erin had a casual way about her that fit nicely with Chapa's often manic life, and he shared things with her in a way he never had with anyone else before—not even with Carla. Sometimes Chapa wasn't sure what he brought to Erin's life, and he wasn't about to ask.

Though they had been together and going strong for more than six months, Chapa's hesitancy to commit further was beginning to cause a strain. With Erin's help he had succeeded in clearing up the financial fallout from his failed marriage, only to find that there were some other lingering issues that were also the product of his past failures.

The restaurant was crowded, mostly by families, and for Chapa the feeling of fitting in with this group was both alien and comforting. Nikki and Mike were getting along well, and Erin gave Chapa a look and tossed a nod in their direction. He knew what she was thinking.

They're cute, aren't they.

And they were, but something else had captured his attention. Chapa had first noticed the man and his car as he and Nikki were walking in the door. The banged-up, late model Ford had rumbled through the parking lot at a speed that was just a bit beyond casual.

Now the guy Chapa had seen behind the wheel was standing by his Toyota, eyeing it, and not trying to act like he was doing anything else. Chapa watched as the man with at least fifty hard years of living on his body circled the Corolla.

"Something wrong?" Erin asked in a way that let Chapa know she already knew the answer.

"Not sure, maybe."

Four days' worth of salt-and-pepper stubble crowded the guy's face, but Chapa sensed it wasn't the beginning of a beard. He looked like he'd dressed himself in the dark, putting on the first clothes his unsteady hands landed on.

The waitress brought a platter of appetizers, but Chapa didn't notice right away. His attention was on the guy who was now staring right back at him from the parking lot.

"Who is he?" Erin had noticed him too.

"No idea. But I have a feeling we'll know soon," Chapa said as he watched the man stride across the parking lot, toward the front door of the restaurant, like he had to be someplace in a hurry. His eyes fixed on Chapa the entire time.

Chapter 13

Alex Chapa had spent much of his career kicking up piles of dirt and pissing off the people who'd built them.

He'd exposed area businessmen who had ties to the mob, cops gone bad, and all variety of cheats, chiselers, and shitheels. Chapa had paid a price for his efforts. His cars had been vandalized more times than he could remember, his front lawn was once set on fire, and there had been three death threats—at least one of which was taken seriously by the police.

But it had been some time—days, maybe weeks—since he'd last written anything that could be considered incendiary. This fact bothered Chapa, made him feel like he wasn't doing his job.

At the moment, it was also a cause for confusion. Chapa could not imagine what he might've done to rile the thin but imposing man who had just burst through the door of the restaurant, rushed past the young lady offering him a table or booth, and was now rapidly narrowing the distance to where they were seated.

Maybe this was someone who'd landed in the joint after one of Chapa's exposés. He certainly had that look. Chapa fought the urge to stand up and anticipate a confrontation. His first instinct was not to avoid trouble in front of the kids. But he was trying to work on that.

"You're Alex Chapa?"

"As far back as I can remember."

It was an off-the-cuff response, probably not the wisest one under the circumstances. Chapa knew that, but over the years he'd made a habit of answering that question with any one in a series of smart-ass lines.

"Then you're the one investigating what happened to Jim."

Chapa took a better look at the man fidgeting by their table. Did he look familiar? Maybe, though he couldn't quite place the face. A waitress whose hands were filled with plates excused herself and did her best to shimmy past the guy who acted as though she wasn't there.

"I'm not investigating, exactly. There's nothing to investigate."

"The hell there ain't," the guy said, then seemed to catch himself as he looked toward the children. "I'm sorry. It's been a bad time."

He looks like a bad time, Chapa thought as he excused himself, got up. and took the guy by the arm.

"Let's go over here," Chapa said and led him to the bar at the other end of the restaurant. "Can I buy you a drink?"

The guy shook his head. "Had too many already."

Based on the stranger's appearance and the way he smelled, Chapa had no reason to doubt that.

"Who are you?"

"I'm Warren Chakowski. I'm Jim's brother."

Chapa looked for a resemblance—maybe that was why the guy seemed familiar—but couldn't find any.

"Were you two close?"

Warren Chakowski looked down, and Chapa had the answer to his question.

"I've had some troubles, you know?"

Chapa didn't, but he could easily imagine, and nodded anyhow.

"I was born with some difficulties that I've fought to overcome," Warren said as he rubbed his forehead. "Some times have been better than others."

"I liked your brother a lot," Chapa said, waving the barkeep away. "I'm sorry for your loss."

"I'm sure you are. That's why you need to investigate what really happened last night."

Now Chapa remembered where he'd seen the guy. Warren Chakowski had been at the crime scene, standing along a tree line at the far end of his brother's property. Even then it had seemed to Chapa like this guy was out of place.

"Look, Warren, I can see you're upset, and hurt, and maybe a little confused—"

"I'm not confused about anything—" Warren said, raising his voice to an uncomfortable level.

Chapa put a hand on Warren's shoulder and tried to settle him down.

"That came out wrong, it sounded condescending, and I apologize. But your brother's death was a terrible accident."

"No accident," Warren stopped him. His demeanor had suddenly changed and he now appeared resolute, certain, and sober. "My brother knew he was going to die, knew they were out to kill him. He warned me to keep an eye out for myself and to watch who I talked to if anything happened to him."

"Did you tell this to the police?" Chapa pulled up a stool and ordered two Newcastles.

"Like I said, Jim told me to watch who I talked to. I got the feeling he didn't trust the police."

The beer arrived quickly, along with chilled glasses and cardboard coasters. Chapa watched Warren take a long, cold sip from the bottle.

"Or maybe, if he really was worried about something or

someone, he was concerned you might implicate anyone you spoke to."

"And here I am now talking to you," Warren said, smiled, and drank the rest of his beer in a single tilt. "Jim and me were supposed to go hunting this weekend."

"I didn't know he was a sportsman."

Warren shook his head and signaled the bartender for another beer. Chapa shook him off, and slid his untouched bottle over to Warren.

"He wasn't. Jim just went along because I wanted him to. Probably just to keep me from accidentally shooting myself."

That sounded a lot like the Jim Chakowski Chapa had known. He wasn't the sort of reporter anyone would ever want to hurt. He handled community news, did his share of feel-good pieces, and had been at the job for nearly three decades. But maybe he'd gotten himself into something.

Chapa doubted it. The cops had this one right. An old house in an even older neighborhood. Bad wiring. Worse luck. But no crime. In a few days the cops would likely reveal that Jim Chakowski had recently installed a new appliance or a new printer, or had started plugging his electric razor into a different outlet. A dozen or more possibilities that made a hell of a lot more sense than someone blowing up a house to get rid of a reporter.

Still, there was a look in Warren Chakowski's eyes, an uneasy combination of desperation and determination that marked him as someone to be taken seriously.

Chapter 14

Chapa followed Erin back to her house, some three miles from his own, so Nikki could see where she would be spending parts of her days. After they all politely took off their shoes and got a short tour of the neatly kept ranch, the kids disappeared into the family room where the game system was.

"Okay, are you going to tell me what that strange man at the restaurant wanted?" Erin asked the moment the children were out of earshot.

As he followed her into the kitchen, Chapa explained who the guy was and dismissed Warren Chakowski's theory about his brother's death, but then added, "I'm meeting him tomorrow."

"Why? What are you trying to get yourself into now?"

"I'm not getting myself into anything," Chapa said, retrieving a cold bottle of beer from the refrigerator. "I feel I owe something to Jim Chakowski. He helped me out a number of times over the years." Chapa downed a long swig. "Maybe I can help his brother get some closure."

Erin was putting pots and silverware away, wiping down countertops a second time, and doing a number of small things that told Chapa she was more than a little uneasy. The kitchen, like much of the house, was a nice mix of functional and decorative. Erin liked bright colors, and Chapa found her tastes charming, and in sync with her personality.

He also got a kick out of seeing Mike's drawings framed and hung on walls as though they were works of fine art. And there were so many photos of Erin and Mike, treated with the same reverence. Chapa was in a few of those, and it made him feel good to be included in that way, but he was also a bit uneasy about it.

Erin had told Chapa that he was, "A man of grays and blues," and that she hoped some of her would rub off on him. Deep down, he hoped it would, too, but feared it might turn out the other way around.

"I thought you were supposed to just be following Jim Chakowski's beat, keeping it all as simple as possible."

"I will, Erin. But I can still ask a few questions, fill in a blank or two. Basically, I'll confirm the official report, and lay this to rest without any of it getting in the way of my work."

Erin turned away from the sink and walked toward Chapa. She had a face that he was sure he'd seen in an adolescent dream, and the legs of a runway model. Chapa liked those legs. Even now, hidden inside a pair of faded jeans, he knew how good they looked, how nice they felt every time she wrapped them around his bare waist. And that made him smile.

She draped her long arms around his neck, pulled Chapa close to her, which made him smile more.

"I just don't want you turning this into one of those things."

"One of what things?"

"You know what I'm talking about."

He did. From the early days of his career Chapa had shown an ability to find the worst kind of trouble, and a willingness to rush head on into it. As a result, he was on a first-name basis with some very bad people.

Chapa was about to reassure Erin that there was nothing to worry about this time. How at its core this was a fairly benign assignment and that he would not end up getting shot at, stabbed, or even punched. Not that she'd believe him anyhow.

But the instant he opened his mouth she pressed hers against it. Their tongues tangled for a hot moment, then she slowly eased her head back.

Erin gave Chapa's lips one more quick flick with her tongue and said, "Mr. beer breath."

"Just pretend this is a bar pickup sort of thing," Chapa said and gave her an exaggerated wink.

Erin laughed. "I don't think you're the sort who ever went for the bar pickup scene."

"Oh, I didn't mean me," Chapa said and slowly smiled.

She smacked his chest, hard, but playful, then laughed and again wrapped her arms around his neck.

Two rooms away, the sounds of their kids playing began to gradually fade, and then everything else went with it. For a perfect moment Chapa's universe consisted only of Erin's lips, her touch, and the warmth of her body pressed against his.

Chapter 15

Chapa had hoped to spend some time with Nikki when they got home. But she fell asleep in the car, and was still groggy when he walked her up to her room. It was the first time in nearly a year that Chapa had put his daughter to bed.

He'd preserved the room exactly as it was when Nikki moved out with her mother, but now realized she had already outgrown many of the decorations and most of her toys.

He pulled back the covers and guided Nikki into her white frame bed. Then Chapa gave her a few minutes to get back to sleep while he walked across the hall to his own room, which was quite a bit messier. He flipped on the lights, kicked off his shoes, and then softly walked back across the hall, the floor creaking under his heavy feet.

Nikki had dozed off by the time he walked back into her room. Glancing up, he looked at the glow-in-the-dark stars and planets that covered the ceiling, and remembered when Nikki was much younger and believed it really was the night sky.

"Those stars come out to glow just for you," he'd told his daughter when she was barely three years old.

They weren't radiating much tonight, the light in her

room had not been on long enough. Tomorrow he'd leave it turned on the entire day, and they'd be a whole lot brighter when Nikki spent her second night in her room.

Sitting at the edge of Nikki's bed, Chapa watched her sleep until she finally rolled over and faced the wall. For some reason, he thought she'd look more like her mother by now, but that wasn't the case. Though he understood that everyone sees themselves or their close family in the faces of their children, Chapa couldn't stop thinking about how much Nikki resembled his father. He remembered a photo of his dad standing by the side of a table during a birthday party. There was a smile on the man's face, a playfulness in his eyes that Chapa had seen in Nikki these past several days.

That made him feel even worse for not playing a bigger role in her day-to-day life. But what could he do? There were only a few options, and none of those were particularly good.

He heard the sound of a car start up and pull out, just a few houses away. Odd in this neighborhood at this time of night. He lifted a Dora the Explorer blanket up over Nikki's shoulders, then walked to the window and looked through the curtains. Nothing. Probably a neighbor putting his car in the garage.

Two decades of regular dealings with lowlifes or worse had made him a bit jumpy, and maybe a little paranoid. His bizarre conversation with Warren Chakowski hadn't helped, and maybe Jim's sudden death hadn't either. He was also feeling more guarded with Nikki in the house. Chapa thought about how long it had been since he'd felt that way as he leaned across and gave her a soft kiss on the side of her forehead. The child responded by shrugging, curling her nose, and disappearing under the blanket.

Chapa took one last look before closing the door to her room, then heading downstairs to make sure all the doors were locked.

Chapter 16

The man has been sitting in his car, parked under the crooked shadows of bare trees. He watched the reporter enter his house with his child. He saw that a few lights had been left on, though they had not been home for some time, and he was certain no one else lived there. He followed the path of movement through the house as the living room went dark, then a light went on in an upstairs window, but not for long. The girl's room. Then, finally, the reporter's bedroom. The man made a mental note of all this.

As he drives away, the man begins to wonder if he's made a mistake, if perhaps the reporter isn't a danger to his child. The man doesn't tolerate mistakes, especially his own. His hands tighten on the steering wheel until pain creeps up both of his arms. Releasing his grip, the man realizes he is speeding down dark, quiet neighborhood streets, and yanks his foot off the accelerator, then gently presses the brakes.

Wouldn't be good to get pulled over for speeding. A bad play anywhere, at any time, but even worse here and now. Sure, he could talk his way out of it. Was there a member of the force that he was not on good terms with? None that he can think of. But the man has a feeling he'll be back in this area, back at that house. Wouldn't be a good idea to let a cop remember seeing him there. Late at night. Driving too fast. Sweating. Anxious. Wouldn't be a good idea.

Besides, he has other, more important concerns. Nervous people to deal with, voices to silence.

But the more he thinks about it, and the longer his mind lingers on the image of that reporter carelessly letting his child wander around a crime scene, the more his frustration swells. It begins to fill him up again, pushing against the man's rib cage, crawling up his spine with sharp boney fingers. And soon he can feel the pressure behind his eyes threatening to break through, ready at any moment to expose him and destroy everything he's worked to create.

Once more, the man clutches the steering wheel in a death grip, though he fights and wins the battle to avoid accelerating again. He has business to attend to. People to bring into line and plans to carry out. The target he's pursued for so long is now within reach, and he has to get all of it right, every detail, no matter how small. No room for mistakes. This is too important. First things first.

But now, as the man leaves the west side of Oakton in his rearview, he knows—in fact he is certain—that he will come back to the reporter's house. And the next time, he will come prepared to do a great deal more than watch.

Chapter 17

St. Louis, Missouri, 1975

The child sits in a cheap chair that lost its padding a long time ago. Its narrow, chipped legs are uneven, and the chair creaks beneath his frail body each time he moves.

He leans over a desk in the narrow room he sleeps in. Disgusted by the stains on the carpet beneath him, he tucks his feet up under his legs. The air is pungent with the smell of body odor and rotting food. The only other piece of furniture in the room is a thin mattress pressed against a paint-chipped wall that's been badly cracked by time and violence.

The child spends hours at that desk, filling page after page of a dime store drawing pad with stick figures. He draws the figures into stories and makes them do terrible things to each other. Then, once he's covered every page with drawings, he slips the pad under the mattress, alongside all the others, and waits for his mother to bring home a new one. That can take weeks, sometimes. But the child doesn't mind. He spends the time thinking of all the things the people in his next set of drawings will do to one another.

But on this night, he still has more than half the pad to fill, and that brings as much joy to the child as he's capable of feeling. He has so many good ideas tonight. So many important things that his stick figures must do to each other.

The pimp and drug dealer who lives with him and his mother and likes to be called Gilley, wanders in to see what the boy is doing. The child can hear his mother in the other room going at it with tonight's second customer.

The child looks up for just a moment, then instinctively looks down at Gilley's hands. He feels only a slight sense of relief when he sees they're empty and unclenched. It's a survival tactic the boy has learned without realizing he was learning it.

Gilley is not the child's father, and he's not the first man in his life. Just the latest, and the meanest, at least as far as the boy can remember. The child looks up at Gilley's face, not always a good idea, and notices that his stringy blond hair is shorter than usual. He's made an attempt to shave, apparently cutting himself in the process, a fact that pleases the boy.

"Hey little punk, those are some freaky people you drew there. Cool, though."

Gilley smells like he's been swimming in stale aftershave, and for a moment his odor threatens to overwhelm the general stench of the two-bedroom shanty in one of the city's forgotten neighborhoods.

"Hey, maybe you're an artist," Gilley says and smacks the child on the arm, maybe a little harder than he meant to. Or maybe exactly as he wanted to.

The child says nothing, but his thoughts are running zigzag sprints through his mind. And the child wonders what this man, a stranger to him by any decent person's standards, would say if he understood that he was the subject of the drawings.

Chapter 18

When Chapa opened his eyes he saw Nikki staring back at him. She smiled, and her face captured every ounce of sunlight that was pouring into his bedroom.

"I woke up more than an hour ago, Daddy."

"Of course you did." Chapa sat up slowly. Most days he felt his age, forty-two, sometimes older. But not today, and not while Nikki was with him. "I need to get you some breakfast."

She nodded, then spoke in measured tones. "Yeah, I looked around in the kitchen, but I didn't find much to eat."

Now Chapa remembered. He hadn't planned on bringing his daughter home when he left for Boston a week earlier. There hadn't been a clearly defined purpose to his visit beyond wanting to see his child. Something that had become increasingly more difficult for him to do as Carla had done all she could to force Chapa out of Nikki's life. So the best he'd hoped for was a smile, a hug, some precious time together, and for his ex to understand that the rules of the game had changed. But then his attorney went to work.

Chapa hadn't thought about stocking the fridge or pantry, or even picking up a loaf of bread.

"We'll find something," he said, feigning optimism.

As he walked toward the stairs, Chapa glanced into Nikki's room and noticed that her bed had been made. He turned to compliment her, and found that she was already smiling back at him.

"Thank you for noticing," Nikki said.

He walked ahead of her down the stairs and into the living room, then started toward the kitchen, but stopped when he noticed that Nikki wasn't following him anymore. She stood in the middle of the floor, carefully scanning every inch of the living room.

Chapa wondered how much of it she remembered. The downstairs looked nothing like it had when a family still lived there. Most of the photos were gone. Carla had also taken the furniture, then let Chapa know she'd given it away. The only thing that was the same was an old tan leather couch that Chapa too often slept in, and his tower of CDs.

"I like what you've done with the place," Nikki said, doing her best to sound sincere.

"All of the toys are up in your room, but you've probably outgrown them by now."

"Some, yes, but not all of them. It's okay, I've got my PSP to play with."

As he led Nikki into the kitchen, Chapa made a mental note to pick up some games at the toy store in town. But as soon as he walked in and started looking around, Chapa knew he had more pressing issues than shopping for something to keep Nikki entertained.

The pantry and fridge looked like they belonged in an abandoned house. But Chapa managed to throw something together, at least enough to convince himself that it resembled breakfast. Twenty minutes later, Nikki was treated to a scrambled egg, a handful of Tater Tots, and some nacho-flavored Doritos.

"Interesting breakfast," Nikki said, her lips gradually turning orange with each new chip she ate.

"We'll have better food tomorrow. Pancakes, and bacon, and cereal."

"It's okay, I like this. It's exotic."

She shoved two Tater Tots in her mouth.

"You know what, those are like potato pancakes or hash browns, only smaller."

Nikki laughed.

"Is this the type of breakfast you usually eat?" she asked.

"I don't eat breakfast all that often. I work late, get home even later, and I don't always get up in time."

"I do, and I have fruit every morning. You know, breakfast is the most important meal of the day."

"Yeah, I think I read that somewhere. Tomorrow will be different, Nik. I promise. There will be fruit."

"Don't worry about it, Dad." The last bite of egg filled her mouth, but that didn't keep her from talking. "And Mom never has to know."

There hadn't been much opportunity for Chapa to worry about what his ex-wife was thinking while Nikki was away from home. Though he didn't want to spend too much time discussing the shaky start to Nikki's visit, he wasn't about to coax her into deceiving her mother, either.

"I don't like lying, Nikki. We talked about this after what you did to that reporter yesterday."

Nikki shook her head.

"I won't, but Mom won't ask, and I won't tell her."

She smiled a big toothy grin, and Chapa sensed he had more to worry about when it came to Nikki than the unconventional meal she'd just finished.

Chapter 19

Through the frosted window that filled the upper half of the closed door, Chapa saw there was someone sitting in Jim Chakowski's office as he approached. It was dark inside, but the smattering of light slipping in through an outside window backlit the visitor, creating a silhouette. Chapa paused for a moment before opening the door.

"Come on in and close the door behind you, Alex. I have something to show you."

Chapa couldn't see the man's face, and he didn't recognize the thick voice, not right away. But he did as asked, anyhow.

"This arrived in my mail this morning," the guy said, then leaned forward and turned on an old desk lamp.

Chapa looked at the man's face, ignoring the envelope he'd just tossed on the desk pad. Maybe it was the low, unflattering light of the single bulb, but Warren Chakowski looked like he hadn't slept since the night before. Probably hadn't bothered to try.

"You look tired."

"I don't sleep much these days, never have. But that's not important," Warren said, pushing the thin package across the desk and toward Chapa.

"What is it?" Chapa asked, lifting the yellow, oversized envelope from the desk.

"You tell me."

It had been torn open in a hurry and folded unevenly, as though Warren had shoved it into a pants pocket. Inside, Chapa found a piece of paper ripped from a yellow legal pad without much care. He unfolded the paper and saw a collection of what appeared to be random notes.

"Was there a letter explaining any of this?" Chapa asked.

"No, just that sheet of paper. But it's Jim's writing all right."

The sheet was cluttered with various brain droppings, but Chapa's attention was drawn to a list of names, some of which were familiar, as well as a list of cities and dates—*Cleveland (1990–1996), Pittsburgh (1997–2002), Baltimore (2003–2005), Oakton, Illinois (2005–)*.

Scribbled in the bottom right corner was a series of numbers: *ND93106*.

"Why would he mail this to you?"

"Because Jim knew what was going to happen to him."

Chapa tried to mask his skepticism, with mixed results.

"I know you don't believe me, Mr. Chapa. But just a week or two ago, Jim told me how he was preparing a will."

Chapa thought about the do-it-yourself kit he'd found in one of Chakowski's desk drawers, but decided to keep that to himself for the time being.

"A lot of people in their fifties have a will, Warren."

"Not my brother, he just wasn't the sort to worry about that kind of thing. I asked Jim if something was wrong, physically, I mean. He said he was fine, but I could tell something was burning him up inside."

Chapa studied the notes on the paper. Where to start?

"Jim was scared, and he wasn't the sort to get scared."

There wasn't much more to say. How can you tell someone he's wrong about a person he's known his entire life? Chapa knew better than to even try.

"I'll check out the names and dates and see if any of it means anything."

Warren stood up from behind the desk and started for the door.

"But please understand, Warren, that this could take a while and will likely lead us right back to your brother's death being the result of poor wiring."

The man nodded, and Chapa continued.

"I know you've suffered a loss, but you have to try to put some of these thoughts out of your head. Give me a few days, and I will call you."

Warren nodded once more as he let himself out of the office, but Chapa was certain he'd hear from him again, and soon.

Chapter 20

Chapa didn't bother opening the blinds or turning on any more lights in Jim Chakowski's office. The lamp on the desk was enough for what he had to do, and he didn't want to draw any attention.

Being in that office was a little like sitting in a man's personal confessional. Whoever Jim Chakowski had been, and maybe all that he had been working on, was right there, somewhere.

Chapa studied the large shelving unit that housed Chakowski's collection of LPs, at least what was left of it since any that he kept at home had been blown to shards. The records were neatly organized in alphabetical order by artist, except for the one that had been pulled out and played most recently. The disc itself, James Taylor's *Sweet Baby James*, still sat on the turntable. Chapa wondered whether it was the last record Jim had ever listened to, or perhaps something his brother had played while he was there. Chapa thought about putting it back on the shelf, but that didn't seem right somehow, so he dropped the needle on the first track, turned the volume down so that only he could hear it, and unplugged the headphones.

He made a call down to the archive room to request

copies of every issue of the *Chicago Record* from the past two months that had included a Jim Chakowski story. After being told that would take a few hours to put together, Chapa decided to focus on the torn piece of paper.

Jim Chakowski's scribbling didn't get any more helpful with multiple readings. But the list of dates and places, that was something Chapa could research.

Cleveland (1990–1996)
Pittsburgh (1997–2002)
Baltimore (2003–2005)
Oakton (2005–)

Three large cities, followed by Oakton, a town of about 150,000. Why not Chicago? Or Milwaukee? Cleveland to Pittsburgh to Baltimore could be a natural progression of some sort. But Oakton?

What the hell did any of this mean?

He searched online for the four sets of dates, but came up empty. Then he began burrowing through Chakowski's computer hoping to locate any stories or notes that might contain further details corresponding to the items on the page. He was ready to give up after an hour's worth of frustration, when the phone rang.

Chapa thought for a moment about how best to answer. Who would be dialing up a dead reporter? Could be an old acquaintance who hadn't heard the news, or had just found out and wanted more information. Probably Warren Chakowski calling Chapa to check up on him. Or maybe it was a source.

That thought made Chapa's pulse race for a moment.

"*Chicago Record.*"

"Mr. Chapa?"

"Yes."

A pause on the other end, then, "Are you in Mr. Chakowski's office?"

"Two for two."

"This is Maya, you know, at the front desk."

"Yes, Maya."

"Mr. Sullivan told me I would probably find you there and asked me to remind you about the Oakton Business Council meeting."

"What about it?"

"You're suppose to cover it, you know, like Mr. Chakowski used to. It starts in just under two hours."

Chapa wondered what the hell he'd signed up for, and why Sullivan would go through someone else to remind him of his assignment. Chapa didn't have to think about that for long. He understood. Fear was a great motivator, and in Chapa's relationship with Sullivan it served to blur the line between writer and editor.

"Hey, Maya, do me a favor."

"Remind you every day about your itinerary?"

"No, I can keep track of that, thank you. I'd like Mr. Chakowski's mail here at the paper forwarded to me, to my office, or just hand it to me when I come in."

There was a brief pause on the other end.

"Okay, Mr. Chapa, I've written myself a note."

He thanked Maya and got back to work. After ten minutes of sifting though Chakowski's stories about the Oakton Business Council meetings, Chapa concluded that his colleague had been writing them on cruise control. Not much in the way of probing news reporting, just a lot of who said what about which. Determined to do better, he spent the next hour taking a crash course in Oakton city business and politics.

The information Chapa found in some of Chakowski's other stories turned out to be far more interesting than he'd expected. But his research came to an end when Maya called again, this time to remind him that the meeting began in forty-five minutes.

Again, he thanked her, and considered marching over to

Sullivan's office and pinning his ears back a bit. Two hours ago he may have done exactly that. Stormed in and reminded Sullivan that he was award-winning reporter Alex Chapa—though all of those awards were stuffed in a box somewhere—and explained that he knew how to do his job better than anyone, and didn't need a reminder, let alone two.

Chapa might have done that earlier, but not now. Having his editor hide behind a receptionist was victory enough. Besides, after reading a few of Chakowski's meatier stories about corruption and shady associations, he was almost looking forward to this assignment.

Chapter 21

This early in the day, the *Record*'s newsroom was a buzzing hive of clicking keyboards, phone interviews, and story meetings. It used to be like this throughout much of the day, but not anymore.

The cubicles and free-standing desks were aligned in rows—more or less—though reporters typically spent little time at their assigned stations. At the busiest times it was sometimes easier to grab the nearest phone or a sheet of paper from a nearby cubicle.

Privacy was not a priority in a working newsroom, except where the more established writers were concerned. They had their work space. They'd earned it, and even if it was just a cubicle or a desk, it was their private turf.

Zach was sitting at his usual workstation, surrounded by loose sheets of paper and ad fliers.

"What are you working on?" Chapa asked as he surveyed the newsroom and saw the usual cast, minus one.

"Research," Zach said, lifting his hands from the keyboard and using two sets of fingers to make quotation marks in the air.

He was wearing a mud brown T-shirt with a cartoon advertising character on it that Chapa recognized from his youth.

"Nice shirt," Chapa said, pointing to the image, "I was a Quisp man myself."

"Why am I not surprised?"

"Where's Wormley?"

"That's who I'm doing research for. He's at Annino's Toys for the big launch of the new Our Heritage Doll line."

"You're shittin' me."

Zach shook his head. "I could not make that one up, boss. I'm researching how much everyone loves these dolls."

"Well here, do this for me instead."

Chapa pulled the yellow notepaper out of his pocket and handed it to Zach. He'd decided it was best to not leave it in Chakowski's office. During the three years that Zach had been working as an intern at the *Chicago Record*, Chapa had come to trust the young man. Zach was a right guy.

"See if any of what's on that sheet of paper matches up to anything."

Zach smiled.

"Ooh, detective work."

"Maybe, of a sort."

Zach was staring at the notes as he brought up a fresh screen on his monitor.

"And, Zach," Chapa started, then waited until he was certain he had the intern's attention, "do not let anyone see this piece of paper or anything that you find out about what's written on it. And don't tell anybody that I asked you to do this."

"I get it."

"I know you do."

"But can you give me a starting point?"

Chapa shook his head. "I wish I could."

"How soon do you need to know whatever it is that you need to know about whatever this is?"

"How many days ago was Jim killed?"

Zach did not hesitate. "Two."

"Then three days ago would've been nice, but I'll settle for as soon as possible."

It took a moment for Chapa's words to sink in. When they did, Zach's eyes got as wide as a startled deer's.

"Oh shit," he said, then hushed, "oh shit."

Chapa raised a hand and Zach only mouthed his next, *Oh shit*.

"It's probably not a big deal. But I'm curious to see what you can turn up."

Zach nodded and looked around the newsroom with suspicion.

"I'm on it. But what should I tell Wormley?"

"Damned if I care," Chapa said, looked at his watch, and started for the door. He had less than twenty minutes to get to City Hall. "Just let him know how I reacted when you told me what he had you doing, and how that made it impossible for you to continue and still have any dignity left."

"That's a relief," Zach said, his voice slowly fading into the background as Chapa left the newsroom. "For a moment I thought you were going to tell me to lie."

Chapter 22

Downtown Oakton was a ten-minute drive from the newspaper office. Chapa parked a couple of blocks away from the city's government complex that included its central police station and court, which bookended the City Hall. A pedestrian mall, stretching two blocks between Clinton Avenue and Marion Boulevard, connected the buildings.

Chapa was surprised by the amount of foot traffic as he tried to remember how many times he'd been down here on official business. The police station, and the court, had at times been part of his regular beat, but City Hall was another matter.

Checking his watch to confirm that he still had a few minutes before the meeting was scheduled to start, Chapa decided to duck into police headquarters. He told himself he was going there to find out if the cops had turned up anything new on the explosion. But deep down Chapa knew he was just trying to delay doing something he didn't want to do.

As always, the Oakton Central Police Station was crowded with an unruly mass of humanity. A dingy dance hall where the cops did their best to waltz with the folks whose lives had been derailed by a single mistake or a wrong turn, and the others who'd been broken down since birth.

Chapa walked past the front desk to where the real business got done, and found a clerk at the records counter who seemed to recognize him. She was tall and slender, with wavy red hair and a nice smile. Her name tag identified her as Jayne.

Through the din of complaints and pleas he managed to ask for Detective Tom Jackson, and got the woman to make a call.

"He says he'll be here in five."

Chapa thanked her, moved aside so she could return to work, and checked his cell phone. There was a text message from Nikki.

> Hi Daddy, I'm having fun and studying here with Erin.
> Hope you're having a great day!

He wondered how the day was going for Erin. Great, probably, this all seemed to come naturally to her. He decided to call and check in with her anyhow, but was interrupted by the sound of a woman's voice. More of a screech, really.

"I'm Gladys Washer, check your records, I've been down here before." She was small and wiry, seventy, seventy-five years old, perhaps older. Despite her age and frail appearance, the taught veins on her neck looked tough as rope. "Don't pretend you don't recognize me."

Poor Jayne was doing her best, but the old woman would have none of it. Chapa put his phone away and walked over toward the two women. But before he could ask Gladys what her problem was or save the clerk in some way, he heard Tom Jackson call out to him.

"Please tell me you're here for something that has nothing to with Jim Chakowski's house."

"I'm just checking in, Tom, just in case there's something new."

Jackson grabbed Chapa's elbow and led him away from the desk and in the direction of the front door.

"Nothing new, and you're persona non grata around here."

"Well that's nothing new either, but I must say I'm impressed by your use of Latin just now."

"It's true, Alex, none of us like you very much anyway. But things are a little worse than usual right now. A lot of folks are really pissed off about the way you got onto the crime site yesterday."

Chapa looked at a large clock on the wall across the room. The meeting was scheduled to start in three minutes.

"I'm pretty sure I didn't break any laws, Tom."

"Trust me, there are some people around here who would love to pick you up for jaywalking."

Chapa let out a small laugh, slapped Jackson on the arm.

"Nothing new about that, either," he said, and turned for the exit.

Chapter 23

Chapa spotted Sean Moriarity first. When Moriarity saw him, the rival reporter's facial expression turned from one of recognition, to disgust, to dismissal, before disgust came back around for seconds. Chapa didn't care. He figured Moriarity would know a whole lot more about the goings-on than he did.

"That seat is taken," Moriarity said as Chapa sat down next to him.

"It is now."

Moriarity shuffled some notes and leaned away from Chapa, damned near turning his back to him. Chapa scanned the meeting room, he'd never been there before. There was a conference table, big enough for the twelve highback leather executive chairs that ringed it. The rest of the room was filled by rows of far less comfortable plastic chairs. All but six were empty.

"Do they draw much of a crowd, Sean?"

After the twenty seconds or so that it apparently took him to conjure a comeback, Moriarity said, "Today it seems like there's one too many."

"Look, Sean, I'm sorry about yesterday. I talked to Nikki

about it, but she was just trying to have some fun. She didn't understand." That wasn't entirely true, but Chapa's apology seemed to break the ice a little.

A few minutes later Moriarity was telling him about the various issues that the Business Council dealt with, including zoning recommendations, business contracts, and deals to bring new commerce into town. He explained that each council member had been nominated by the mayor or some other official, and approved by the City Council, which, according to Moriarity, "rubberstamps everything."

As each member of the council wandered in and took a seat at the table, Moriarity would give Chapa the skinny on who was who.

"The tall guy with the horn-rimmed glasses is Dex Ferguson, a former alderman."

"I remember, he resigned after they caught him in his car at the Sunset Drive-in with an ounce of coke on the dash and a nude college girl on his lap."

"Yeah, but then he went on to make a couple mil and all was forgiven. The guy next to him is Charles Stoop, owner of the Chicago area's largest landscaping firm. He does all of that sort of work around here."

Stoop had a flat, pasty complexion, which Chapa thought seemed odd for a man in the landscaping business. Apparently having noticed the two reporters talking about him, Stoop walked over and handed Chapa his business card.

"I've already got a few, thanks," Moriarity said as Stoop fumbled for another card.

Stoops nodded, then returned to his chair.

"The chubby guy is Tony Villanueva," Moriarity said, continuing his roll call.

"Oh, I know Tony. Used to be a hack writer for the *Oakton Observer*. I heard they rewarded his bad work by kicking him upstairs."

"That's right. He's head of some department there now and sits on boards like this one."

"And why would he do that?"

"Because it keeps someone from your paper or mine from sitting there."

That made sense. As far back as Chapa could remember the *Observer* had been as passive about reporting the news as its name suggested. Though it had a decent circulation, especially by present-day standards, it was more of an extension of the city's public relations department than a real newspaper.

"Who's the old guy from soap opera central casting?"

"He's a doctor."

"Of course he is."

"That's Dr. Walter Bendix, a former surgeon who made a lot of money buying and developing land."

"He looks important."

"Oh, Dr. Bendix is. And he works with all sorts of charities, even volunteers his time."

A middle-aged woman of Amazonian proportions walked in, and appeared to disrupt Moriarity's train of thought.

"That's Vanny Mars," he said, lowering his voice. "She's one of the Clinton Avenue Cougars."

"The Clinton Avenue what?"

Vanny Mars was as tall as any man in the room. Her hair looked like it had been dyed so many times it was no longer a clearly defined color, but instead something between dark beige and burgundy.

When she sat down Chapa noticed that her shoulders were wider than the chair's broad backrest. Moriarity explained that Vanny was the city's numbers cruncher, the person who made sure the deals worked on paper. A former CPA with dreams of grandeur. But her true claim to fame came a year ago when she thought up the slogan *Oakton—It Sizzles!*

"That slogan is on signs all over town."

"Maybe I should go ask her for an autograph," Chapa whispered to Moriarity.

"I'm sure she'd give it to you without batting one of those ridiculous false eyelashes."

They kept making their way in, and Moriarity continued to play the role of the know-it-all at the ballpark who's committed every player's batting average to memory. There was Greg Vinsky, a man Chapa guessed to be in his late thirties or early to mid forties, with light features and thick dark hair. According to Moriarity, Vinsky owned a consulting business, and had helped broker a number of deals for the city. And Franklin Gemmer, who'd moved there just a few years back and started a successful security alarm company.

"Clay Hunter runs an insurance firm, Harvey Nestor owns a chain of drugstores, Mario Melendez is a consultant, Ted Bruce is a PR guy, and Dick Wick provides legal counsel for the city."

Chapa was still listening, but he'd been distracted by a new member of the gallery.

"You may not realize this, Alex, but more than half of these people moved here in the past few years, after the new mayor was elected and reached out to businessmen beyond Oakton's borders."

"Um hmm." Chapa was staring at the man sitting alone in the back row. He was wearing a slate gray suit that reminded Chapa of the one Cary Grant wore in *North by Northwest*. The suit fit him so well that it almost seemed organic, a part of his body like a second skin or outer shell. He had deep set eyes that were fixed on Chapa. Just as they had been the first time Chapa noticed him.

"But what this council actually does," Moriarity, still in a zone of his own, whispered, "is make sure no competition moves in and hurts their businesses."

"Sean—" Chapa blurted, stopping Moriarity in midsentence. "The guy in the expensive suit, back row, far right, who is he?"

Chapa hoped Moriarity would be cool, assumed he wouldn't have to tell him to be. He was wrong.

"Him I don't know," Moriarity said after pivoting all the way around and looking straight back. "Nice suit, though."

"But he's looking right at me."

"No, not really. He appears to be reading the newspaper on his lap."

"Yours or mine?"

Moriarity squinted, then the expression on his face withdrew into disappointment.

"Can't tell."

Chapa figured he would have the entire length of the hourlong meeting to decide whether or not to confront the guy in the suit. But Mr. Brooks Brothers in the back row became a secondary concern after Chapa recognized the last council member to arrive.

"I've seen him before. He was knocking around the crime scene."

"Sure he was," Moriarity whispered. "That's George Forsythe, he's the area's leading electrical contractor. The city's safety and standards division, and the police always call him in when there's a problem or an incident."

Chapa spent the next several minutes fixed on George Forsythe, almost forgetting about the curious man in the back row. He would approach Forsythe when the meeting was over, and this time there would be no police to stop him from asking his questions and getting some answers.

As the meeting was drawing to a close, Chapa checked the batteries on his tape recorder, and turned to a fresh page on his notepad. Vanny Mars was bellowing about a zoning issue when she was interrupted by the sound of even louder voices in the hall outside the room.

Chapa looked back in the direction of the noise, purposely

avoiding eye contact with the man in the gray suit, and assumed that the next gaggle of white-shirted warriors had started their meeting a bit early. But when Warren Chakowski burst into the room clutching a hunting rifle, Chapa knew he was wrong about the noise, and any conversation with George Forsythe would have to wait.

Chapter 24

Though he'd never owned one, Chapa knew a little about rifles and shotguns, and the difference between the two, from a series he'd written back in the 90s about militia groups. The stories earned him an award that he didn't care about, and a raise that wasn't big enough. But they also earned him some hate mail and several sleepless nights as Chapa waited for some gun nut to show up at his door seeking retribution.

As far as he could tell, the weapon Warren Chakowski was pointing at everyone and no one in particular was long and powerful and probably loaded.

"Somebody here knows something about what happened to my brother, and we're all going to find out what it is."

Warren jerked the weapon from side to side like he was expecting a target to emerge at any moment. Chapa slowly raised his hands and eased out of the chair.

"This isn't the way to do this, Warren," Chapa said in a voice so calm that for an instant he wondered if he'd actually spoken. "Nothing good is going to happen this way."

Warren, confused, looked as though Chapa had just spoken to him in a foreign language. But a moment later the fog seemed to clear.

"Why are you here, Alex?"

"Same reason as you. Just trying to get at the truth." That wasn't the truth, not entirely. But at this moment, *truth* was whatever it took to disarm Warren Chakowski. "And bringing a gun into this building is not the way to go about it."

"Yeah, you better put that gun down, numbnuts." It was Vanny Mars. "You got a choice of either cutting this crap out right now or getting your ass kicked by the men in this room."

A few of the men at the table looked at one another, they appeared confused. Chapa gestured to her with an open palm, as if to say, *I have this under control.*

"After I talked to you this morning, Alex, I started thinking and thinking, and the more I thought about it all the more angry and scared I got."

"You should be scared, dickhead." Vanny hadn't sat back down, yet.

Chapa decided to give her a little more encouragement. He turned away from Warren and marched toward the table.

"Lady, will you please be quiet, huh? Really. Shut the fuck up!"

She flashed one of those *people don't talk to me that way* looks that people who should be talked to that way sometimes cultivate.

"Fine. I don't have to help at all," Chapa heard her say as he turned his attention back to Warren and the rifle he was now pointing at someone, anyone, his finger coiled around the trigger.

Chapa took a breath, then stepped into the line of fire. Warren refused to make eye contact.

"No, Warren," Chapa said, shaking his head as he took measured steps toward the rifle. Warren began to tremble.

What Warren couldn't see, in the doorway behind him were two police officers, guns drawn and trained on his back. Tom Jackson stood behind an officer who was squatting, arms extended toward Warren, a large black pistol in his hands. Jackson was signaling Chapa to move away, but he had no intention of giving them a clear shot.

When Chapa was just two or three feet from him he caught a whiff of Warren's cologne—Jack Daniels's, Old No. 7. Now Chapa knew how Warren had spent the hours after their conversation in his brother's office.

"Seems a little early to be communing with the spirits, Warren," Chapa said as he slowly reached up and put his hand around the gun barrel.

Warren looked at him, but his eyes, so red with hurt Chapa feared they might burst, refused to settle on any one thing. A drop of sweat slid down Chapa's cheek, and he heard the sound of ceiling fan blades swooshing above. Had those been there the whole time?

"They're gonna kill me too, Alex. I'm next, I know it."

Chapa came up close, put an arm around Warren's back, and watched Jackson's face shift from healthy pink to just a shade shy of crimson.

"No, Warren, no one is going to kill you. I won't let them."

Warren made eye contact with him again, and Chapa shook his head in a way that was gentle but confident. When Chapa tightened his grip on the rifle, Warren offered no resistance.

As his fingers slowly retreated from the weapon, Warren leaned in close to Chapa and whispered, "Damn thing ain't even loaded. I never shot any animals, either. I just liked tracking them. Jim knew that."

Chapa knew what would happen the moment he took the gun from Warren.

"Do you have any other weapons on you?"

"No. Of course not."

"Then I want you to give me this rifle and get down on your knees and put your hands behind your head."

Warren's face was awash with confusion.

"Please trust me, Warren."

"I do," he said, then handed the rifle to Chapa and did exactly as he'd been told.

Everything changed in an instant.

Police rushed into the room. Chapa stopped counting how many after five of them tackled Warren and pushed his face to the floor.

"He's not armed!" Chapa yelled as one of the officers screamed at him to drop the rifle. "It's not loaded," Chapa said, tossing him the weapon.

"Tom, really. Is all this necessary?"

"Just stay out of the way, Alex."

Warren was moaning softly as they lifted him by his arms, hands cuffed behind his back, and walked him out of the room. A plainclothes said something to Chapa about having to ask him a few questions, but he was already headed down the hall, calling after Tom Jackson.

"Tom, I consider you a friend, but let's be clear about this. I will make damn sure anything that happens to Warren Chakowski will also happen to your department."

"Alex, I'm only here because I was available and responded. But I will try to look after him like he was my own. Is that good enough, Alex?"

"I'll let you know."

Chapa watched Warren Chakowski, broken, lost, and under arrest, being hustled away by nearly as many cops as had been investigating his brother's death the day before. Chapa's mind was racing from one thought to another as he walked back toward the conference room.

But there was one thing of which he was now certain. If someone was responsible for Jim Chakowski's death, Chapa was going to do a great deal more than just track them.

Chapter 25

George Forsythe, a small but solidly built man in his late forties who had moved to Oakton four years earlier after his wife died, seemed nervous and fidgety. Chapa had seen this sort of response before, and chalked it up to the anxiety some folks felt around reporters.

He was wearing a dark blue polo with a small patch stitched on the left side that read POWER 4 OAKTON. Chapa had seen the trucks emblazoned with that insignia all over town. Until now he'd assumed they belonged to a utilities company, at least as much as he'd bothered to assume anything.

But standing with its owner in a far corner of the conference room, Chapa now knew that *Power 4 Oakton* was an electrical contracting firm that had grown very quickly in a few short years. He'd gleaned some of that info from eavesdropping on the statement Forsythe had given the police. It hadn't taken long for the cops to get their statements. Each council member had told a variation on the same story.

A guy they'd never seen before came storming into the room with a gun and might've shot all of them if Vanny hadn't confronted him.

Chapa had no professional reason to be talking to George Forsythe, no story to write that begged for an electrician's quote. Chapa simply had a few unanswered questions poking around in his head, and that was reason enough. Besides, Warren had inadvertently given him some cover. After all, he'd have to write the news story of the most eventful council meeting Oakton had seen in some time.

He'd just started talking to Forsythe when Dick Wick walked up and offered his hand.

"Alex Chapa, right?"

"That's what they keep telling me."

"Yeah, I know who you are, seen you around. Nice work today, you seem to have a way with troubled people, like you know what's going on in their minds."

Chapa was trying to remember what Moriarity had told him this guy did, while keeping an eye on Forsythe. Wick was about the same age as Chapa, maybe a year or two older. The grooves in his face, some the product of age, others not, suggested that he'd spent some time on the wrong side of the street.

Wick reached in his pocket, pulled out a small thin silver case and removed a business card, which he handed to Chapa.

"I serve as legal counsel for various businesses and organizations in the area."

"Good for you."

"Hey, I'm sorry about what happened to your fellow journalist, that was too bad."

Chapa nodded, but said nothing as an uncomfortable silence followed.

"Well, I'm going to lunch," Wick said finally. "You coming, George?"

"Right behind you."

Chapa put a hand on Forsythe's shoulder, felt it tighten under his touch.

"I just need a minute, Mr. Forsythe. I'd like to get some background for my story about the explosion."

Forsythe looked lost at that moment.

"Okay, but just a minute," he said, looking in every direction but Chapa's.

Wick stepped between them.

"You know, George, you don't have to talk to this man," he said, then turned to Chapa, winked and smiled as though he was just joking.

He wasn't joking.

"No, it's okay, Dick. I'll be along in a minute."

Wick nodded—the smile was gone now—and walked out of the room.

Though it didn't take long before their conversation began to resemble a high-speed Ping-Pong match more than an interview, Chapa had no intention of giving up and letting Forsythe off easy.

"Everything that happened is already in the police report."

"How do you know that?" Chapa asked, noticing how Forsythe would rhythmically click the pen in his hand.

Click, click, click.

"Because I'm the one who advised them on it."

"And what led you to such an easy and speedy conclusion?"

"I've been at this for a long time. I know what I'm doing."

The answer had come a bit too quickly and maybe too easily, Chapa thought. Most pros would've taken issue with the question, that was the reason Chapa asked it. Maybe he was one of those unflappable, eternally calm people, but Forsythe didn't come across as that sort.

Click, click, click.

"Have you seen a house explode like that before?"

"A couple of times, yes."

"Really?"

"I do have to go, I've been here much too—"

"Ever been wrong about something like this?"

"Never."

Click, click, click.

Up until now, Chapa had resisted the urge to record this conversation, concerned that doing so would have the same effect on Forsythe as a bright light does on a scared rabbit. But now he wanted to press a few of Forsythe's buttons.

He drew the small black Olympia from his pocket like it was a natural extension of his hand, and pressed RECORD.

"Walk me through it, George. What did you see that made it all so clear in your mind?"

Forsythe's eyes were fixed on the recorder. The clicking had stopped.

"Some of the surviving wires in the house were frayed, many were still original." Forsythe now seemed distracted, his mind likely drifting in the direction of an escape plan. "You know what, Alex—it's Alex, right?"

Chapa nodded slightly.

"I'm starting a big job today, so I really do have to get going."

"When can we continue this conversation?"

Forsythe was on the move.

"Maybe next week or the week after, I'm gonna be real busy for a stretch."

"I suppose it wouldn't matter if I gave you my card," Chapa said as Forsythe opened the door and hurried out without looking back or answering. *Click, click, click,* fading into all of the other sounds from the hallway outside.

Then the door closed with a loud *snap,* and Chapa was alone in the room. He looked around and wondered how much Chakowski could have told him about what went on here and how horrified he would've been by what his brother had done for him today. A lifetime of learning snuffed out by a single spark.

"What a waste."

He flipped open his cell phone and tried to call Erin, but the old building refused to let a signal sneak inside its thick plaster walls. Maybe out in the hall. Chapa stepped though the door, but he didn't get far before someone got his full attention by grabbing his arm and yelling at him.

Chapter 26

"You!"

There was a look of the crazy in the old woman's eyes. The sort that you sometimes see at political rallies, racetracks, or Vegas night at the local social club.

"You write for one of those useless papers that are letting them get away with it!"

"I know, I do. Don't you hate that? I know I do. Damn it."

"I . . . what? Huh?"

Apparently, Chapa had succeeded in confusing the woman, usually a good play in these situations. He knew that one option when confronted by someone who has jumped the rails is to make them think that your train wasn't on a track to begin with.

"What can we do about it, Gladys? It's Gladys, right?" Chapa remembered her screeching at the poor woman by the info desk over at police headquarters. Apparently, Gladys had migrated down the street in search of a warmer reception. Didn't she have anything better to do?

"Um. Well, you can start by writing some honest stories about this town."

A political nutcase. Chapa hated politics, never trusted anyone who made their living off broken promises.

If he'd had a moment to think about it before the woman rushed him, he would've guessed that her harangue had something to do with politics. But he would've been wrong.

"It's those houses with the peeling paint and the weeds and the garbage cans that are visible from the street." Her breath smelled like stale coffee and dentures. "There are ordinances, you know. But some people, the ones who have no pride in anything, they don't care about any of that."

Gladys Washer was worse than a political loon. She was a civic-minded loon. Chapa had to get away, now. He started looking for a means of escape, then looked back at Gladys and realized she was still talking.

"I'm sorry, ma'am, but I've got to get go—"

"No, you don't."

Chapa was almost resigned to having to stand there and reason with her when a face from the past gave him a better idea. He wondered how long she'd been staring at him from across the wide hall.

She was older than her body was willing to let on. A sky blue top, the sort that manages to look both simple and expensive, smoothed its way down to her trim waist and around the kind of breasts that young women believe will be theirs forever and middle-aged moms have long given up on. She was wearing neatly pressed gray slacks, and expensive black shoes with two-inch heels. Her hair had been pulled up and back.

"Leah?" He knew it was her, but it came out sounding like a question.

She smiled like he remembered she could. But then the smile was withdrawn and replaced by a much less inviting expression. He remembered that look too, along with all the others she'd shown him during their time together.

He made a nifty move and slipped out of Gladys Washer's clutch.

"I'm sorry, Gladys. But I promise I'll get right on all those important things you're concerned about."

"Do your job!" Chapa heard Gladys screech, followed by the sound of her loafers squeaking down the hall.

Chapter 27

Chapa met Leah Carelli more than fifteen years ago when he was just beginning to settle into his first job. He'd started making a habit of going out after deadline with writers from the other papers, usually to a smoky bar and grill called Peck's, where the burgers were fresh, even at two in the morning.

She was waiting tables and seemed genuinely friendly, even at such a hostile hour. Leah had recently lost her job at a software company in Naperville, and was working two of them just to pay the bills and keep from having to move back in with her parents.

Their conversations were small and brief at first, but things progressed from there until Chapa realized he had started looking forward to seeing her. He began stopping by on nights when she was working, even if he wasn't.

They soon discovered a mutual love of old movies, and when Chapa asked her to go with him to see a screening of *It Happened One Night* it didn't really feel like a date. Though every cell in his body was attracted to her, and he had noticed how she'd begun to wander into his thoughts at any hour of the day.

Several nights out passed before they kissed, a few more

until it went any further. But once they reached a tipping point there was no going back. They'd gone to see *Random Harvest* at the old Parkway Theater, then picked up some Chinese carryout and a bottle of wine. It was about 9:30 when they got to Leah's place, but they didn't get around to eating the Kung Pao chicken until well after midnight.

"I don't think I've eaten Chinese food in my robe before," Leah said, dipping a fortune cookie in her glass of wine.

All Chapa could think about at that moment was how she wasn't wearing anything under that baby pink terry cloth robe, though they had already made love twice that night.

They saw each other regularly after that, through the spring and into summer. But just after Labor Day, Leah landed a job in Spokane, where she had some family. She asked Chapa to move with her.

"I'm pretty sure they have newspapers in Washington, Alex."

But he had already begun to establish himself in the Chicago area. And besides, they agreed to stay in touch and travel to see each other as often as possible. That lasted a couple of months, though they did spend two days together later that year over the holidays.

Fifteen years had passed, and seeing Leah now, Chapa was surprised by how much he remembered about her. It was never clear to Chapa who let go of whom. Not that it mattered, at least not for long. He never saw or heard from Leah again after they lost contact, until a card arrived a few weeks after he married Carla.

Inside the card she had written simply, *Congrats . . .*

Chapa spent weeks trying to figure out what the hell that ellipsis was meant to imply, knowing full well that it was anything but random.

"Alex Chapa," she said now, nodding her head in a way that meant something, though he had no clue what that could be. "I understand you're divorced."

"You do?"

She allowed herself a quiet laugh, and Chapa remembered that, too.

"How did you know Carla and I had—"

"People talk, you hear things."

"I hadn't heard you were back in town."

"You must not have been listening too hard. I've been working here for almost five years."

"I don't spend much time at City Hall."

"Really? By the way you seemed to be drifting around like you were waiting for someone to recognize you, I would've thought you were a regular. Did they send you down here because of the crazed gunman?"

"That's not exactly the correct order of events, no."

"Well, it's too bad Vanny stopped him. Between you and me the world would be a better place without a couple of the assholes on that board."

Chapa figured it out right then. Leah's job probably gave her access to all sorts of files and records. He wondered how much more she might know and saw an opportunity.

"So which department do you work in?"

"Community and Property Standards. Sorry, nothing juicy that could someday make me your unnamed source."

He followed her through a large door that led to another part of the building and a series of offices.

"Actually, you're wrong. I'm not looking for a source."

Leah smirked, and Chapa understood that she knew he was always looking for sources.

"But I was wondering if you could get some info about the accident at Jim Chakowski's house."

The smirk evaporated. "I read about that. Sad thing. I spoke with Jim a few times, and he seemed like a nice man."

"He was a nice man, and a good reporter too."

"And after not seeing me for so long the first thing on your mind is how I can help you?"

Chapa flashed a smirk of his own.

"Well, it's not the first thing," Chapa said, and instantly

realized that what he'd meant as a clever comeback actually came over like a flirt that he had not intended.

"Okay, Alex, because I know you're wondering—I'm not married, never have been," she held up her left hand and wiggled a set of bare fingers. "No kids, both parents still alive, sister too. I own a house, have one cat, and became a Republican after 9-11."

"Wow, you could be a hell of a speed dater."

"Some of us don't have to go to those kinds of extremes."

She smiled again, and this time a few lines gathered around her eyes and conspired to betray Leah's age.

"If I find what you're looking for, you'll buy me lunch, we'll catch up."

Chapa hesitated for a second, wondered if there was a way around this, then accepted there wasn't.

"Sure."

He explained about the workman who'd been seen around Chakowski's house not long before the accident and asked Leah to find out if it had been someone from the city.

"I doubt it, but I'll check."

Chapa followed her through a set of double doors that opened to a large office area to their left and another door on the right.

"I also need to know if there are any records of repairs or city inspections at that house."

"It would have to be something pretty significant for us to have records for that sort of thing. What are you trying to stir up, Alex?"

"I'm not trying to stir up anything. I just promised a guy that I would look into it. And it's the least you can do when one of your own goes down."

She leaned the way she used to back when they spoke on a daily basis, tossing a firm round hip to the side.

"And you always keep your promises, don't you?"

Chapa tried to remember what promise he might've made to Leah Carelli. But he came up empty.

"I try."

"Yes, you do, sweetie," she said, patted him gently on the cheek, then opened the door on their right, leading to a set of offices labeled COMMUNITY AFFAIRS, and stepped inside. "Give me just a few."

From the doorway Chapa watched her disappear down a narrow hall. All the while he was struggling to remember whether Leah had always been this elusive, or if the behavior was a more recent affectation.

Chapter 28

A well-lit room stretched far to Chapa's left. He wandered away from the door Leah had disappeared through a few minutes ago. The office was at least as big as the *Chicago Record*'s newsroom, though not nearly as manic, and much more orderly than any place Chapa had ever worked. The people here were also much better dressed.

White blinds lining a far wall glowed neon bright as the midday sun fought to push through. Perfectly aligned cubicles created long rows of organization and structure.

The smell of detergent suggested that the light brown carpeting, so bland as to almost not exist, had been recently cleaned. The sounds of printers and clacking keyboards were drowned out by office chatter. Chapa caught snippets of the sort of corpo-political office speak that is at once familiar and superficial. All of it spoken at a polite volume level.

A door opened and closed down the hall to the right. Chapa turned, expecting to see Leah, but instead saw one of the members of the Business Council walking his way.

"That was some meeting you guys had," Chapa said. "Is it always that action packed? Should I wear a bulletproof vest the next time?"

"A bulletproof vest?" The guy actually seemed to be weighing the idea. "No, I don't think that's necessary."

Chapa liked to use humor as an ice breaker, but knew that it was lost on some people. Then the guy smiled and extended his hand.

"I'm Greg Vinsky, I help out around here."

"Alex Chapa, *Chicago Record*."

Vinsky nodded as though one of his questions had just been answered.

"Are you planning on becoming a regular?"

Chapa hesitated before answering, but knew there was power in the idea that he might be around for a while.

"I expect I will, yes. What is it you do, exactly?"

"What do I do, exactly? Well, Alex, mostly I bring parties together, make deals happen."

He pulled out a business card. Chapa had always been amused by businessmen and salespeople who were trained to act like PEZ dispensers and give their cards to anyone they met. Chapa took this one and tucked it in his pocket without looking at it.

"Did I see you at Jim Chakowski's house yesterday?" Chapa asked.

"At the house, yes, I was there taking pictures, Alex."

Vinsky was a little taller than Chapa, with broad shoulders, and gentle features. He had an easy, comfortable manner about him. But the way he spoke, repeating what was just said and using the name of the person he was talking to, told Chapa that this guy had been to a few business and sales seminars. Maybe even walked on coals once or twice.

"Why were you taking pictures?"

"The pictures, I'm something of a photographer, I guess. So I photograph parades and other events, or in the case of that house, I took some shots to give to the police. Just in case."

"I'd like to get a look at those pictures."

"I'm sorry, Alex, I know you're a quality newsman and

I'd like to help, but you'll have to talk to the police, they have those pictures now."

"You didn't keep copies for yourself?"

"Copies for myself?" Vinsky seemed confused. "No. Why would I?"

Chapa shrugged and shook his head.

"I guess you wouldn't."

"No, no one would. Those were some very disturbing images."

There was a softness in Vinsky's eyes, but Chapa sensed the guy was trying to figure out how to sell him something.

"Tell you what, Alex, if the *Record* ever needs a freelance photographer, I might be able to help. I've had some pictures run in the *Observer* before. They seem to do more community oriented stories, no offense."

"No offense taken." Chapa looked down the hall to check if Leah was on her way back yet. "And I'll mention to my editor that you're available."

"Yes, I'm available. And you have my business card, Alex."

"And I have your business card, Greg."

They shook hands again, then Vinsky left. Chapa had always thought of downtown Oakton as being little more than a pile of dirt populated by self-important ants. None of what he'd seen thus far contradicted that belief.

He surveyed the workers scurrying about. The administrative assistants were always the easiest to spot since they were usually the hardest working. Chapa spotted a couple of women he decided were middle managers of some sort because they were too fidgety to be anything else.

Then he eyed someone who didn't seem to belong there, or fit into any of the standard categories. In a corner, along the far end of a long blank wall, sat a young man at a lone desk. Apparently, he did not merit a cubicle, though it seemed he'd made an effort to claim his turf by using the wall behind him as a bulletin board.

Chapa knew from experience that it was often the outcast, the solitary man, the *quiet ones*, who knew the most about what went on. He took a glance down the hallway, and seeing no sign of Leah, decided to approach.

He guessed the guy to be in his late twenties, perhaps a little older, but not much. His white shirt and thin black tie reminded Chapa of the new wave look of the early 80s. Medium brown hair rested in a shiny tangle above pale, angular features. There had been an effort to grow a beard, maybe a goatee, but it hadn't taken and there was no evidence that it would anytime soon.

Chapa pulled up a chair in front of the desk, passing on the one along the side, which seemed a bit too familiar.

"How you doing, I'm Alex Chapa," he said, and extended his hand around a wide computer monitor and across the cluttered desk.

"Okay," the guy said, releasing his fingers from the keyboard's grip just long enough to shake hands. "Can I help you?"

"What's your name?"

"I'm Tim."

"Just 'Tim'?"

"Haas, Tim Haas."

Chapa reached over and took one of Tim's business cards.

"So tell me, Tim, why is it that you're isolated over here? Why don't those other folks like you?"

The young man's eyes doubled in size, and he looked around like a meerkat on alert.

"Are you from Internal? Because if you're from Internal then you should've told me that right off. That's what you're supposed to do."

"It's okay, Tim. I'm not from Internal."

Chapa pulled out a business card of his own. Tim's hand was trembling as he took it. Chapa watched Tim read it as closely as he might the warning label on a medicine bottle.

"I can give you someone else's business card if you'd prefer. I've got a bunch of them."

Tim shook his head as though he'd taken Chapa's offer seriously.

"Things have been a little tense around here," Tim said in a low voice.

"I kinda get that feeling."

"And now with what happened this morning. Are you here because of the gun—"

"No. But really, why are you over here at the office equivalent of the little kids' table? What do you do?"

Tim wiped his brow with a napkin that had the name of a local pasta restaurant printed on it, then reached in a drawer. There was a *pop-shoosh* sound from behind the desk.

"It's my energy drink, would you like some?"

"No thanks." *No wonder the guy is high-strung,* Chapa thought.

"I'm the head computer tech around here, though you won't find that on my job title. I'm not part of the In Crowd."

"No shit."

"It's my job to coordinate with the other techs around the city offices, make sure files and forms are up to date, that sort of thing."

"And that doesn't earn you better accommodations?"

Tim let out a heavy sigh, and Chapa knew he'd jabbed a sore spot.

"The cubicles go to the friends and supporters of the mayor, their wives, mistresses, and I'm none of the above. Besides, I replaced the husband of one of the office directors down here. The guy had cut his teeth on a Commodore, didn't know shit."

"Let me guess, he got moved up to a better job."

"Um hmm," Tim grunted through a long sip, then asked, "Are you here doing a story?" Chapa's business card still in one hand, his rocket-fueled beverage in the other.

"Why, do you have one to tell?"

"I got a bunch of them." Tim lowered his voice. "I may be hidden away in this crappy little corner now, but that won't last. I'm going places."

"How do you figure?"

Tim smiled but didn't answer right away.

"So, honestly, are you here for a story?" he asked, rocking back in his tight little office chair.

"No, I'm just friends with Leah, and she's helping me with something."

Tim gave Chapa a broad, bar buddy smile.

"Ah, Leah," he said.

"You know the song?"

"Not as well as I'd like," Tim said, his smile even wider now.

Chapa remembered he'd once bought her a CD that had the old Donnie Iris hit from the 1980s on it, only to learn she hated the song.

"Did I just hear my name?"

Chapa hadn't heard her walking toward them.

"Maybe," Chapa said as he stood, his attention focused on the red file folder in Leah's hand.

She signaled for Chapa to follow her, and led him away from Tim's high tech island. Chapa looked back to say good-bye, but Tim had turned his attention back to his monitor.

"So what do you have?" Chapa asked as they turned a corner and started down the hall.

"Not as much as I should, it seems."

"What's that supposed to mean?"

She opened the file folder. It was empty. Chapa took it from her and looked at the label. It read *James Chakowski, 806 Dwight St.*

"He had a file, but there's nothing in it."

"That's really strange."

"You're telling me."

Chapa looked into Leah's chocolate-brown eyes, saw that they were not hiding anything, and was surprised by how certain he was of that. She seemed to have all sorts of questions for him that had nothing to do with Jim Chakowski's empty file.

Up until now Chapa had a pretty good idea about what he was going to say to Warren Chakowski. How he was going to explain that bad luck, poor timing, and deco-era wiring were the only villains in his brother's death. He might've gotten philosophical on him, talked about the forces of the universe—not exactly Chapa's strong suit, but what the hell. Whatever it took to help the man begin the internal process of burying his brother.

But looking at an empty folder that might've had vital papers in it just a few days earlier, Chapa knew that version of the truth wasn't going to cut it anymore.

Chapter 29

Things had quieted down considerably in City Hall. But Chapa was leaving with much more on his mind than when he'd arrived, less than two hours earlier. The fuzzy images and curved lines that seemed to lead nowhere were stubbornly refusing to form a picture in his mind.

Warren Chakowski was in police custody, and Chapa's commitment to finding out what had happened to his brother carried a lot more weight now. How could he brush off a promise he'd made to a man who had given up his freedom in a crazed attempt to get at the truth? He couldn't.

That meant devoting more time that he didn't want to take away from Nikki, and legwork into unfamiliar territory. Chapa was processing all of it as he dodged a few folks who were on their way to one meeting or another, when a meaty paw slammed into his chest and abruptly halted his forward progress. In a single swift move that was part gymnastics, part sumo wrestling, a hand clutched Chapa's left bicep as an arm swung around his back and directed him into a corner, away from view of others.

Chapa quickly got his bearings again, and after a moment of confusion he recognized the man in the gray suit. The same one he'd seen sitting in the back row of the conference room before Warren busted his way onto the minutes of the meeting.

There was no hint of letup in his vise grip on Chapa's arm, even when their glares met. And now, as Chapa looked into the man's eyes for the first time, he saw something that he could not have seen from across the room. There was a well of darkness inside this man, and Chapa sensed that if he got too close or stared too long he might fall down into it.

Though the guy's build was no broader than Chapa's, it was clear he was big enough to create a roadblock that could put the state police to shame. If that didn't work, the bulge by his left shoulder suggested he had other ways of getting a person's attention.

"Am I right in assuming that you've taken over for Jim Chakowski?"

"And who might you be when you're back home?"

The man in the gray suit leaned away a little and sized up Chapa with no more subtlety than a tailor uses when measuring an inseam.

"I asked you a question." His sharply pressed suit crinkled a little as he rubbed up against Chapa.

"Good for you. But you already know the answer to yours, now answer mine."

After another bit of sizing up, he leaned away from Chapa, eased up on his grip, and reached inside his suit coat.

"My name is Martin Clarkson, FBI," he said and produced a thin, weathered leather wallet which he then flipped open to reveal an official I.D.

"You look better in your photo than you do in real life."

"Yeah, I must've gotten some sleep the night before."

Chapa rolled his shoulders, trying to coax the circulation back into his arm.

"So why the heavy-handed crap?"

"I wasn't sure about you."

"Christ, I'm not sure about you now. You don't see me shoving you into a corner."

Clarkson smiled as if to imply, *I'd like to see you try.*

"Let's go someplace and talk, Alex. I think you'll find we have several things to discuss. My car is right outside."

"So is mine. I'll follow you."

Clarkson looked him over again. Chapa was starting to tire of this.

"Tell you what, sport," Clarkson said, jabbing Chapa's chest with a thick index finger, "you pick the restaurant, I'll follow you, and lunch is on me."

Chapter 30

Chapa drove out of Oakton, then several miles through newer subdivisions, all of them offering great deals on homes that were supposed to have sold two years ago, and eventually into Naperville, then Warrenville. Clarkson's silver Chevy Impala remained in tow through turns, stoplights, and swelling traffic.

A few times along the way, Chapa thought about trying to lose him, maybe just to see if he could, or maybe because he didn't like being roughed up for no reason. But Clarkson did not come across as someone you screwed with.

He put a call in to Joseph Andrews at the Chicago office of the FBI, but got his voice mail, as usual.

"Hey Joe, give me a call when you're back from catching bad guys. I was confronted by one of your agents today. In fact, he's tailing my ass right now."

Chapa had purposely left out the part about how Clarkson was merely following him to a restaurant, knowing Andrews would be far more likely to call back quickly if he thought his friend had done something foolish. Again.

The two had been friends as far back as it mattered. They'd stayed close through the good times and the not so, in spite of the occasional dustup.

The downside of leaving a cryptic message with an FBI agent was that it still left Chapa unprotected, with an armed and determined man in his wake, and no one knowing about it. So after sorting through his options while waiting for a stoplight to turn, Chapa decided to call Erin.

"Hey, how's Nikki doing?"

"She's great, a sweetie, but also a complex little girl."

"Well, she's led a complex little life."

The light changed, and Chapa's Corolla rolled through. Clarkson followed without hesitation, like he'd had one foot on the brake and the other on the accelerator.

"There was something of an incident at City Hall today," Chapa said, then told her a bare-bones version of the morning's events, having decided it was best to keep the drama to a minimum, and downplay his role in disarming Warren Chakowski. There would be time for a more complete account later.

"Please tell me you're not planning to take up his cause."

"I'm not planning to charge into any conference rooms with a rifle in my hands."

"Well, thank goodness for that, Alex. C'mon, you know what I mean."

As he drove past a patrol car that was parked in front of Brinkman's Pharmacy, Chapa thought about how some people feel a sense of comfort and security at the sight of police on the job. But Chapa had never felt that way. His occasional run-ins and long-standing feuds had done nothing to ease his discomfort around local law enforcement.

A lot of folks would have at least considered flagging a cop and letting them know about the armed guy claiming to be an FBI agent. But that thought entered Chapa's mind for just a swift and unwelcome moment.

"I'll make sure Warren is treated fairly. I owe that to his brother." He heard Erin begin to object, then withdraw. "As far as I'm concerned, Jim Chakowski's death was no one's doing. Tragic and weird, yes. Criminal, no. I'm going to try to learn as much as I can about Jim's work because that will make it easier for me going forward."

"So what have you learned so far?" Erin asked.

But before he could answer, Chapa's phone started buzzing in his ear.

"Gotta go, Erin. Joe Andrews is on the other line."

Chapter 31

"Hey, Joe, do you know an agent named Martin Clarkson?"

Chapa's eyes were on the rearview, where he saw Clarkson's car emerge for an instant behind a large black Dodge pickup, then disappear again.

"Can't say that I do, but there are quite a number of us out there."

Chapa explained how Clarkson had approached him, and how he'd played the heavy hand.

"That doesn't sound right, Al."

"Which part?"

"Any of it. Did you get a good look at his I.D.?"

"I did, and it appeared to be standard issue."

"I'll look into it. At the very least he should've checked in with our office, and I'm finding no record of that."

Chapa eyed his rearview again, and saw there were more vehicles separating him from Clarkson. He could lose him now if he really wanted to. Chapa knew these streets, could draw a fairly detailed map of the area from memory alone.

But as he weighed that option, Chapa decided he was curious about the man in the gray suit. It was best to keep

Clarkson dangling on the line until Andrews could confirm who he was.

"So when are you going flying with me, Al?"

This again. The latest obsession.

Andrews made a habit of immersing himself in one thing after another. From scuba diving, to hiking, to spelunking, Andrews had devoted himself to the point of becoming an expert. He'd mastered each activity, then moved on. And for some reason, he always seemed compelled to drag Chapa along.

As far as Chapa could recall, Andrews caught the flying bug about three years ago after a fellow agent had earned his pilot's license.

"One of these days, Joe."

"I promise you'll love it, even more than spelunking."

"I hated spelunking."

"Well, there you go then."

Chapter 32

The Burger Stop had been in the same location along Butterfield Road, past a strip of newer restaurants, since the 1950s. It was one of Chapa's regular haunts. The sort of place that's found throughout the Midwest, except only locals know to look for it.

Chapa pulled into one of the few empty spots, looked back toward the parking lot entrance, then in his rearview mirror, but saw no sign of Clarkson's silver Impala. Chapa wondered whether he'd somehow lost the guy until his door swung open and he saw Clarkson standing on the other side.

"This the place?"

"Yes, and please don't slam the door when you close it for me, or the rest of the car might crumble from the impact."

Clarkson scoffed and started toward the restaurant, leaving Chapa to shut the door himself. They were greeted by the smell of fried food and soft music as they stepped inside.

Carmen recognized Chapa right off, like she always did. He nodded in her direction and followed Clarkson to the last booth in the row.

"Hey stranger," her usual hello whether she had last seen him two weeks ago or earlier that same day.

"You know what I want, Carmen," Chapa said to the twenty-five-year-old waitress who'd been working there since before her high school graduation.

"How 'bout your overdressed friend?"

"Turkey sandwich, coffee, and privacy," Clarkson said without looking at the menu or making eye contact with Carmen.

"I'll bring you the sandwich and coffee, but for real privacy you may have to get a room."

She gave Chapa a *What's his problem* look. He responded with a shrug.

As soon as Carmen walked away, Clarkson started right in.

"How much do you know about what Chakowski was working on?"

"Only what I read in his stories. He had a beat, I'm a columnist, at least I *was*. Our paths rarely crossed, and only professionally when they did. Why?"

Clarkson glared at him, and didn't break eye contact when Carmen brought two cups and filled them with fresh coffee, then left without saying a word.

"Look, Clarkson, or whoever the hell you are, I already placed a call to the FBI offices in Chicago. They have no goddamned clue who you are or what you're doing here."

Clarkson ran his heavy fingers around the rim of his cup.

"You shouldn't have done that." Clarkson's cool faded like the steam from his black coffee. He looked around as though everyone in the place posed a threat.

"This is simple. You're going to tell me what's going on or I'm going to inform those nice policemen by the door that there's an armed man claiming to be a fed in this restaurant."

Looking smaller now, like he was slowly fading into his suit, Clarkson nervously shook his head, but said nothing.

"All right then," Chapa said and started to get up.

"Sit down. I'll tell you some things."

"Give," Chapa eased back into the chair and tried to hide how pleased he was with the way he'd turned the situation around.

"My name is Martin Clarkson. I'm a special agent, but I'm not with the Chicago office. I've tracked a man, a killer, to this area. By my count he murdered at least seven people in Pittsburgh, and another nine in Baltimore."

Chapa casually slipped a palm-sized notepad out of his pocket and flipped it open like it was no big deal.

"I believe there were some similar murders even earlier in Cleveland, back in the 1990s. But the evidence on those is a bit sketchier."

"You got a name for this guy?"

"No."

"Description?"

"Male, in his forties."

"That's it?"

Clarkson nodded.

"Then how do you know—"

"He leaves a signature."

Many of them did. Chapa had spent more time studying mass murderers than he cared to admit. He'd learned that a lot of them left behind some sort of common detail. It could be a word or marking, or even the way the crime was committed, or how the body was disposed of.

"What kind of a signature?"

Clarkson reached into his sport coat. As he did, the lapel bowed just enough to reveal a dark brown leather holster. He drew a pen from his inside pocket and made a series of crude markings on his napkin.

"It's a stick figure. You know, like in the kids' game Hangman."

He rotated the napkin and slid it toward Chapa.

"Aw, somebody lost the game." Carmen was back with their food. "Let me guess, the word was 'big tippers,'" she said, smiling as she carefully placed the food in front of them, waited, apparently for some sort of response, then seemed to get the message and left.

"He leaves this somewhere in the vicinity of the body."

"Not on the body itself?" Chapa asked and took a bite of his Philly cheesesteak with provolone and extra onions.

"No. It's drawn on a sidewalk or carved into a wooden bench twenty feet away."

"Could be coincidence."

"It's not."

"So what makes you think he's here, in this area?"

"There have been a couple of murders in the past year—"

From under the table, Chapa's phone started playing "Daydream Believer."

"I'm sorry, let me turn this off," he said, reaching for the phone in his left pants pocket, then randomly pushing buttons until the music stopped. "But why this area? Why the western suburbs instead of Chicago?"

"I believe he came here for a reason. This isn't some common criminal, not the sort of guy anyone could easily pick out. I believe he's been a successful businessman of one sort or another, perhaps even a community leader, everywhere he's lived."

"So you're saying this killer is nomadic."

"Exactly."

"That could make him very difficult to track."

Clarkson nodded. "Could be he has a history here," he said.

Chapa's phone emitted a short and happy chime, indicating that he had received a message. It seemed to throw Clarkson off-stride for a moment, but then he continued.

"Or maybe he thought it might be easier to establish himself in an area like this. You live here, Chapa, how much do you know about Oakton's business and political leaders?"

"You tell me what you know."

"This town has seen a lot of turnover since the new mayor moved in and got rid of the old establishment."

Chapa followed enough of it to know that Jessica Breen, a successful attorney, had been elected mayor in a landslide six years ago, then re-elected by an even wider margin. She was sharp, hardworking, and popular, and many folks believed the city was heading in the right direction.

"Think about this, Alex, Oakton's Chamber of Commerce board has twenty members, twelve of whom weren't around here five years ago. The Business Council, that meeting you were at, twelve members, eight are relatively new. And it goes on and on."

"So that's where Jim came into it."

"He knew who the players were, old and new. But there was more to it than that. He was supposed to meet me the night he died, but he never made it. There was something that he wanted to show me."

"Maybe it had something to do with the new network that seems to be in charge now."

"Could be, sure. I think I might have a contact, someone in the middle of it all, who's willing to cooperate. I'm hoping to meet with them in the next couple of days."

Chapa took one last bite of his half-eaten sandwich. His appetite was gone. He thought about the piece of paper Warren gave him, wondered if it was meant for Clarkson, but decided to keep that to himself for the time being.

"So you've been chasing this guy halfway across the country?"

Clarkson looked off toward the large, bright windows that lined the front of the restaurant. "Yes, and I was close to getting him, once."

Carmen came over and refilled their cups.

"Tell me, Alex, what do you know about Dr. Walter Bendix?"

"Why, is he a suspect?"

"Oh no, fifteen, twenty years too old, I think. It just seems like all roads lead either to or through him."

Chapa was about to ask whether Dr. Bendix was Clarkson's contact, when he felt the buzz against his leg before he heard the chiming.

"I'm sorry, that's a text message, probably from my daughter."

Clarkson nodded and downed a long sip of coffee. Chapa flipped the phone open and checked the number. It wasn't Nikki's. The message came from Joseph Andrews, and though it was very brief, Chapa read it three times before he could finally manage to look away.

> Martin Clarkson isn't who or what he says he is. Be careful.

Chapter 33

Joseph Andrews didn't answer his phone, but the message he'd left for Chapa contained a fair amount of information. Andrews explained that Martin Clarkson was a former FBI agent, though it wasn't clear whether he'd quit or had been thrown out of the Bureau. There was some concern about his mental stability after he began obsessing over a case that did not officially exist.

"He has no authority or jurisdiction, and he probably shouldn't be carrying a gun," Andrews had said in a voice that sounded a little less steady than usual.

Chapa tried calling Andrews twice more from his office, then gave up and went to work on the two stories—the one he'd set out to write that morning about a business council meeting and the one Warren Chakowski's desperate and foolish actions forced him to write.

He was almost done with the first story when Zach knocked on the door before letting himself in.

"It's a zip code," Zach said, pointing to the number at the bottom of the yellow note page. "93106 is a zip code for Santa Barbara, California."

"What makes you think it's a zip code?"

"At first I thought it was a password of some sort, you know, for his computer."

"Maybe it is."

"Have you come across any files that require a password?"

"No, not yet."

"Well, keep it in mind, in case you do, but I tried looking it up online, I tried everything I could think of, and got that hit for Santa Barbara."

"What about the *ND* in front of the number?"

"Maybe the initials of someone who lives there, or a business? Don't know."

His mind still wound around the story he'd been working on, Chapa decided not to try and make any sense of this right now.

"Thank you, Zach. Now I need you to build a list of local movers and shakers—male, under fifty—and see if any of them have a connection to Santa Barbara, or even California. Maybe they went to college there, who knows, could be anything or nothing."

The young man's shoulders sank just a little.

"You can do this, and it may turn out to be something big." Chapa didn't actually believe that last part, but it never hurts to make someone who's helping you feel good about what they're doing.

Zach nodded, almost smiled, then turned and started to leave Chapa's office.

"You know, Zach, a good journalist goes where the story takes him—wherever it takes him."

The young man stopped in the doorway.

"What if the leads and the story go in opposite directions, or no direction at all?"

"Sometimes you've got to make an educated guess. I've found that my guesses got better over time."

"And hunches?"

"Those get better too," Chapa said, and got back to work.

It was just after six when Chapa filed his second story, which meant he was already late for dinner. He thought about calling Erin to tell her, but knew that after months of missed meals, cold food, and canceled dates, she'd come to expect this.

Still, that didn't make things right in Chapa's mind. He felt bad about it, and not just this time because Nikki was waiting too, but every time. He phoned Erin on his way across the parking lot and began to give her an explanation which she, as always, assured him wasn't necessary.

Chapter 34

Chapa heard the oven's timer go off just as he walked in the door, twenty-five minutes late. The warm smell of Erin's cooking filled his senses as Nikki came running at him an instant later, her smiling face flush with excitement. She wrapped her arms around him and squeezed.

Erin stuck her head out into the hallway. She'd hastily drawn her chestnut hair back into something resembling a bun, though a few renegade strands dangled freely by her left ear.

She mouthed the word *lasagna*, then smiled, so casually, as though she had no idea how much that smile meant to him.

Perfect.

It wasn't the sort of thought Chapa typically allowed himself. But this was so close to what he'd long ago imagined his life would be. The complete package.

He could hear the sound of Mike racing a loud and fast car on a computer-generated track, coming from a room in the back of the house. Erin flashed an open palm to let him know dinner would be ready in five minutes, then called to Mike, telling him to finish his race and turn the game off.

Ten minutes later they were sitting down to dinner, with

Chapa at the head of the table, Erin's gentle eyes looking at him from the other end. The kids sat along the sides, and jockeyed back and forth in a contest to tell him everything that had gone on that day.

Mike's dad had left shortly after his birth, and remained out of the child's life. So in the months he'd been with Erin, Chapa had inadvertently become something of a stand-in. It was a role he did not take lightly.

Erin had made it clear to Chapa that she wouldn't have wanted her son's father to stick around, anyhow.

"I want someone to stay in my life because that's where they want to be. I don't want them to feel they're doing it for me or Mike."

She was giving without being needy. Chapa was reminded of this as he watched her talk to Nikki in a way that erased boundaries and barriers. He marveled at the genuine sense of friendship that seemed to be emerging between the two of them.

Chapa allowed himself a moment to dwell on the image of what a life with Erin and Mike could be. A life that Nikki might better fit into. Here was the family he'd always wanted. The one he had lacked growing up without a father. Home for dinner. Spending time with the ones he loved. In bed at a decent hour.

But as quickly and easily as those thoughts had drifted into Chapa's mind, they were chased out by harsh truths. After this week was over, he would have no idea how long it would be before he could again spend some quality time with Nikki. He had an ex-wife who sometimes behaved as though her sole reason for being was to make his life difficult. And he was barely clinging to his job in an industry that was grasping to hold on to its dwindling vitality.

Even if he could work out some of those issues, there was still the one that followed him around and routinely found its way into Chapa's relationship with Erin, even when it had no business there. Chapa's life had been marked by a series of professional successes, and one great personal failure. And Chapa knew that until he could find a way to move beyond the wreckage of his marriage, he would not be able to fully invest in a future with Erin. That had not happened yet, and he hoped it would before her patience ran out.

Once dinner was finished, they shooed the children off to the playroom and began cleaning up. After Chapa had carried the last of the dirty dishes to the sink, he cornered Erin.

"We need to stop meeting like this in your kitchen."

"You're right, c'mon," Erin said and clutched Chapa by the wrist.

She led him out into the hall, pressing a finger to his lips when he started to ask what they were doing. Peering down in the direction of the family room, then toward the front door, Erin turned back to Chapa and smiled.

"Coast is clear, let's go."

"Where?"

Erin tiptoed down the hall and into her bedroom with Chapa in tow, still holding his wrist. She led him inside the dimly lit room, and slapped at his hand when he reached for the light switch.

"Did you miss me today?" she asked, erasing the space between their bodies.

"You have no idea," Chapa said, and held her close.

"Umm, yes I do."

She smiled, and in the glow of a night-light, Chapa saw a look of surrender and unguarded passion in her eyes that made him want to never leave her side. He kissed Erin's smooth neck, and felt her body respond, pressing even closer to his than before.

They kissed in a way that was at once both passionate and full of affection, holding back nothing. When Chapa finally pulled away from her soft mouth, he was instantly captured by Erin's tender eyes. They told him everything and offered so much more.

He could hear the children laughing in the other room.

Chapa was desperate to throw this beautiful woman on her bed and spend the rest of the night and much of the next day making love to her in every way she wanted, and maybe even inventing a few new ones. And though that couldn't happen tonight, the combination of elements seemed right, perfect.

Passion and love and security and the sense of family were one at that moment. For the first time since he could remember, Chapa felt at peace.

As he searched Erin's face, he understood that she was waiting for something. Something he had struggled to say, though he'd felt it since their third or fourth date. Knew it long before they'd slept together.

He'd imagined this moment, though not that it would happen tonight. But when the moment came and Chapa finally spoke the words he knew Erin had been waiting to hear, they didn't come out like Rhett Butler wooing Scarlett O'Hara, or something out of a scene between Bogie and Bacall, or any other classic romantic couple, and it wasn't anything like what Chapa had intended.

When that small parcel of time arrived, the kind of memory that couples recount for their grown children, grandchildren, and eventually anyone who will listen, Chapa looked deep into Erin's eyes and unwittingly channeled David Cassidy.

"I think I love you."

She withdrew a little, smiled, and Chapa knew he'd blown it.

"You mean you're not sure? The jury is still out?"

"No, of course not." He tightened his arms around her and tried to ignore the voices rushing down the hall. "That did not come out the way—"

There was the sound of a small hand knocking at the bedroom door.

"Daddy, you have a call. Your phone has been playing that music, twice."

"I took it out of your coat pocket the second time," Mike jumped in. "But Nikki made me put it down on the table."

"Because it's none of your business," Nikki responded, as Erin opened the door, looked at her son, and nodded in agreement. "I looked to see who it was, Daddy, and it said *Chicago Record*. Maybe it has something to do with that house that blew up."

"What house blew up?" Mike seemed concerned. "Do houses blow up just like that?"

"No, Mike, no they don't," Chapa said, squatting down to the boy's eye level. "Houses are very safe."

Nikki was tugging at his shirt.

"C'mon, I bet it's something important."

Not as important as some other things, Chapa thought.

Instead of what might've been and almost was, Chapa would have to settle for Erin's soft touch on his shoulder and her slight giggle as the children led him out of the room, his eyes on her the whole time. She looked back at him and grinned. It was a broad, sweet smile, and Chapa knew she meant all of it. But the moment was gone.

Chapter 35

"Why did Mommy dump you?" Nikki asked as they sat on the couch and watched their fourth straight episode of *SpongeBob SquarePants*, one of the few children's shows that Chapa not only tolerated, but actually liked.

"That's not quite how it happened, sweetie. It was more of a mutual thing. We sort of dumped each other."

The call from the *Record* had turned out to be of little purpose or significance. Just Maya, probably on Sullivan's direction, again reminding him of what he was supposed to do tomorrow.

Nikki had just about fallen asleep when Chapa pulled into his driveway. He'd thought about driving around the block a few times and giving her a chance to nod off entirely, but the truth was that he wanted to have a few minutes with Nikki before her day ended.

She was sitting with her legs crossed in front of her. A large cardboard bucket of microwave popcorn by her side.

"Why did you guys get married in the first place, then?"

SpongeBob and his squirrel friend were karate chopping one another all over town, and Chapa would've preferred to focus on that bit of silliness. But he had known these questions were coming, and even looked forward to answering them. Though he now wished he'd been better prepared.

Chapa opted for the high road, while at the same time wondering if Carla had any idea of what the high road was.

"I loved your mother very much, and we were happy for a time. We were happiest when you were born. But we reached a point in our lives where we were changing, still working to try and figure out who we were. Once we did, your mother and I discovered that we weren't right for each other."

"That's kind of sad in a way."

Chapa nodded, his eyes fixed on the TV screen though he was no longer paying any attention to the cartoon.

"In a way, I suppose."

"Why does she hate you so much?"

She asked it as casually as a child might ask for a mid-afternoon snack or to play outside on a lazy summer day. Chapa muted the TV, and turned to face her.

"I think there's a part of your mom that wishes I would've been able to make her happy. But I wasn't."

Nikki offered a grin that was lined with pain, and Chapa slid over and draped an arm around her narrow shoulders.

"You two are never going to be together again, are you?"

"No. But we'll always be with you. Even when we're apart."

"And what about Erin? I like her a lot."

Chapa took the popcorn bucket off her lap, set it down on a coffee table alongside unread magazines and empty CD cases, and helped Nikki to her feet.

"I like her a lot, too."

"Are you going to marry her?" This time Nikki's smile held nothing but joy and mischief.

"That's another discussion for another time."

He put his hands on Nikki's shoulders, directed her toward the stairs and told her to brush her teeth before climbing in bed. A few minutes later, after he'd checked and double-checked that the doors were locked, Chapa walked up to her room and tucked Nikki in.

"Tomorrow, will you tell me about one of the stories that you wrote?"

"Sure." He pulled the comforter up to her shoulders and kissed her forehead.

"Erin told me you've won a lot of awards."

Chapa reached down and flipped on a night-light without asking Nikki if she wanted him to.

"Well, there's no accounting for taste."

"What does that mean?"

"It means that you need to shut off your agile little mind and get some sleep."

She snuggled into her sheets and looked up at the ceiling.

"Those are cool," Nikki said, pointing at the stars glowing above her.

"They've been there a long time." Chapa was watching his daughter's face.

"I don't have anything like that at home, but I do have some glow-in-the-dark markers that I brought with me in my backpack, and—"

"Goodnight, Nik." Chapa stood, then blew her a kiss.

"Daddy?"

"Yes."

"You make me happy."

He stood still for a moment, not able to respond, then leaned in, kissed her on the cheek and whispered, "I love you."

Chapter 36

A little more than a mile away from Chapa's house, in a neighborhood whose best days came and went with the 60s, Gladys Washer was settling in for the night after a satisfying day.

She poured herself a cup of tea from the same pot her husband Elmer once used to make hot chocolate, and walked back to her living room. Measuring each step and every move so as to not spill on the carpet or herself, Gladys sat down in her favorite living room chair just in time to watch the last of her nighttime game shows.

Elmer would've liked most of the newer shows, especially the one with all the suitcases and the pretty young women. He never stopped liking pretty young women. Even as Elmer lay in the hospital, his life measured in hours, he still had enough energy to flirt with the nurses.

Gladys took a sip of tea, which proved a bit hotter than she'd expected, and looked at the empty chair across the room. Elmer would've been proud of her and all that she'd done to make sure the minorities and the trashy people weren't allowed to drive their town into the gutter.

Oakton had changed so much since they bought their first home back in '52, and all for the worse. In a way, Gladys was relieved that Elmer hadn't lived to see some of what was going on in the world today.

She was determined to do all she could to make certain that decent standards were maintained. Elmer would've wanted her to do that. Over the past several years she had reported numerous violations by home and property owners. And she knew Oakton was a better place because of all she'd done. Maybe that reporter she'd spoken to would write a story about her. That would be nice. Most of what she read in the papers these days was so ugly.

If he did do a story about her, maybe one with a picture, Gladys planned on cutting it out of the paper, for that scrapbook she'd been wanting to start. She would include all the other clippings of her letters to the "Common Voice" section of the *Chicago Record*.

For a time, Gladys had the page almost all to herself. And then some other person started sending in smart letters about how it wasn't a bad thing that criminals were dying violently in Oakton. But Gladys didn't mind sharing the page with someone who felt the same as she did about her community.

The contestants were introducing themselves when the doorbell rang. It startled Gladys, and her first impulse was to ignore it, figuring it was probably some high school kid trying to sell raffle tickets, magazines, or who knows what other nonsense. Though it seemed kind of late for them to be out doing that, especially on a school night.

But what if it was someone checking to see if she was home? Would they try to break in if she didn't answer the door? There had been some burglaries in the area over the past few months, maybe this was how they did it. Could this be how the burglars found out if a house was empty?

Gladys was wishing she still had some of Elmer's guns in the house when the doorbell sounded again. Maybe it was an emergency of some sort, someone needed help. If that was the case, she'd agree to make a call for them, but she would not open the door.

She set down her tea, clutched her phone, and slowly walked to the window but did not draw back the curtains. Instead, Gladys slipped a peek through the narrow slit in between. No need to let them know an old woman lived here.

Gladys was surprised when she recognized the tall, distinguished older man standing outside her door. He must've seen some movement at the window, though she'd been very careful to not touch the curtains, because he smiled at her.

What was he doing at her house? And at this time of night? She had seen Dr. Bendix at some of the city meetings that she'd been to. He was a very important man in the community. But why was he here?

Perhaps it had something to do with that complaint she'd filed. He too was a concerned citizen, and maybe he'd come to thank her for her diligence.

I bet he's noticed that house too. As well as all the others with chipped paint, cars on the lawn, or broken fences.

As she opened the door, Gladys wondered if the doctor was married. Widowed, probably, she decided. All alone now. No one should be alone in their final years. It's just not healthy.

"Dr. Bendix," Gladys opened the door, smiling. "What a pleasure and a surprise."

He returned the smile, though Gladys thought it looked a bit forced, then stepped inside and closed the door behind him. The doctor looked tired and worried, and she'd never seen him look this way before. She was about to ask what he was doing there, when she saw the device he was holding.

Any thoughts about receiving recognition for her community work, or whatever fleeting fantasy she may have had about the good-looking doctor on her doorstep, vanished the way dreams often do. But now those thoughts were quickly being replaced by something else.

She recognized the device as a stun gun, like the ones she'd seen in her favorite cop reality shows, and wondered why Dr. Bendix would have one. Had the neighborhood gotten that bad?

"Why do you have that?"

He didn't answer, which left Gladys even more confused. Maybe he'd mistaken her for someone else. But who? And why?

Gladys was still trying to figure it all out as she watched the expression on the doctor's face shift in a way that terrified her, an instant before he pressed the stun gun to her chest and squeezed the trigger.

Chapter 37

After making breakfast for Nikki, Chapa dropped her off at Erin's house and drove to the *Record*. Along the way he gave serious thought to calling in sick, something he'd done no more than a half dozen times over the past ten years.

It wasn't right that Erin was using her vacation time to care for his daughter while he wasted these precious days. Chapa knew in his gut that a year from now he would not be working for the *Chicago Record*. And all the good soldiering in the world wouldn't be enough to change that.

Zach jumped out of his chair when he saw Chapa walk into the newsroom.

"Not much info on any killings in Cleveland, but there might be something to the murders in Pittsburgh and Baltimore that you told me to look into."

Knowing Wormley had to be lurking somewhere nearby, Chapa tilted his head in the direction of his office. They shuffled over to it, slipped inside, and Chapa closed the door behind them.

"What do you mean there might be something to it?"

"There was a spike in the numbers during those years that were listed on the page, mostly criminals killing criminals."

Chapa sat down behind his desk, flipped the switch on the lamp, and started writing down some notes as Zach spoke.

"Gang war?"

"Probably. That's what the papers reported, for the most part."

"For the most part?"

"Yeah, there was a cop in Pittsburgh, I found a couple of stories where he was quoted. He had a different opinion."

"His name?"

"Conyers, but you won't be able to talk to him. He was killed, banger style, a few years ago."

Chapa stopped writing.

"Cops don't just get themselves killed."

"Well, there was some suggestion that this one was dirty."

The door swung open and Sullivan walked in.

"Alex, you're supposed to be—"

"Yeah, I know, interviewing an important member of the community."

Sullivan raised his palms toward Chapa as if to suggest there was no problem between them. Chapa had another opinion.

"Look, Matt, I am very good at my job and part of that means making sure I'm where I need to be when I need to be there."

"Alex, I certainly in no way meant—"

"I'm talking now," Chapa interrupted, raising his voice just enough. "If you have anything to say to me you come to my office and say it, or pick up the phone and call me yourself. You don't ask Maya to do it, and especially not when I'm on my own time."

The quiet that followed had a physical presence, much bigger than any of the men in the room. After an uncomfortable stretch that seemed longer than it actually was, Sullivan silently nodded and left the office.

"Hardcore," Zach said after they'd watched Sullivan walk back to his own office and close the door.

"I had to get rid of him."

"I hate to have to tell you this, but he might get rid of you." Zach had a crooked grin on his face.

"That's pretty much a given," Chapa said as he closed his door. "I need you to find out everything you can on a man named Martin Clarkson."

"Is he a bad guy?"

"Well, I have a feeling he just happened to be in those towns during those times."

Chapa slipped Zach's notes into his satchel, double-checked the battery power on his tape recorder and headed out of the office.

"Also, see if there's anything on a killer who leaves drawings or carvings of stick figures at murder scenes."

Zach's face contorted until his expression was equal parts confusion, bewilderment, and concern.

"You're serious?"

"Couldn't be more serious. And now I'm off to do some hard-hitting journalistic work."

"You are, really?" Zach said, following him.

"Maybe by Wormley's standards."

Chapa didn't have to look back toward Wormley's desk to know he'd gotten a reaction. He could feel at least one set of angry eyes tailing him all the way out of the newsroom.

Chapter 38

Charles Stoop, age forty-seven—a "*young* forty-seven," as he'd boasted to Chapa—seemed to have two facial expressions in his arsenal. There was the full-on smile, like someone seeing a long lost friend or favorite uncle for the first time in years, and the look of compassionate concern, which came complete with a furrowed brow, but stopped just short of suggesting worry.

His dark hair looked like it had been colored that way to cover much of the gray, though Stoop wasn't trying to fool anyone by making it all the same shade. He was starting to give ground in the battle of the hairline, and trying to compensate by combing it straight down over his forehead. He was also losing the fight against middle-age sag, though not as much as most men his age.

"You know, I'm something of a journalist myself," Stoop said with a smile, his teeth whiter than white.

"Are you really?" Chapa was busy with his notes, counting up the number of useable answers and trying to determine whether he had enough to build a sandcastle of a story.

"That's right. I'm a columnist for *Lawn Times*. It's a trade publication that all the big commercial landscapers subscribe to."

Chapa was still trying to figure out why he was doing a feel-good piece on a guy whose apparent claim to fame was that he could, "sell anything to anybody," a boast he'd already made three times during the first ten minutes of the interview.

"I'll tell you what I like about Oakton. Here everybody works together. The various businesses and agencies help each other out. We don't fight or compete with one another."

"Isn't competition a good thing?"

"Not for business, it's not. I don't need to be protected from competition—I can sell anything to anybody. But this is just a good environment for everyone."

Chapa now understood why he was here. Stoop and Carston Macklin were cronies. Macklin golfed and went out for cocktails with people like Stoop, and they both belonged to any number of social clubs and organizations. Anything that might help the *Record* box out its competitors. Not exactly high-integrity American journalism. But then again, the concept of an independent press had died long before Carston Macklin took over the paper his father founded.

"And everyone has their role to play. Me, I handle the landscaping. It's Willie Blair who scouts out potential deals as well as anyone. If you need to make sure all the insurance forms are filed you go to Clay Hunter. Gotta have a security system, that's Frank Gemmer's thing. Greg Vinsky makes sure all the *i*'s are dotted, and Wick is there to handle any legal issues."

"And Vanny Mars?"

"Vanny is a whole lot of everything. She makes sure the accounting is right, and then there's Teddy Bruce who handles the PR for all the area business groups."

Chapa had wondered why Stoop wanted to meet him downtown, in a city hall conference room and not at his business office. Now Chapa knew. Stoop's business office *was* at City Hall.

"Look at how this city has changed for the better since

we've weeded out those people who simply refused to get with the program."

"Some might call that corruption."

"Let them call it what they like. Those are disgruntled people, air takers who don't know how to thrive in a vibrant, changing business community."

Stoop reached across the table, took hold of Chapa's tape recorder and slid it closer to his side, as though he wanted to make certain his words were recorded clearly.

"They've got their petty accusations. We've got before-and-after pictures," Stoop said, then pushed the recorder back across the table. It *swooshed* against the laminate top and came to a stop by Chapa's hand.

"It's like a cozy little network," Chapa said, doing his best to make his assertion sound neutral.

"That's right. We communicate with one another, and that's a key. I'm all about communication, I tell everyone that."

"How 'bout George Forsythe? How does he fit into the mix?"

"Yeah, George is a fixture around here," Stoop said and grinned. "Get it, fixture? He's an electrician."

"I got it."

"That's the sort of thing I'd put in one of my columns, you know."

"Um hmm," Chapa said, tucking his tape recorder away and closing his notebook.

"We should write something together sometime, you know, collaborate. You're a pretty good writer too."

"Speaking of good writers, did you know Jim Chakow-ski?"

Stoop put on his best solemn face.

"I didn't know him as well as some of the other folks who've been around here longer did. But he seemed like a good man."

"He was." Chapa started for the door.

"Hey, I'm serious about that collaboration. I'll give Carston a call and talk to him about it."

Chapa did his best to suppress a laugh.

"I'm sure you will."

Chapter 39

It had been years since Chapa had spent this much time at the office. There were a number of reasons for that. None of them were good.

In the early days of his career Chapa enjoyed simply being a reporter, got a charge out of calling himself one. He was proud to be part of a great tradition of newspaper writers who played an indispensable role in the lives of Americans.

His job, as he saw it, was to tell the truth in print, even the hard truths. *Especially* the hard truths. He bonded with colleagues and peers, who enjoyed each other's company more than anyone else's because they understood one another.

But many of those writers were gone now, some for years. They had retired or left for a more stable line of work. Others had been forced into writing bullshit stories that wallowed in nonsense or bordered on tabloid.

A few more had died. Heart attacks seemed the most common deadly weapon, an exploding house less so. It wasn't until this moment, as Chapa sat in his office thinking about how the last members of a dying species must feel, that he understood for the first time how comforting it had been to have an old school reporter like Chakowski nearby.

There were a few others like him still kicking around at the *Record,* like Jerry Rossiter in sports, Lisa McCleary in international news, and Lloyd Nomer in business, but not many. And Chapa knew, just as they did, that management was already looking for a cheaper, less independent option for filling its pages with words.

Zach had done some good work in researching as much as he could. He would've made a good reporter twenty years ago, when good reporting still mattered. But Zach didn't know how to connect the disparate dots. That was Chapa's specialty.

Oakton and some of its surrounding communities had seen a jump in the murder rate. Most of the killings involved gangbangers and street thugs, so no one much cared.

Gang wars were bad for business and worse for tourism. It was the sort of news which guaranteed that young women from Naperville, Wheaton, or Geneva, clad in doll-sized outfits, would not party and spend money in your town on Friday nights. There was always pressure to downplay those kinds of stories, or define the violence as gang-on-gang crime.

Zach had printed out photos, most of which were head-shots of men in their teens or twenties who were working on a hundred-mile stare they had not yet earned and now never would. But one photo in particular caught Chapa's attention. It was a shot of an alley on Oakton's seedy south side. The body that someone had sliced up and left there was already gone, but the *Record*'s photographer had decided to document the crime scene anyhow.

It was an alley much like any other in a blighted section of a town. The bricks along the building's exterior wall were cracked and faded. Broken glass and weeds filled the countless gashes in the pavement.

The victim's throat had been cut, probably by someone who'd come up behind him. A hell of a trick no matter how dark it might have been that night, Chapa thought, in a long alley like this one. But the fuzzy details of the crime's how and why were not what grabbed Chapa's attention.

Along the left side of the photo, where the wall began to taper off into the distance, a large NO had been crudely scratched into the bricks by an unsteady hand. There may have once been another word after it, perhaps PARKING or DUMPING, but that must have been covered over by grime or weeds, because Chapa could only make out a few uncertain lines.

Chapa leaned in close to get a better look at the grainy photo, hoping to confirm what he thought he was seeing inside the two-foot high letter O. But he couldn't be sure.

Zach walked into the office a few minutes later as Chapa was getting off the phone with Dana Taylor in the art department.

"I just requested an actual print of this photo. Take a look. Do you see anything unusual inside the letter *O*?"

Zach leaned in just as Chapa had, stared at the image for a moment, and shook his head.

"Maybe a bug or some vines or snot or could even be a speck in the print, I don't know."

Chapa knew he was probably seeing something that was not actually there. Dana had promised him a fresh print within the hour, though he was starting to wonder whether that would clear up anything.

"What are those?" Chapa asked, pointing to the small stack of papers Zach was holding.

"This is why I came in here. These are letters that were printed in the 'Common Voice' section."

Chapa was familiar with that page in the *Record*. It was where anonymous letters to the editor, or ones that were too out there for any serious news page, were printed. Letters from loonies had been around since the advent of the printing press. In the old days they were passed around the newsroom, mocked, and given the burial they deserved in the circular tomb. Today, however, they were collected and given precious column inches that once belonged to real news.

The letters Zach handed him all fit a pattern. They were written in defense of the killings of some of the area's bottom feeders. On one level, Chapa could understand the sentiments, but on another, he was troubled by the sense of satisfaction that bled between the lines.

> *What would these insects have done if they had been allowed to live? They would have brought more misery to the lives of good people. The only thing Roberto whatever his name was ever did right was bleed to death.*

"I wonder if the cops ever follow up on letters like that," Zach said.

"No, they're busy chasing legitimate leads."

Chapa was starting to read the last of the letters when Marcie Conrad, an attractive young woman who did a bit of everything around the office, arrived with the photo. She handed it to Chapa, then smiled at Zach and left.

"How long have you two been, you know . . ." Chapa asked, smiling as he laid the color photo on his desk and shifted a lamp, shining more light on the image.

"We really haven't been, you know, but there's something about her, isn't there?"

"Umm hmm . . ."

Chapa studied the picture. There wasn't as much contrast as he'd hoped. But as it turned out, that didn't matter anyhow.

"There's something here, too," he said, pointing to the small stick figure that had been etched into the brick just inside the letter *O*.

Chapter 40

St. Louis, Missouri, 1977

The child has had his face buried in his pillow for more than an hour. The thin fabric is sticky and cold with tears.

It started earlier, in the afternoon as the sun dropped below his window ledge. He heard the yelling in the other room, then his mother's screams. Then silence.

Looking around his room now, he sees the Halloween costume he wore just two nights ago. He'd wanted to be Superman, but his mom brought home an old Frankenstein costume, the vinyl kind that ties in the back.

The child didn't like it, not at all. The plastic mask that came with it was cracked along the bottom, held together on the inside by a piece of scotch tape. It smelled bad, too, like spit and sweat.

"That's the best I can do, Sugar," his mom explained. "But I tell you what, we'll hop the bus and go trick-or-treat in a real nice neighborhood, where the people give out good candy."

The child likes riding the bus, always imagines it will just keep going, won't stop until they're somewhere else. Anywhere else.

They were on the bus for a long while that Halloween night, and the child loved every minute of it. His mom told the child to ignore how some of the folks looked at his costume when they opened their door.

"Just say, 'Trick-or-treat,' and 'Thank you,' and ignore everything else. Those folks may be all high and mighty, but someday their kids will be working for you, looking up to you."

He looked at his mother's face, her difficult smile. Then he reached up and brushed aside a strand of her thin yellow hair that became darker toward the top of her head until it was almost black. And the child knew this meant a lot to her for some reason. He returned the smile and watched her face blossom, if only for an unguarded instant.

That turned out to be a magical night, as he and his mom walked up one block, then down another, until she told him they had to catch the bus back. The child stalled, hoping they would miss it and never go back, but that just made his mom angry.

He didn't say a word to her on the way home, and right now the child was feeling very guilty about that. Things had gotten real bad between his mom and Gilley, and the child wishes he'd had the courage to call for help, or the strength to go find a knife in the sink and jab it into Gilley's back.

But he didn't do anything like that. The child hid in his bed, trying to make himself invisible. Like he'd learned to do.

The child finally works up the courage to go check on his mother. He knows Gilley isn't there anymore. He heard him run out the door, lock it tight from the outside. Then the sound of Gilley's car raging to life before it roared away.

Still, the child gets out of bed slowly, one foot on the floor, then the other. Stopping for a moment to stare at the Frankenstein costume draped over the back of a chair, its broken mask laying facedown on the seat. He tiptoes to the door of his room, and calls out.

"Mommy?"

Silence.

"Mommy, you okay?"

When there is no response, the child knows he has to be brave and walk into the other room. He closes his eyes, opens the door, and steps through.

But the child stops when he feels a thick dampness on the bottoms of his socks. He opens his eyes and sees his mother sprawled on the floor in what to his young mind appears to be an ocean of blood. Her neck has been cut so savagely that as he reaches for her the child fears his mother's head is about to come off.

Touching her blood-smeared face with delicate fingers, the child is stunned by how cold her skin feels. He puts his arms around her and starts sobbing, then crying, then screaming. First out of fear, then out of sorrow, and finally out of rage.

The child screams for a very long time.

Chapter 41

The alley was located in what was once Oakton's industrial corridor, back when companies still thought it was a good idea to have plants in the Midwest. It was down the street from an abandoned metal works, and across from a liquor store that was still thriving the way they always seem to in places where folks don't have a lot of cash.

Two street toughs, one sporting a black-and-white bandanna, the other weighing three hundred pounds, easy, sat on the curb in front of the store drinking cheap beer. Chapa stared at the two long enough to make it clear he was aware of them, but not long enough to pose a threat, or issue a silent challenge.

Even under the bright midday sun, Chapa felt the grip of desperation and the promise of violence it often produces. He parked on the street, just beyond the mouth of the alley. The littered corridor seemed to lead nowhere in particular, and Chapa guessed it might have once been used by factory workers as a quick route for transporting material from one end of the building to another.

The passageway itself was in even worse shape than the photo revealed. Nature had long ago taken over much of the pavement and gravel, its growth hampered only by pieces of broken glass that might've been there for years, and discarded paper bags and food wrappers of a more recent vintage.

At some point there had been a passing attempt to patch things up a bit, maybe in the hopes of selling the buildings. But apparently those efforts were abandoned shortly after they began. Chapa's footsteps crunched the gravel beneath as he tried to avoid the glass and ignore the odor of waste, both human and undefined.

Walking down the alley, Chapa searched for gaps or doorways, anywhere that a killer could've hidden, waiting to attack. But the passageway was narrow, and its walls appeared solid and revealing. Nowhere to hide. And coming up from the far end without being heard would be nearly impossible, even if darkness had provided enough cover.

The area he had seen in the photo was about a third of the way or so into the thirty-yard-long corridor. Chapa made a point to carry himself like a man with a purpose from the time he got out of the car to the moment he reached his destination. All certainty, no fear. His don't-fuck-with-me attitude, the one that he'd learned long ago and employed many times over, was his only weapon against anyone who would harm him. And he knew it was a piss-poor defense.

The brick wall was veined with cracks, many so small that they had not been captured in the photo. The writing was less clear than in the image, and it took Chapa several tries to locate where he'd seen the stick figure.

Was it still there? Chapa couldn't be sure now. He compared it to the photo, and identified what he thought might have been the legs forming two-thirds of a triangle. But what he'd believed to be a head looked more like a pockmark now, and Chapa began to wonder if Warren Chakowski's theories and Martin Clarkson's claims had conspired with his imagination.

Did he want to believe? Why?

He stepped back, examined the photo again, then the

wall. There was an area inside the O that had been scratched in a deliberate way. But the closer he got, the more the image, if there indeed was an image, became distorted and open to any number of interpretations.

"Daydream Believer" started playing in his pocket. He took his phone out and the song gently echoed off the beaten walls. The number was unknown to him.

"This is Chapa."

"Yeah, Martin Clarkson here. There's something I need to show you."

"Is there?"

"I just told you there is. How soon can you get to the Fletcher Forest Preserve? Do you know where it is?"

Chapa did. As a child he'd picnicked there with friends and family. There was always something mysterious about the park. It was the sort of place that could easily spark a child's imagination.

"I know where it is."

"You know that big windmill on the west side of the park."

Actually, it was closer to the center of the park, but he saw no reason to correct Clarkson. They agreed to meet in half an hour, though Chapa's attempts to learn more about what was going on all failed.

Chapa took one last, long look at the wall. He couldn't be certain about anything, but figured it couldn't hurt to show the photo to Clarkson. As he emerged from the alley Chapa realized that two pairs of eyes were on him from across the street.

The duo had finished their beers, and that was bad. But they were still sitting on the curb, which meant Chapa might be able to get to his car before they made their move.

"Hey man, you find what you was looking for?"

It was the guy with the bandanna. Wiry and oozing 'tude. His narrow but taut, prison-honed muscles weaving their way down from tattered T-shirt sleeves.

"Guy got killed in the alley earlier this year," Chapa responded.

Then he heard the big guy whisper to his buddy, "I think he's talking 'bout Gato."

"Lot of guys got killed there, and some got cut up, or fucked up. All of it, man. You some sort of cheap-ass cop?"

"No, I'm a reporter."

The big guy laughed, then said, "Clark fucking Kent came to pay us a visit."

Chapa watched as the two men then went through a series of choreographed fist bumps and complicated handshakes.

"So who uses this alley, or whatever is on the other end of it?" Chapa asked, knowing the bandanna guy would be the one who answered.

"Ain't nothing on the other end of it, just another alley that don't go nowhere. Nobody goes in there unless they got to."

"And why would anyone have to?"

The big guy jumped in. "I piss in there sometimes, like this morning, right where you were standing just now."

They laughed and went through the whole hand-slapping ritual again as Chapa headed for his car.

"Hey, you gonna put us in the newspaper?"

Chapa smiled, opened his door, then turned back toward them.

"The cops said someone had snuck up from behind the victim. Was Gato the sort of guy you could sneak up on?"

"No fucking way." It was the big guy, and he didn't seem interested in cracking any jokes now. "Nobody ever got the drop on Gato." His buddy was silently shaking his head. "Nobody. Ever."

As he sped toward his meeting with Clarkson and away from two men who under different circumstances might have ventilated his chest, Chapa thought about how that exchange would likely be the highlight of their day, or even their week. *Some fucking reporter was down here, man, he talked to us and shit.* He also thought about how hard his mother had worked to keep that from becoming his life as well.

With that in mind he decided to call Nikki. Just to say hi, and let her know he was thinking about her.

Chapter 42

Martin Clarkson looked up at an unblemished blue sky and decided it just wasn't right, as he slumped in the only remaining patio chair. He'd reached the same conclusion twenty minutes and two drinks ago, but had forgotten in the process.

Nothing about the day suited his mood. Not the flawless weather, or the expensive scotch, or how the movers, like everyone else it seemed, managed to go about their work. Like nothing had happened. As though life could somehow drag on beyond this place, this moment.

Through eyes that were blurred by emotion and made unsteady by liquor, Martin stared at the empty swimming pool. Again. He could almost see Kimberly, smell the lotion on her shoulders, watch her dive in and marvel at the way her body seemed to slip inside the water leaving barely a ripple.

His wife had grown up with a swimming pool in her yard, another down the street, and one at her grandparents as well. She was not supposed to die in one.

Martin should've been there that afternoon. It was a

scheduled day off. The sort that used to mean spending hours at the movies, or a museum, or just kicking back by the pool before and after making a mess of the sheets in the bedroom.

He should've been poolside, watching her, talking with her. There to help when her head somehow slammed into the side. In the water, pulling her out, before she could even begin to drift away.

Kimberly had been drinking, not a lot, but enough. They often enjoyed a bottle of wine by the pool. But never to excess.

Martin looked at his shot of scotch and saw his own, distorted reflection in the small glass. Unshaven, unwashed, his hair a tangle of gray and black.

But he had not been there that afternoon. He was in the field chasing what turned out to be a useless lead on the stickman murders. Goddamned stickman murders. Martin wondered if he even believed in them anymore. He had to. The price he had already paid for his certainty that a serial killer had been responsible for at least two sets of murders was far too high to allow any doubt.

Having doubts would mean he'd been wasting his time chasing shadows of his own creation while his wife lost her life. For Clarkson, doubt would mean he'd been somehow negligent at best, and responsible for her death at worst.

He'd been dismissed from the Bureau after being labeled a *rogue agent*. He was out of work, and didn't care. Kimberly would've found the right words, she would've told him what he needed to do next. But now there was only silence on an otherwise perfect day. How could the sky be so goddamned blue?

"Mr. Clarkson? You okay?"

It took Martin a moment to respond. Sensing that the man might've been trying to talk to him, he began by apologizing.

"That's okay, Mr. Clarkson. I know this can be a difficult day, moving out of your home and with what happened to your wife and all."

Martin nodded and willed his eyes away from the swimming pool.

"You want a drink . . . what's your name again?"

"I'm William, sir, and thank you, but no, I don't drink."

A gut-punch smile flared across Martin's face as he lifted his glass in a toast. "Here's hoping you never have a reason to." He drank until there was nothing left, then slapped the glass onto the patio table and poured himself another.

"Sure, okay, Mr. Clarkson, I thank you for that. Me and my men, we've got all of your stuff loaded on the truck, and we're almost done."

Clarkson tipped the bottle, looked to see how much was left.

"Me too."

"Right. Well, all that's left to go is this table and that chair you're sitting in. Do you want us to just leave them, or are you ready to go?"

Martin thought about it for a moment, then without fully realizing his arm was in motion, threw the shot glass into the pool. An instant later he heard it shatter against the bottom at the far end.

After an uncertain attempt, Martin managed to stand up as he clutched the bottle by its neck.

"Take it. Take all of it."

As he stumbled toward the pool, then sat down at the edge, Martin thought he heard William say, "Yes, sir," and call to one of his fellow movers.

Martin looked out over the empty pool, and through the haze filling his mind and clouding his eyes he could almost see her emerging from the still water. And then Kimberly wasn't there anymore, no matter how hard he tried to picture her.

It was time to go.

He rolled onto his side, making certain to hold the bottle steady, and pushed himself to his feet. The table was gone, the chair too. The moving truck's engine bellowed to life at the end of the long driveway. They were waiting for him.

Martin straightened up, told himself that what was over, was over. Committed in that moment to do his best to believe it. Then started to walk in the direction of the driveway, heading for the moving truck. Away from this place and the pain that now defined it, and toward a different direction for his life.

Until something caught his eye.

He stopped and looked at the small dark blotch on the concrete, where the table had been. Then Martin walked over to that spot, no stagger or uncertainty in his step now.

The outline of a table leg, painted in rust, created a misshapen circle around the small stick figure. As he squatted to get a better look at the grotesque ink drawing, the bottle slipped from Martin's hand. Its contents washed across the area by his feet. Bathed in scotch, the figure appeared to come to life as it glistened in the afternoon sun.

It seemed to be mocking him.

Whatever resolve Martin Clarkson had managed to build up in the weeks since his wife's death vanished that instant. It was buried under the shards of blue sky that were crashing down all around him.

Chapter 43

Chapa eased off the gas as he passed through the last of several speed traps on his way to the park. He scanned a mental list of questions he now had for Martin Clarkson, while doing his best to not get too pissed off over the ones he should've already asked.

Why haven't you coordinated your investigation with local authorities? Have you created a list of potential suspects? And why the hell are you dragging me out to a park on the outskirts?

Getting information from people who didn't want to give it was one of Chapa's special talents. But then again, it was probably one of Clarkson's, also.

Nikki had been thrilled to hear from him. Maybe because it pulled her away from schoolwork for five minutes. Maybe because she truly missed him. Chapa settled on the latter.

Erin too was happy that Chapa had called, at least until he told her where he was going and where he'd been.

"You're not doing what you're supposed to be doing, which I thought was following in Chakowski's footsteps."

"I'm not so sure about that, Erin. I think this may be exactly what Jim was chasing."

"Okay, and look what happened to him."

Having Nikki around seemed to be having an effect on her. It was as though Erin was now acutely aware of every bad thing that could happen to him. He was too. Over the many months since Carla had moved Nikki to Boston, Chapa had become more accustomed to the feeling of not being tethered to anyone. Not that he would act any differently under other circumstances.

There had been some reckless moments after Nikki's birth and before the divorce. Of course he'd feared for his safety, worried that he might never again see the people he loved, recoiled from pain or danger on several occasions. But Chapa feared something else, too, perhaps even a little bit more. He was scared of losing his edge. Worried that if he ever flinched away from a story or stepped back from trouble, he might never be the same.

Besides, how much trouble can you get into while writing about changes in zoning laws, or negotiations over the building of a new grocery store? That's what Chapa was telling himself as he pulled into one of the forest preserve's parking lots and began searching for Clarkson's silver Impala.

Chapter 44

Martin Clarkson had been pacing the same nine feet of weathered pavement for nearly ten minutes. Clarkson wasn't waiting for Chapa, he expected that guy to be late. Members of the press usually were, it was some sort of industry-wide epidemic. Calling Chapa had been an afterthought, anyhow.

But the contact from downtown that he was supposed to meet, Clarkson's real reason for being there, didn't seem like the sort to keep someone waiting. Clarkson circled the windmill again, just as he had done when he first got there. It was some thirty feet in diameter, narrowing at the top like a funnel, in decent shape for its apparent age, and entirely out of place in the middle of a forest preserve.

He'd hesitated calling out, for fear that some hiker or vagrant might hear him. That could mean trouble in this area where everyone seemed to know someone who knew everybody else.

The hell with it, Clarkson thought, and was about to head back to his car when he heard a sound coming from inside the structure. He was certain they'd agreed to meet by the windmill, not in it, but maybe there had been a misunderstanding.

He walked up to the main door and pulled on the handle.

But the old wood, misshapen by seasons of expansion and contraction, groaned against Clarkson's effort and refused to budge.

"Hello?" he whispered, but his voice was carried off into the wilderness by a stiff gust.

Clarkson remembered seeing another entrance around the backside. He started in that direction. As he came around the curve, Clarkson noticed that this oak wood door, smaller in height and width than its partner on the other side, was open just slightly.

Why hadn't he noticed that before? Looking around from side to side as he approached, Clarkson wondered where Chapa was. He should have been there by now.

He pulled on the door, letting it go as the wind grabbed hold and yanked it open. As sunlight streamed inside and became refracted by the dust floating in the musty air, Clarkson saw a pair of legs in dark slacks sprawled out on the floor.

"Hey, what happened, are you okay?" Clarkson asked, rushing inside and over to check on the man he was supposed to meet there some fifteen minutes ago.

Clarkson leaned in, looking for any signs of consciousness. The man's back was pressed against an inside wall, his legs spread out in front of him. Clarkson was reaching for his face with one hand, and the man's left wrist with the other.

Then the man's eyes snapped open. Clarkson was relieved, but that feeling lasted only an instant. It vanished when Clarkson felt the sting of sharp metal puncturing the side of his neck.

He froze. Years of FBI training weren't doing him much good now, as the blade was dragged along the width of his throat.

In that frenzied moment Clarkson couldn't decide whether to cover the expanding wound in his neck, fight his assailant, or reach inside his holster. So he did all of these, and none at all, reaching for his throat as the blade was making a return trip and feeling it bite into his palm. He fumbled inside his coat for a weapon, but managed only to clutch his wallet instead.

The pain was beginning to overtake him now, and Clarkson felt the warm blood dripping out of his body as chills swept through every limb. He felt the pulse in his temples grow until it pounded like a bass drum, as his chest hardened.

And then he felt nothing more.

Chapter 45

The way to the old windmill curved for a half mile down a tree-lined trail. Sunlight filtered in through high branches that stretched to meet across the recently paved path.

Chapa checked his watch and saw that he was ten minutes late. Clarkson would be waiting for him. That was okay. Chapa didn't mind being a bit late. There was something about Clarkson, a lot about him, actually, that made the guy hard to trust. He was hiding something, and Chapa wondered what that was.

The sounds of kids playing in the distance seemed to dance among the leaves. They were just on the other side of the trees, in one of the park's play areas. The Fox River ran through the middle of the park, splitting the forest into east and west halves. It was a safe bet that even on a weekday like this one there were old men in their boats, casting a line and testing their patience.

The Fletcher Preserve had always been a popular destination for families and hikers. It was not unusual to pass students from nearby Randall College doing the sorts of things college students do in the woods.

As he came around a narrow bend, Chapa spotted the windmill in the distance. The slow movement of its large

blades made it appear alive, like it was waving, warning anyone who came near to stay away.

It wasn't a modern windmill, not the sort that consists of
little more than a fan blade on top of a tall pole. The century-
old structure at the center of a large clearing reached up as
high as many of the trees surrounding it. A long time ago it
had been a fully functioning windmill. But time and decay
had stripped it of its usefulness. Now it was little more than
a curiosity for young people who'd never seen anything like
it in person, and a shelter for any wildlife that burrowed its
way inside.

Chapa was surprised to see no sign of Clarkson as he arrived at the clearing. The windmill's main door appeared to
be locked tight, and Chapa wondered how many weeks or
even months had passed since anyone had been inside. He
recalled being brought here on a field trip when he was in
grade school, and getting a tour of the inside. But that probably didn't happen anymore. He remembered the spiral stair-
case that wound around the inside and led to the top, and
wondered if it was still there.

The building had undergone a bit of restoration in the
90s, but the positive effects of that were now a thing of the
past. The wood was cracking and flaking. Its dark brown
stain had faded several shades in those places where there
was nothing to get in the sun's way, and weeds had chewed
through the foundation.

"Clarkson?" Chapa called out as he scanned the area.

A bird fluttered above, moving from one branch to another as though intent on getting a better look. The sounds of
children and boaters were gone now. Too far off to be heard
in this remote part of the preserve.

Chapa checked his phone to see if he'd missed a call from
Clarkson, delaying the meeting or changing its location. If
that was the case, Chapa decided, he would be the one to determine the next where and when.

No calls. And no service.

He looked up at top of the structure. Its weary blades rotating unevenly, more out of habit than purpose.

Chapa cupped his hands to his mouth as he circled around the backside of the windmill.

Louder this time. "Clarkson?" he called out again, facing the opposite direction from his first attempt.

Through the dense forest, about twenty yards away, maybe closer, Chapa thought he saw some movement. Was Clarkson screwing with him? Could this be some sort of bullshit power play?

Make the reporter wait. Serves him right for not being here on time. Shows him who's in charge.

Chapa decided right then that he didn't like Clarkson. Then realized he'd never liked him. Something about his too-perfect suit, and the darkness within that it seemed to be hiding.

Movement again. This time from a slightly different direction, maybe a little closer.

That's it. Time to go.

Chapa continued around the backside of the windmill, knowing he'd emerge right by the path. From there it would be a brisk and determined walk to his car, followed by an angry phone call to a federal agent, or former agent, or whatever the hell Martin Clarkson was.

He was about to come around the last turn behind the windmill when Chapa noticed a back door. This one had a latch, but no padlock. As he got closer, Chapa saw that the door was open just a crack.

"Clarkson, are you in there?" he said in a flat, measured voice.

No response. Just the crunching of dead leaves and broken twigs, some twenty yards into the woods. Probably a raccoon or possum, or even a deer hiding somewhere in the shade, staring at the dumbass walking around the windmill.

This door was not as solid as the one along the front. It consisted of a series of wide oak slats held in place by three other large pieces of wood, one across the top, a similar one across the bottom, and another connecting the two, forming a backwards Z.

Chapa angled around as he approached, hoping to sneak a glimpse inside and have some sense of what he might be getting into. The door was open an inch, maybe two, no more. It appeared to be slightly warped, suggesting that it might've been hanging this way for some time.

Chapa stopped a few feet shy of it, extended his right arm, and reached for the door, cupping his hand around the uneven edge. The splintered wood bit into the palm of his hand as he took hold and gave it a tug. The door trembled but did not budge. He looked down and saw that the bottom half was sticking.

Setting aside any thoughts of safety or hesitation, Chapa wrapped both hands around the edge of the door, near the top, and pulled hard. It popped free, then wheezed open.

He stepped back and tried to look inside from several feet away, but saw only darkness.

"Clarkson," Chapa said, and was troubled as much by the hint of fear that he heard in his own voice as he was by the silence that followed.

An empty windmill in a long forgotten section of a large forest preserve. Chapa wondered what the hell he was doing here. Clarkson had blown off their meeting, maybe because something had come up, or because he wasn't the most stable or reliable person. He might've given up after Chapa was a few minutes late. Whatever was the case, Chapa was done being spooked, and pissed off that he'd had to make that decision in the first place.

A fistful of wind punched its way through the trees, shifting empty branches enough to allow a grasp of sunlight to slip inside the darkness and touch something black and shiny within.

Chapa forced the door open as wide as it would go. An instant later, the sun reached inside the structure again, just enough to reveal a pair of legs sprawled across the dirty concrete floor and wearing expensive gray slacks that led down to a nice pair of black shoes and back up into the shadows.

"Clarkson!"

He was sitting up, but in an unnatural way, folded not at the waist, but higher, around his rib cage. Chapa rushed inside, squatted, grabbed Clarkson's shoulders, his suit coat still crisp to the touch, and shook him gently.

"Martin?"

Clarkson's head swung from side to side like a broken toy.

Then Chapa saw the blood, caked on Clarkson's collar, coloring his white shirt. Chapa recoiled when he spotted the gash across Clarkson's neck, so long and wide it looked like a grisly smile.

The blood appeared slick, which meant it was still fresh. Though Chapa figured Clarkson's heart had stopped pumping it ten, maybe fifteen minutes ago, tops. It was an educated guess, based on years of reading coroners' reports and attending more autopsies than he wanted to remember.

Clarkson could just as easily have been killed ten minutes after Chapa spoke with him, or ten minutes ago. And that's when Chapa felt a cold chill surge through his body and into his mind.

The killer might still be in here.

From his squatting position, the open door behind him, Chapa pivoted left, then right, and tried to peer into the darkness.

Nothing.

Remembering that Clarkson had carried a gun under his sport coat, Chapa carefully took hold of a lapel and began to peel back the blood-soaked cloth. He'd just about succeeded in exposing the holster when another swipe of sunlight revealed that Clarkson was clutching something in his left hand.

Chapa leaned in for a closer look, knowing better than to

touch it. It was a snapshot of a woman, attractive, nicely put together, wearing a discreet swimsuit and standing by a backyard pool. A fresh finger-streak of blood split her image in half. Clarkson's wallet lay open on the concrete by his side.

From above, Chapa heard the windmill's blades squeal into motion, then a rushing sound behind him an instant before the door slammed shut, and darkness took hold.

Chapa fumbled for the holster inside Clarkson's coat, felt sticky, half-dried blood smear across the back of his hand, didn't care. From the other end of the darkness, a rustling. He grabbed the handle of the weapon and pulled on it, but the holster was snapped shut and his effort tipped Clarkson's body sideways, toward Chapa.

Clarkson's head bobbed to the side and came to rest on Chapa's thigh, but he wasn't about to let that concern him. Reaching inside the coat with both hands, his back now turned toward the sound he'd just heard a second time, then again, closer now, Chapa unsnapped the holster, withdrew the gun and spun around.

Two eyes stared back at him. They were small and belonged to someone or something that was tucked into a far corner, behind the ladder that led to the top of the windmill. Arms extended outward, gun clutched in his left hand, Chapa slowly stood.

The eyes followed him up, but remained near ground level. Chapa felt foolish, now, realizing that a raccoon, or possum had sent him into a panic.

Chapa's heart was working his chest wall over like a cheap punching bag, as he forced himself to breathe and took stock of the situation. He needed to find a park ranger, or get back to his car, where he'd have a cell phone signal again.

He took one last look at Clarkson, knowing now that whoever he'd been chasing was as real as the brutal slash across the dead man's neck. Then Chapa yanked the door open and hurried to get out.

He didn't get far.

Waiting for him outside were eight police officers, some in uniform, some not. Four were pointing guns at him, one had a rifle. Another was yelling for Chapa to drop his weapon and get on the ground.

Chapter 46

Chapa, his hands still in cuffs, sat across from a wide mirror in a small, dimly lit room that smelled of perspiration and cheap cigarettes. The cup of coffee they'd insisted on giving him during four or five minutes of civility still sat in front of him, untouched, cold.

The first hour of questioning was difficult on Chapa—the three plainclothes playing bad cop, worse cop, and dangerously unhinged cop made sure of that. But it wasn't especially rewarding for them, either. Chapa made certain of that.

It wasn't that he didn't want to cooperate. He did. But he'd dealt with this sort of treatment from the police in the past and learned that rewarding hostility only begged for more bad treatment.

The worst of the three, a hateful bit of spit named Dixon, was itching to get his hands on him. Chapa knew that, and had managed something of a balancing act. Dancing just to the edge, then slowly stepping back.

Everything changed when Tom Jackson walked in the room.

"What the hell, Chapa?"

"Hey Tom, thanks for stopping by," Chapa said, then turned to the three would-be interrogators, his eyes on the one who'd led with his mean streak. "You guys can leave now, go to a restaurant, get a bite to eat. And you, Dixon, you're free to go beat up the waitress, or whatever your kink might be. I'm ready to tell Detective Jackson the whole truth and nothing but."

Jackson shook his head, then nodded to the other three, who got the message but took their time leaving the room, anyway.

"They're just doing their jobs, Alex."

"I know, Tom, and I'm certainly capable of being an asshole sometimes."

"You think?"

"But some members of the law enforcement community seem to enjoy doing their jobs on me a little too much."

Jackson dragged a chair across the tile floor until it squealed into place alongside the table.

"So tell me, Alex, why did you murder Martin Clarkson?" Jackson asked with absolutely no conviction in his voice.

"I'll answer your questions, but first tell me this, who tipped the cops off to what had happened at that windmill?"

"An anonymous call from a cell phone. We just ran the number and found it belonged to—"

"Martin Clarkson."

Jackson nodded.

"We figure someone found the body, the phone was with it, so they made a call, but didn't want to get involved. Probably tossed the phone away after they used it. Happens that way sometimes."

Chapa smiled. It sounded plausible, a good story, but he had a better one.

He asked for a fresh cup of coffee, then spent the next forty minutes putting as many pieces in place for Jackson as he could. All the while, Chapa was fleshing out the story he would write later that day for tomorrow's paper.

Chapa explained how he'd first seen Martin Clarkson at

the council meeting, and how he was muscled out of the building. He filled Jackson in on how Clarkson had left the bureau under circumstances that could, at best, be called dubious.

Jackson already knew all about that, but Clarkson's theory about a series of murders was new to him.

"That's the sort of thing the FBI does really well," Jackson said.

"Usually, but one or two do slip by from time to time. Believe me, I know."

"Yeah, yeah, Alex, you don't have to remind me. I'm one of your loyal readers."

"You're the one."

"But look, that area, right where Clarkson was found, can be pretty rough. There have been attacks there before, a couple of killings, too, had one last year. That quaint old windmill, which should've been ripped down years ago, sits in the middle of a big expanse of wilderness, and we get squatters there all the time."

"And one happened to walk up to a federal agent who was carrying a loaded weapon and cut his throat?"

"A former agent."

"My point is still valid."

"Maybe it is, but at any given time there are bikers and ex-cons living in those woods. Bodies turn up in forest preserves every year. The rangers do their best to patrol them, and we get at least one call per week about some bad guys making trouble. But you can only do as much as you can do."

"Why did Clarkson want to meet me there?"

"You're asking me?" Jackson shrugged, then got himself a fresh cup. "Here's how it went down, Alex—he wandered into some vagrant's makeshift home, got jumped, got his neck sliced. It isn't exactly the most sophisticated killing of the month in these parts, let alone something suggesting a grander scheme."

Chapa downed the last swig of flaccid coffee and tossed the Styrofoam cup in a small metal wastebasket.

"There's just one problem with your theory, Tom."

Jackson flashed a look of exasperation at Chapa.

"What now?"

"The wallet. The type of person you're describing would've taken it."

Jackson didn't look exasperated anymore, so Chapa continued.

"But the only thing taken out of it was that photo of a woman."

"Clarkson may have fought the assailant for his wallet, and pulled that photo out as he was dying. You probably scared off his attacker."

"Who's the woman in the picture?"

"We believe it's Clarkson's wife. She died accidentally a few years ago."

"Really?" Chapa picked up a clean cup and poured himself some fresh coffee.

"Drowned in a swimming pool. It happens."

"Sure, and federal agents—sorry, *former* federal agents—get themselves murdered in park windmills. That happens, too."

"Yes, Alex, apparently it does."

Chapa finished off another cup, and walked over to the door.

"Don't worry, Tom, I won't be leaving town or anything."

"That's too bad," Jackson said as he opened the door for Chapa.

They walked down a crowded hall to Processing.

"Alex, do me a solid here. Promise me you'll go light on this pattern killing thing. At least until we've got more info one way or another."

Chapa couldn't make him that promise, even if he'd wanted to. But that's not the reason he didn't respond right away. A form attached to a clipboard caught Chapa's eye.

"What is this?" he asked a clerk behind the counter. The old guy looked like he might've been there when they erected the building eighty-five years ago. His name tag identified him as Larry.

"It's a death notice."

Apparently Gladys Washer would not be serving as the local watchdog anymore, she'd moved to that gated community in the sky. She'd been found early that same morning by a neighbor who came by for a regular visit, looked through a window when there was no answer at the door, and saw Gladys lying on the floor of her living room.

"Cause of death?"

Larry seemed bothered, but something told Chapa that was just his normal state.

"It says heart attack, you see that," Larry said, poking at the paper with a tobacco-stained finger. "Heart attack. What the hell is it to you?"

He yanked the clipboard out of Chapa's hand and disappeared through an office door.

"Alex, really, keep this all in check," Jackson was still asking for a favor.

Tom was a hell of a good cop, a better man, and Chapa liked him. The look on his face was so sincere that Chapa had to turn away.

"I'll see you around, Tom," he said and left the station.

Chapter 47

Leah Carelli misinterpreted the reason for Chapa's phone call, exactly as he'd feared she would.

"You didn't use to move this fast, Alex. Maybe if you had, way back when, we might've—"

"Leah, you know how much I like talking to you—"

"Do you? Are we going to have that lunch we talked about?"

"Absolutely, but first I need your help."

He was driving toward Gladys Washer's house, though that was not his true destination.

"Oh, I can help you, all right. You sound tense."

"Do I? I don't feel tense. No more than usual, anyway. I need an address."

"Really? What time are you picking me up?"

Chapa tightened his grip on the wheel and exhaled. Leah's cute and flirty way was starting to become annoying, and just a little creepy.

"Not *your* address, Leah, the one Gladys Washer was there complaining about a couple of days ago."

Silence.

"You're kidding."

"No, I really need that address. I thought I remembered it being on Grove Stree—"

"You called me for info?"

Chapa rifled through his options, searching for the best one. It didn't take long.

"Yes, and I will be grateful."

"How grateful?"

He could almost hear the naughty smile on her face.

"Leah, please."

It sounded like she was walking, at least that's what Chapa wanted to believe was causing the soft panting on the other end. A moment later he heard the sound of paper rustling.

"I have what you want, right here, Alex."

He decided to play along.

"I bet you do," Chapa said in what he hoped was his best lounge lizard voice. "Are you going to . . . give it to me?"

"Oh, I'll give it to you."

And she did. But then Leah had a question of her own.

"Alex, why did you dump me?"

"What?"

He remembered the end of their relationship being more of a drift than a split. Anyhow, this wasn't a conversation he wanted to have—now or anytime soon.

Chapa signed off, and five minutes later he pulled up in front of the house on Elm Grove Street, still uncertain why he was there or what he was hoping to find, and sensing that little good could come from what he was about to do.

Chapter 48

On the sidewalk across from where he was parked, Chapa saw a series of children's chalk drawings and scribbling, most having to do with Halloween. When he turned back toward 414 Elm Grove, the last address Gladys Washer had complained about, he felt certain he was looking at the house those same kids probably thought was haunted.

Every older suburban neighborhood has one. The street Chapa grew up on certainly did. And he remembered the Wallace house with its thick bushes in front, vines creeping up the stone front, and the rarely seen but eternally angry people inside. He recalled the time the neighborhood punk stomped all over the Wallace's flower garden, then blamed it on him, explaining, "You know, he's one of those Spanish people."

That seemed to be proof enough for Mrs. Wallace, who immediately grabbed Chapa by the arm and dragged him to his house. But she left five minutes later and just ahead of a torrent of angry profanity the likes of which Chapa had never previously heard come out of his mother's mouth.

This neighborhood's haunted house had no bushes or vines, and not much paint. Much of what there was, white mostly, had flaked off, exposing patches of bare and rotting wood. Fistfuls of grass and weeds had punched their way through the narrow walk that led to the front door. It didn't take much work to figure out why this property had gotten Gladys Washer's attention.

Chapa saw no car in the driveway as he walked down the street toward that side of the house. At the far stretch of the uneven concrete, Chapa saw a garage that appeared to be leaning just a bit. The yard was fenced on three sides, though it was unclear whether any of the fencing belonged to this property, or if each of the neighbors had put it up for their protection.

This section of Oakton was, as a whole, more beaten down than most. But even here, in this mixed neighborhood populated by day laborers, service workers, and third shifters, this property was way behind the curve. The closer he got to the house, the worse it looked, and Chapa wondered which of the paint chips, if broken off, would bring the whole thing tumbling down.

Chapa had hoped to get a look at the home owners, though that would've been unlikely on a weekday afternoon. He couldn't shake the thought that Gladys Washer's death seemed a bit too sudden and unusual, especially in light of all that had been happening these past few days.

Chapa tried to carry himself like a man with a purpose as he walked across the patchy lawn spotted with dead leaves, some dry, others rotting. Arcing around toward the side of the house, still not sure what he was looking for, Chapa glanced through an opening in a set of frayed and faded curtains. Though the area beyond was dark, he caught a glimpse inside at what appeared to be a folding table and a chair near the center of the room. He leaned in closer and saw that the large room was otherwise empty.

There were some papers on the table, a notebook, perhaps, and Chapa was about to step forward to get a better look when he heard the crunching of leaves underfoot. He turned to find a large man wearing work clothes, gripping a crowbar and moving swiftly in his direction.

The guy's hairline was all but gone, but he was compensating by growing what was left down to his crooked shoulders. His nose was bent, and it may have been broken at least once in each direction. There was something wrong with his left eye, but Chapa was sure he could still see well enough to take his head off with a swing of that crowbar.

Chapa knew right then that running wasn't going to get him very far, maybe to the tall wood fence that stretched down the length of the backyard, no farther. If he fought, he was going to end up badly injured, or worse. And if this guy called the cops, Chapa was going to jail, this time for a reason.

So Chapa decided to try something he was very good at—talking his way out of a shitty situation of his own making.

"Are you the home owner, sir?" his voice steady, neutral, but authoritative, no hint of the churning in his stomach.

"And what the fuck would it be to you?" The guy spoke with one of those Midwestern white trash accents that are often laced with a hint of the rural South. He was still advancing, shortening the distance between Chapa and that crowbar.

"I'm from the city. There have been a few complaints regarding the upkeep of this house. I'm required to let you know that."

"And so you have. Good day now."

He was wearing what had once been a blue jean jacket, but the sleeves were crudely cut off, turning it into a vest. He had no shirt on underneath, revealing a narrow but muscular midsection. This guy looked like he could've emerged from a prison yard yesterday.

"Look buddy, I'm not some hard-ass from downtown who's here to bust your balls," Chapa lowered his voice, the way a stranger sitting on the barstool next to you does as he cozies up. "But if I can't go back to the office and tell them I had a serious and productive conversation with someone who lives here, they'll send some prick next time."

"And that would be bad."

"Hell yeah it would. They'd probably send Wormley down here, and he's a real piece of work."

"I don't want no Wormley poking around my yard." The crowbar was now down at his side.

"You're damn straight you don't."

The guy looked down and shook his head. Without taking his eyes off him, Chapa slowly started wandering toward the back of the house, but stopped when he saw the man tighten his grip on the crowbar.

"Look, um, what's your name?"

"Cal."

"Just get the house painted in the next few months, Cal. Nothing too fancy, just slap some whitewash on here and there."

Cal nodded.

"Do enough so that we don't get anymore complaints about the place. You know, these old women who complain all the time have nothing better to do than drive around town looking for ways to—"

"Stick their noses in other people's shit," Cal said, completing Chapa's sentence, though not exactly as he would have. "Yeah, okay, it'll get cleaned up and painted some."

Cal tilted his head to the side just enough, as if to ask, *So now what?* Over time Chapa had developed a sense of when it was time to go—and that time was now.

Chapa thanked Cal, then walked past him and started for his car, anticipating an attack at any instant. When it didn't come, Chapa stopped in the middle of the yard and turned back toward the house.

"By the way, Cal, are you the owner?"

Cal was holding the crowbar like a barbell, one hand on

each end, down by his waist. He lowered his head the way a bull does before charging, then slowly moved it from side to side, indicating *No*.

Chapa knew better than to ask the owner's name. He walked the rest of the way to his car without hesitation, knowing the guy was still standing there in the yard with a weapon in his grip and the wheels beginning to turn in his head.

Before getting into his car, Chapa looked back toward the house as a sliver of sunlight pierced a cloud, illuminating a figure standing at the edge of an upstairs window. He appeared to be holding a rifle.

Chapter 49

As far as Chapa could determine, the letter Jim Chakowski had sent his brother wasn't giving up any more of its secrets. It wasn't even a letter, really, more like a collection of notes, the sort of disjointed thoughts that some people mindlessly scribble on a desk pad.

Some of the names on it were now familiar to Chapa, and maybe he understood the significance of the dates and places. But so what? There wasn't enough to put anything together.

Could be Chakowski was on to the stick figure killings. Or he may have been coming at it from another direction. And if he was in contact with Martin Clarkson, perhaps even working with him, why wasn't his name anywhere on the paper or in Chakowski's notes or files?

Thinking about all of this, and flipping it around in his mind until separating fact from speculation became nearly impossible, reminded him of something. Chapa tracked Zach down in the archives, a crowded storage room located in a back corner of the second floor.

"Did you have a chance to look into the stickman murder connection?"

"Oh yeah, I did some online searches. There's a whole

urban myth surrounding it, dating back to the 1980s, but not a lot of hard info."

"So it predates the Internet."

"Pretty much. Check out the blogs, it's all there."

Chapa thanked him and headed back downstairs. On the way to his office he passed a guy whom he recognized, but not as a member of the staff.

"I'm Ted Bruce," he said, though Chapa had not asked.

"Right, I saw you at City Hall."

"I run a public relations firm that does a lot of good work with the city and its leading businesses."

He gave Chapa his card.

"Of course," Chapa said.

Ted Bruce vibed former jock, or he could've been that guy who was built like an athlete but never got into sports. He had high cheekbones and a hard chin. Chapa sensed the guy's strong blue eyes were trying to read him like a security scanner.

"I'm here to see your boss."

"Matthew Sullivan?"

"No," Bruce smiled, but only the middle third of his lips got in on the action. "Bigger."

"Oh, of course."

"I assume you know where his office is located," Chapa said, then started to point in the right direction.

"Of course," Bruce said as he walked away.

Chapa continued to his office and did just as Zach had suggested. He found a couple of blogs that mentioned stick figures and pattern killings. One even had a photo of a purported crime scene.

There was one blog that he found of particular interest. It made mention of the Traveling Serial Killer Museum, another urban legend. In this case, one that Chapa knew to be true. But it did not connect back to anything like the stickman murders. A dead end.

Chapa looked over at the clock on his desk. It was a compact travel version he had picked up some years back while on assignment. A small plane attached to the end of the second hand was rotating around the dial. When he bought the clock at a shop in the terminal at Midway, Chapa hoped it would inspire him to travel more. It hadn't worked out that way, but ten years later the thing still kept good time.

It was just after three. He was supposed to meet Erin and the kids at his house in a couple of hours.

He had finished two stories for the next day's paper. One was the sort of space filler he was supposed to be writing, the other a vintage Chapa piece about Clarkson's death, and the former agent's theories about the stickman murders. He had done his best to keep that aspect of the story as low-key as possible. But ignoring it altogether would've been dishonest and irresponsible, and Chapa's writing was never either of those.

Why had Clarkson asked Chapa to meet him at that park? Clarkson's death fit the pattern he himself had identified, but only to a point. He wasn't one of society's lost souls. Maybe this killer doesn't follow a strict pattern. Or maybe . . .

Chapa started searching through the notes that Zach had put together for him, placing the various sheets of paper across his desk in a chronological order.

What followed the killings in Baltimore? A cop turned up dead, then a respected businessman died in a car crash two days later. And the earlier murders in Pittsburgh may have ended with the *accidental* death of Clarkson's wife.

Maybe those were unrelated, and two really were accidents. Or maybe this killer broadened his scope whenever he felt threatened. If that was the case, no one was safe now.

Then Chapa remembered something Tom Jackson said about a college student being killed at Fletcher Woods. He examined the *Record*'s computer files until he located the story. The man's name was Wade Marshall. He'd been found with his neck split open on the east bank of the river, the opposite side of the park from the windmill. Police determined that the deceased had been involved in minor campus drug deals and a bit of bookmaking, and decided that he'd probably crossed the wrong person.

Chapa printed out a newspaper photo of the crime scene. A uniformed cop stood in the foreground, near the spot where the body was found. A wooden, curved footbridge angled off into the distance. Chapa wasn't familiar with that area of the large park, but figured he could use the landmarks in the photo to find it.

He slipped the picture and story into his notebook, and turned his attention back to his own work. Twenty minutes later, Chapa had revised and filed his two stories. He turned off the computer, closed down his office, and headed off to Fletcher Forest Preserve.

Chapter 50

The man sits at a desk in his house, filling a legal pad with neatly drawn stick figures. Line by line, page by page. He hears the pen scratch another simple corpse into the paper.

He is still wearing the business clothes he wore at a board meeting earlier that morning. The same clothes he had on when he worked on a major deal just after lunch.

The room he is in, like the rest of his house, contains only what he needs, nothing more. And he doesn't need much. Things like furniture, clothes, or any personal items can create a trail, and leave behind a mark. Make it easier for others to understand who you are. Not a good idea.

There's a stale smell from the old air that fills the house. It's the same air that's been trapped there since the man moved in a few years ago, since he's never opened a window or walked through a door without immediately shutting it. Can't risk letting the outside in.

He continues his work, it soothes him. Line by line, page by page. He thinks about the stick figures he's erased. The pimps, the pushers, the gangbangers, the thieves, the liars, and the cheats, and those who've shielded or defended them.

Not human, really. Just two-dimensional creatures driven by their base urges.

The man believes he can see behind the masks that people wear. He sees the stickmen for what they actually are inside, whether they're hiding behind a title or a weapon, expensive clothes or homeboy tattoos. He gets a special rush from cutting them open and letting the evil pour out.

He thinks about the community leaders who still don't appreciate his efforts to make their town a better place by eliminating the worst of the worst. They need to learn the importance of appreciation. And they will. Soon. He's already forced two of them to kill for him. They remind him of the men who used to pay to spend time with his mother.

The man is almost done with the last page, the last line, but stops when there's only enough room left for a few more figures. Then the man slowly fills in the space he imagines had been reserved for Martin Clarkson.

He knows who the last space is for, it's the reason he chose this place. Then he thinks about Alex Chapa and how he allowed his daughter to wander where she should not have been. And how he keeps digging around, even though he isn't getting anywhere. Though he did find Clarkson's body. What was he doing at the park?

The man was there, hiding in the trees, watching the police move in from the other direction. He planned it so well, but he had not planned on Chapa. Maybe the man should have taken both of them out. He could have finished Chapa with one quick cut.

But he had already phoned the police. He could not have known how long it would take them to get there.

The man can't be certain, but he wonders if Chapa was the person who showed up at his workhouse after that old woman filed a complaint. The man wasn't there at the time, but his associate told him all about it. *A guy from the city.* Only a simple creature like Cal would fall for that.

He wonders if that's why Clarkson asked Chapa to meet him there at the park. Could've had something to do with the dead reporter. Maybe it was about the punk he killed there last year.

Could there be any traces left of that killing? The man considers whether he should go back and see. He'd been very careful, as always, then made certain police came across some of the details about the victim's life.

But could he have missed something? That was months ago, but Clarkson was once a good agent. He might have found something.

Again he thinks about Alex Chapa, and how the reporter keeps turning up where he shouldn't.

The man digs his nails into the wood table as if he's trying to scratch an itch he just can't get at. Again and again. The table is scarred with the remnants of old frustrations alongside newer ones.

Perhaps he should go back to Fletcher Woods. He could go right now, get there before sunset. Then he'd know for sure. There would probably still be some police milling around the area where Clarkson was killed, maybe even a TV reporter or two, but that was a separate area of the park.

He could go right to where he'd made the kill and left the body that a boater found the next day. No one would see him. And what if they did? Wouldn't matter. He's a vital member of the community, just out for a stroll after a big day of meetings and deal making. Just winding down.

The man thinks about this for a while, and decides it's a good idea. He's not clawing at the table now. He thinks about the other reporter who got too close, the one they're putting in the ground tomorrow. Then his mind rushes back to Alex Chapa.

A smart reporter would've stayed away from Chakowski's death, just like a good father would've left his daughter at home. He decides that Chapa is not a good father, but he might be too good of a reporter.

The man resists the urge to dig his fingernails into the table again by focusing on the inch-long blank space at the end of the last line. He decides to leave it that way, with enough room for three or four or more figures. Then he grabs his car keys and heads out the door.

He figures it should take him no more than ten minutes to reach the forest preserve.

Chapter 51

Fletcher Woods, as everyone in the area called the preserve, hugged the Fox River for nearly five miles on the east side and three on the west. But Chapa was only interested in a few yards down near the waterline.

He parked in a small secluded lot off Culverson Road, not far from a deserted picnic area. There were four other vehicles there, but Chapa didn't see anyone. This half of the park was a favorite destination for runners and bikers, because the kids and the families didn't find it as appealing.

His cell phone signal was low and battery power lower. So he plugged in the charger and stashed the phone under the dash.

Examining the crime scene photo, Chapa determined that the small bridge and the area he was looking for should be about a half mile to the north. He started down a paved path, which eventually became gravel, then dirt, and finally matted grass. He soon realized this wasn't a well-traveled area.

The gusts that had blown shut the windmill's door earlier that day had given way to a far more agreeable breeze, which brushed against the branches and shook the surviving leaves. The sun was in full descent, and Chapa had no interest in crossing the woods after dark.

Chapa first saw the footbridge from a distance of roughly forty yards through a small clearing. He resisted the urge to cut through the trees, and instead remained on the path, which had turned into dirt again. When he emerged from the woods, Chapa saw that he'd been wrong about the location of the crime scene.

The bridge was much smaller and farther from the river than it appeared in the photo. It was more ornamental than anything, traversing only a pond so small that it probably dried up altogether during droughts.

The mental image that he'd formed of the area from the photo seemed distorted now that he was actually there. Some landmarks were too far away, others closer than imagined.

Holding the photo out in front of him, his back to the river, Chapa walked away from the bridge until it seemed to be about the right size as in the picture. He looked around at the area where he was standing. There was nothing unusual about it. The tree line curved past, about thirty feet away. Forty yards or so downriver, the sun shone off a large metal bridge connecting one bank to the other.

Chapa imagined folks fishing off it on weekend mornings. Fathers dropping a line into the dark, rushing water while sharing memories with their kids, having no idea of the violence that occurred just a few feet up along the shore.

But in a sense, that made this place no different from many other places. Chapa figured out long ago that there wasn't a square mile of land that had not once been home to death.

Chapa was wondering if the killer and victim came here together, or if one was waiting for the other, when he heard a sound that seemed to be coming from beyond the trees, away from the path. He turned in that direction, looked for movement, waited, but saw none.

The woods were home to a variety of wildlife. Every couple of years someone would get arrested for hunting deer in this area, and that thought made Chapa think about the clothes he was wearing. Maybe something bright and orange would've been better than the dark jeans, dark green polo, and black jacket he had on.

When a minute had passed and nothing jumped out of the woods, Chapa resumed his search, though he wasn't entirely certain what he was looking for. He walked over to the foot-bridge, and started up one of its steep curves, searching for a stick figure. The wood was old and darkened by time. It appeared that this structure, like the area surrounding it, didn't merit much attention from park keepers.

As he squatted to get a look under a six-foot-long stretch of a railing, Chapa wondered how Clarkson would've gone about this. He probably had it down to a science, and knew exactly where to look. Maybe he had already found something here, and this crime scene was the reason Clarkson had wanted to meet him by the windmill.

Then why not just ask Chapa to meet here? Too remote. Chapa glanced over at the large bridge and wondered how far of a walk it would be from the windmill. Five minutes, maybe, depending on the sort of trail that connected the two areas. Though it was difficult to say with any certainty, especially after the disorienting experience of winding through the path from his car to this place.

Movement. Something large. A quick wave of shadow just inside the woods.

Chapa stood quickly and scanned the trees, doing his best to look through them and into the brush beyond. But he saw no more sign of movement, nothing other than October leaves waving their last goodbyes.

Could be what he'd seen out of the corner of his eye was actually farther away, up along the path. A jogger, perhaps. He walked down the other curve and away from the small bridge, then stopped and turned back to look at it.

Was that the sort of place where a killer would leave his mark? He had no idea.

There was no pavement or path along the river where the body had been found. Nowhere to scratch a figure like the one Chapa thought he had seen in the alley photo.

Chapa kept looking toward the trees as he walked along the water's edge in the direction of the larger bridge. He considered the possibility the killer might have sliced a stickman into the bark of an old maple. But there were so many of them, and it was probably safe to assume he wanted his signature to be found. Not easily, perhaps, but not too well hidden, either.

A patch of white gravel led the way to the bridge, which was wider and not quite as well-maintained as it appeared from a distance. Its silver aluminum sides knifed through the air like long sabers, and reached across the river. The deck was made of a series of oak slats that creaked underfoot as Chapa walked to the middle.

He stared down into the Fox River, which in his youth had been too polluted to fish or swim, evidenced by the way it had once looked and smelled on steamy summer days. The kids would make up stories about monsters rising up from the foul water, taking to land and attacking anyone in their path.

But years of highly funded clean-up projects made that largely a thing of the past. Even now that the river was suitable for fishing, its swift waters were dark and deep, and Chapa remembered a friend once telling him about how the riverbank fell off after just a yard or so, with no footing beneath.

He looked upriver and toward the muddy area where the body was found. An ideal place for a murder, assuming you could find someone gullible enough to meet you here. Chapa felt his chest tighten a bit. Had Clarkson been his killer's only target? Had the cops arrived at that windmill just in time to keep Chapa from becoming the next victim?

It was time to go. He took one final panoramic look across the area. A small bridge, a narrow riverbank, the woods, the river. No picnic tables or benches, this wasn't that sort of place.

A sign on the bridge read NO DIVING. There was another one down along the river, apparently for anyone too smart to dive in the river, but dumb enough to go wading in it.

Chapa left the bridge and walked back to where he estimated the body had been found. The seasons had come and gone three times over, taking with them any residual evidence that a crime had been committed here. If the killer had left his mark anywhere on the six-inch-tall grass or along the shifting riverbank, it was long gone.

He started back toward the path, frustrated about having learned nothing new in the past half hour. Something caught his eye as he came up on the small rectangular sign he'd seen from the bridge. This one was different—it did not read NO DIVING.

The elements had chewed away at the metal, leaving its edges uneven and discolored. The sign leaned toward the river about three feet off the ground and read NO SWIMMING. There was nothing unusual about that. But when Chapa drew in and got a better look at the rest of it he felt something primal claw at his spine as his senses jolted into full alert.

Squatting to get a better look at the remnants of paint, Chapa discerned that the sign had originally shown a simple black figure of a diver going headfirst into the water, which was represented by a series of wide, squat *U*'s, the way a child draws the ocean. There was a small red *X* covering the diver, making sure no one got the wrong idea.

Except the diver wasn't there anymore, only a faint outline. A significant amount of force and determination had gone into scratching him away, so much that it exposed the bare untreated metal beneath. A small stick figure had been drawn in black permanent marker, its head sticking out of the water, its body dangling beneath the cartoonish waves.

There was something about it that was oddly fascinating. Despite the damage to the sign, the figure blended in so well. No wonder the police investigators missed it.

But Chapa realized something else, too. The killer had chosen this place. Staked it out, knew the sign was there. Knew what he was going to do to it.

Plop.

The sound came from behind Chapa's right shoulder. He pivoted and spun around too quickly and nearly lost his balance. His eyes were fixed on the ripples that appeared a few feet into the river as they multiplied and reached for shore only to be swept away by the current.

The branches of a dying tree hung down, close to the river, and Chapa knew that something, a small branch, a clutch of leaves, could've been responsible for the noise. But Chapa also sensed that he was working a bit too hard to conjure up comfortable explanations.

He scanned the large bridge. Empty. And the tree line revealed nothing. Chapa knew he was an easy target for anyone hiding in there with a gun.

Then he heard a different sound.

This one traveled on a trail of wind, the way fine dust can so that you don't see it until it slaps your face. It sounded like a whisper.

Chapa had heard the sound of wind whistling through bare autumn branches his whole life, and this was probably just that. He knew he'd spooked himself—an easy thing to forgive under the circumstances—but he needed to get out of this place and back to his car.

He thought about crossing the bridge to the other side, just to be safe, just to avoid going back through that narrow path. But he wasn't sure where that would take him. He could end up miles from where he needed to go.

The wind started hissing through the trees again, and this time the sound was much crisper. But then he heard something so inexplicable, that instead of doing what he should—running, fast, now—he stood locked in place, somehow certain that he would hear it again.

And then he heard it once more. Clearer. Closer.

Aaa—lex . . .

Chapter 52

A few weeks after Alex Chapa's tenth birthday his mother informed him that she'd saved up enough money to take them both on a two-week trip to see their relatives in Miami.

Except for field trips to Springfield, it would be the first time Alex left the Chicago area since moving there shortly after arriving in the U.S. For the next four weeks his mother showed him photos of second cousins and third uncles once removed. There were some postcards, too, that had been sent from Florida over the years.

Sunny photos of happy people, sandy beaches, and orange groves. Paradise in all its glossy glory.

So by the time the weeks shortened to days, Alex had become convinced he was going to visit someplace magical. Like his mother, Alex was looking forward to taking a trip, and to playing in the ocean, and spending some time with a few of his relatives. But he also had a reason for wanting to go that was all his own. A quiet cause that he kept close and refused to share.

Alex thought—hoped—that maybe his father would be waiting for them there. That the stories about his death were all wrong, or that somehow this city where Cubans had found refuge and a better future had brought Francisco Chapa back to life. Was that his father, there in that picture of a beach fronting an impossibly blue ocean?

He didn't share those thoughts with his mother. In part because he didn't want her to tell him that he was wrong, but also because he didn't like that look of hurt in her eyes whenever he brought up his father.

Alex didn't sleep the night before they left, stayed awake the whole way on the plane, too, despite his mother's prediction that he would nod off the moment they were in the air. They touched down that afternoon at Miami International, his mother explaining how this was the airport they had flown into when they arrived from Havana.

As the days came and went and there was no surprise appearance, just the unfamiliar faces of people who seemed very happy to see him, Alex began to get angry and felt stupid for that and for expecting anything else. But he still refused to give up altogether.

On the morning of his sixth day in Miami, several hours before his family had planned to leave for the beach, Alex asked his mom if he could go to a drugstore a block away from his uncle's house, along busy Calle Ocho, and buy a couple packs of baseball cards. His uncle assured Alex's mother that he'd be safe on his own.

"That store is owned by Emilio Gomez, who used to have a store on Calle Paredes near our house in Havana. I'll call ahead and ask him to keep an eye out for Alex."

On his way to the store, Alex thought about how different this place was from home, though his mother kept telling him it was a lot like Cuba. He used the fifty cents his mother had given him to buy two packs of Topps Series 3, exactly what he wanted.

But he had an ulterior motive, too. Alex thought if he had the chance to look around the area a bit he might find . . . well, he wasn't exactly sure who or what he might find.

He didn't go back the way he came. Alex instead walked

out of the store and headed in the opposite direction, then crossed the street, and walked another three blocks.

Shoving a pink flat rectangle of baseball card bubblegum into his mouth, he quickly flipped through the cards before slipping them into a back pocket. He still had his bearings, knew exactly where his uncle's house was, more or less, when the man wearing the Dolphins T-shirt and a week's worth of stubble said hi to him from behind a screen door.

"What's your name?"

A cigarette stuck out from under the guy's mustache and bobbed up and down as he spoke.

Alex did not answer.

"Do you live around here?"

Why did he want to know that? Alex shook his head, chewed the gum, which had already lost most of its flavor, and kept walking past the man's house and his overgrown fenced-in yard. A BEWARE OF DOG sign hung crooked on the chain links, but Alex didn't see a dog.

"I can help you find what you're looking for. Help you get home if you're lost."

Alex kept walking, picked up the pace some when he heard the screen door open then shut, but he didn't look back. When he reached the corner, instead of crossing the street and heading back, Alex turned right, deciding that he did not want the man to know where he was going.

This street was narrow and crowded with cars. It seemed to go on forever, and Alex started walking faster, even jogged a few strides. When he reached the end, Alex turned left, sensing that was the way back. But this new street curved around to the right, and soon Alex was lost in a seedy maze of palm trees, long alleyways, and pastel-colored concrete. None of it looked like any of those postcards.

Searching for anything that looked familiar, Alex turned down a short street, then another, then cut through an alley thinking that was the way back to where he'd started, but nothing looked like anywhere he'd been before.

Alex stopped at a deserted intersection, looked around and wondered how far he was from his uncle's house. He tried to think back and count the blocks. Twelve, in more directions than he could remember.

That's when he started getting scared. At first he'd managed to push his fears aside, thinking of himself as an explorer walking through uncharted territory. But now Alex knew he was in trouble.

He spit out the flavorless gum, watched it stick to the curb. Maybe he could use it as a marker, so he'd know if he walked past here again. This idea made Alex feel smart. He pulled out the second pack, opened it and popped the gum in his mouth without bothering to look at the cards.

At least the man in the Dolphins T-shirt hadn't followed him. Alex felt good about that, certain that his decision to take a side street had somehow convinced the guy to leave him alone.

Looking up and down the next intersection, Alex noticed a cross street where the traffic seemed steady, several blocks away. He started in that direction, his steps getting faster as he got closer, no longer trying to convince himself that he was just out for a walk.

When he reached the busy intersection, Alex spotted something he was sure he'd seen before. Across the street on the next block was a small park surrounded by palm trees. He'd noticed it while looking out through a second-floor window in his uncle's house.

As he walked toward it, Alex thought about stopping and playing for a few minutes, almost as a way of proving to himself that nothing bad had happened and that he was never really scared. He decided to do it—jump on the swings, or go down the slide a time or two—but then thought better of it when he saw the man in the Dolphins T-shirt sitting on a bench at the far end of the park.

Alex kept his head down, and fought the impulse to start

running, but watched the man out of the corner of his eye. When he reached the next intersection, Alex sprinted across the street and kept running. Five minutes later he stood on the corner of Calle Ocho and Miranda, the street his uncle lived on.

For a moment, he worried about that piece of gum he'd left stuck to a curb somewhere back there. He wondered if the man in the Dolphins shirt might find it and use it to track him down somehow. But then Alex decided not to think about that anymore.

He didn't get in trouble, which was a relief. His mother hadn't even noticed how long he'd been gone. But as those concerns drifted away, Alex was left with the fear he'd felt while walking past that man's house, and seeing him again at the park. But it was the disappointment of not finding who he was really looking for that lingered.

That was when Alex decided there was no such thing as magic. That the dead stay that way forever. And that there are certain things you should never go searching for, and some places that are best avoided.

He never told his mother, or anyone else for that matter, about that day. And while he could not be certain, even now, whether or not the man was some sicko who might've done terrible things to him, or just a guy offering to help a lost child, Chapa knew he'd made several dangerous mistakes.

The biggest of those, he concluded years later, was leaving the busy and well-traveled street in favor of the narrow and secluded ones. It's there, in those shrouded places, that you run into people who aren't all that nice.

That thirty-year-old event had stayed with Chapa the rest of his life. It flashed through his mind now as he weighed his few options. It came back to him the instant he considered rushing into the forest in the hope that he might be more difficult to find in there, and thus safer.

Chapa waited and listened for the voice again as he

scanned the tree line for any movement. Nothing. He could just as easily have been completely alone, but Chapa didn't believe that.

Deciding that he would feel better with a weapon in his hand, Chapa began looking for anything he could use to defend himself. But there was nothing in the immediate area.

"Who's there?" Chapa called out, expecting no answer. He received none. "You don't have to answer—I already know who you are."

He studied the tree line, listened for any unusual sounds. The sun was closing in on the horizon, so there wasn't much time left for Chapa to decide what he was going to do.

"Clarkson and I talked a lot. He had a whole bunch of theories, but I have something better," Chapa said to whomever might be there. "I have information. I know who you are. I know about all these little stickmen you leave. That's pathetic, you know. It's something a child would do."

Some movement down near the small curved bridge. Chapa drew back toward the riverbank and prepared to defend himself.

If the guy had a gun he would run straight into the forest. But based on the M.O. he'd seen so far, Chapa was certain he'd come after him with a knife.

The wind slapped the branches around a bit again, and Chapa heard the whistle and hiss, but none of it sounded human. He decided to make his way toward the large bridge, cross it, and get away from this side of the forest.

Stealing a glance downriver, he saw something he could use. A long, thick branch was resting in the mud along the bank, just fifteen feet away.

Without taking his eyes off the tree line, Chapa carefully walked down toward the water. His shoes sank about an inch as he tried to find footing in the soft, wet soil, just five feet from the branch.

As he squatted and reached for the makeshift weapon,

Chapa again scanned the trees for any sign of movement. But all was still, even the wind seemed to be taking a break.

He pressed his hand against the cold damp wood and tightened his grip, but it did not feel right. Instead of the rigid piece of wood he'd expected, this branch turned out to be spongy and fragile.

Chapa looked down and saw that it was also longer than he'd thought, and much of it dropped off into the river, just a short distance away. He was frustrated, and beginning to get angry, as much with himself as anything.

Then Chapa saw the figure. Someone tall, and wide, just inside the trees, where no jogger would go. The shadow was moving fast, and with purpose.

He glanced upriver and eyed the defaced NO SWIMMING sign. How deep into the ground did the post go?

If he could coax it free, the jagged metal edges would be capable of doing some serious damage to anyone who came at him.

But could he reach it in time?

Chapa scrambled to free his feet from the mud, but his right foot slipped and the left one gave way. Falling backwards, unable to find footing or stop himself, he grasped at the air and came up empty.

He heard the splash as the river rushed around him. But the sound seemed to be coming from somewhere else. This had to be happening to someone else.

Chapa reached for the shore, but it wasn't there. And now the current was pulling him in and away from safety.

He rolled over once, and then again. Getting farther away from shore with every move. Lifting his head out of the water and looking back toward where he'd been, Chapa saw the NO SWIMMING sign upriver. The distance growing by the second.

A darkness blotted out the sky for a moment, and when

Chapa looked up he saw the bridge passing by above him. And then he was past it.

He rolled and looked back toward the bridge he'd been standing on just a few minutes ago. Through water-soaked eyes Chapa thought he saw a figure standing on it, watching him.

Then the current pulled him under, and Chapa knew he was in for a fight. How many drownings had there been in this river? Over the years he'd heard about a dozen or more.

River water filled his nose and mouth. Its smell was foul, its taste worse, like swallowing sewage.

His clothes were getting heavier with each stroke, but swimming with the current was easier than he'd expected, and Chapa began to gradually work his way back to shore. He'd almost cut the distance in half when the sound of rushing water started getting louder.

Struggling to lift his head far enough out of the water to look ahead, Chapa noticed the steady flow of the river seemed to change again. It appeared to end some twenty-five yards up ahead.

Then he got a better look. It didn't end—it dropped. Chapa didn't know how many dams there were in this part of the Fox River. But he remembered seeing one in St. Charles, and another in North Aurora, so it was safe to assume they were found at regular intervals along the way.

From the shore, or the safety of a bridge, those drops appeared small, just ten feet or so. But rushing toward one now, those ten feet seemed a great deal more significant.

He began swimming hard toward the near shore. His arms heavy, being dragged down by wet clothing. But the river was moving faster now as the dam closed in, and Chapa understood why the current had pulled him under and carried him off.

The shore was no more than a dozen feet away now, but the river was racing faster. Despite his determination and effort, as he battled the current and fought to swim faster than he ever had before, Chapa knew he wasn't getting anywhere.

Then he felt something under his right shoe, then beneath his left. There was footing of some kind, not entirely solid, but firm enough that Chapa was able to stand and start wading through the neck-deep water.

But the current was pressing harder against his side now. And then the footing was gone.

Chapa was rushing headlong toward the drop, wondering if there would be rocks at the bottom of the dam. He got his answer an instant later.

Chapter 53

For a moment, Chapa wondered if someone, anyone, was watching all of this from the safety of the shore. On a busier day at the park there might've been a boater nearby, or a quick-thinking forest ranger with a rope.

But there was no one who could help him now.

As Chapa tipped over the edge of the dam he felt himself flip sideways on the way down, pushed by the short waterfall into the white water below. No rocks were waiting for him at the other end of the drop, but the river was much deeper, and Chapa felt himself being pulled down into the mud-green darkness.

Five feet under, ten, maybe more.

Righting himself, he started swimming for the surface, letting the current carry him forward—it didn't matter how far. Chapa felt like he was dragging a trailer with just his shoulders and thighs. His muscles burning against the cold water.

Then, in a single desperate lunge, he came up for air and saw the riverbank just twenty feet in the distance. The water was not as turbulent now, as it began the process all over again on its way to the next dam. Chapa had no desire to find out how far away that would be.

He began to gradually swim toward the shore. Managing two feet in that direction for every five he was carried downriver. Finally, the tips of his shoes pressed into the soft muck along the river's edge.

Ignoring the pain in his shoulders and back, he willed his body forward, and was trudging up the muddy bank a minute later. As soon as he found dry footing, Chapa stopped and took off his waterlogged leather jacket. He checked to make sure his wallet and keys were still there, then draped the coat over his right arm and began searching for the path to his car.

A group of children stopped playing four square as they stared, openmouthed, at the man who had emerged from the river and was now walking toward them. Chapa knew how he must have looked to the kids, and realized that he'd just given them a strange story to tell for the rest of their lives.

Chapa leaned down and picked up the red ball that was bouncing away from the children, tossed it back their way, and smiled. He could still feel their eyes on him as he started down a gravel path he assumed led back to where his car was parked.

He knew that if someone had been stalking him back there, upriver, they could still be around now. Though his clothes felt heavy, there was also no hesitation in his step. Chapa thought back to that day in Miami as he realized he'd have to cross the woods to reach the safety of his car.

Back in the forest now, and on the gravel portion of the same path he'd walked earlier, Chapa came to a dead stop when he heard what sounded like the crunching of gravel. Then the sound was gone, like it had never been there.

The sun was almost down, and soon its afterglow would be all that separated Chapa from darkness. It was getting difficult to see as he reached the paved section of his route. The forest, thick with blackness and strange undefined noises, wasn't revealing anything now.

Then the crunching sound returned. Behind him this

time. Chapa estimated that the gravel path lay twenty yards in his wake, and he wondered whether he could make it to his car before someone could reach him.

He turned to look back more times than he should have over the next several minutes, until the forest gave way and the parking lot appeared in the distance. Chapa's car was the only one that was still there, which gave him an odd sense of security.

Maybe he'd been alone the whole time, with only the knowledge that a killer was indeed out there, and a troubling memory from his childhood haunting him, clouding his thoughts.

Chapa took off his shoes and socks and tossed them in the backseat along with his coat, then got in his car, locked the doors, and waited. His eyes fixed on the forest and the path, he didn't see the man approaching his car from the rear, coming up fast along the driver's side.

There was a sharp tapping on his window. Chapa sprung just a bit, then felt stupid when he saw the park ranger on the other side.

"It's time for you to go, sir. Park's closing," the guy said, trying and failing to hide his amusement first over Chapa's reaction, then his appearance.

Chapter 54

Chapa was no more than a mile or two from home, and doing his best to lean forward and avoid soaking both the backrest as well as the seat, when he realized he'd forgotten something.

He called Tom Jackson, hoping he would still be at the station.

"C'mon Chapa, I'm damn near out of here and on the way home to a decent meal. What do you want now? And what's that noise, is it windy where you are?"

"No, I'm just driving with the window down and heater on."

"Why are you doing that?"

"I'm trying to dry off some. Listen, you need to go over that windmill and the area around it very carefully."

"That's brilliant, Alex. Don't you watch all those forensics shows on TV? We've got our own version of that, and they've already scoured the place."

"I don't doubt that, Tom. But they weren't looking for the right thing, may have ignored it even if it was obvious."

Jackson was silent for a moment, and while Chapa hoped that meant the cop was taking notes, he sensed that wasn't the case.

"Oh no, no, Alex, don't say it."

"There's going to be a stick figure," Chapa said, ignoring Jackson's ongoing objections. "It could be carved into a corner of the windmill, inside or out, etched into the walkway around it, or hell, maybe spray painted on that possum or whatever it was that lives there."

"It was a raccoon, and no one spray painted anything on it."

"Well, I'm relieved for the animal's sake, but you'll need to go get a better look at the area."

"We already discussed this, and I told you that—"

"Yes, I know, it's dangerous there, lots of bad people and what-not. But I found one of those figures at another murder scene on the other side of the park."

Sensing that he'd finally gotten Jackson's attention, Chapa described the sign that he'd seen by the river. Jackson told Chapa that he remembered the murder, though it had not been his case, and promised to check out the crime scene photos tomorrow.

"And maybe I'll take a drive there and check it out for myself."

"Maybe? Really, Tom? That's all I can get from you on this?"

"Fine, Chapa, goddamnit, I'll go check out the sign. It's probably some bullshit gang symbol, or a frat house thing, or just old-fashioned vandalism. But I'll waste part of my day and drive there to check it out just for you. Because I obviously failed to get through to you earlier."

Jackson was still droning on as Chapa turned into his driveway, some of the same spiel as before about how Fletcher Woods can be a dangerous area and any one of a thousand or more people could be responsible, and that it probably had nothing to do with any murder.

But Chapa wasn't listening anymore. His eyes were

locked on the silhouetted figure of a man, hands on hips, shoulders broad and even, standing by his house.

"I gotta go, Tom. There's a man in a suit in the middle of my driveway, and I have a feeling he's been waiting for me to get home."

Chapter 55

The last time Chapa saw Joseph Andrews they were witnessing a killer's execution. That was a little over two weeks ago, and though Chapa was happy to see his longtime friend now, he was surprised to find Andrews waiting in his driveway, wearing a blue suit that looked just like the one he had on the last time he saw him.

Chapa got out of his car, shoes and socks in hand, dripping a trail of river water as he carried them up the driveway.

"New suit, Joe?"

"Yes, it is."

"Looks right on you."

Andrews was the only man Chapa had ever known who seemed more comfortable wearing business clothes than anything else. He'd been an FBI agent for nearly twenty years, a good friend for much longer. Though the two didn't see each other very often because of their work schedules, Andrews' family obligations, and geography.

"Is that a new look for you, Al?"

"It's a long story."

"The wet leaves and mud on those pants, all over that shirt, and in your hair are a nice touch, sort of completes the style."

"When's the last time you were at my house?"

Andrews shrugged. "Been a while, hasn't it? I figured I'd stop by and say hi to Nikki."

"Yeah, right." Chapa smiled and keyed the lock on his front door. "You're here to make sure I'm not getting my ass in the chopper over the Clarkson thing."

"There's that. The way you look and smell right now makes me think I got here just in time."

Chapa told Andrews to make himself comfortable, not that he had to, while he ran upstairs to change. He took his river-soaked jacket with him, and tossed it into the bathtub along with everything else he'd been wearing, then did his best to get cleaned up. After dousing his hair in the sink and putting on some fresh clothes, he came back down ten minutes later feeling a bit better and hoping the layer of deodorant would hide the smell of the river.

He poured a couple of rum and Cokes and carried them into the living room.

"So where is Nikki?"

"Erin should be bringing her home any minute now," Chapa said, and pressed a small button on the side of the door, to keep the dead bolt from clicking shut.

He handed Andrews a drink and looked out through a living room window as a car drove past. Seeing that it wasn't Erin, Chapa let himself fall into his couch, across from the plush upholstered chair Andrews had opted for. Both pieces of furniture were purchased the day after Carla sent movers to take away everything that had been there.

"All right, Al, what about Martin Clarkson?"

Chapa kicked a copy of *Sports Illustrated* off the coffee table that came with the couch, and put his feet up.

"I saw him two, or I suppose three times, including the time when he couldn't see me."

"What do you know about him?"

Chapa shrugged, then took a slow, soothing drink, letting

the liquor wash down his throat, and waited for the burn which never came.

"Not enough rum. I may have given you my drink."

Andrews smiled and knocked back all that was left in his glass.

"I know what you told me, what Martin Clarkson told me, and what the cops told me, which wasn't much. Former FBI agent, half out of his gourd, packing heat while chasing a pattern killer who likes to draw but doesn't have a great deal of artistic ability."

Andrews pulled a tissue out of an inside pocket, folded it into a perfect square, then leaned forward and set his empty glass on the makeshift coaster.

"Did he tell you about his wife?"

"No, but I think I saw a picture of her."

Chapa laid out the details of the crime scene, including the bloodstained photo in Clarkson's hand.

"A lot of folks who knew him believe that her death is what set him off, what really sent him over."

"Maybe, but it doesn't mean he was wrong," Chapa said as he placed his damp, empty glass on the bare table.

"Wait, hold on, Al—are you saying that you believe him? You think Martin Clarkson was right."

"I do now."

Andrews buried his face in his hands, it disappeared behind long thick fingers.

"Is that a new watch, Joe?"

"What?"

"That watch you're wearing, it's not government issue, it's cool."

Andrews looked at the timepiece on his wrist like he'd never noticed it before. It was one of those with exposed gears and mechanisms as part of the design.

"No, it's not new. Jenny gave it to me two years ago, on my fortieth birthday, and you've noticed it before."

"Well, I probably thought it was cool then, too. I'm not a fickle man, Joe."

Andrews shook his head as though he wanted to free something stuck inside.

"You do understand that a slew of very good, very capable investigators looked into Clarkson's claims."

"I don't doubt that. But here's the thing, clever killers have eluded the law before, and are doing so right now as we sit here." He watched Andrews bristle just a little at that thought.

"There were even some at the Bureau who suspected Clarkson might be pursuing himself."

"Sure, I considered that possibility too, Joe." Chapa got up to get himself another drink, pointed to Andrews' glass, but got waved off. "A killer like that, one who is able to change appearance, maybe even identity, and then integrate himself into a community could be especially difficult to track."

"That's all hypothetical, Al."

"Okay, but what I found today by the river wasn't," Chapa said and left to pour himself another drink, this one without alcohol since Nikki would be home soon and he never wanted her to smell liquor on his breath. He was feeling pretty good about walking out of the room on a cliffhanger line like that one.

When he returned with a fresh glass in hand, Andrews was waiting for more. Chapa explained what led him to go back to the forest preserve. He told Andrews all that he'd learned about the murder down by the river, the sign, and his sense that someone was watching and screwing with him just before he fell in.

"The thing with the sign, there are a lot of possible explanations for that. You don't even know when it was vandalized. Could've been a year before the murder, could've been last week."

Chapa heard a car pull into the driveway, Andrews tilted his head toward the front door.

"I pushed that little button on the door that leaves it unlocked, so Erin can let herself in. For some reason she likes doing that."

"Then like I was saying, Al, the sign might not mean anything. Hell, maybe Clarkson was crazy enough to do that himself."

"Why would he?"

"To make you think he was right. It doesn't hurt to have one of the area's leading investigative reporters on your side."

"*One* of the area's leading reporters?"

"You know what I'm saying, Al."

A series of car doors opened and shut, then the sound of laughing children bounced around the front lawn.

"As for your sense that someone was watching you, that, just like a lot of the other dark shit, was probably all in your head."

Chapa thought about it for a moment. Everything Andrews was saying could very easily be true. But he wasn't ready to give in to that.

"No, Joe, it wasn't all in my head. And way too many pieces are starting to fit together."

Andrews leaned forward in his chair, like a shrink with a troublesome patient or a priest confronting a fallen parishioner.

"You do understand that when it comes to chasing something like this, your job is a lot easier than mine."

"I'm sure it is," Chapa said, then knocked back the rest of his drink as Andrews was standing up and straightening his suit coat.

"You win either way, Al. If there is a serial killer moving through the Chicago suburbs, leaving corpses and crude drawings in his wake, that's a good story."

"No, that's a *great* story, and one that people need to know."

"And if there isn't a killer out there, but a former FBI agent lost his life chasing what he believed to be one, that's a great story too."

"True. But, Joe—"

"What?"

"There *is* a serial killer operating in Oakton."

Andrews let out a long sigh as Erin came through the door. They had never met, though she had been the topic of many of Chapa's conversations with Andrews.

He introduced them to one another.

"From everything Al has told me, you sound like a wonderful, sensible person, which makes me wonder why you're dating him."

Erin feigned a serious expression, then said, "Out of pity."

Nikki and Mike came rushing through the front door.

"We're going to go play in my room until supper is ready," Nikki said, her voice trailing away as she and Mike ran up the stairs.

But Chapa stopped Nikki before she made it to the top and told her to come back down and say hi to their guest.

"You were only this tall the last time I saw you," Andrews said, holding his palm up to about Nikki's shoulder.

She smiled politely, but Chapa wondered if she actually remembered him.

"What are you going to be for Halloween?" Andrews asked.

"A princess," Nikki answered.

Mike jumped in. "I'm going to be a pirate."

After a few rounds of adult-child small talk, Nikki and Mike were headed back up the stairs.

"Erin picked out the costumes," Chapa said and put his arm around her. "Took Nikki shopping at one of those seasonal Halloween stores."

Erin withdrew a little.

"You smell . . . different, Alex. Did you get ready for dinner by slathering on a bottle of aftershave?"

"Actually, it's deodorant, scented," Chapa said and smiled. "And dinner, hadn't thought about that."

"Erin, here's hoping that you can straighten this guy out, get some sense into him."

"Not an easy task," she replied without missing a beat.

"No, it isn't. But Al isn't a bad person, not really."

"I'd been wondering."

"He's not. And that is why if you give me a couple of days' heads-up, I'll be there for the intervention."

Chapa had heard enough. "Hey guys, I'm right here."

They ordered pizzas and ate them together in the dining room. Andrews finally took off his suit coat, but Chapa was certain that had more to do with not getting food on it than making himself comfortable.

As they sat and talked for a couple of hours after dinner, Andrews and Chapa took turns telling war stories, and Erin seemed to enjoy every minute.

"I'm taking notes, you know, for future reference," she said after Andrews was done recounting the time during their college days when the two of them sneaked up onto the roof of a prominent Chicago museum, drank beer until they passed out, then woke the next day and had to figure out how to get down without getting caught.

Nikki stayed up for another half hour after Erin and Mike left, then said goodnight to Andrews, and Chapa went up and tucked her in. When he came back downstairs, Andrews had his suit coat on.

"Stick around a while, Joe."

"I wish I could, but it's been a long one."

"Yeah, tell me about it. I've got Jim Chakowski's funeral to go to tomorrow."

"What about Erin?"

"She's not going. Nikki will be over at her house."

"What I meant was are you going to marry her? Are you going to let her make a decent man out of you?"

Chapa started cleaning up, well aware of how that uncharacteristic behavior let his perceptive friend know he wasn't comfortable with this conversation.

"I don't know. I'm still too concerned about getting lost down the rabbit hole again."

"Erin is not Carla."

"Not even close."

"Carla was just plain wrong in too many ways to count."

"And Erin is right in a lot of ways."

"Al, you need to get your head straight, or you're going to lose Erin, I can see it in her eyes," Andrews said, following Chapa into the kitchen with a plate and two dirty forks in his hand. "Her priorities right now are different than yours, and they're the right priorities, so that's not going to change."

"I've thought about all that."

Andrews nodded and followed Chapa back to the living room.

"I'm supposed to be spending time bonding with my daughter, and instead I'm dancing back and forth between stories I don't give a shit about and one that is potentially bigger, but that probably won't add up to anything." Chapa could hear the weariness in his own voice. "It feels like everyone is a step ahead of me, and I don't like that feeling."

"Here's what you need to do, Al. They're going to can your ass, probably after this week, or next, maybe in a month, but it's going to happen, right?

"That's where the smart money is."

"No one ever bet smart money on you one way or another."

Chapa smiled.

"When the *Chicago Record* finally gets around to putting you out of your misery, I'll give you the keys to our condo in Key Largo. We won't be using it until next year, so you can spend two weeks, a month—hell, go join the tribe of colorful, eccentric beach bums down there, whatever. Just get away for a while."

Chapa thought about his friend's offer. It wasn't a bad idea.

"But isn't this hurricane season?"

"C'mon, Al, with you around it's always hurricane season."

Chapter 56

There was no visitation for Jim Chakowski. No one was around to plan it. Even if his brother wasn't being held in custody on weapons charges, there was very little chance Warren would've been up to the job.

But Jim Chakowski, though he'd left no will, had made funeral plans, bought a plot, and paid for it in advance. So four days after his death, Chakowski's remains were buried in a short but surprisingly well-attended service.

Chapa dusted off his black suit, picked a simple tie off the rack, and dressed to honor his colleague's memory.

Warren was brought to the gravesite in handcuffs by two uniformed policemen, which Chapa found distasteful. He thought they should've sent a couple of plainclothes cops, and planned to write about that in his column. Several of Jim Chakowski's friends and neighbors walked over to offer their sympathies to Warren, who struggled to raise his head in acknowledgment.

Carston Macklin, the *Record*'s managing editor, was there along with several of the newspaper's leading suck-ups. Sullivan was there too, doing his best to avoid eye contact with Chapa.

None of that came as much of a surprise. What Chapa

hadn't expected, however, was how many local businessmen and politicians showed up.

The mayor didn't make it—she rarely attended this sort of thing—but Monica Brown, her chief of staff, was there, along with an alderman or two. Dr. Walter Bendix stood nearby, looking at Chapa like he had something on his mind.

Huddled off to one side of the burial site like some sort of teenaged clique were Frank Gemmer, Clay Hunter, Greg Vinsky, Richard Wick, Charles Stoop, Ted Bruce, and a few other serious-looking men, one of whom Chapa guessed had to be Willie Blair. They stopped talking to one another when Vanny Mars showed up just before the graveside service began.

After a pastor, whose church Jim Chakowski may or may not have attended, finished a dull and uninspired service, most of the personal acquaintances filed by Warren once more. All of the community leaders headed in the opposite direction.

Chapa watched Carston Macklin walk over to Warren and try to comfort the man. His effort appeared to be genuine, and that he meant whatever he was saying. Maybe Macklin was capable of human emotions after all. But Chapa needed a lot more proof before he'd sign off on that bit of revision.

Macklin was heading toward Chapa now, and the look on his face was anything but consoling.

"We need to have a meeting, Alex. Today."

"I'll be in the office later," Chapa said and walked away.

He saw Sullivan watching them from what the editor probably hoped was a safe distance. Chapa wasn't sure there was such a thing where he and Macklin were concerned.

Warren looked up as Chapa approached. He didn't know what to say to a grieving brother. But then again, who does?

Before Chapa could say anything, Warren reached up and clutched his arm.

"Hey, none of that," one of the officers, a man with a gentle face and a voice too soft for a policeman, said as he yanked on the cuffs.

"It's okay," Chapa said, trying vainly to wave off the cop's attempt to protect him from his prisoner.

Warren responded by tightening his grip until it hurt, though Chapa wasn't about to let the officers know that.

"Help me, Alex. Help me."

He looked much worse than he had in the restaurant a few days ago. The skin under his bloodshot eyes was a mix of red and violet.

"I'm working on it, Warren." *I'm working on a lot of things right now,* Chapa added in his own mind.

Chapter 57

As he left the cemetery, Chapa couldn't stop thinking about the gaggle of community leaders who had shown up at Jim's funeral. Maybe they were fond of him because of the way he did his job. Or maybe there was something else.

Chapa couldn't get over the way they congregated together, like some sort of animal pack. Okay, so they didn't want to be close to the guy who'd barged into a meeting at City Hall carrying a rifle. He got that. But still, there was something odd about the whole thing.

Maybe they were just comfortable around one another. Or it could be that they were keeping an eye on each other.

He needed to get more insight on who the players were. After all, Clarkson had speculated that the killer he was tracking had woven himself into the fabric of every place he'd lived. Chapa was on his way home to change into some more reasonable clothes when he decided to make a call.

Tim Haas answered his phone on the first ring. Chapa hoped he could take advantage of what he sensed was Tim's desire to be a big shot. When he tossed a lunch offer Tim's way, it sealed the deal.

"Do I get to pick where we eat?"

"Well, yes, sort of. I want to go someplace where a lot of the people who work at City Hall go."

"I don't know about that." Tim's voice carried a combination of disappointment and concern. "I want to help you, and I'm sure by now you know I'm the sort of person who can, but if they see me talking to you—"

"So what? I'm not doing any sort of trash piece on city government, you're not going to be quoted anywhere. I won't take notes or record our conversation. I just need you to point out who's who, so I can do my job better."

"I can tell that to anyone who asks?"

"Absolutely, tell anyone who asks that you painted them in a good light."

The silence let Chapa know Tim was thinking it over. The young man's hunger for significance had its own scent. It was a need that would either get him to the top or in a whole lot of trouble one day.

"Let's meet at The Dancing Clown, that's where a lot of them go."

The Dancing Clown, a newer restaurant located in downtown Oakton, had something of a split personality. By day it was a popular lunch destination for area professionals who came tumbling in around noon to escape their banks and office buildings. But after hours, as the downtown was abandoned to local street gangs, hookers, and the homeless, the place underwent a seedy transformation.

Chapa saw Charles Stoop wave to him as he walked in, ten minutes before Tim Haas was supposed to get there. Chapa responded with a polite but neutral tip of the head, then watched as Stoop tried to process why he was here and whether to invite him over. He appeared to eventually decide against asking Chapa to sit at the table he shared with Franklin Gemmer and Clay Hunter.

A tall, slim man in his early twenties, who smelled like he'd just finished sneaking a smoke, seated Chapa at a cramped half-sized table near the other side of the large room. Chapa took off his light-brown suede coat—the one he'd decided to wear while his leather jacket was convalescing—and slid into the tight space.

Across the crowded restaurant, Chapa could hear Franklin Gemmer talking about some new security system, but he couldn't figure out whether the guy was pitching or merely boasting.

Chapa was splitting his attention between the menu and the door, as he kept an eye out for Tim. Gemmer was still holding court at the power table when Chapa noticed a familiar face smiling at him from the other end of the room.

Leah Carelli was sitting in a crescent-shaped booth overlooking the rest of the room. She was flanked by Vanny Mars on her left, and a blond woman whom Chapa did not recognize on her right.

When Chapa didn't return the smile, Leah slipped a wink at him in a way that no one else would notice. The gesture across a crowded restaurant belonged to just the two of them, and filled the moment with a certain intimacy.

But Chapa knew that in a sense Leah had been winking at him since the moment he saw her at City Hall. Turning his attention to the other two women at the table, Chapa immediately and involuntarily determined that Leah was easily the most attractive of the three.

He was trying to decide just how certain he was about Vanny's original gender when Tim dropped into the other chair.

"Wow, couldn't they find you a smaller table?"

"You kidding, this is an upgrade from the serving tray they first offered me, though not much of one."

A waitress wandered over. She looked tired and bored like she'd lived this day thousands of times before, but at least she didn't smell like Marlboros. Tim ordered without opening the menu, Chapa took a little longer before settling on something called the Chicken Del Rey sandwich.

"Who's the third member of the Oakton City Supremes?" Chapa asked and tossed a glance toward Leah's booth.

"Let's see . . . Oh, you mean Tammy Trench, right? The one who's not Leah or Vanny?"

"Yeah."

"That's her. She runs a tile and carpeting business."

Tammy glanced over and noticed Chapa and Tim. She smiled, softening her severe, high-maintenance looks.

"She's the third member of the Clinton Avenue Cougars. There are a couple of others who come and go, but those are the founding members."

"Yes, you mean the thirty-plus women who go for young guys. I've heard of this group before but didn't know who all the members were."

"I don't think any of those chicks have been thirty for some time. But yes, that's what they do."

"Do you have firsthand knowledge of this?"

"Well, let's just say I've made Tammy smile before."

"Thank you for sharing that, Tim."

"They get around, at least Tammy does. Leah might just be more of a flirt. They say Vanny's been married six times or so, Tammy twice. Leah is more of a mystery."

Chapa was trying to process the idea that Leah Carelli, the same hot, shapely, young lady with whom he'd shared a number of memorable nights was now a "cougar," when Dick Wick walked in, followed a minute later by Greg Vinsky. They headed straight for the power table, and pulled up chairs alongside their associates.

"And those guys over there, are they ever seen apart?"

Tim didn't have to turn around to know who Chapa was talking about.

"That's who makes the decisions in this town. Every time there's a photo of a ground-breaking ceremony you're bound to see one or more of those guys in the background horning in."

"Have you dealt with many of them directly, Tim?"

"Four of those men know me by name. That's what matters around here. Three have asked me for help with their websites or computer systems." Tim smiled like someone keeping a special secret. "I know some things."

Chapa had met guys like him before, and felt certain Tim didn't know half as much as he liked pretending he did.

Greg Vinsky and Charles Stoop were joking and laughing like lifelong friends. Chapa had no stomach for that sort of phony corporate chumminess between men who probably wouldn't cross the street to say hi to each other if they didn't have to. He remembered when Carla left her job at the law firm she worked for shortly after Nikki was born. How certain she had been that all of her work friends would stay in contact with her. That lasted two weeks, maybe three.

"Are all those guys really friends?"

Tim shrugged. "Not sure. They each disappear into their private lives only to reemerge when the time comes to get their name in the paper, or on some new contract or regulation."

He glanced back at the power table, then inched toward Chapa and lowered his voice. "I'll tell you what, though, you don't cross those guys."

"What happens if you do?" Chapa asked as the image of Jim Chakowski's house flashed across his mind.

"Take a look at that guy." Tim pointed to a solitary man sitting across the room at a table that was even smaller than theirs. "That's Brent McGraw, he used to be a quasi-big shot, but not anymore. Those guys pretty much ran him out. You should talk to him sometime."

Tim was done with his sandwich, and Chapa could tell that he was getting a little uneasy about being there.

"How was your sandwich?"

"Good. It's always good here. How 'bout your Chicken Del Rey?"

"Fit for a king. Look, Tim, don't try to be a big shot, not

here in this town. Only bastards and suck-ups thrive in this town, and I don't believe you're either. Stay under the radar."

Tim nodded, then got up to go, and Chapa knew his words had failed to register. He watched the young man leave, then signaled the waitress to come over.

"Could you do me a favor?" he asked, straining to read her name tag, "Amanda, could you bring my check to the small table over there? I'll be joining that gentleman."

Chapter 58

"You're taking a chance, Mr. Chapa."

"I do that sometimes, and it's Alex."

Brent McGraw looked like he'd just climbed out of a thrift store donation bin. His white shirt was badly in need of a run-in with an iron, and his hair could've used a trim anytime last month.

"I used to be one of them, but not now."

"What happened?"

"I challenged the system, spoke up against a bad zoning change. They didn't like that and cut me off."

"They can do that?"

He smiled, and the wrinkles across his forehead lined up in formation.

"Every major decision in this town that involves money is made by those men plus a couple more, and maybe Vanny Mars and Tammy Trench, and always in concert with the others."

Chapa kept looking over at the two tables, couldn't help himself. He watched as Greg Vinsky said his goodbyes and left, and then Charles Stoop did likewise a couple of minutes later. Chapa waited to see if Stoop would look his way, but he seemed to make it a point not to.

"But it's a big town. How can just a handful of people—"

"No, it's not a big town, not really. Oakton is a little speck of nothing that's grown like a weed. Most folks here live at one end of the city or the other and don't give a shit about what goes on downtown."

"That's an old story, Brent. Rockford, Aurora, Joliet, Elgin, and probably hundreds of other towns across the country have struggled with that problem."

"Yes. But it's different here in Oakton, and Jim Chakowski knew that."

Chapa was starting to realize that Jim Chakowski had known a lot of things. He reached in his pocket, pulled out a pen and began casually doodling a stick figure on his napkin, like Clarkson had done. He made sure McGraw could see it, and watched for a reaction, saw none.

"You do understand, don't you, that Oakton couldn't function this way if your employer wasn't in bed with those people over there?"

"You're saying the *Record* is in the tank for these guys?"

"Maybe I wouldn't go that far, but I believe Jim got pressured from time to time to spin a story one way or another or kill it altogether."

Chapa was thinking back through his own stories and remembering a few that he'd been nudged off of, or that had wound up getting marginalized when they finally saw print. At the time he hadn't spent too much energy worrying about it. There's always the next story to move on to.

"Look, Alex, in Oakton, everyone works together. This is a go-along-to-get-along city."

"Don't most cities and towns operate that way to some extent?"

McGraw appeared to get lost for a moment as he stared at the three men who remained at the table.

"Sure," he said, turning back toward Chapa. "Only here, the price for not going along can be very high."

Knowing that silence is often the greatest tool in getting

someone to volunteer information, Chapa didn't say anything. He sensed that McGraw had more on his mind.

He was right.

"Look around, Alex. Each of the neighboring towns have buildings going up or businesses opening their doors. But the only way that happens in Oakton is if one or more of the men at that table have something to gain from it."

The waitress brought McGraw's bill, tossed it on the table by his drink. Chapa reached across, picked it up, and checked the total. It wasn't much. He reached in his wallet and dropped two fives.

"I don't need the charity, Mr. Chapa."

"Charity my ass, consider this an investment in your comeback."

McGraw laughed a little, like it hurt to do so, then mouthed *thank you*.

"Tell me something, how far would those people go to protect their way of life, their style of doing business?" Chapa asked, nodding toward the other tables.

"As far as they had to."

Chapa lowered his voice.

"Might one of them be willing to kill?"

"*One* of them? If it meant protecting the matrix that they've built here in Oakton, their own mothers would not be safe."

Chapter 59

Chapa's story about the funeral functioned as a second obit for Jim Chakowski, and came as easily as anything he'd written in months. The other piece he wrote in the two hours after lunch, the story that would fill his column space in the next day's paper, took quite a bit more thought and time.

He'd decided to begin the process of reexamining the murder of Wade Marshall, the college student whose life was stolen from him alongside that lonely stretch of river in Fletcher Woods. Wade Marshall—he had a name. Chapa had looked it up in the original story, and then written it on a small lime green Post-it note that he then affixed to the edge of his monitor.

It was easy to forget some discarded corpse, a lot harder to ignore a person whose name you knew. With that in mind, Chapa wrote the name Martin Clarkson on another note and put it next to the first. Then he went into some of the research Zach had done and found a few more names from Baltimore and Pittsburgh and paid those folks the same tribute.

Maybe they weren't all good people, no doubt a few were anything but. Still, had they all deserved to die? That thought triggered another, and Chapa wrote one more name—

Kimberly Clarkson—and added it to the bottom edge of his crowded monitor screen. He had no reason to assume her death had been anything but an accident—except for one—Chapa did not like coincidences. A husband and wife each dying the way the Clarksons had, for example.

He stopped and looked at the small paper squares ringing his monitor like florescent petals. There was still enough room for two additional notes, and Chapa was certain he'd missed at least that many more murders, but this would do for now. He had plenty of motivation.

His story revisiting the murder of Wade Marshall raised many more questions than Chapa could hope to answer. And in a final stroke, Chapa added a sentence that he knew could make the difference one way or another.

> *No matter what anyone may have thought about Wade Marshall's death, or even if you were not concerned about it, even for an instant, if his murder was indeed part of a pattern, a pattern that continues today, then all of us have reason to be concerned.*

Chapa quickly revised the story, then sent it off to editorial. His phone rang twenty minutes later as he was planning his next few days in a way that would allow him to spend much of the time with Nikki.

"Alex, you're needed in Mr. Macklin's office right now."

"What's up, Matt?"

"Just stop whatever you're working on and come down here, will you?"

Chapa agreed, then emailed copies of the day's stories to his home computer before shutting down. Creating a backup of his work in that way was a precaution Chapa did not like having to take. And he knew it spoke to how badly his situation at the *Record* had deteriorated.

Macklin's office occupied the most visible space in the building, filling a prominent corner and extending half the entire length of an adjoining wall. It was strategically located in a place that made it nearly impossible to avoid, coming or going.

Chapa opened the door and walked in, then looked at the three solemn faces staring back at him. Under different circumstances he might've gone for a cheap laugh and asked if someone had died, but of course someone had, and there was no room for humor anymore.

Sullivan was seated along one side of Macklin's SUV-sized desk. A sour-faced man whose wrinkles came naturally and extended beyond the rim of his glasses, was sitting off to the side of the room, as though he was there to observe.

"You know Barth Morton, the *Chicago Record*'s counsel, don't you Alex?" Carston's voice didn't fill the room, it merely trickled across his desk, its significance left somewhere behind, like distant thunder.

Chapa nodded to the attorney, whom he did not know personally, but his greeting was not returned.

"We seem to have a problem. Why don't you sit down and we can talk about it."

Chapa looked at the chair Macklin was pointing to, the one directly in front of the desk. It appeared to be a few inches shorter than the others.

"I'll stand."

Macklin was not pleased, but he appeared to decide this wasn't worth any further debate and turned his attention to some papers on his desk. He flipped through them, pulling out a few and separating them across his desk pad.

The office décor had changed somewhat since Chapa was last there. The air was scented with a woodsy aroma that had greeted him at the door. Macklin had redecorated the place in a golf motif, complete with framed autographed magazine covers of Tiger Woods, Phil Mickelson, Vijay Singh, and a few others Chapa didn't recognize.

Mixed in were several pictures of Macklin at various

courses around the world. A small brass plate at the bottom of each frame indicated which course it was and what year he'd been there. A photo of Macklin with Greg Norman, inscribed by the golfer, *From one shark to another*, was framed with one of the Australian's used gloves.

A small rug, meant to simulate a putting green, lay in a far corner. Chapa had noticed a putter leaning against the doorframe as he walked in. The name *Mack* was embossed on the handle.

Macklin's old man would never have gone for any of this shit.

"Do you golf?" Macklin, no longer sifting through his notes, had apparently noticed Chapa taking in the surroundings.

"Oh hell no," Chapa responded and watched Sullivan sink in his chair just a little.

Macklin silently stared at Chapa for an uncomfortable length of time before saying anything.

"You were given an assignment."

"And I've been doing it."

"Not exactly. You were supposed to take Jim Chakowski's beat, and no more."

"I've been doing my job."

"Not exactly." Macklin leaned back in his leather throne, loosened his shoulders a bit, and Chapa sensed a different approach was coming. "Let's have a talk among men, man to man, men to men. How about that?"

"I know I'm up to it."

Macklin smiled, though his pale blue eyes did not join in the fun. Each strand of his thinning light brown hair looked like it had been carefully put in place that morning. He had his usual tan, even though it was October in the northern Midwest.

"We are part of a vibrant, growing community. And that community is, in turn, vital to our own growth."

"This paper hasn't grown in eleven years," Chapa said,

picking that number intentionally. That was how long it had been since Carston Macklin took over and began running his father's greatest achievement into the ground.

Macklin raised his palm toward Chapa.

"Please, Alex, let me continue. It's the community that pays our bills, and allows us to pay our employees. We, in turn, need to make sure that the community is happy with our work, and that we play a part in its continued success."

"That's not a newspaper's responsibility."

"That's how it works around here."

"Okay, Carston, well how 'bout this, someone is carving up members of your community."

"You don't know that, and these irresponsible claims you're making aren't of any value to anybody."

Chapa stepped forward and leaned on Macklin's desk, a confirmed no-no for any staffer.

"They're not irresponsible, and if a single life is saved because the police go out and find who's doing this, or folks around here are a little more cautious, then my story will have value."

"Look, Alex, will you have a seat, please?"

"I'm good."

Macklin let out a heavy sigh. Chapa knew he was more than just accustomed to being in complete control—he *needed* to be.

"I know you miss Jim, I do too."

"You didn't give a damn about Jim Chakowski, you don't give a damn about me, or Sully, or—" Chapa pointed at the attorney. "Okay, that guy, maybe."

"Alex, you're off your game. You were given a specific assignment."

"I've taken Jim's beat, I can't claim to be as good as he was at it—"

"Not even close," Macklin said, cutting him off.

"Well maybe that's what your dad said when he saw what you were doing to his newspaper."

Out of the corner of his eye Chapa saw the lawyer writing something down. Macklin remained a tidy package of tightly controlled anger tucked behind a desk that didn't seem quite as big now.

"Alex, are you trying to get yourself fired?"

"I'm trying to do my job, something that you seem to keep getting in the way of. Maybe it's because you're not sure what you're supposed to be doing."

"Here's what I have been doing," Macklin spread a dozen or more sheets of paper across his desk. It was clear that he'd regained his composure. Chapa felt like he'd lost some sort of temporary edge he might've had a moment ago. "I've been reading the stories and columns that you've written over the past five weeks, and I want to go over a few of them with you."

"We're done here," Chapa said and turned to leave.

"The hell we are!" Macklin was out of his chair. "You're going to sit the fuck down and go through these stories with me!"

"No, Carston, you're wrong about that. Watch." Chapa looked over at Sullivan, who appeared to have developed a sudden fascination with his own shoes. "Matt, I've got a whole shitload of vacation time, yes?"

Sullivan looked up, and seemed relieved that he'd been asked a nuts-and-bolts question, one that did not require an opinion.

"That's right, Alex. I can never get you to take any, so—"

"In fact, I'm technically on vacation right now."

"Well, technically yes, but—"

"Then like I said, we're done here."

Chapa turned and left. He stopped by his office for a few of his things, and was already on the phone with Erin when Maya handed him the mail on his way out of the building.

Chapter 60

Chapa flipped through his as well as Chakowski's mail on the way to Erin's, found nothing of value, and tossed it all in the glove compartment. He was leaning into his car, and cleaning the interior, having finally gotten the driver's seat reasonably dry, and making room for Mike's car seat when Nikki hugged him from behind.

"Are we really going to a special park, Daddy?"

"Well, it's special to me."

Chapa had never known the place's actual name. As long as he could remember, it was referred to as "Rocket Park," thanks to the thirty-foot slide that served as its centerpiece.

"Is the slide really shaped like a rocket?" Mike asked as they pulled out of the driveway.

"Yes, it is. And you have to climb up through the rocket to get to the top and slide down. When I was a little boy it was my favorite place to go, and I would ask my mom to take me there almost every weekend, even in winter."

Nikki leaned forward as far as her seat belt would allow, until her face was almost between the front bucket seats.

"And did grandma take you every time you asked?"

Chapa laughed. "Oh no, not even close. Your grandmother worked a lot."

After a brief pause, Nikki said, "Just like you do, Daddy."

He knew she'd meant it as a compliment, but the words stung, anyhow. This moment, this afternoon, driving Nikki, Erin, and Mike to a park, this was how the entire week was supposed to be.

There had been a chill in Erin's voice when Chapa called to tell her he was picking them all up. Maybe it was there last night, too. Some of what Andrews had said about priorities was gnawing at Chapa now.

But he was starting to sort through some things on his way to Erin's. Andrews might've been right. Maybe Chapa did need to kick his priorities around a bit. He wondered if that was happening already.

After all, if he lost his job he'd find another. There were all sorts of opportunities for unemployed journalists. Weren't there?

If his stories didn't run in the next day's *Record* he might be the only one who would notice, anyhow. And if a killer was operating in the Chicago suburbs the cops would eventually catch him, or he'd move on and become someone else's problem.

At the moment, Chapa's biggest concern was finding a park that he hadn't been to since Nikki was five. He wound down curved residential streets that crisscrossed and doubled back until finally stumbling across it on the fourth try.

As soon as he'd found a parking spot and switched the ignition off, the kids barreled out of the backseat. Chapa smiled as he watched Erin chase after them.

"C'mon, Daddy."

Nikki had beaten everyone to the rocket slide, but was now waiting for her dad to get there. Built during the height of the space race, the slide had been restored a number of times over the past several decades. The park wasn't as popular as it once had been, but the slide still served as a reminder of a time when kids still dreamed of becoming astronauts and blasting off into the unknown.

They climbed up steps that angled toward a platform near the tip. While Mike and Erin watched from below, Chapa and Nikki rushed to the double slide, sat down, and let go, full speed to the bottom.

"Let's do that again!" Nikki was racing back around to the steps. Mike had decided that the swings were more his speed, and as he and Erin headed in that direction, Chapa trailed his daughter around the rocket and back up again.

This time they paused at the top, sat on the edge of the metal platform, and let their legs rest on the red slide.

"What did you want to be when you were you my age and came up here to play?"

Chapa didn't have to think about his answer for long.

"I wanted to write for a newspaper. I wanted to be a reporter. Just like some boys wanted to be astronauts, or baseball players, though I wanted to be both of those, too."

"And you've been able to be a reporter."

"Yeah, for a while, anyway."

Nikki raised her arms in the air, screamed, and let herself slip down the slide. Chapa didn't.

"C'mon Dad," Nikki called from below in her small voice.

"You go on and play. I'll be down in a minute."

She shrugged and ran over to the swings to join Erin and Mike.

From somewhere in the distance, maybe one of the houses that fronted the park, Chapa heard an up-tempo piano rendition of "Someday My Prince Will Come." Leaning on his knowledge of jazz—which was not quite extensive, but not bad, either—he guessed it was Bill Evans on keyboard. Whoever it was, the music was a perfect fit with everything else around it.

Chapa thought about all that had taken up so much of his time and attention over the past several days. How much of it actually meant anything? Everything Chapa had been focusing on, the stories he had been chasing and the people he'd been spending his time on, now seemed to belong to another universe.

For possibly the first time since he became a journalist, Chapa began to give serious thought to simply walking away. Not just from the *Chicago Record,* but from newspapers altogether. What was left of the newspaper business anyway? He didn't recognize it anymore.

Maybe he could get a job teaching, work normal hours, and fly off to Boston once a month to see Nikki. Or would Erin consider moving to Boston? That would be a lot to ask, too much, maybe. But then so many things could fall into place if they could make it work.

Nikki, Erin, and Mike had timed their swings so that they rose and fell and swung back in unison like perfectly synched pendulums. Chapa looked at the empty fourth swing, and knew what he needed to do next.

Chapter 61

Chapa put away the rest of the Chinese food, and started heating up some milk to make hot chocolate. He'd been disappointed when Erin chose to go home, but she probably wanted some time to be alone with Mike. There had not been much of that over the past few days.

Nikki had left her chopsticks, along with a piece of sweet and sour chicken on her plate. Chapa was amused when his daughter boasted that she knew how to use those things, but pleased when she proved she could.

His feelings changed a little when Nikki explained, "Stephen taught me how."

All through dinner he was still thinking about life after the newspaper. How things would be different if he could see Nikki twice a month, every month. That would be so much better for everyone, except maybe Carla, but to hell with Carla. He would start looking at other jobs tomorrow while Nikki did her homework, not at Erin's, but in her own house.

He poured two cups of hot chocolate and carried them to the living room, stopping at the foot of the stairs to call up to Nikki. She came down from her room a minute later wearing a pair of pink pajamas with the word *Princess* stitched across the front of the shirt. That reminded Chapa of her Halloween costume, and it felt good to know he'd be with her on that night.

The TV was turned on, but the sound was muted and it had been that way since dinner. That was fine as far as Chapa was concerned.

They talked about school and her teachers and classmates, and whether she was having any trouble doing her homework this way, with the lessons arriving via email.

"Not really. Erin has been very helpful. She knows a lot of stuff."

And then Nikki was back on the subject of his relationship with Erin. Chapa felt more comfortable talking about that now.

"You two should get married someday," she said, blowing away some of the steam from her cup. "She's certainly crazy about you."

Chapa smiled.

"What has she said to you about me?"

"Not too much, Daddy, just some girl talk. But she has a couple of friends that she emails, and they talk about you."

It took Chapa a moment to process what Nikki had said.

"How do you know that?"

"Because I read them. She forgot to sign out once and I—"

"Nikki!"

"Aren't you curious? Mommy gets into Stephen's emails all the time."

"I don't care what your mom does. Decent people don't snoop around others' emails. That's a terrible violation of Erin's privacy."

"But Mommy says it's important to know other people's secrets, so that you can get to know them better."

"Well your mother is wrong."

Nikki put her mug down on the table and pushed it away.

"I'm sorry."

"That's not going to be enough. You're going to have to apologize to Erin tomorrow."

The mood had shifted, suddenly and in a direction Chapa did not want it to go. But he knew better than to ignore this, though a big part of him would've liked to.

"Oh no, please." Tears ringed her eyes, as the sides of her mouth tilted downward.

"That's how it's got to be, Nik. You and I have a few things to talk about."

She stood up, shoulders slumped.

"Can we talk in the morning? I just want to go to bed now."

Chapa sighed as he grabbed the remote and turned the television off.

"That's fine. Give me a hug and go up to bed."

He almost felt like apologizing for some reason. She draped her arms around him in something that was not quite a hug.

"You know I love you, no matter what. Even when I'm not happy with something you've done."

"I love you too," she said, and headed up the stairs.

Chapa picked up the mugs and carried them to the kitchen sink. He decided to give Nikki a few minutes to think about what had happened before going up and calmly talking to her about it. Then he would call Erin, and get her take on this.

He walked back to the living room and turned off the two floor lamps at the far end. He'd gotten in the habit of leaving a lot of lights on because Nikki had a slight fear of the dark. Besides, Chapa wasn't too fond of dark houses himself.

When he reached for the small lamp at the other end of the room Chapa noticed a strange marking on the wall. It was faint, and could easily have been mistaken for a shadow.

But it didn't go away when Chapa put his hand up to block the lamp. Instead it grew in intensity and clarity, and appeared to be surrounded by a few friends.

What Chapa saw resembled two neon yellow lines forming an upside down V. For an instant, he wondered why Nikki would've drawn on the wall like that, remembering her glow-in-the-dark markers.

Deep down, Chapa knew what this was, but he was having trouble processing the vile thing he was seeing. When he turned and looked back toward the darkened half of the room, Chapa knew there was no time to do anything but grab his daughter and get out of the house.

The walls, the ceiling, and even one of his tables were covered in stick figures. Drawn using Nikki's glow-in-the-dark markers, the figures beamed back at Chapa, mocking him and all his sense of security.

The three-inch-tall yellow-green stickmen littered almost every inch of the walls. Neatly drawn, and each roughly the same size, they appeared to be dancing all over the room and closing in on him.

Chapa heard the floor creak upstairs, but not in Nikki's room, or in the hall that led to the bathroom. This sound seemed to come from directly above him—where his bedroom was.

"Nikki, come down here please."

"Can't we talk in the morning, Daddy?"

"No. I need you down here now."

"Daddy, I'm sorry I did that, but why do we—"

Chapa heard the creaking sound again and rushed up the stairs, two at a time. For an instant he thought about running into his bedroom and confronting whomever might be there. But that would leave Nikki unprotected, and her safety was his only concern.

Startled, Nikki bolted upright in bed. Chapa pressed an index finger to her lips and shook his head in as calm and controlled a way as he could.

He took Nikki's arm and helped her out of bed, then walked into the hall. His bedroom was only fifteen feet away, just beyond the bathroom.

Maybe he could send Nikki outside and over to a neighbor's house, then confront the intruder on his own. Bad idea. What if no one was in the house, and someone was waiting outside?

Only one choice, he'd have to get Nikki out, then come back.

Chapa pointed at the steps and signaled for Nikki to walk down. He could tell she was a little disoriented by the situation. Of course she was. He was too.

She walked slowly, taking each step carefully, as though she was trying to be quiet. But this was taking too long. And Chapa realized that if someone was upstairs they had already figured out what was happening.

"Hurry up," Chapa whispered. "And go right out the door."

Nikki looked back at him, her face awash in confusion.

"And don't stop for your shoes, or jacket."

Fear replaced the confusion, but she moved faster down the remaining steps, then straight to the door, just as she'd been told to do. Nikki was about to step outside when she looked back toward the living room and froze.

Her mouth open, she pointed at the figures. Chapa could see the mix of dark emotions in his daughter's eyes. He knew right then this was a moment she'd carry with her forever.

He picked Nikki up by the waist and carried her out into the October night, taking one last look back at his living room. The sheer number of stickmen threatened to overwhelm him, but he refused to let that happen.

As the screen door closed behind them, Chapa wondered how his daughter had managed to avoid screaming. Something any sane adult would have been justified to do.

Chapter 62

Chapa was rushing Nikki to Mrs. Steinmetz's house, right next door. The elderly woman usually stayed up late, or at least her television was on deep into the night. Chapa would often notice the flickering blue light as he came home after a midnight deadline.

But then he saw Jim Martin pulling into his driveway across the street, and carried Nikki in that direction.

"Jim, I need your help right now."

"Why are you carrying a child?" he asked, with no apparent sense of urgency.

"This is my daughter Nikki, and I think someone is in my house."

"Oh damn. I'm sorry, Alex and Alex's daughter, didn't mean to swear. Get inside."

He ran to the door, opened it and hurried them inside, then slammed the door shut and locked it behind them.

"Call the cops, tell them there's a break-in going on, give them my address."

"Why don't you do that, Alex?"

"Because I'm going back to see who the hell is in my house."

"No, Daddy don't go."

Nikki threw herself at him and wrapped her arms so tightly around his waist that it hurt.

"She's right, you belong with her," Jim's wife Alice said as she draped a blanket around Nikki's shoulders.

Chapa thought about it for a moment and realized they were right.

"Give me your phone, please," he said and headed to their front windows to keep a watch on his house.

Chapter 63

Chapa heard the sirens in the distance, cutting through an otherwise tranquil night. Two cruisers showed up a moment later and parked in front of his house. It had taken them eleven minutes to get there. Chapa had kept track of the passing time by watching a grandfather clock that stood near the front windows. Those few quick glances had been the only times he'd broken eye contact with his house.

There had been no movement. No one came skulking through the front door, or across the yard. No suspicious shadows in the windows.

Chapa walked out to meet the four officers who'd emerged from their cars and were now standing in the middle of the street. He pointed to his house, explained what had happened, and after a brief hesitation retreated to the neighbor's yard when one of the cops told him to.

Two officers headed toward Chapa's front door while another circled around the back of the house. Ten minutes later, they were all standing in the front yard.

Chapa didn't wait to be asked to cross the street and join them.

"We don't see any sign of forced entry, and there's no one

in your house now," a uniformed policeman named Root was saying. "Did you know you left your back door unlocked?"

"But my back door shouldn't have been unlocked." Chapa was trying to remember if he'd taken out the garbage or unlocked that door tonight for any reason.

He could sense these officers had little if any interest in pursuing this. Still, when Chapa remembered the unlock button on the front door, the one he'd pushed the night before so Erin could let herself in, and then forgot to push again, he told them about it. And they stopped searching the grounds.

They walked with Chapa back over to his house and let him point out the drawings, something they had already seen. Chapa noticed how one cop in particular, a skinny bit of nothing, was trying not to laugh. Nobody likes a comedian at a crime scene.

There was nothing missing in the house. No open drawers or empty file cabinets.

"So apparently someone broke in here, except they didn't have to break anything to get in," Sergeant Mark Slattery said and turned to his underling, the comedian, who responded with a smirk. "Then, once inside, they decided to get artistic."

Slattery was a heavyset man with multiple chins that he must've shaved on a rotating basis because no blade had touched two of them that day. He had thin red hair, narrow eyes, and more than a hint of B.O.

His fellow officer, the guy with the sense of humor whose nameplate read simply OFFICER BORIS, didn't seem too interested in being there anymore.

Chapa remembered these two slowly emerging from their vehicle. He remembered sensing right then that this wasn't going to go well.

Slattery spoke for both of them

"Look, Mr. Chapa, we found nothing unusual besides the graffiti."

"Graffiti?"

"What else you wanna call it?"

"How about a death threat?"

Another squad arrived, lights flashing, and Slattery told them to drive around the area.

"Look for someone really skinny who glows in the dark," he said with a thick laugh, then waved them off.

"This is funny to you, Sergeant? I have a ten-year-old daughter who is terrified right now. You think this is funny?"

Slattery waddled up to him until his belly pressed against Chapa's. Nikki had just wandered outside and was observing all of it. That was one reason, maybe the biggest reason, why Chapa refused to give ground.

"No, it ain't funny. Not at all. But what the hell you want from me?" Slattery said and took a step forward, adding pressure against Chapa's body. "Some homeboy of yours got pissed off and inked up your crib. You understand better now?"

"What the hell are you talking about? Homeboys? My house was broken into and you're trying to muscle me? Really, tough guy?"

Boris walked back from the cruiser and whispered something in Slattery's ear.

"A newspaper reporter, huh? Well heck, you could've ticked off all sorts of people."

"Could be. Sounds like a possible motive. Doesn't it?"

"Watch your step, Mr. Chapa. You don't impress me."

Chapa was ready to respond by telling him the feeling was mutual, but he was aware of how upset Nikki was after all that had happened. The last thing she needed to see was a shouting match between her father and a three-hundred-pound policeman.

Slattery turned to leave, taking a step forward as he did,

assuring that the full girth of his gut shoved up against Chapa and knocked him a little off balance. This seemed to pass for amusement with the sergeant.

"You come down to the station and fill out a report if you want," Slattery said on the way back to his car. Then he turned back toward Chapa and added, "Or not," before wedging himself into the passenger's side.

Chapter 64

Chapa watched Nikki walk up the stairs and into her room as though she'd never been there before. He understood how the child must have felt. The house seemed different now.

He'd turned on every light in the living room before bringing Nikki back over, which made the stickmen fade back into the paint. But he could still *feel* their presence, lurking just beyond reach and waiting to return with the darkness. Chapa sensed Nikki could feel them, too.

"Did the policemen wash the drawings away, Daddy?"

"No Nik, but I will do that before you come back here. Now you need to get set to go."

Nikki did as she was told and with her father's help packed a suitcase with three days' worth of clothes. Chapa planned to call a house painter in the morning, and wanted to make sure Nikki stayed away until all traces of this night were gone. The physical ones, anyway.

Chapa called Erin back to tell her they were on their way. He had gotten her out of bed with a call a half hour earlier. Though he'd done his best to sound calm, Erin had immediately volunteered to rush over. She sounded calmer now as Chapa assured her all was okay.

"I've got everything ready for Nikki, and I'll stay up with the two of you all night if you need me to," she said in a voice that was all crisis management.

Chapa thanked her and promised they would be there soon. But he didn't tell Erin he wasn't planning on staying.

Nikki was quiet for most of the drive over. Chapa's efforts at any sort of dialogue were met with "um hmm," and "I guess so." He refused to give up trying, feeling the need to get some sense of what his child was thinking, and he was still struggling to have a conversation as he turned into the driveway.

Erin met them at the door. She threw her arms around both Chapa and Nikki, and they returned the embrace.

"You okay?" she asked Chapa in a low voice.

He nodded, and she knelt down and gave Nikki another hug.

"I'm okay too," Nikki said, then looked up at her father. "Daddy, do we have to tell her now?"

Chapa had forgotten about Nikki's reading of Erin's emails and the argument it had caused. Maybe that was another reason why she'd been so quiet on the way over.

Erin looked up at Chapa. "Tell me what?"

He shook his head just a little, and mouthed, *Later.* That seemed to ease the tension in Nikki's shoulders, and she grinned at him as they walked inside.

Nikki was hungry, prompting Erin to heat up some oatmeal. Chapa sat next to his child as she lay on the couch, and by the time Erin walked in with a bowl, its steam trailing back toward the kitchen, Nikki had fallen asleep.

"She had a tough day," Erin said, gently placing the bowl on a side table by the couch.

Chapa nodded, then slipped his arms under Nikki and carried her to the bed in the guest room. Even under these strange and troubling circumstances, this made him feel like a father, and there was a fragment of comfort in that feeling.

After Nikki was tucked in and the night-light had been

switched on, Chapa walked out of the guest room, leaving the door open just a crack.

"Take off your coat and stay a while," Erin said as Chapa walked into the living room. "I know you won't sleep in my room because you're concerned about what the kids might think."

"I'm not staying, not just yet, anyway."

"What are you talking about, Alex?" Her voice was laced with confusion and frustration.

"I'm going to go to the station, give them a statement, and find out if they know anything more."

"How much more of a statement can you possibly give them?"

"I have to go down there, Erin. Someone invaded my home and threatened my daughter and me. I need to follow up on this."

Erin folded her arms and looked away, then turned and started back toward Chapa.

"Right now your daughter needs you to be here," Erin said, reaching out and putting her hand on his arm. "And I need you to be here."

Chapa closed the distance between them and put his arms around her. Erin was reluctant to give in to his embrace.

"I know Nikki needs me, and I'll be back before she wakes up. But I also know that whoever did this, and killed Clarkson, and who knows how many more, isn't going away."

Erin looked into his eyes, searching them, then seemed to give up as though she'd failed to find something that should have been there.

"In the time we've been together I have seen you hurt, injured, and been scared that I would never hear your voice again. And I've sensed that sometimes you hadn't told me just how much danger you'd been in. I've felt threatened myself, my son too, and I've stuck with you, Alex, because you're the best man I've ever known."

The raw honesty in her words made Chapa look away, though he did not want to. She gently placed a hand on his stubbled chin and pulled his face back to hers.

"Alex, you're a father, and a man I want to be with and who I want my son to grow up around, and yes, a reporter too. But you don't have to go into dangerous buildings, or track killers into the woods, or do the things that put you in harm's way. Do you?"

Chapa reached up and slowly ran two fingers across Erin's temple, brushing back a few strands of hair and continuing down the side of her face and across her cheek.

"Yes, Erin," he said in a voice that was just above a whisper. "Sometimes I do. But this has nothing to do with chasing a story."

She drew in a breath that was much deeper than normal, then turned away without letting it go.

Chapter 65

The scene at the Oakton City Police Headquarters reminded Chapa of a big city emergency room at one in the morning on a Saturday night. Except this wasn't a Saturday night, and Chapa had been here after hours before, and knew that it was always crazy time between midnight and morning.

He used his knowledge of the place to bypass the front desk and get right to someone who would find Slattery for him. The sergeant waddled through a doorway fifteen minutes later, his sidekick, Boris, in tow.

"Now what?"

"You need a statement from me."

"Got one already, goes like this—being an idiot, you left your door unlocked and some punk who's got it in for you walked in while you weren't home and drew on your walls."

On the drive over, Chapa had told himself that he wouldn't lose control, wouldn't get out of line by anyone's definition.

"It isn't that simple, Sergeant."

"Yeah, it is," Slattery said, cutting in. "You may not want it to be, but I do, so it is."

Chapa could feel his cool, limited as it was to begin with,

wandering off, down the hall, past the front door, and out into the night, never to be seen again.

"What's it take to get you to do your goddamned job?" Chapa heard the words come out of his mouth, knew they shouldn't have, but then a few more escaped. "No, it's not that simple, though you apparently are."

Slattery erased the gap between Chapa and himself, then started doing the bully bit with his gut again while Boris laughed to himself. It was all such a joke.

"Hey asshole," Slattery was in Chapa's face. His breath smelled of last night's fast food. "I'm sorry we don't have a better story for you to put in your paper tomorrow, which I could then use to wipe my ass."

"Tomorrow is Saturday, Sergeant."

"So it's Saturday, so what?"

"I'd think your ass would require the Sunday edition, including the comics, and all the sale fliers."

The veins in Slattery's fleshy neck began to bulge more than Chapa would've thought possible.

"Go home now," Slattery said in a no-nonsense voice that was thick and meaty.

Chapa got the message, got a grip, was ready to retreat. But Boris wasn't about to let that happen.

"You know what, Sergeant, I think this prick is disappointed that more didn't happen over at his house tonight." Boris produced a crooked grin, left it there on his face as he continued. "Maybe if someone had broken in while he was home and carved his kid up some, that would've made for a better story." Boris leaned his face toward Chapa's and smiled more broadly now. "Look Sergeant, he's thinking about it. That would've sold a lot more papers, huh?"

There was no thought directing Chapa's movements as he lunged for the smirking weasel hiding behind his superior. No concern over how this might turn out or how badly it could all go down.

As Chapa rushed Boris, fist cocked and set to punch his smile into the next county, Slattery shifted his weight with surprising agility and slammed his gut hard into Chapa's side, knocking him off balance and down to the floor.

Chapa started scrambling to get up, but that ended abruptly when Slattery dropped a knee onto his chest and pinned him to the filthy, cold floor.

"You fucking shithole, I could have your ass for assaulting an officer," Slattery said, then pivoted and brought even more pressure down on Chapa.

"Get the hell off me." Chapa's chest ached as he pushed out each word.

Slattery laughed and called over to a pair of cops who'd been watching from across the room.

"Lake, Preston, take this piece of shit out of here and toss him in a holding cell for an hour or a day or a week. However long it takes for him to learn what's what."

The two uniformed officers grabbed Chapa off the floor and threw him face first into a wall, then pressed hard against his shoulders and yanked his hands down behind his back. The cuffs went on an instant later without Chapa being aware that they were there. His mind was spinning like a roulette wheel that refused to stop.

A few heads turned in his direction, and some of those same broken people he'd noticed on the way in now looked at him with disgust.

Slattery yelled, "This is for your own good, asshole," as they led Chapa through a heavily secured door and down the hall toward the holding cells.

He managed to steal a look back before the heavy door closed and saw Boris staring at him, smiling like he'd just won some sort of prize.

Chapter 66

The other guy in the holding cell was sleeping on a thin cot, but that didn't make Chapa feel any more safe or comfortable. Just the opposite.

What sort of a person would feel so at home in this place that smelled of rot and human waste, that they could fall asleep here? One who bears watching, that's who.

The man's slender back was turned to Chapa, his long black hair draped over the side of the cot. He was tall and wore a black denim jacket, blue jeans, and a pair of brown leather boots that looked like they'd been around, and into and out of all kinds of situations.

Chapa sat on a bench that was tucked between a grime-encrusted sink and the cell bars. Once he was sure the cops who put him in there were gone, out of sight and beyond earshot, Chapa pulled out his cell phone and called Joseph Andrews at his personal number.

Hi, this is Joseph Andrews. I'm probably out flying right now . . .

"No, Joe, you're not flying, you're home sleeping," Chapa began after the beep. He left Andrews a message explaining what happened and asking for his help.

Then Chapa started to call Erin, but changed his mind.

The evening already had more than its share of tension, no need to add to it now. There would be a time for him to tell her all about his visit to prison, but this wasn't it.

Instead, Chapa put a call in to Tom Jackson, figuring that his best friend on the force might be his only hope of getting out of there anytime soon. Not that Tom would ever think of Chapa as a friend. Not that Chapa had given him much reason to lately.

He left messages on both Jackson's cell phone and his voice mail at the station. It seemed odd to be calling a cop from jail when his desk was just across the building, but it sure wasn't the strangest thing Chapa had done this week.

Chapa thought about calling an attorney, but decided he didn't want to go that route just yet. It was best to keep this on the down low as long as possible. He hadn't been booked or fingerprinted, so it was safe to assume that no official record existed of his arrest, not yet, anyway.

Getting thrown in jail can sometimes be a good career move for a journalist, but not under these circumstances. And never when your paper is already trying to figure out a way to get rid of you.

Two guys in a cell down the hall were speaking Spanish, comparing notes on the women they'd had. Another guy at the other end was talking to himself, engaging in a session of self-loathing and speculating on the stupid shit he'd done to get himself tossed in jail.

So what the hell am I doing in here? Chapa thought.

As he slipped the cell phone back in his pocket, Chapa noticed that the other guy wasn't asleep anymore. He was sitting up in his cot, staring at him.

"They let you keep your phone? Why?"

"Because they didn't exactly follow standard procedure when they put me in here."

The guy had strong features, rich tan skin, and Chapa guessed he was in his mid to late twenties, though his dark, heavy eyes belonged to someone older.

"Before they put me in here, those assholes took my belt, laces, and bandanna," Chapa's cellmate said with a lot of street in his voice.

"Did they believe you were suicidal?"

"No, just very good at what I do."

"And what would that be?"

He smiled at Chapa and ignored his question.

"But you. You've got technology on your side."

Chapa sensed that his phone could become a liability in this place. He decided that if it came down to some sort of a challenge, he wasn't going to die protecting it.

"I'm not exactly a typical prisoner," Chapa said, then realized he didn't like the way his words had come out. "I didn't mean to say that you were."

"Sure you did, Alex Chapa."

"How do you know me? What's your name?"

The guy leaned back against the cracked gray wall behind him as he pushed several long strands of hair away from his face.

"Everyone calls me Ladrón."

"Ladrón? *Thief?* You go by 'Thief' in Spanish? Why don't you just tape an *Arrest Me* sign to your back?"

Ladrón was laughing, and Chapa hoped this was a good thing.

"I got the nickname back when I was a teenager because I could steal anyone's girl away. Though I suppose I've earned it in other ways, too."

Chapa had no trouble believing both claims. Ladrón could've been a Hollywood heartthrob, but he also looked like the wrong guy to line up against.

"How do you know who I am?"

"I was a kid in seventh or eighth grade when you came to my school and talked about what it was like to be a journalist." Ladrón leaned forward on the edge of the cot. "It was inspiring and I went home that night and told my aunt, she's the one who raised me, that I wanted to be a newspaper man when I grew up." He looked toward the floor, his straight, shiny hair hanging down like a black curtain. "But things didn't work out that way."

"How did they work out?"

Ladrón offered Chapa a pained smile as he got up off the cot and walked over to the other side of the narrow cell. He was even taller than Chapa had thought.

"Is this off the record?" he asked, and sat down next to Chapa. "That's the term you guys use, right?"

"Yes, we're off the record, way off the record."

Ladrón searched Chapa's eyes for a moment, then having apparently seen what he was looking for, nodded. In a hushed voice he explained that he'd been a career thief, a damn good one. He hadn't done any real time since his days in juvie, and the only reason he was being held now was because there had been a series of robberies on Oakton's west side.

"I'm one of those special people the cops pick up any time they don't know who else to pick up. I'll be out of here later today. It's just the routine. I'm used to it. How 'bout you, why are you in here?"

"I was about to beat the shit out of a cop who suggested I'd be happier if my daughter had gotten hurt tonight."

Ladrón took a moment to process this, then nodded and said, "Works for me."

That admission seemed to buy Chapa some sort of street cred. He did not ask Ladrón if he'd been involved in those robberies on the west side, figuring that there might be a kind of jail cell etiquette involved.

Over the next several hours they shared stories about their lives as Chapa gradually realized he was talking to someone who was almost as good at getting information from a stranger as he was.

"You would have made a damn good reporter."

Ladrón looked off toward a blank wall.

"Maybe in another lifetime. I'd like to believe in that sort of thing."

The conversation kept winding back around to their two kids. Ladrón had a son he rarely saw, a choice he'd made in the hope that the boy would avoid repeating his father's mistakes.

"He's got a good mom, and she tells him I work for the government, so I'm away a lot. My real life is no place for a child."

"But you're not going to be able to keep that lie going forever."

"I can sure as hell try. No, look man, I know that someday my son will learn the truth about his old man, but maybe by then he will be on the way to a life that has nothing in common with mine."

It was just before noon when a guard who led with his aftershave and the sound of his heavy feet came by and told Ladrón he'd be getting out in a few minutes, then looked at Chapa like he'd just remembered something.

"You're that reporter guy Jackson told me about."

"That's me."

He had a gray buzz cut and a face that had been through more than one war.

"You were supposed to be out a couple hours ago."

"Yeah, well you know, I just couldn't tear myself away from this fine establishment."

The guard tilted his head to one side, his face now transformed by a scowl. It was a look Chapa knew well.

"I was hoping you'd invite me to stay for lunch. Are you here to take my order, officer?"

Over his shoulder, Chapa heard Ladrón laugh quietly.

"I'm gonna go double-check, but you'll be getting out too," the guard said as he turned and left.

"You wonder why I've told you all this?" For the first time there was some urgency in Ladrón's voice.

Chapa shook his head.

"Not really. People need to tell their stories. It's carved into our DNA. Some talk to a priest or a psychiatrist, others talk to me."

"I understand what you mean, but that's not my thing. I'm not exactly a candidate for that Dr. Phil's show, you know what I'm sayin'?"

Chapa did.

Ladrón reached over to a battered wall and tore off a two-inch-wide paint chip.

"I know you got a pen."

Chapa pulled out a Parker from his pocket and handed it to Ladrón, then watched as he wrote a number on the light gray chip.

"You call me if you ever need a favor," Ladrón said, handing the paint chip to Chapa. "I can be a good person to know sometimes."

That was not a difficult thing for Chapa to believe.

"And that's it? You've told me all this about yourself because you want to offer your services?"

"Not exactly. Maybe you'll do something for me, too." Once again Ladrón searched Chapa's eyes, this time apparently finding something that made him smile. "Don't worry, it wouldn't be anything too bad. Nothing illegal, you know, like beating the shit out of a cop."

Chapa slipped the paint chip inside his wallet, then asked for his pen which he'd seen Ladrón discreetly slip into a pants pocket.

After a moment's hesitation, which Chapa assumed was Ladrón trying to figure out a way to claim he did not have it, the pen appeared.

"You know, a pen can be a very useful thing, Alex."

"You're telling me," Chapa said as he took it back from him.

"A man can do a lot of things with a pen. It's very powerful."

Chapa caught a whiff of the guard as he approached their cell.

"All right, Chapa, you first."

He offered his hand to Ladrón, who at first seemed poised for a more complicated exchange, but settled for a traditional shake, then gave Chapa one of those single-shoulder hugs he'd seen athletes do on TV.

"Take care, bro."

Chapa nodded and walked out of the cell.

He was heading for the door of the station, anxious to get the hell out of there and uncertain whether he'd ever be able to come back, when Tom Jackson called to him.

"Slow down, Chapa. We need to talk."

Jackson was rushing in his direction.

"Don't scold me, Tom. I know I screwed up."

"You think?"

Chapa shook his head and made for the doors.

"C'mon, Alex, I'll walk you to your car."

A sharp pain stopped Chapa the instant he stepped outside as a shaft of cold air piped through his system. He pressed his hand to his side and imagined he could feel the imprint of Slattery's knee.

For a moment, Chapa lost his bearings and could not remember where he'd left his car. It seemed like days ago that he'd driven here in the dark, determined to get some answers. He had parked on the street, a logical choice late at night when the meters aren't running, not so good now.

"Can you take care of these for me?" Chapa asked, yanking two parking tickets from under his windshield wiper and offering them to Tom Jackson.

"No, I can't. I've done enough for you, Alex."

"None of this would've happened if those two cops had shown just a little interest in what went down at my house last night."

"That may be, but you also played a role in this. Anyway, I've sent officers out to canvas your neighborhood today."

Jackson waved off a meter reader who was closing in on Chapa's car. "Look, I know Slattery is an asshole. The saying around here is 'Slattery will get you nowhere.' "

"That's good, Tom. Can I quote you?"

"No. The only reason you didn't get booked last night is those two have had so many incidents like this one that they couldn't afford another."

"I was provoked."

"Of course you were, dumb ass. That's what they do. You gotta get a whole lot smarter, Alex."

"I'll get to work on that right away," Chapa said, then offered the tickets to Jackson a second time. "C'mon, Tom, you know I'm not going to pay them anyway."

Jackson grunted something under his breath, snatched the two long yellow slips of paper out of Chapa's hand, and started to walk away.

"See, I'm starting to feel smarter already. Lunch next week, Tom, my treat?"

"I'm free on Wednesday, call me," Jackson said without looking back.

Chapa saw Ladrón walking out of the station and heading the other way, past City Hall and into the shadows that led to the rest of the town. He thought about how comfortable the man had been in that cell, in this environment, and wondered what sort of person would find any of this, *routine*.

Chapter 67

Erin didn't seem especially happy to see him by the time Chapa got to her house just after three in the afternoon, still wearing the same clothes he'd left in more than twelve hours earlier.

"I didn't think you were going to make it," she said.

"Make what?"

Her face curled up and she was about to answer him when a princess and a pirate came running into the living room.

"Hey, I think it's Halloween," Chapa said, making a fast recovery.

"Can we go, right now? Can we go?" Mike was saying, more as a demand than a question.

"Official trick-or-treating time begins at four-thirty, and that's when we can start," Erin said, lifting the large, black felt hat off her son's head. "Now go play for a while."

Mike reluctantly did as told, but Nikki grabbed her father's hand and dragged him into another room.

"C'mon, I want you to see my homework," she said, pointing to a computer monitor.

Chapa spent the next forty minutes reviewing several days' worth of math problems and geography questions. There was something very rewarding about seeing Nikki's work, though he'd been hoping to get some alone time with Erin. Something was happening between them, or maybe it had already happened. Whatever it was, it wasn't good.

The sun was starting to sink when someone rang the doorbell at around four-twenty. Chapa and Nikki heard the trick-or-treaters at the door, prompting the young princess to leap out of her chair and run to the living room.

"Time to go!" Nikki said.

Chapa and Erin walked along the sidewalk as their children ran from door to door, cutting across front lawns and around the occasional scarecrow or plastic tombstone.

"I have a feeling we need to talk," Chapa said, half an hour and six blocks into their trek.

"Maybe we do. I'm not sure I want to know what happened to you last night."

"I'm not sure you do."

She looked him over, more like an acquaintance than a lover or even a friend.

"You didn't even change your clothes, Alex. You look haggard, like you got roughed up or something."

Chapa nodded. "Something like that."

They walked another half block in silence, trailing the children by a house or two.

"Yes, we do need to talk," Erin said, finally. "Maybe figure out where we go next with all of this. But not tonight, please."

Chapa understood. He wasn't one to put things off, but last night had been long and complicated and very unpleasant for all involved. Erin looked weary, something Chapa had only seen once or twice before. And he'd gone more hours without sleep than he cared to count.

Erin called it quits around six-thirty, and they returned to her house. Nikki had decided she wanted to sleep in her own bed that night. Chapa saw a look of resolve in his ten-year-old's eyes. She wasn't about to let some stranger drive them out of their house again.

Chapa hesitated at first, worried about the possible effect that taking her back there so soon might have on Nikki. But when he saw Erin nod to him in approval, he gathered his daughter's things and said goodnight.

"Did you have fun?" Chapa asked Nikki on their way to grab a burger before heading home.

"Yes, I guess so."

"Okay, so you didn't have that much fun."

Nikki hesitated, and Chapa watched in the rearview mirror as her expression shifted and changed.

"I was hoping to be out longer. And, I hope this doesn't come out wrong, but I wanted to be out trick-or-treating just with you."

Chapa had noticed that there were still dozens of kids out walking along every street they'd driven down.

"Then I guess we're not finished yet," he said, then drove an extra three miles past his street to the Ridgewood Heights neighborhood, one of Oakton's most exclusive areas. He parked his beat-up Corolla on a wide, well-lit boulevard, and got out.

"Let's go. Grab your pumpkin."

Each block had only five or six houses on either side of the street, and only a couple that were giving out candy, but Nikki's demeanor changed immediately.

"I got a full-sized chocolate bar," she squealed as they walked between the pillars of a two-story brick house that was at least three times bigger than Chapa's. "I didn't realize there were houses like these in Illinois. This reminds me of my neighborhood."

Chapa did his best to smile and make it appear genuine. Half an hour later they had exhausted the area, and filled Nikki's plastic pumpkin to the brim.

"Ready to call it a night?"

Nikki nodded, and didn't bother trying to speak through a mouth that was crammed to capacity with chocolate.

As he turned into his driveway, Chapa told Nikki to wait

in the car for a moment. He got out, locked her in, then walked to the front door and opened it. Without looking at the walls any more than he had to, Chapa quickly moved from room to room, turning on every light on the first floor. Then he went back to the car and got Nikki.

He wasn't sure what to expect, or how his daughter would react. But she seemed more curious than afraid—until it was time to go to sleep. That was when Nikki's resolve began to fade.

"Will you leave the lights on all night, Daddy? She asked, holding her hands together near a wall in a way that blocked out enough light to make one of the figures appear.

"Yes. I will. And I've already double and triple-checked that all of the doors are locked and bolted."

They went upstairs soon after, and Chapa tucked Nikki in bed, as he encouraged her to go to sleep. He was looking forward to taking a much needed shower before heading back downstairs to do some research online.

But he'd barely made it back to his room when Nikki called out to him.

"What's the matter, Nik?"

"It's those stars up there, glowing, can you make them go away?"

Chapa's heart sank. Something had been stolen from his daughter, though she was too young to fully understand just how much.

Half an hour later, Nikki crashed in her father's bed. As he was dozing off, half sitting, his back against the headboard, Chapa thought about turning off the lights in the bedroom. But he couldn't decide whether or not that was a good idea.

Chapter 68

The man did not sleep last night.

He sat in a chair in the middle of his otherwise empty living room. Lights turned off, curtains drawn, silent. He sat there from the late afternoon when the sun was dying its next death through its rebirth a dozen or more hours later.

A few of the neighborhood kids rang his doorbell last night. Trick-or-treaters scrounging for a piece of candy. Children who are still too young to know what horror truly is, out celebrating manufactured fear.

The man knows. He first met horror as a child, swallowed it whole, devoured it before it could devour him.

And then as yesterday slipped away and turned into last night, he became the darkness. Letting it move through him like a spirit until it washed away everything he did not need to perform his task. Until he wasn't anyone, anymore. None of the names he'd gone by suited him now. And once again, the darkness took shape within him, filling him up until he was sated.

His belongings have been reduced to a single suitcase, the clothes he is wearing, and his bag of *tools*. All else has been given away to charity, or disposed of entirely.

He will no longer exist in twenty-four hours, and in time

some will wonder whether he ever had. This is a day the man has been working toward his entire adult life, maybe longer. Yes, longer. Ever since that night he cradled his mother's lifeless body in his arms.

The man hears her voice sometimes, but never responds for fear that he might scare her off. But things will be different after today. After he's avenged her murder. Not squared it, no, that could never be possible. What the man who then called himself Gilley stole from him can never be equaled.

But he's going to make him pay in blood and pain, and then with his life. After that, the man will be finished with Oakton. There's more work to be done here, no doubt about it, but the walls have started to close in again, and a few loose ends have been threatening to unravel over the past week.

There's no fall guy or stand-in this time. No corpse to leave behind for misidentification. But that's okay. There's a finality to what he's planning to do here, and the man senses that peace is within his grasp for the first time in his life.

The cops in this town never got close, not really. For a time he actually considered staying here a lot longer, making a life for himself, just like other people do. But he understands now that after tonight that will not be possible.

He sits quiet and still until the sun rises up over the trees across the street, then muscles its way through the narrow slits in the curtains and into the man's empty house.

It's November 1st. All Saints Day to some, the Day of the Dead to others.

As far as the man is concerned, it's a little bit of both.

Chapter 69

Chapa's story ran in that day's *Chicago Record*, though not quite as written. A few of the more scandalous details, those that he'd put in to stir things up and maybe shake a killer loose from his safety zone, were gone.

No doubt Macklin would claim legal concerns, and that guy in his office, the one with a look of terminal constipation on his face, had signed off on those decisions. That's what he was paid to do.

Still, there was enough in there to rattle a cage or two. The discussion was now on the table, though Chapa was unsure where it would go next or whether he'd be with the *Record* long enough to follow it.

He dropped Nikki off at Erin's, planning to pick her up after lunch, once she'd finished her schoolwork. Chapa needed to clear his head for a few hours, so he put Tom Petty's *Highway Companion* in his car's CD player, and just let the road take him away for a while.

Around eleven, he decided to grab something to eat. He checked his cell phone messages, then called home to find out if there were any on his machine. Nothing from the paper, which in this case was probably good.

He thought about checking in with Erin, but decided that

could wait. She was angry with him, something that hadn't happened too often, and Chapa knew things were going to get edgier between them once he told her about his night in jail.

Jake's Bagels was starting to fill up as the lunchtime crowd wandered in. Office workers and guys who got paid to do the heavy lifting converging for thirty or forty minutes to eat and swap stories.

The deli was a local legend, home to Chapa's favorite sandwich, and one of the best places in the area to get an honest cup of coffee.

Millie behind the counter was already preparing his usual—ham and provolone on a garlic bagel, warmed not toasted, with onions and lettuce—when Chapa stepped through the door.

"What would you have done if I wanted something different today?"

"Probably dropped dead from shock, Chapa," she said without looking up at him.

Millie had been at Jake's longer than the many years Chapa had been stopping in for breakfast, lunch, and the occasional bagel fix. In that time Chapa had come to believe she existed only within the confines of this building in Aurora, along the river. That she probably vanished as soon as the lights went out, only to return the next morning in time to start baking that day's batch.

Chapa had once asked her why they had not yet named the sandwich after him, considering that he'd ordered it dozens, maybe hundreds of times.

"You could put it right up there on the menu," he said, pointing to the large sign that hung behind the counter. "Call it, 'The Alex Chapa.'"

Millie had responded with a smirk, and said, "Because, Chapa, the idea is to bring customers in, not to scare them away."

Chapa paid for his sandwich and coffee, confirmed that the fireside seating was already taken—it usually was—and sat at one of the tables along the front windows. He studied the paintings by local artists that decorated the walls of the restaurant, tranquil scenes of the Fox Valley area.

He had just finished half of his sandwich when a man he'd never seen before pulled up a stool, sat down across the table, and introduced himself as Merv Olsen.

"I'm an assistant medical examiner, Mr. Chapa."

"Here in Aurora?"

"No, over in Oakton."

"That's nice. Good job?"

"Not bad, decent benefits and all. Can't complain, especially during these times."

Chapa nodded, punched back the last of his second cup of coffee, then signaled to Millie that he needed more. She responded by pointing to the self-serve coffee counter.

"I wanted to tell you something about that story you wrote in today's paper," Merv said and leaned in closer as Chapa braced for a round of criticism. "You're spot-on about something being strange with those murders. You know, the college kid, the former cop in the windmill, and the guy in the alley."

"Why do you say that? Was there something in my story that tipped you?"

"No, not what was in your story. It's what wasn't in there."

Chapa quickly thought through some of the material that had been edited out hoping to anticipate what this guy was going to say next.

"It was the wounds themselves," Merv said, his voice even quieter than before. "I've looked at my share of neck wounds, you know, cuts." He ran a long, thin index finger across his neck for emphasis. "They're always a quick slash, uneven, you know, and they usually start near the middle of the victim's neck."

This wasn't anything Chapa had considered.

"You see, Mr. Chapa, one of the reasons they go for the

neck—assailants, I mean—is because it's not too difficult to kill someone by cutting them there. It doesn't take a lot of strength or effort to inflict a fatal cut to someone's throat."

"And these wounds?"

"From jawbone to jawbone," he said, pressing against either side of his face, just beneath his ears. "And deep, too. Like they used a sawing motion."

A pair of cops walked in. Chapa instinctively paused and checked to see if he knew them. He didn't, but lowered his voice anyhow.

"You said you're an assistant medical examiner, have you shared your thoughts about these wounds with your superiors?"

Merv checked his watch, then gave the place a quick scan, as the expression on his face became more solemn.

"I've told a few people, yes," he said, lowering his voice just as Chapa had. "But there seems to be some heavy pressure coming down. A lot of folks don't want any of this to be true."

"What kind of folks?"

"The kind who can reshape reality," Merv said and gave Chapa a simpatico look as if to say, *I know you get me.* He reached across and smacked Chapa on the arm, then left the table and pulled up a stool at the far end of the room.

Chapa was thinking about asking Merv Olsen to meet him for dinner later in the week, or maybe coffee someplace where they could talk, when "Daydream Believer" started playing in his pocket.

I have to do something about my ringtone, he thought as several heads turned his way. He checked the caller ID, expecting to see Erin's name, or the paper's, but it read simply CELLULAR CALL.

"This is Chapa," he whispered as he waved to Millie and made for the door.

"Alex Chapa?"

"That's right." He was outside now, with a finger in his right ear, blocking out the traffic noise.

"This is Walter Bendix, Dr. Bendix. We need to talk."

Chapter 70

The doctor's directions were too good to be spontaneous. The more Chapa followed each prescribed turn and noted every landmark, the more he sensed that Bendix had known exactly where he'd be coming from.

The only time most people in the Chicago area ever thought about Kendall County was when it flashed across the bottom of their TV screens during a tornado warning, which happened about once a week during the spring and summer. Now Chapa was racing past vast farmland, and ready-made subdivisions where barns and silos stood not too long ago, on his way to a large parcel that Bendix owned on the county's western end.

Chapa turned left off the main highway and onto a narrow two-lane just past a place called The Chicken Bin that had been boarded up and abandoned years ago despite a sign promising, OUR GRILLED BREASTS WON'T GO TO YOUR THIGHS. Two miles later he passed through a tall wooden gate that read, BENDIX, in large, no-nonsense letters.

He followed the rest of the directions past a stretch of cornfields to an enormous storage shed. As he drove up, Chapa saw Dr. Bendix standing by a small white plane along the backside of the aluminum building.

Bendix was walking toward him as Chapa stepped out of his car.

"I'm Walter Bendix," he said, extending his hand.

"You wanted to talk about something," Chapa said, accepting the offer.

"That's right. I read your story in today's *Record*. I think there are some things you need to know."

Chapa nodded, and waited to be asked into an office inside what he now realized was a hangar.

"C'mon, let's go up."

Chapa stopped walking and stared at the small plane. He wondered where the rubber band that made it go was.

"I know you probably didn't plan on flying in a private plane today, Mr. Chapa."

"Or yesterday and probably not tomorrow, either."

Bendix smiled.

"With the weather being what it is, today's a good day to survey my properties, and it's a lot easier and faster to do that from the air. Don't worry, you won't be up too long."

He was trying to remember whether Bendix was someone he could trust. There was nothing about the guy in any of Chakowski's files, only stories detailing his entrepreneurial achievements and dedication to various charities. Walter Bendix seemed to have a hand in just about everything that went on in the area.

Chapa now understood that could be good, or bad, but this guy seemed to be as clean as they came.

"The sky is a great place to talk, Alex. You don't have a fear of heights, do you?"

"None that I know of."

For an instant, he thought about calling Erin and telling her where he was and what he was about to do. Then realized doing that would probably lead to another conflict, and though the sky was clear and the temperature was in the low sixties, he could still feel the chill that had recently permeated his relationship with her.

Bendix was walking around the plane, performing what Chapa assumed were routine preflight preparations. After another moment's hesitation, he pulled out his tape recorder, checked to make sure he had enough battery power left, then walked over to the plane, climbed in, and buckled himself into the copilot's seat.

Chapter 71

Walter Bendix had become a surgeon for only one reason—to make money. Sure, it felt good to save lives and
help people, that's why he'd always wanted to become a doctor. But the decision to go into surgery was strictly driven by
money.

"The difference can be significant, especially if you're
good, and I was good," he explained as they flew over Route
30. "Don't get me wrong, it gives one a sense of personal
contribution. That's a part of it, too."

The doctor's big financial break came twenty years earlier
when he removed a badly ailing appendix belonging to the
son of a savvy land developer named Paul Montgomery.

"He's the one who got me started in all this. Changed my
life in a way."

Bendix had spent the next decade securing chunks of
land in six counties throughout northern and central Illinois,
and a couple more in Indiana.

"You own any land, Alex?"

"Not really. The bank still owns my house."

"A man should own land if he is to truly be a man."

Chapa resisted the urge to start listing all of the great men
who've never called an undeveloped plot in LaSalle County

their personal source of pride. He was focused on the controls, and the ease with which Bendix was manipulating them.

The plane felt a bit more secure than he'd expected. But any sense of safety vanished whenever Chapa thought about the drop that could await them if this fragile piece of human ingenuity suddenly gave out.

"I've worked very hard for everything that I have, and all that I've been able to provide for my family."

"I don't doubt that, Walter."

"I prefer that you call me Doctor."

"Will do, Doctor."

They were starting to climb. Chapa felt the surge through his body as he watched rectangular patches of farmland below shrink to the size of postage stamps.

"I've done a lot of good in my life. I've saved others, given my time and money to a variety of charities and good causes."

Chapa now couldn't stop wondering why the hell he was up here in a plane with a guy who apparently thought of himself as a combination of Ward Cleaver and Superman.

They had been silently cruising above Route 47—at least that's what Chapa assumed the thin gray thread below was—for nearly five minutes. Finally, tired of drifting along at a high altitude with no clear plan, Chapa asked him where they were going and why.

"And I'm not sensing that you're surveying any parcels of land, Doctor."

Bendix stared straight ahead into the horizon, motionless. If it hadn't been for the single drop of sweat cruising down the side of his face, he could have passed for a wax figure.

"But I've made some mistakes, too." His voice was different now, deeper, older, tired. "Most of my mistakes weren't too bad. But then one day you cross a line, and—"

The plane took a sharp dip, and in that instant Chapa felt himself lunging forward, his hands clutching at nothing, as though they were trying to hang on to the sky. But as quickly as he'd lost himself and damn near lost control of the plane, Bendix seemed to get a grip, and managed to steady the aircraft.

As Chapa did his best to coax at least two, maybe more of his vital organs back to where they belonged, Bendix reached over, and pressed a button on the control panel. The plane immediately leveled out, and Chapa assumed he'd switched on the autopilot.

Chapa watched in silence as Bendix struggled to gather himself. Not exactly the sort of behavior he wanted see from the man who was piloting a plane, three thousand feet above the hard Midwestern soil.

Then Bendix unbuckled his seat belt and turned to face Chapa.

"Most of what I've done wrong has been victimless."

Chapa had no clue where this was heading, but just to be sure he reached inside his jacket pocket, clutched his tape recorder, and pushed RECORD.

"It's funny how one thing leads to another."

"What led to what, Doctor?" Chapa asked trying to get some control over the situation, though it was clear he had none.

"It started about three years into my working as a volunteer at the prison hospital over at Pennington Correctional. The system didn't have a lot of money to pay big shot doctors, so I volunteered to stop by once or twice a month and help patch up guys who'd been cut up or had their bones broken because they looked at the wrong guy the wrong way. I've done some good work there."

Bendix pressed a series of buttons, steered the plane west, leveled it out, and switched on the auto again.

"Then I met a guy there, a prisoner who was back in. I knew him from his first stint, and he wasn't a bad guy, not really. He just needed a chance, a new start. He'd tried to make it on the outside, but his record followed him around.

He wished he could just have a different name, a new identity."

As the plane continued to split the sky on its way to nowhere in particular, Chapa started searching for the reason this conversation was taking place up here, instead of in a warm, well-grounded office, or the middle of an open field—there were certainly enough of those to choose from down below.

"As soon as his parole time was up I helped him change his name and history. Made him promise to leave the state and never come back. Which he did."

But the bigger question remained—Why was this conversation happening at all?

"You might be surprised how easy it is to create a new identity for someone when you're a respected person in an important profession with access to personal records. So easy to change a detail or two, if you know which ones are the most vital to an individual's identity."

Then Chapa figured it out—maybe. Could Bendix be concerned that Chapa was wearing a wire? That could explain the meeting in a lonely hangar in Kendall County, as well as their present altitude.

"You did this for free?"

"No. You do something for a person and don't charge them, it has less value. That's why handouts to the poor or minorities are a bad idea. I charged him, told him he could mail me the money in cash when he had it."

What the hell? Was one of Oakton's leading citizens, a man with several lifetimes' worth of civic awards, confessing to a major crime? Chapa was accustomed to working hard for his scoops. This was way too easy.

"A few months later, I did it for someone else, then someone else the year after that. And you know, except for two of them, they all paid me eventually. They all did exactly what I told them to do. The payments would come from California or Texas or Alaska, or wherever."

Chapa shifted in his seat. The ride was becoming more uncomfortable by the minute.

"It felt good, what I was doing. I told myself I was helping guys get their lives straightened out."

"You were making some bucks on the side, Doc, helping convicts elude the authorities."

"They weren't convicts anymore, and they were all off parole." Bendix said, raising his voice for the first time, and Chapa was surprised by how much hostility had been hiding behind that measured tone he'd been using up until now.

"Do you really think I needed the money? I own this plane that you're sitting in, which is more than you can say for your house."

Chapa watched as Bendix took a deep breath and struggled to regain his composure.

"Please don't rile me like that again. I don't like it."

Okay Doc, I won't, Chapa thought. *Not right now, anyway.*

"In time word got around a little bit, and eventually made it to the wrong person. And I helped a guy change his identity, start over, and he showed up at my door a few years later and threatened me, threatened my family, and he forced me to help him change it again. But he didn't leave after that."

Wait, this was much more than an admission of guilt. Chapa remembered what Clarkson had told him about the stickman killer changing his appearance and his name. Was that where this was headed?

"This guy wasn't your standard simple criminal. In fact, as far as I could tell, he didn't even have a record. At first I told myself it would be okay, that he'd disappear like the others. But then he started joining civic groups and getting invited to all sorts of things. He wasn't going away—he was putting down roots."

Up until now Chapa had resisted his reporter's urge to interrupt with questions, but that restraint wouldn't hold much longer.

"I still thought it was going to be okay, until the day he told me I needed to do him a favor. I looked into his eyes and knew he wasn't asking, he was telling me. I thought he was going to tell me to change someone else's future, but it had nothing to do with an identity."

Chapa was sorting through the recent murders. The guy in the alley? Wade Marshall, the college student? Clarkson? He remembered what Merv Olsen had told him about the fatal cuts, hardly the work of a surgeon.

"I refused to cross that line, but he threatened to destroy me, and all that I've built for my family. He forced me to accept just how deep I'd be willing to go to protect everything I care about."

Bendix was waiting for something from Chapa, but it was not clear what that was.

"You understand, Alex, he knew everything, all of it. And he made it very clear that he'd make it all public before vanishing again."

"I'm not the guy to ask for absolution, Doc."

"That's how he got me to do it, understand?

"Who got you to do what?"

Bendix's face underwent some sort of transformation, like he was seeing Chapa for the first time.

"Good Lord, you don't know." He looked into Chapa's eyes as though they held the answer to a puzzle he was desperate to solve. "Here I thought you were ahead of it all, like Chakowski was, but you're not."

"What did Chakowski know?"

"I thought you were the cat in all this, but you're not. You're just another mouse."

What was Chapa supposed to know? What didn't he understand? Had Bendix killed all of them? He couldn't have. Maybe there was some other crime. Then Chapa remembered there had been one other recent death. He had alluded to it in his story, but only in passing.

> *The situation has become so grave that for those of us who have been paying attention even the heart-related death of an old woman can merit a closer look.*

"Gladys Washer."

"You're guessing."

"Why do you say that?"

"Because you seem to know so little about so much. I thought you were toying with me when you mentioned her in your story. Now I realize that wasn't the case."

Bendix rubbed the side of his face, then turned and looked out toward the horizon.

"I thought you had something, Chapa. Maybe even enough to stop him before he does whatever he's been working toward."

"Who? Who am I going to stop?"

"I thought we would negotiate, work something out, an agreement that would have benefited both of us."

Chapa was about to ask him again, but then he realized Bendix wasn't listening anymore.

"But it's over anyhow, Chapa."

Bendix reached under his seat and produced a handgun. It was big enough to do a great deal of damage, especially at close range. Chapa wasn't sure about its make or caliber, but it was just the sort of weapon a lot of regular people own, believing it will protect them. He was pointing it at Chapa.

"I've run through a number of scenarios. Most of them end with one or both of us dead."

"I'm a writer, I can probably help you come up with a bunch of better scenarios."

Bendix almost smiled, but the change in his expression seemed driven by pain, not humor.

"I brought you up here because I thought you might be wearing a wire, working with the feds like that Clarkson guy."

"I figured that was it."

"But now I know you're not. And that's too bad in a way. Because he's been building up to something, and it's going to happen soon."

Chapa thought about the recorder in his jacket pocket, hoped it was still running and picking up most of this conversation.

"Look, Dr. Bendix, I *can* help. I'll expose what's been happening in Oakton. We can work on this together, you and I."

Bendix nodded in a way that seemed neutral, almost involuntary, and Chapa read it more as a gesture of resignation than agreement.

"You're an important person in your own way, I guess, and killing you would ultimately just make the situation worse for my family," Bendix said as he looked out toward the horizon. "He'd make sure of that."

"*Who* would make sure of that?"

Bendix responded with another pained smile.

"As long as I'm alive he's got something to hold over them. He will hurt them to get to me."

Uncertain of what was happening to Bendix, and having no idea what would happen next, Chapa slipped his hand across the seat belt buckle.

"Do you believe in God, Alex?"

The gun was pointed at Chapa's chest, again.

"I've never thought about it much, maybe I should have," Chapa responded. "But you won't find too many committed atheists among two men squeezed into a small plane when one of them is holding a gun."

"I've done a lot of good, saved lives." Tears were starting to fill Bendix's eyes. "But none of that matters once you've taken a single life."

"All of this has been off the record, Doc, so there is another option. Let's land the plane, and walk away like we never met."

Bendix seemed to be considering Chapa's offer. It wasn't genuine. Chapa's first stop would be the Oakton police station. Or, considering how his last appearance there was received, he'd call first.

"We've never met, not formally," Bendix said, still processing.

"That's right."

"We've only seen each other in passing, and just once or twice at that."

"Exactly."

"And I never noticed you before, had no idea who you were."

"Okay."

"So when I saw you sneaking around my plane, I naturally rushed back to my office in the hangar and got my gun."

"Wait, what?"

"I called out to you, but you seemed to have a weapon of some sort, and I pulled the trigger, meaning to fire off a warning shot, but it struck you in the chest."

Chapa was certain now that Bendix had snapped, gone completely over. Not a bad man, necessarily, not too bad, anyway. But he'd killed once already, and no matter how much remorse he may have felt, the second kill would be much easier than the first.

"Are you forgetting we're at close range? They won't buy that story."

Bendix withdrew a little, and Chapa quietly started unbuckling his belt.

"You're right. No, it wasn't a warning shot. I saw you by the plane, didn't know who you were, got my weapon, called to you, and you came after me, hostile, yelling something about that reporter who got killed a few days ago. You lunged for the gun, and it went off."

Chapa was looking for an in, any twitch or other movement that would give him the chance to make a grab for the gun. The plane was buzzing over a long stretch of trees. Route 47 and all that Chapa knew was a distant memory now.

"A few of the other leaders around the area will tell police that you threatened them too. We watch each other's backs, you know."

"I've heard that, but this is a pretty big favor you'd be asking of them."

"There have been bigger, believe me."

Bendix leaned back against the door and raised the gun so that it was pointed at Chapa's face. His finger coiled tight against the trigger.

If Chapa dove at him, low, a shot might ride high and miss. But that would make it difficult to go for the gun. And the cockpit was much too snug to allow for a horizontal dodge.

No, getting out of the way of a bullet wasn't a good option at the moment. Chapa needed to create an opening.

"Think for a moment, Doctor, this isn't who you are."

"Maybe it's who I've become," Bendix said, then straightened his arm and prepared to fire.

Chapter 72

Chapa thought about Nikki and Erin and all the things they could be doing right now.

What had he been doing the moment his father was murdered? Probably playing with his toys or being read a story, or asleep in his room. Maybe he was outside enjoying a clear blue sky and the dying sun's warmth, unaware that someplace else, someone who was a stranger to him was about to squeeze a trigger and change his life, a vital part of it ripped away while he was off doing something ordinary.

Still no flinch from Bendix. The end of the gun was no more than three or four feet from Chapa's face.

Any in, any at all, Chapa thought, his eyes fixed on the doctor's trigger finger.

He saw the muscles in Bendix's neck tighten, pushing against the man's sagging flesh. Chapa was readying himself to make a move, probably the only chance he'd have. He locked eyes with Bendix, trying to get a read, but came up empty.

But something else was happening. The doctor's arm was trembling just a little now, barely noticeable, but it had not been a moment ago. Was this good or bad?

Chapa kept his eyes fixed on Bendix, trying to give him a

hard look, worried all the while that his fear might show through. Would that be good or bad?

The shaking was becoming more obvious now. So much that Bendix himself must have been aware of it, and known that Chapa was seeing it, too.

There was a struggle going on inside the man. But there was one raging in Chapa as well. Part of him wanted to keep watch on the trigger finger, but looking into Bendix's eyes, so deep that Chapa felt like he might see all the way through him to the door beyond, was having some sort of effect.

The plane hummed across the empty Midwestern landscape as Chapa struggled to find the right words to say, uncertain whether he should say anything. But before Chapa could think of something, Bendix withdrew the gun, pulling the weapon back until he was holding it sideways against his chest.

Chapa had flinched at the first hint of movement, but now he thought he saw a chance. He slowly began to slip his fingers under the seat belt release.

"She had that look in her eyes, just like you did a moment ago." Bendix was still trembling.

"Gladys Washer?"

"You tell yourself she's just an old woman who doesn't have much time anyhow. That she has a heart problem and could go any day, anyhow. That she's a widow who won't be missed much."

Chapa was pulling back on the buckle, almost loose now.

"I've crossed a line, and there's no going back anymore. And you, you know enough to hurt my family. He won't care once I'm not around. He'll forget me like I never existed. But you can still hurt the people I love."

"Like I already explained, this conversation never—"

"Save it," Bendix interrupted, then reached back with his free hand, slipped his fingers inside the armrest, and pulled up on a silver handle.

Chapa heard the pilot's side door open slightly, and felt

the change in cabin pressure. A swirl of wind rushed through the plane, shuffling papers around in the tight cabin.

"What the hell are you thinking of doing?"

"Something for my family," Bendix said, then forced the door open a foot or so.

"No!"

Chapa wasn't being coy anymore. He fumbled with the buckle until it popped open, then threw the belt to the side.

But as he looked back toward Bendix and started make his move, Chapa saw the gun pointing in his direction again. Not much conviction in the doctor's face anymore, but still enough to push Chapa back into his seat.

"Easy to think about jumping, harder to do it," Chapa said, looking straight into the doctor's eyes.

Bendix nodded. "I've never been a coward, and this is the only way out for my family."

"No, no it's not. Your family needs you."

Bendix let out a shallow laugh.

"The hell they do."

"They do."

"No. My son and I are barely on speaking terms, and my daughters have each found better men to look up to. My wife and I have been little more than acquaintances the past ten years. And now I've hurt all of them."

"But you don't know what the loss of a father and husband will do to them."

Chapa could see that the man's mind was drifting off to a dark place that few ever visit and from which even fewer manage to return.

"Your wife will blame herself. Your son, your daughters, they will mourn you every day for the rest of their lives. They'll struggle to remind your grandchildren of who you were. And if they succeed, then your grandchildren will mourn your loss as well."

"There's no need for them to do that."

"No, there isn't. You can just land this plane, and we'll figure out—"

"No, I meant there's no need to mourn the dead. They have no worries. They can't hurt anyone. They have no deadlines or commitments weighing them down. Don't mourn the dead. Mourn the living."

Bendix slipped the end of the gun inside his mouth. His eyes grew wide as he bit down on the shaft, until he slowly eased them shut.

And pulled the trigger.

Chapter 73

The back of Walter Bendix's head splattered against the window an instant before the force of the blast slammed his corpse into the door, forcing it open. The dead man's face was unusually flush, though his eyes had nothing more to reveal.

Chapa could only watch as the doctor's legs flipped up, the left one just missing Chapa's chin before slamming into the plane's T-shaped steering column. Then the body took a pratfall, backwards through the opening and out into nothing.

The outside air raced into the cabin, creating a whirlwind, but the plane seemed to be holding steady—at least for the moment.

Chapa jumped from his seat and rushed over to the pilot's chair as the door swung shut, without closing all the way. Specks of blood and brain matter from the small window flicked against the side of Chapa's face.

He looked out through a window toward the rear as the aircraft turned just enough for him to get a glimpse of the doctor's body tumbling to the cornfield below.

He'd seen Bendix switch on the autopilot. That meant he was okay for the moment. Right? Chapa had never set his hands on the controls of an airplane, not even a simulator. He had no idea what to do, but knew he had to keep his cool, or at least try his level best to not let panic take hold.

Hoping that he could get a signal out here, fifteen miles west of the middle of nowhere, and a few thousand feet in the air, Chapa punched in Joseph Andrews' cell number.

Hi, this is Joseph Andrews. I'm probably out flying right now . . .

No, Joe. I'm the one who's out flying, Chapa thought as he abruptly ended that call and made one to the FBI offices in Chicago. The nice operator who took his call refused to transfer him directly, but was kind enough to forward it to the general office.

"Agent Eisenhuth."

"Eisenhuth, this is Alex Chapa. I need to talk to Special Agent Andrews right now."

"Ooh, that's gonna be tough, Alex. You see he's in a meeting, and—"

"No, it's not tough—it's necessary, urgent, vital. Get him on the phone. Now."

There must've been something in Chapa's voice—maybe a large dose of fear—because Eisenhuth said, "Hold on, I'll transfer you to his phone," and nothing more.

Less than a minute later, Andrews was on the line.

"This better be good, Al. I got pulled out of an important meeting and into my office."

"I'm in an airplane, a small private one, probably two or three thousand feet above Illinois farmland. I'm alone, no pilot. Help me, Joe."

"This is some sort of scenario you're working out for a story?"

"No, this is real. I *am* up in a plane, alone. The pilot is dead, somewhere below. I'm in trouble."

For a moment, all Chapa heard was the sound of the airplane's engine buzzing, and a high-pitched hiss coming from the tiny gap where the door had not closed tightly.

"How the hell did you—" Andrews started, then caught himself. "You need to call Air Traffic Control. They will talk you down. I don't have the experience to do it."

"How do I do that? And what are they going to need to know?"

"Um, shit, please tell me the autopilot is on."

"Yes, I saw him turn it on."

"Good. That's very good. That will make it easier for Air Traffic Control. I'm finding their number for you now. What's your altimeter reading?"

"My what?"

"Altimeter, your altitude? It's a big black dial with numbers on it, looks like a clock."

Chapa found it.

"Okay, the big hand is on the three and the little hand is on the six."

"That's thirty-six-hundred feet. That's good. How about fuel?"

"Nearly full."

"That's good too."

"Glad to hear it."

"But it could also turn into a problem on impact."

Chapa understood—the more fuel, the greater the possibility of an explosion. He took a deep breath, maybe the first since Bendix had pulled a weapon, located both ends of the seat belt, and strapped himself in. He then pulled the blood-stained door shut and pushed down on the handle, locking it in place.

"Okay, you ready for the phone number?"

"Sure."

Andrews rattled off the number for Air Traffic Control in Aurora, but Chapa was only half listening. His attention was on something else altogether.

"Hey, Joe?"

"What, Al, were you listening? Did you get that number?

You need to talk to them right now. I will call them and confirm that you—"

"The altimeter is moving."

"What do you mean?"

"The little hand isn't at six anymore. It's now closer to four. Now it's right at four."

"I thought you said—"

"Now it's just below four. Is this a bad thing?"

"Did you turn off the autopilot?"

"No," Chapa looked over to where he'd seen Bendix switch it on. "The orange light isn't on now. It was before, but I haven't touched it."

"Did you bump the yoke?"

"The what?"

"The yoke, the steering mechanism, sometimes that can switch off the autopilot."

Chapa remembered seeing Bendix's foot clip it on the way out. He also remembered feeling the plane turn slightly to the left.

"Yes, I think that's what happened, Joe. But I'll just flip it back on."

"No! Don't do that. You may have changed the plane's trajectory. If you turn it on now the plane will maintain whatever course you're on now, even if it's one that's headed straight into the ground."

Whatever small and fragile fragment of confidence Chapa had felt a moment ago was now in tatters.

"Can you get me out of this, Joe?"

"I don't know. We don't have a lot of time."

Chapa allowed himself a glance at the altimeter—twenty-nine-hundred feet.

"Al, you need to do exactly as I tell you."

"You need to get me out of this, Joe."

"I don't know how—I've had my license for just over a week."

"Right now, that makes you an expert."

Silence.

"C'mon, Joe."

"Okay. Are you buckled in?"

"Yes."

"The shoulder harness, too?"

"No, wait, hold on." Chapa looked up over his left shoulder and found the strap, yanked it down, locked it in place. "Got it."

"Do you know if you're near an airport?"

"No idea. But I might be able to find a paved highway, land it there."

"Bad idea. I know there are stories about planes landing on highways, but that's a tough go. You've got power lines on both sides, road signs, and of course cars to worry about."

Chapa had imagined that would be his best option. Now his heart sank a little more.

"Let's start by trimming for level flight. I want you to grip the yoke and gently raise or lower the nose until the horizon is about two inches above the bottom of your windshield."

"It's about six inches above it now."

"You need to pull back on it, then. Remember, pull back on the stick and the trees get smaller."

Chapa switched on his cell phone's speaker, turned up the volume as loud as it would go, and set it down on a narrow ledge above the control panel. Then he gripped the two upright sticks so tight his hands felt like they were one with the mechanism. He pulled it back and watched the horizon shrink in front of him.

"I think I got it, Joe."

"Now find the throttle. It's a black handle with a round knob at the end."

"I see it."

"Locate the tachometer. It will be labeled among a series of gauges on the control panel."

Chapa had been studying the controls since boarding the plane, so it took him only a quick scan of the panel to find it.

"Yep."

"Pull back on the throttle until the tachometer reads fifteen hundred RPMs."

Chapa did as instructed and watched the reading drop as he felt the plane slowing.

"I think it's slowing down, Joe."

"It should be, but we're not going to let it get too slow, or . . . remember, air speed is life right now."

"Sure, okay, sounds good."

He was amazed by how steady Andrews' voice was now. Chapa knew that came with years of training and field work, but still. He was damn good.

"As long as your wings are level you should be descending at about eight hundred feet per minute."

Chapa did the math—that left him just over three minutes.

"Do you know if this plane has fixed landing gear, or retractable?"

"I have no clue."

"Let's hope the wheels are tucked under."

"And if they're not?"

"Then you might cartwheel. Look, Al, our best chance is a controlled crash landing."

That sounded like a contradiction in terms. Everything ahead of him was getting bigger, and Chapa knew it wouldn't be long now.

Eleven hundred feet, now one thousand.

"Do you see an open field somewhere? A cornfield is good—it will slow you down once you're on the ground and maybe keep you from rolling over."

The cornfields below were pale yellow, the change in seasons having come and gone, bleaching the stalks of their summer colors.

Eight hundred feet, now seven.

The plane began to rock a little, and Chapa told Andrews it felt like he was sitting in the middle of a teeter-totter.

"Don't let that happen, Al. Keep the wings level."

Chapa struggled to do that. Then everything got quiet.

Five hundred feet, now four.

"Um, Joe, I think the engine shut off. I don't hear it anymore."

"Did you stall out?"

"You're asking me? I'm drifting down and the ground seems to be coming at me faster now."

"Oh shit. The carburetor heat. I didn't tell you turn on the carburetor heat."

"No, you didn't. How bad is this?"

"I've never done this before, Al, I studied and read a lot, but I just forgot about—"

Andrews' voice wasn't as steady now.

"Shut up and get me down in one piece, Joe."

Three hundred feet.

"Right. Sorry. Push the nose down."

"How much?"

"So that it's about a foot below the horizon."

Chapa dropped the nose as the plane dipped to one hundred and fifty feet.

"Al. You still there?"

"Yes."

"You're gonna have to pull back when you think the plane is about to hit."

"I'm less than one hundred feet off the ground, heading for a wide field."

Individual stalks of corn flashed by.

"Pull back when you're about thirty feet from impact, and level the wings out."

Chapa saw the tops of a row of trees in the distance, saw that he was now closer to the ground than they were.

"And then what, Joe?"

Silence. Then in a voice that was just above a whisper, Andrews said, "Hang on."

As the first of the stalks swiped the bottom of the plane Chapa whispered, "I love you Nikki, I love you Mom, I love you Erin, I love you Mike."

It was the closest he'd ever come to saying a prayer in his entire adult life.

He was dropping toward the middle of the field now as cornstalks battered the plane on all sides.

Then he felt the impact an instant before it threw him forward.

The seat belt held him in place, but he felt it knot against his lower abdomen, knocking the air out of him.

The small plane rocked from side to side as it skidded through the field. Tossed in one direction, then the other, like a runaway thrill ride.

Then the fuselage slid sideways, and Chapa heard a loud crash as he saw the right wing being sheared off.

The plane was slowing, it had to be, but not quickly enough.

Chapa still had a grip on the yoke when he caught a glimpse of something coming at him through the air, an instant before it slammed into the right side of his head.

He slumped forward and a silver metal rectangle, about the size of a shirt box, tumbled toward the copilot's chair. Chapa started feeling woozy, his head doing cartwheels.

The craft spun once more, like a Tilt-a-Whirl getting its final licks in before letting riders get off. And then Chapa felt the ground to his left give way.

The horizon began tilting, as up became down and everything that had been bouncing around on the floor tumbled to the ceiling. Then the sky vanished altogether.

Chapa just let go—there was no use fighting anymore—and drifted away into a deep blackness.

Chapter 74

Alex Chapa's first plane trip was from Havana to Miami. It was relatively short and uneventful, except for when his mother had to convince customs officers that her son was not sick. He remembered smiling for the tall man in the dark blue uniform, the way his mother had told him to if anyone asked any questions about his health.

Whatever it took to hide his hundred-and-two temperature and get out of Cuba and begin a new future.

His second flight, just a few days later, ended in a more dramatic fashion as the Delta jet survived a rough landing in the middle of a January snowstorm in Chicago. It was the first time he'd seen snow, and unlike most kids who look forward to the next blizzard, Chapa never liked the stuff.

Chapa was thinking about that storm from nearly four decades ago, now. Through eyes that were only half open and barely able to focus, he struggled to see the snow that was sliding down the cracked windshield of the small plane. It drifted aimlessly across the glass, like it was unable to stop itself from falling.

Chapa knew the feeling.

But this snow was dark, like city street slush. And for a

scrambled moment Chapa wondered if smaller planes some-how attracted a different sort of snow.

Then he realized it wasn't snow at all.

The plane had kicked up a wave of dirt as it rolled over, and now that fine Illinois soil was headed back where it be-longed.

How long had he been out?

The plane had flipped, at least once, and came to rest up-side down. Chapa was suspended, still strapped into the pilot's seat. He reached around to where his head was throb-bing, just above his left temple, and felt a bump, but no sticky blood.

His head was sore to the touch, as were his ribs, left side, and abdomen. He breathed in as far as his lungs would allow and felt an ache in his chest and back.

But that didn't concern him as much as the faint smell of gasoline.

Chapa had to get out of there. He had no idea whether a plane could catch fire after it had plowed into the ground and sat half-buried, but he had no intention of finding out, either.

He raised his knees and wedged them against the instru-ment panel, then pressed his left forearm against the ceiling. Once he felt as secure as he could hope to, Chapa slowly un-buckled the belt and harness, and instantly rolled to his right side, then his shoulder slammed against the ceiling.

Chapa grunted as he twisted himself into a kneeling posi-tion, and started searching for his phone in the dark cabin. Wading through various pieces of debris, he found it a minute later, tucked into a back corner of the plane, then located the battery pack resting on the underside of a back-row seat.

Andrews was probably still on the line asking Chapa if he could hear him. Chapa snapped the battery pack back in place and slipped the phone into a front pants pocket.

The plane jostled slightly as he made his way toward the front and over by the copilot's chair. On the ceiling that was now beneath the seat, Chapa spotted the silver rectangle that had crashed into his head on impact.

It was some sort of thin metal case. Chapa picked it up and coaxed the latch open. Inside he found a leather bound flight log. Turning to the last page, Chapa saw the most recent entry was from early that morning, it read: *Surveying of land parcels.*

Chapa flipped to the beginning and saw that the log went back more than a year. Checking through a few earlier entries, he found a number of familiar names listed as *passengers*, and wondered how many private meetings had taken place above the cornfields of Kendall County.

The smell of gas was getting stronger now. He closed the case, then slipped his hands inside his jacket sleeves, and carefully wiped down every part of the plane he could remember having touched. He wasn't sure how he would play this yet, but it made sense to leave *I wasn't there* as an option. Even though a federal agent knew otherwise.

Chapa grabbed the flight log and kicked the jammed copilot's side door open, then rushed out of the plane and onto the soft topsoil. He willed his aching body away from the wreckage. The smell of gas wasn't as strong now, replaced by the subtle odor of post-harvest rot.

Looking back, some sixty crooked yards, Chapa saw the damage the plane had done to the cornfield. It looked like a runaway reaper had slashed and rolled its way through. He imagined how this must appear from the air, like a crop circle gone awry.

Checking his watch, Chapa saw it was just shy of three in the afternoon. He wondered if anyone had witnessed the plane go down. There was nothing but farmland all around him as far as he could see.

Remembering a road he'd flown over as the plane was going down, Chapa started in that direction, fighting his way through dormant but stubborn cornstalks as his cell phone searched for a signal.

Chapter 75

"Damn it, Al, you *must* get to a hospital." Andrews was pleading his case for a second time. "You're probably concussed. You might have a broken rib or two or worse."

Chapa had walked in the direction of a tree line, then emerged on the other side of it, before he had a signal, and managed to get a call to go through. Now he was heading for a row of power lines in the distance, the sort that Andrews had warned him about on the way down, the kind that flank a road.

"Listen, Joe, I'm a little beat up, but I'm okay. What I need now is time. Something is going down, soon. The cops here don't want to know about it, but a very bad thing is about to happen and I'm worried it may change Oakton forever."

"Well, I'll put a call out to the sheriff in Kendall and have them find that plane."

"No."

"What do you mean, *no*?"

"I know it's wrong of me to ask you to do this—"

"Then don't ask."

"I need you to forget the last hour ever happened."

"I can't do that."

"Does anyone else there know?"

"That's not the point, Al."

"I'm fine, Bendix killed himself, then his plane crashed. I was never here."

There was silence on the other end, and Chapa checked to make sure they were still connected.

"Joe?"

Silence.

"C'mon Joe, I hear you breathing."

"I can't do what you're asking me to do, Al. I just can't."

"Then just give me some time. A few hours. The authorities are bound to find the body and the plane by then anyhow."

"You do understand their first conclusion will be that you murdered the guy."

"That would have been like committing suicide."

"Except I can clear you, Al. But I've got to make a phone call in order to do that."

"Two hours. If they pick me up now they'll just throw me in a cell again."

"One. And I'm sending an agent your way for protection."

"Send them to Erin's," Chapa said and gave Andrews her address.

"Fine, I'll send someone to Erin's."

"Deal. I do understand that what I'm asking is—Joe? Joe? Are you still there?

Chapa still had a signal, but the conversation was over.

Chapter 76

Fifteen minutes after he'd reached a nondescript country two-lane, Chapa arrived where it intersected with Kingfisher Road, a major thruway that connected three counties. He wondered how long the walk back to Oakton would be from here and decided not to find out.

Calling Erin for a ride was not an option. The past few days had put a strain on their relationship. Chapa understood that if he told Erin everything now this could turn into an evening of wound salving, which would be nice, but then again it could just as easily prove to be the last straw.

For the first time since he was a child struggling to learn English, unable to understand why the other kids were laughing every time he spoke, Chapa felt like he'd fallen off the grid. Left on the outside looking in.

All of the safety devices he'd worked his entire adult life to build—a family, a career, a home—had been gradually stripped away. He felt naked and alone. But there was also something strangely liberating about that feeling.

These thoughts were moving through Chapa's aching head as he reached into his wallet, pulled out a gray paint chip, and punched up Ladrón's number.

"Who's calling me?"

"This is Alex Chapa, we met yesterday at the—"

"Yeah, yeah man, I know you."

There was an edge in Ladrón's voice, which led Chapa to assume he had a couple of his guys with him.

"What's up, A.C.?"

"I need a ride. And I need you to come alone."

"What? Pick you up at your house to go run some errands?"

"Not exactly. Are you alone?"

"No."

"Can you change that?"

Ladrón did not respond, but Chapa heard the sound of a thin door squealing open, then shutting in the background.

"I'm good now. What's up?"

Chapa explained that he needed to be picked up, no questions asked. Told Ladrón he was out in the middle of nowhere, gave him directions.

"I know that area real well. Used to be a place out there that we called The Pit. It was just a clearing in some woods, but a bunch of us smoked a whole lotta weed there, back in the day."

He told Chapa he could be there in twenty-five minutes, and that he'd be driving a burgundy Chrysler LeBaron.

"Now, I do this for you, Alex Chapa, and you'll do something for me."

"Sure, why not."

"No, you gotta be sure. I'm serious about this shit. Man to man. You down?"

Chapa shook his head as he processed the idea of entering into an oath of honor with a career criminal.

"Yes, we have a deal, as long as it's not illegal."

"No, no, nothing like that. I get the feeling your side of it might be a bit more dubious," Ladrón said in a way that drew attention to the word *dubious,* as though he knew that using it might buy him some lit cred.

"Then I'll see you in half an hour," Chapa said, ducking behind a large oak as a car appeared in the distance.

"Less."

Chapter 77

Ladrón wasn't kidding. Twenty minutes after their call ended, Chapa saw Ladrón's car, heard it a moment later. He stepped out from his hiding place, a small but dense grove of oak trees, then crossed a four-foot ditch and climbed up onto the gravel shoulder.

The Chrysler came to a hard stop right next to where Chapa was standing, and idled loud enough to be mistaken for a large piece of farm equipment. No doubt a familiar sound in these parts, though the thumping hip hop music that was punching its way out from inside was another matter.

Chapa opened the heavy car door and climbed inside.

"You got here in a hurry," he said, settling into his half of the wide seat.

Ladrón turned down the volume. He'd cleaned up some since leaving prison, though his look was still all street.

"Hey man, it's what we do. You look kinda fucked up, though, bro."

"I feel kinda fucked up."

Chapa rested the silver box on his lap. He thought about buckling his seat belt, but that part of his torso still ached, so he decided to take a pass.

"What's that thing?" Ladrón asked, pointing to the box.

Chapa just stared back at him, did not answer.

"Oh hell, yeah, that's right, no questions. My bad."

He noticed how Ladrón checked his rearview every few seconds, almost out of habit, or maybe a survival instinct born of experience.

"It didn't take you long to ask for a favor," Ladrón said as Chapa shifted, struggling to get comfortable on the vinyl seat.

The car was old but immaculate. Not a single fast food wrapper or cigarette butt on the floor or a speck of dust on the dash. Chapa had never owned a car that looked this clean.

"I have this bad habit of getting into shit."

Ladrón nodded like he knew.

"Seems to me that a man who doesn't get into shit isn't really much of a man. You know what I'm sayin'?"

Chapa knew. He gave Ladrón directions to where he'd left his car, the hangar belonging to the late Dr. Bendix.

"If that's the only trouble you got, that you're here and your ride is somewhere else, then you got no troubles at all."

Chapa smiled. He wished that was all.

"How's the love life of a big time reporter?"

"I have no idea, ask a big time reporter."

Ladrón laughed. "You're all right, A.C. But really, you got a lady? You're divorced, right?"

"I told you that back in the cell."

"That's right," Ladrón said and smiled, which made him look young.

"And yeah, I've got a lady."

"Troubles?"

"Maybe."

"Um hmm, troubles. She a keeper or just another slice of foolish time?"

"A slice of what?"

"Foolish time. It's like time expired. Like it was there, but then it got used up, wasted, never to return." Ladrón turned and looked at Chapa for emphasis. "Foolish time."

"She's not foolish time, not even close. She's a keeper."

"Then don't let her go, bro. Or it's gonna hurt something fierce. Losing the good ones always does. I know." Ladrón pounded a fist against his chest a couple times.

Chapa was starting to believe what Ladrón had told him about the origin of his nickname. But he had a lot of other things on his mind. The state of his relationship with Erin was eating away at him. But that was tomorrow's problem.

"So what do you want from me in return for this?"

"Just like that, bro? No chitchat? No thank you, Ladrón, you saved my ass from the children of the corn, Ladrón."

Chapa was starting to like this guy. He was troubled, but in a very real and honest way.

"Thank you, Ladrón."

"Don't mention it."

"Now, what do you want from me?"

Ladrón hesitated, and his expression changed. He didn't look young anymore.

"It's my kid, you know, my son. They have these career days at his school where dads show up and talk about what they do."

"Sure."

"I can't go, man, you know. But I want to."

"I can understand." Chapa didn't understand, had zero idea where this was heading.

"Right. So what I need you to do is to go, you know, as yourself."

"I'm good at that."

"Right. And explain how you know me, being a reporter and what not, and that I've been a high-level source on shit. Right?"

"You're a source?"

"Yes, my work is of a sensitive nature and shit, so you're there to speak for me."

Chapa had imagined being asked to do any manner of things, from turning his back on a troubling story to providing some sort of information. But this?

"You want me to lie?"

"I want you to help me give my son a chance. That's not a lot to ask, Alex. It really isn't."

No, it wasn't.

"It's not that big of a favor, either," Ladrón added.

It wasn't. A coach Chapa had looked up to back in high school had once told him that it's wrong to kick a man who has fallen on his sword. It was a piece of advice that Chapa had found useful through the years.

"I'll figure out how to do that, Ladrón."

Ladrón smiled broadly and slapped the wheel as though Chapa has just given him his one moment of true joy for the month. There was nothing wrong with that. The guy was okay.

As they drove toward the hangar, Ladrón told Chapa all about his various theories of life and the things that mattered most. Some of it made sense, the rest was mildly amusing, bizarre, or both. But Chapa's mind was on another track.

"If I needed to hide something from a thief, say in my home or office, and I didn't have a safe, where would the best place be?" Chapa asked as Ladrón pulled up to his car.

"Why are you asking me?" He responded with a half grin.

"Maybe because you get around, you know people."

"And people talk."

"That's right, they do."

"Except for friends like you and me, who talk to each other about shit, but that's where it stays."

"Exactly, that's where it stays."

Chapa wondered whether Ladrón realized he was about to actually become a source.

"It depends on the size. If it's a big thing, that's tough to hide. But if it's something small, then you want to slip it in with stuff that you have a lot of, so that it just blends in."

"Sounds obvious enough."

"Right, but it can't be in with anything valuable that someone would steal, because that's exactly what's gonna happen."

Chapa was trying to remember what he'd seen among the remains of Jim Chakowski's house. If he could only get inside and look around.

"Here's the thing, A.C., if you want to understand a person you gotta look at their stuff, where they keep it, and what they have in a special place, or the things they take good care of and treat like valuables. That will tell you a hell of a lot more about them than any journal or diary. I remember one time—"

Chapa let out a heavy sigh as he pressed the base of his palms against his forehead.

"Goddamn it. It's not a zip code or a password," Chapa said under his breath.

Chapter 78

Chapa didn't see Chakowski's office the same way as before. The cramped, shady space was not quite familiar to him, but more revealing now.

The office was so quiet, so still, locked in that moment when Jim Chakowski left for the last time. Like the place was waiting for him to return.

But Chapa understood Jim Chakowski a little better now. He felt something of a kinship with his fallen colleague.

Besides his brother, Jim had no family or much of a life outside of the paper. Maybe that had been a decision he'd made at some point. But more likely it was the product of many other decisions. Those would have included chasing leads into compromising and dangerous situations. It meant occasionally having to put an arm around the irredeemable and not worrying that some of their tainted DNA might rub off on you. All because something useful might come of it.

Chapa understood now that Jim Chakowski had done his best to pantomime a normal life. Going through those motions that he'd read about, or doing many of the things others do, and faking the rest.

Ultimately, it had been Chakowski's need to know that got him killed. When he was a child, Chapa's mother had

often told him that information was the most important com-
modity in the world. What she'd failed to mention was that
it's also one of its most dangerous.

Chapa stuck his head out and took a look down the hall,
confirmed Macklin's office was dark, then closed the door.
Pushing Chakowski's chair aside, he began sifting through
the LP collection, searching each spine for record album
number ND93106.

He quickly figured out that the letters were not random,
they were initials, and that narrowed things down in a hurry.
Chakowski owned four Neil Diamond albums, all were from
the late 60s and early 70s. Serial number 93106 belonged to
one titled *Stones*.

As he pulled it off the shelf, Chapa wondered why this LP
had been singled out from the three or four hundred in
Chakowski's collection. A personal favorite? The artist was
pictured on the cover sitting on a bench, barefoot. Then
Chapa flipped the record over, and began to understand why
Chakowski had chosen this one.

Instead of being flat, the back cover had a flap at the top,
and a tie clasp with a string attached. It looked a little like
one of those large interoffice envelopes that can be tied
closed.

Chapa had never seen an album cover like this before.
Clever, he thought. He unwound the string, pulled the flap
back, and found more than the record.

Several sheets of stark white paper had been folded
neatly in half and tucked inside. Chapa removed them, revealing a manila envelope pressed against the vinyl record.

He opened the envelope, turned it on its side, and four
crudely cut pieces of paper tumbled out. One landed on
Chapa's lap, two more on the floor, and another fell onto the
desk pad, flipping over to reveal the image of a man's leg,
clad in dark pants. The dress shoe pointing to the left told
Chapa which leg this was. He collected the other pieces,
placed them on the desk, and built the small puzzle.

One arm—the left, a torso, two legs, no head. The subject had been dressed for business or church, or maybe he didn't differentiate between the two. It had been a simple photo of a man standing in place against a wall. Each part of his body cut out of the picture, most of the background trimmed away.

Who the hell is this supposed to be?

Chapa turned his attention to the quarter-page-sized photo. The black-and-white image was fuzzy, a cheap copy machine duplicate of a group shot that had been taken at some meeting or business event.

Despite the low quality, Chapa instantly recognized the nine men and one woman standing side by side in what he assumed were their favorite power poses. For once, Vanny Mars wasn't the tallest or widest one in sight, but it was still a close call.

Chapa now knew every one of Oakton's power elite by name, title, and reputation. Their names were printed in caption form across the bottom.

Franklin Gemmer, Clay Hunter, Charles Stoop, Richard Wick, Vanessa Mars, Greg Vinsky, William Blair, Dr. Walter Bendix, Ted Bruce, George Forsythe.

But what held Chapa's attention wasn't the super-serious looks on their faces, or the way that Vanny Mars seemed to have the middle to herself, as none of the men apparently dared to brush up against her. It wasn't anything actually in the photo that prompted Chapa to put it under the desk lamp and lean in for a closer look.

Something had been scribbled across the bottom in red ink, maybe by a source or by Chakowski himself. Chapa realized he would likely never know which, but he also understood it might not matter.

Chapa read it again, then looked at the men in the photo and compared them to the broken and uneven figure he'd pieced together on the desk. His attempts to match those pieces to anyone in the picture failed, and Chapa began to wonder if those body parts all came from a single photo, or even a single person.

He couldn't know. But Chapa was certain that he had to find out what that handwritten sentence in the lower margin meant. His eyes were drawn to the writing again. Chapa could not stop looking at it, then letting his eyes wander up to the group photo, then back again.

As Chapa read it once more, he noticed that the bottom edge had curved under a bit, enough to obscure the line underscoring the first word. He flattened the thin piece of copier paper against the desk, and looked at it again.

<u>He</u> is one of them.

Chapter 79

Playing a hunch, Chapa called Jan Boll, a reporter at the *Baltimore Tribune*.

"Damn, Chapa, must be a dark day in hell if I'm hearing your bark on my line."

Boll, whom Chapa knew was a damn good reporter, had worked at several different papers in the Chicago area back in the 90s, before relocating to Maryland. It wasn't the prospect of a better job that lured her to the Eastern seaboard but rather a cure for her teenaged daughter's illness.

She found it at a clinic near Baltimore, and then managed to land a job, albeit one that came with a pay cut. In time, the move and the strain of having a sick child cost Boll her marriage. But Boll would spend the rest of her life telling anyone who asked that she was okay with that trade-off.

They exchanged the customary friendly questions about family, health, and work before Chapa got after it.

"I need your help, Jan."

"Oh shit, Chapa, how much is this going to cost me?"

"Just a few minutes of your time. It's not as though there's anything to write about in Baltimore anyhow."

Boll's big laugh made Chapa flinch away from the earpiece. He hadn't heard it in a long time, and realized now that he'd missed it.

"I need you to track down a photo from five years or so ago, and fax me a copy."

"I might be able to do that, in spite of the fact that you're the schmuck who's asking."

He reminded Boll of the car accident in 2005 that had resulted in the death of a prominent businessman.

"I believe his name was Roland—" Chapa started.

"King," Boll said, completing the thought before adding that she remembered it well. "But if memory serves, you won't get much out of the photos from the wreck. The vehicle was burned like charcoal, not much there."

"That doesn't surprise me."

"It was a one-car deal. Poor guy smashed into a pole, and the car blew. Not much left of him or the vehicle."

This was info Chapa already had. But hearing a closer account of it made him feel a little like he'd been there.

"Cops investigate the fire?"

"No, not much. Man hits pole at high speed, car blows. Pretty easy to put together that cause and effect. Case closed."

"Here's the thing, Jan, I'm more interested in what the guy looked like. Maybe if your paper ran a headshot with the story or alongside the obit."

"Yeah, yeah, okay. I'll try and run those down. Now tell me why."

Chapa wondered why it had taken so long for a newshound like Jan Boll to ask him that. Boll was a veteran journalist, a solid one at that. She had probably been waiting to see how many cards Chapa was willing to show before pressing the issue.

He would've done the same thing.

"All I can say at this point is that there may be more to that accident than anyone realized back in 2005."

"Suicide? There was some talk about that at the time, I remember. C'mon Chapa, give."

"I'm way out on a limb right now, Jan, and some folks seem to think I'm busy sawing it off."

"Knowing you, I'm surprised you haven't brought down the whole damn tree."

"I honestly cannot go deeper into this with you at the moment. But as soon as I break the story, assuming there is one, you will be the first reporter I tip."

"Full disclosure?"

"Absolutely."

Chapa could almost hear Boll drumming her fingertips on her desk.

"How soon after you break it, Alex?"

"Within twenty-four hours."

Another silence, but Chapa wasn't worried. He knew where this was headed.

"I'll get back to you in about an hour, two max."

As he was hanging up with Jan Boll, Chapa's cell phone started playing its tune. He checked the caller I.D. and saw Erin's number. Chapa paused for a moment, wondering if he should tell her about what happened that afternoon.

Chapa still didn't know what to say when he picked up, midway through the second chorus.

"Alex, there's a man standing in my front yard. He's well dressed, wearing a suit, and he has sunglasses on. I've never seen him before." Erin lowered her voice to a whisper. "But he keeps staring at my house."

"What is he doing?"

Chapa could feel his heart punching away at his chest as he waited to hear Erin's voice again.

"He's . . . just standing there, by the street, near a large dark blue car."

"How old is this guy?"

"Probably a few years younger than us. Alex, if I didn't know better, I'd think he was . . . posing."

"Come again?"

"He's wearing an expensive suit, really nice shoes, too. He's got one hand on his hip, and—"

Now Chapa remembered what Andrews had told him about assigning an agent to watch over Erin and the children.

"Erin." She was still describing the primping federal officer. "Erin, it's okay, that's FBI Agent Sandro, that's just how he is."

"Really?"

"He's a good man."

Chapa had met Sandro a few weeks earlier at the FBI's Chicago offices. He was relieved that Andrews had sent one of his best men. Not only did that give him a sense of security, but it also let him know Andrews was taking all of this very seriously.

"But what's he doing here, Alex?"

He hadn't counted on this question. Never thought that his friend's attempt to protect the people he cared about would force him into this discussion before he'd prepared for it.

Chapa had never lied to Erin, wasn't going to now. But he decided that telling her the entire truth at this moment would not be good for anyone.

"Joe Andrews sent him, you know, because of all that's happened these past few days."

"And we need an FBI agent at our door to protect us? Who from?"

"It's just a precaution, Erin. You know how Joe is."

"Yes, I do," Erin said in a grave voice.

It told Chapa that she understood a great deal. And he knew then that things between them were going to get much worse before he had the chance to make them better.

Chapter 80

Chapa stuck his head out of Chakowski's office and got Zach's attention. The young man spun out of his chair and hustled down the hall.

"What are you still doing here?" Chapa asked, inviting Zach inside and shutting the door behind him.

"This is my long day."

"Do you ever have a short day?"

Zach pretended to be giving the question some thought.

"What's a short day?"

"This isn't one, that's for sure. I need you to keep an eye on the fax machine in the newsroom. I'm expecting something in the next hour."

"Does it have to do with what happened to Mr. Chakowski, and that note you gave me?"

"Yes, maybe. Trust me, I'll fill you in on all of it over a beer."

"Or two?"

"At least."

Zach smiled and nodded, then headed back out into the newsroom. There were very few people left from the day shift, and the night crew had barely started stumbling in.

Zach should not have much trouble retrieving an incoming fax, assuming Jan Boll managed to track down a photo.

Chapa sat down in Chakowski's chair. It was not nearly as malleable and soft as his own. This one had been used by a man working against unforgiving deadlines. Chapa knew that sort of pressure as well, but he'd also spent his share of time rocking back, trying to work out a story in his head before committing it to paper or computer screen. Chakowski had never struck him as the pensive type.

He looked over the notes, focusing his attention on a list of names next to their businesses or the roles they played.

Charles Stoop–Landscaping
Richard Wick–Legal counsel
Franklin Gemmer–Security systems
Clay Hunter–Insurance
Walter Bendix–Doctor, land developer
Greg Vinsky–Logistics analyst
George Forsythe–Electrical contractor
Brent McGraw–?
William Blair–Deal maker
Ted Bruce–Public relations

One name was missing—Vanny Mars was not on the list. Probably because she was a woman, and Chakowski, like Clarkson, had been tracking a man.

Chapa studied the names, first individually, gathering up all that he'd learned about each of these people, then collectively, trying to decipher how they might operate as a single unit. Were they all willing participants? Probably not. Chapa mentally drew a line through the names *Walter Bendix* and *Brent McGraw.*

That left eight of then. *Eight men in.* Were they like players in the old children's string game of Cat's Cradle? Tied together by their individual ambition, fear, and guilt.

He was beginning to form a flimsy pecking order in his

mind, and understand that he didn't have enough concrete information to do any better, when his cell went off. He assumed it was Nikki calling, and answered in something approximating a calming voice.

"This is Alex Chapa."

"Mr. Chapa, Mr. Chapa."

"Yes."

"Good, you're there."

The voice on the other end sounded like it belonged to someone in the fourteenth mile of a marathon that they had not properly trained to run.

"This is Tim Haas. I need to meet you right away."

"Why Tim? You sound anxious. What's—"

"No. I can't do this over the phone, not right now. I have something to show you, but we need to meet someplace public. Safe."

"Okay. How 'bout a hint?"

Tim Haas responded with more heavy breathing. Chapa wondered who or what he'd been running from.

"Meet me at Lansford's as soon as you can."

"The big supermarket?"

"Lansford's."

Chapa was about to explain how he'd had enough of mysterious meetings and that he needed to know more. But all he heard now was dead air.

"Tim? You still there?"

Chapa pressed the redial button, but his call went straight to Tim Haas' voicemail. He grabbed his coat, checked the batteries in his digital tape recorder, and headed out of the office. He was almost to the door of the newsroom when Zach caught up to him.

"Here's the fax from Baltimore. It's a photo, but it's not very big or clear."

Chapa took the papers from him. There were two—a cover letter with a message from Jan Boll that read simply, *I will look forward to hearing from you,* and the picture.

Zach was right, the waist-up shot wasn't very good. The stark and grainy image of the man identified as Roland King stared back at Chapa as if asking, *Do you know me?*

"Is it what you were expecting, Mr. Chapa? Does it help?"

"Yes, maybe, not sure. He would not have been my first guess."

Chapter 81

Chapa figured it would take him about fifteen minutes to drive to Lansford's Megamart, a store as big as some shopping malls, surrounded by a new housing development on Oakton's far north side. The big-box store was built with the idea that it could anchor a large shopping complex which would serve the thousands of people moving in.

Except they didn't move in, and the other stores never came. The houses stopped selling when the economy slumped, and developers responded by halting all new construction.

Oakton had become an increasingly more difficult and complicated place to do business. The downtown masters made demands of anyone seeking to make it in their town. And not everyone was willing to pay what amounted to a form of protection money.

Chapa wondered how many of the businesses he was now driving past were part of the game, either out of choice or need. Almost everything that he'd learned about his hometown over the past week had made him want to move away, go anywhere else, take Erin and Mike, and possibly even Nikki with him, and never look back.

Maya had given Chapa several pieces of mail on his way

out of the building. Most of it was his, except for one envelope addressed to James Chakowski. Chapa opened that one
at a red light and found an invitation to speak at a small college graduation in the spring. He wondered if it would be
tacky to call the organizers, explain the circumstances, offer
to act as a stand-in, and insist that any payment of a
speaker's fee be sent to Warren Chakowski. Why the hell
not.

The parking lot, large enough for a stadium and tailgat-
ing, was about half full. Chapa spent a few minutes driving
up and down the aisles, giving Tim Haas an opportunity to
spot him. Were they meeting outside? Inside? In the men's
room?

Satisfied that Tim was not waiting for him outside, Chapa
found a space along the far right half of the block-long store-
front, turned the car off, then checked his cell phone for any
new messages, hoping that Tim had gotten back to him.
Nothing.

The overhead light switched on as he opened the door
and started to get out, drawing Chapa's attention to an envelope that had slipped away from the others, off the passenger's seat and onto the floor. He reached down, picked it up,
and flipping it over noticed there was no return address. His
name and address at the *Record* had been neatly centered
and typed on a white label affixed to the front.

Chapa held the thin envelope up to the light, but could
not see through it. It felt flimsy, as though it was empty.
There seemed to be another name under the label, typed directly onto the envelope, but he could not be certain.

He tore it open and reached inside for a letter, but found
none. Then Chapa squeezed the top and bottom edges, puck-
ering it open, and shook out a small piece of paper that
drifted down and came to rest on his lap.

Pinching it between his thumb and index finger, Chapa
picked up the thin scrap and looked at it under the light.

It was a cutout of a man's right arm.

Chapter 82

Lansford's Megamart was a Midwest-based chain that had originated in Rockford, Illinois, and expanded to six states. The one in Oakton opened in 2002, promptly forcing a handful of locally owned stores out of business.

Chapa didn't care for the place. Yes, it was open twenty-four hours, offered lower prices on account of being non-union, and carried everything from power tools to mayonnaise, but it had absolutely no soul, or feeling of uniqueness. Chapa wondered if over time those things rubbed off on the people who regularly shopped there. Besides, he had little use for power tools and hated mayonnaise.

He'd been in the store no more than five minutes, when he began to realize this one also offered something that wasn't on the department directory—a stalker. The moving shadow had been tailing Chapa since they both passed the office supplies, then around the corner and beyond the eight aisles of cleaning products.

If this guy was working passive security he might want to start looking for another job. Just out of curiosity, Chapa cut through the children's wear, past pink sweatshirts and sequined tops that were far too revealing for a woman in her twenties, let alone a tween-aged girl.

Stealing a glance in a mirror along a column, Chapa confirmed that his newest fan was still hanging around and doing a piss-poor job of appearing to be interested in some *iCarly* T-shirts. The guy was tall and slender and fidgeted a little, like someone in need of a fix. The bottom half of his face was pocked with uneven stubble, not enough to be a beard but too much to suggest any other intent.

Where the hell was Tim Haas? And was it a good idea for Chapa to try to find Tim as long as he had a tail on him? Probably not.

Chapa walked by a small café along the front of the store, scanning the tables as he passed. He considered taking a seat at one and waiting. But then what?

He continued walking down the main aisle that ran along the front of the store, leading to the registers. When Chapa saw the sign for the men's room, he cut through an empty checkout lane and rushed past a store employee who looked at him as though he couldn't decide whether he was a shoplifter or someone who had to go real bad.

A set of ripe odors invaded Chapa's senses as soon as he pushed open the scuffed and finger-marked red door. It was a mix of industrial cleaner and shit, and he couldn't tell which one was covering up the other.

"Tim," Chapa said, not quite yelling.

No response. Chapa had not expected one, and quickly left the men's room.

Something was very wrong. All of it was wrong. Tim's anxious phone call, this meeting place, the guy trailing him—wait, where was the guy?

He scanned the area, then walked back through the still empty checkout lane, smiling at the confused cashier as he passed. Again, he surveyed his surroundings. The guy was gone.

Maybe Chapa's imagination had overtaken his better judgment. Could be the guy had not been trailing him. Or if he was security, he might've called the cops as soon as he saw Chapa rush past the cash registers.

He decided to give the store one last thorough search. Just in case Tim Haas was cowering in sporting goods, or had forgotten why he was here and was shopping for auto supplies.

Chapa was tired of this runaround, had been even before he walked into the store, before he got that call from Tim, too. He wanted to be with Nikki, and Erin, and Mike, and that was all he'd wanted for most of the past few days.

It seemed like the folks in downtown Oakton had created their own little fiefdom, and someone was butchering anyone who threatened it. Chakowski stumbled into that, Clarkson too, maybe. And Chapa now felt like he was lost in the middle of a maze that he didn't recall ever walking into.

He started at one end of the store and weaved through the aisles, turning anytime he hit a dead end, scanning each row for a man that he'd spoken to just twice before tonight, but one who chose to call him when he was in trouble.

But was Tim Haas in trouble? Chapa stopped asking that question when he noticed that his persistent friend was back. He seemed to have picked up Chapa's scent just past housewares, and was now in lockstep pursuit.

This guy was no security officer. Chapa glanced up as he passed a circular security mirror near the jewelry counter. The guy had his left hand tucked inside a coat pocket. He was looking down, as though he wanted to avoid eye contact with other customers, store employees, or . . .

Now Chapa understood why he hadn't been followed through the checkout lane—security cameras. The pay areas were littered with them, blanketing every square inch. The cameras throughout the store were there to spy on shoplifters, but the ones by the checkout spied on everybody, customers and employees alike.

This was not good. The guy was a pro, and he had a plan.

One that involved not giving the cops a look at his face after the fact.

Chapa thought about finding store security, telling them about this man following him. But then what? His shadow would vanish. He'd walk out with the next group of people leaving the store, then wait for Chapa by his car, or worse, at his house.

The idea of running held no appeal at the moment. Something had happened to Tim Haas, probably something very bad.

Chapa didn't feel like running, especially when he wasn't sure who or what he was running from. Besides, what had Bendix said to him just a few hours ago? *It's going to happen soon.*

Maybe it was happening now.

Chapter 83

Alex Chapa's last year in Cuba was the most trying for him and his mother. The man in their lives was gone, and food shortages had become as common as government crackdowns.

Toilet paper and toothpaste would vanish from the shelves of government-run stores, not to return for weeks at a time. Even basic items like milk and bread were often hard to come by.

Chapa's memories of that time were incomplete. Not only was he a young child, barely four, but he was sheltered from much of the hardships by his mother and grandparents. A fact he would learn only later in life, and one that made him feel both grateful and a bit guilty.

He understood that the people who loved him had constructed something of a false narrative, shielding him from much of the horror that was taking place just outside the front door of his home in Havana's Vedado neighborhood.

One thing that he remembered with great clarity was the abundance of avocados and how his mother used them as a fallback meal anytime there was nothing else to serve. The fruit was easy to grow in Cuba, and he recalled seeing some of his neighbors picking them off trees in late summer and early fall.

The West Indies variety of the fruit was not small and dark like the avocados most Americans are accustomed to. These were larger, sometimes as big as a small child's head.

Chapa wasn't finding any quite that large now as he stood in the grocery half of Lansford's Megamart, sifting through a basket in the produce department. But he was more concerned with firmness than size. He found three that were heavy and felt solid, slipped them into the plastic bag, and then confirmed that his unwanted company was still standing nearby. Chapa spotted him pretending to be checking out the green apples.

If Chapa was going to confront this guy, it was going to be when and where he chose. Would not be a good idea to do anything that might set him off. Picking up a series of more clearly useful devices could result in the man attacking before Chapa was prepared for him. That's why he had refused to give in to a deep urge that swept through him as he passed the aluminum baseball bats display and then the golf clubs back in sporting goods.

After double-bagging the avocados, he headed toward the kitchen supplies. Chapa wasn't worried about keeping an eye on the man—he didn't have to. The guy had passed on at least two opportunities to take him out, which meant he was either waiting for some sort of signal, or planning to jump him in the parking lot.

Chapa wasn't going to let it come to that.

He picked up a cheese grater—a large one with cutting areas of various size and shape—like it was nothing at all. Then it was back to the bathroom supply area of the housewares department.

Chapa allowed himself a quick sideways glance and confirmed the guy was still there. It took about twice as long as he'd wanted to find a towel bar that was the right size. The one he grabbed off a shelf wasn't perfect, a bit too small, just eight inches long and about five deep, but close enough to do the job.

He walked back into a main aisle and turned his attention to the store's ceiling. To a casual shopper or bored employee, Chapa looked like someone who was scanning the various department signs. But Chapa wasn't searching for any specific grouping of items. He was looking for a blind spot.

A few years earlier he had done a story on modern retail theft protection. Specifically, cameras and sensors. The store managers and security experts who served as sources on the story had shown him the inner workings of various systems. Chapa never stopped being amazed at the secrets people will tell a guy with a byline.

One secret, however, didn't make it into the story. Chapa promised he'd keep it out. Every store he visited had blind spots, areas the cameras simply could not cover. And the bigger the store, the more difficult it was to secure.

Some unsecured areas were the result of the surveillance equipment's limitations, others were created by the store's layout or displays. He knew nothing about this store's system, but it figured to be fairly elaborate.

But he did know how to find a blind spot, and when Chapa saw a large beige banner that read *Where the Good Life Becomes Great,* hanging over the small furnishings department, he made a quick turn in that direction.

Chapa walked under two dark Plexiglas ceiling panels, the kind used to hide security cameras. There was another in the ceiling about thirty feet to the right and one more some fifty feet to the left.

The department appeared deserted, which was good. The smell of scented candles drifted down one aisle and crossed into another.

As soon as he passed under the banner, Chapa looked back and saw how it blocked all of the possible surveillance options. He double-checked that this store did not have any other devices tucked into the corners and edges of the ceiling. It did not.

Chapa then turned a corner, rushed down an aisle of shelves lined with lamps and fancy frames. Turned another corner, passed two aisles before hurrying down the third, which was home to all kinds of shelving units, ducked around the end cap, and waited.

A moment later he heard the sound of hard shoes slapping the tile floor in an uneven pattern. Not someone browsing, but rather the sound of a predator who'd misplaced his prey and was beginning to panic.

Chapa leaned back against a series of uneven shelves of clearance items as well as he could manage, and waited. For several more seconds, he stared at the rows of wall clocks in front of him while listening for the man's footsteps.

Then it sounded like he'd started to leave the area, and Chapa realized he'd done far too good a job of hiding. Reaching blindly and grasping the first thing his hand landed on, he lifted a small plastic container of furniture polish and tossed it back on the shelf.

The noise it made wasn't much, but the footsteps stopped immediately. Then they began to retreat, heading in his direction.

Chapa waited and listened, clutching the bag of avocados in his left hand, the grater and towel bar in the other. The sound was growing louder as it got nearer. Now even closer. The guy was heading down the aisle to Chapa's left—not the one he'd prepared for.

Without hesitating, Chapa switched the three items from one hand to the other, so that his makeshift sling now dangled from his right hand. A moment later he saw the man's crooked reflection in the curved crystal of one of the large clocks in front of him.

Could the man see him, also? That was Chapa's first concern, but it didn't last.

He was no more than twenty feet away, now. Chapa watched as the guy's silhouette quickly filled the clock's face.

In one fluid motion Chapa leaped into the aisle and swung the bag of avocados at the man's face, putting all of his weight and strength behind the blow. For a *what-the-fuck* instant, there was a look of absolute confusion on the man's face.

Then Chapa connected, hard to the chin, cheek, and up into the left eye. And the guy's face wasn't the same anymore.

A bloody flow erupted from his nose as his eyes drifted north. He stumbled backward, his right hand clutching his battered face while the left fumbled around in a coat pocket.

Chapa prepared to strike again, but the guy was dancing on ice, looking for someplace to fall. Chapa decided to oblige and kicked his feet out from under him.

The guy went down hard, but in doing so he appeared to get a grip on the object in his pocket. Chapa saw the zip gun, a small, crude single bullet device favored by low-level bangers and small-time thieves, an instant before the guy fired it.

He spun to the side as the bullet struck a large body pillow covered in a leopard skin pattern. Knowing it was a safe bet this guy had more weapons tucked away, Chapa dropped a knee on his chest, sending a fresh spray of blood arcing through the air.

Dropping the bag, Chapa got a firm grip on the towel rack and pressed it against the guy's neck, slamming his head against the floor and pinning it there. Chapa then brought the cheese grater up and ground it against a fresh wound along the side of his face.

"You know, Buddy, I never imagined I had it in me. But someone gave my little girl nightmares, and that makes me want to cross all sorts of lines."

"Fuck you."

"Where is Tim Haas?"

He was drifting in and out, and Chapa knew he didn't have much time. The only question was whether this guy would pass out before a store employee found them.

"Who are you?"

"Nobody," he responded with great effort in a voice thick and moist with blood and pain.

"Why were you following me?"

He seemed confused by the question, then his eyes rolled back. Chapa was about to try to shake the guy back to consciousness when he heard the sound of a cell phone.

"You're in deep shit now," the guy gurgled, then smiled, revealing a front tooth that dangled to one side like a broken pendulum.

Chapa brought his left foot up, pressed it against the bar, and reached inside the guy's coat. The cell phone buzzed and sounded again the moment Chapa touched it, and he flinched just a little.

The guy let out a slow, labored laugh that got slower near the end, like his batteries were running down. Then he drifted off.

Chapa carefully retrieved the phone and flipped it open.

"You there?"

He remembered what the unconscious guy had said—*You're in deep shit now*. An already bad situation could get a whole lot worse in a hurry if the caller on the other end didn't get an answer.

Chapa responded, holding the phone a few inches away from his mouth.

"Yeah," he said in as indistinguishable a voice as he could manage.

There was a pause, and that made Chapa more than a little uncomfortable. Then Chapa realized that he might've held the phone too far from his mouth.

He brought it closer to his face and was about to respond again. Then he heard the caller ask, "You got him?"

"Yeah."

There was another extended silence, and Chapa feared that this time the guy on the other end had figured out something was not right.

But the voice returned a moment later.

"Then bring him to the house."

Chapter 84

As he drove out of the Lansford's Megamart parking lot, Chapa repeatedly glanced in the rearview for any car that might be tailing him or to see if a security guard came running out of the store. He kept looking back during the first half mile driving down busy Remlinger Road, until he felt certain no one was following and nobody was coming after him.

Two thoughts invaded his mind.

One was a question—How did the guy know what he looked like? Chapa had never seen the man before.

The other was an assumption—He was never supposed to make it inside that store. That was where it all began to break down for the third-rate thug Chapa had left passed out and tucked neatly into a shelf, hidden behind large, soft body pillows.

Chapa had paid for the towel rack, grater, and avocados at a self-checkout lane, used cash, kept his head down as much as he could without drawing attention or suspicion. When he saw a 7-Eleven store up ahead, Chapa pulled into the parking lot, and drove up to a large brown wastebasket. He lowered his squeaky window and threw the bag away.

Chapa knew he'd been off his game all week. Maybe it

was because Nikki had been around and his attention was divided. His recent troubles with Erin were also having a big effect. Whatever the reason, he'd been a step behind, and everyone else had seemed to know a little more than he did.

The house on Elm Grove Street was about five miles away. He understood now why Gladys Washer had been murdered—she'd stumbled across some very ugly people. Probably had no idea. Just another longtime resident concerned about her town, or an old woman making one last grasp at relevance.

Either way, she hadn't deserved to die, just like Chakowski's life should not have ended as it did. Chapa's colleague understood he'd uncovered deadly information, knew his life was in danger. That had made things much worse for him.

Chapa didn't want to think about what Chakowski's last hours must have been like. He felt a wave of acid roll through his gut as he turned onto Maryvale Avenue, and into the neighborhood he'd first visited just a few days ago.

Chapter 85

Eight blocks away, Charles Stoop is bound to a wall in a small, second-floor room of a house he'd never seen until a little over an hour ago. Has it only been that long?

He came to this neglected corner of Oakton on the promise of a possible landscaping deal. One that he was told could extend to every property in this forgotten neighborhood. It wasn't the sort of business Stoop typically threw himself into, not big enough for him to bother with. But he was asked to look at it by a member of the business core, who convinced him it could lead to something bigger.

Charles Stoop believed he could sell anything to anyone, everyone knew that about him. He believed in his ability to turn any situation into a win. He'd spent much of the drive over devising the best way to say *no* if the deal wasn't right, and still make it seem like he was doing everyone a favor. He was good at that.

Stoop's cocksure swagger had slowed some as he walked up the cracked driveway, though he'd regained it by the time the front door opened. But Stoop has turned down enough dark and narrow streets in his life to know what trouble looks like—and as he stepped inside this house every cell in his being told him something was not right.

There have been times in Charles Stoop's complicated past when he has been the source of darkness. Jagged nights and twisted days that he'd long ago put behind him came racing back when he felt the stun gun burning him from the inside out. And then Stoop knew that he'd been invited into someone else's nightmare.

He also understood that the landscaping deal was only a ruse to get him out there. And he now fears that he will experience a great deal of pain without ever learning why.

Thoughts had danced into and out of his mind as two men—one whom he thought he knew, the other a stranger—carried him upstairs, pressed his limp body to a wall, and fastened his hands and feet using some binds that Stoop could not focus his eyes on well enough to see clearly. Before he could say anything, a ball of some sort was shoved into Stoop's mouth and duct taped in place.

A face that had become familiar to Stoop over the past several years appears from out of the darkness. He has looked into those eyes from across boardroom tables, and while they sat at adjacent bar stools. And Stoop now realizes that he's never been able to read those eyes. Not in the same way that most people unwittingly reveal themselves.

Such simple creatures. But not this one.

Stoop struggles to move his head, but that only tightens the clasp around his neck and brings a smile to his captor's otherwise empty face. If only he could talk, Stoop is certain this could be resolved.

A win-win for everybody.

But he can barely make a sound, can't form words to ask questions. So many questions. They are getting in the way. A salesman never asks questions, not really. Oh sure, it might sound that way.

What is it that you're looking for? What can I do to close this deal today?

Those seem like questions, but they are not, actually. Just part of the game, another play.

If only he could communicate, get the tape off his mouth and coax his way out of this. But even then, Stoop has too many questions of his own.

When he sees the hunting knife in the man's hand, the edge of its blade painted in shades of blood that range from dark brown to glossy red, Charles Stoop fears his questions will soon be answered.

Chapter 86

Chapa pulled over and parked three houses down, along a pitch black stretch of curb, turned the car off, and dialed Tom Jackson's number.

Wanting to make certain he didn't miss anything, Chapa had decided to wait until he'd reached the house before calling the cops.

"What now, Alex?"

"I'm parked four houses down from 414 Elm Grove Street. It's a house Gladys Washer filed a complaint about. That's what got her killed."

"What the hell are you—"

"I'm not going to pretend I have all the answers. But I know something real bad has been taking place here, and it's probably still going down while we're wasting time arguing."

Chapa heard Jackson slurping what he assumed was coffee.

"Alex, if you're screwing me on this, or if you're as full of shit as we both know you can be, you and me are through."

"Get here, Tom."

The connection dropped. Chapa looked at his watch and figured it would take at least twenty minutes for Jackson to finish his coffee, decide to check things out, round up a couple of officers, and drive to the house.

Chapa knew he'd talked the detective into action, but not into hurrying. It could take them as long as thirty minutes to get there.

With that in mind, Chapa slouched down in his seat, made himself comfortable, and kept an eye on the place. He'd gone along on stakeouts in the past, even conducted one or two of his own, but this situation was different.

The house was dark, except for a dim light illuminating a white shade in an upstairs window. There were no cars parked in the driveway or along the front curb.

Chapa wasn't sure who or what he was looking for. The plan was to wait until he saw Jackson's unmarked car, or a cruiser pull up, then he would get out and join the party.

Those plans changed when he saw a white Ford sedan drive up and park near the house. A man got out, eased the driver's side door shut, and began a measured advance down the sidewalk, in the direction of the house.

Chapa watched for a moment, straining to make out the dark figure moving through darker shadows. There was something familiar about him, but Chapa couldn't see well enough to make out who it was.

Only one way to be sure. Chapa reached up and flipped off the overhead light inside his Corolla before easing the door open and quietly getting out, then shutting it just as carefully. Without hesitation, he crossed the street and headed for the house.

Chapter 87

The man looks into the eyes of his mother's killer.

He never forgot those eyes. They loomed over him in that shabby home back in St. Louis. Haunted his dreams. Until they stared back at him in a magazine photo five years ago.

The man had memorized the caption: *Charles Stoop of Oakton, a genuine overnight success in the corporate landscaping industry.*

"Remember when your name was Gilley?" the man asks, letting the name *Gilley* slither down his tongue and out of his mouth for the first time in years.

Stoop furrows his brow, then narrows his eyes, as though he's trying to bring the man's face into focus. He tries to shake his head, but stops when the metal clasp begins to eat away at the soft flesh of his neck.

"You called me 'Little Punk' back then. Probably didn't even know my name," the man says, then leans in close enough for a whisper. "You still don't. Never will."

The man is distracted momentarily by the sound of a car driving up and stopping near the house. He edges toward the window and slips a look through a thin gap in the curtains.

He sees nothing but darkness beyond the reach of a

streetlight, halfway down the block. The man watches, searching the shadows. Sees no one.

"My mother was not a bad person, just someone stuck in a bad life," he says, turning away from the window. "She would've gotten out of it in time, but you ended her life, Gilley."

Stoop's eyes grow large, forcing his hairline to recede some. That gives the man an idea.

He can feel his mother's presence, like he has his entire adult life. He can almost see her over there in the corner, looking at him from beyond the shadows. Imagines her face as he remembers it the last time he saw her alive. Smiling.

"I've looked for you for thirty years, Gilley."

Stoop is trying to say something. Probably a denial of some sort. The man expected that.

In time he'll slice his throat, just like Gilley did to his mother. But there's no rush.

The man calmly clutches Stoop by the chin to hold his head in place, and trims a couple inches off the man's hairline to give himself a bigger canvas to work with.

"The more you struggle and try to move, the deeper the blade will go," the man says, and sees a look of bottomless resignation in his captive's eyes, and knows that he's made a sale.

Then he presses the tip of his knife against Stoop's pale forehead and begins carving a stick figure.

Chapter 88

Chapa's route to the house was determined by the shadows from trees in the front lawns and the vehicles parked in driveways. When he was just a yard away, he crossed the street again, back to the side opposite the house, the same one his car was parked on, half a block down.

He didn't care if a neighbor saw him crossing their property, or huddling behind an oak tree. What would they do? Call the cops?

It was an unusually warm night. November typically arrived with frigid temperatures and sometimes snow. But Chapa felt warm under his jacket and could feel the sweat gathering along the back of his neck. Though he knew it might have nothing to do with the temperature.

When Chapa was just past the driveway, he decided to take a chance and cross a well-lit section of Elm Grove Street, instead of continuing on another thirty-five feet to where the darkness took over again. He stayed low, like a soldier crossing a trench, until he got to the other side, close to where the white Ford was parked, then slipped around a tall fence and started up the drive.

Had he seen someone come this way? The man who got out of the sedan? Chapa had thought so, but looking back down the street now, he couldn't see his own car, and decided the guy he'd seen was likely the next door neighbor getting home.

Gravel crunched softly underfoot as he approached the front corner of the house, and Chapa felt the muscles in his back stiffen when he tried to limit the noise.

The near half of the narrow drive offered only a smattering of moonlight that fought its way through branches and dying leaves. The long, bowing path was bookended by the house on one side and a fence on the other. Light from another yard rubbed up against the last few feet of the house and spilled onto the gravel and concrete. The shadow of the chain-link fence painted a slanted crisscross grid on the broken concrete, creating a madman's game board in dark and light.

Chapa stayed close to the house as he worked his way up the driveway. Ducking under the first window he passed, Chapa then turned to sneak a look inside. The room was as dark as the rest of the first floor. He paused for a moment and watched for movement, but saw none.

Maybe he had been wrong about the house. He'd already been off about so many different things during the past week. Was he still several days' worth of news behind everyone else?

Turning away from the window, he started up the driveway again, this time with far less hesitation or concern about being seen or heard. Chapa was some thirty feet from the back of the house when the shadows from tall trees gave birth to a silhouette of a man.

He was not very tall or physically imposing. But Chapa stopped and retreated a few steps, not because he was surprised or scared, but out of respect for the gun the man was holding.

"Are you following me? Have you been following me?"

Chapa squinted, trying to get a better look.

"I asked you a question," George Forsythe said, stepping into the meager light. The shadows painting a complex pattern across his face.

"No, George, I did not know you'd be here."

"Then why are you here?" He spoke in a low, controlled growl, punctuating his words with tight jabs of his gun hand.

Chapa extended his hands as he spoke, open palm, to show Forsythe he wasn't armed.

"I followed a couple of leads to this house. Had a sense something might be happening here tonight."

Forsythe lowered his head, but the weapon remained pointed at Chapa.

"Too many people have died already, Chapa. This ends tonight. But it's got nothing to do with you. Get the hell out of here."

"But, George—"

"No," Forsythe said, then recoiled a little, as though his voice had escaped with more force than he'd intended. "Listen, Alex, turn around, walk away, and keep walking."

"Will you talk to me after all of this, whatever this is, is over?"

Forsythe's shoulders slumped as he shook his head. "No. But if I were you I'd round up the people I love and leave this town for a while."

Chapa took cautious steps toward Forsythe, until he could start to make out his features.

"Let me go with you, George. I spoke with Bendix, he told me how—"

"Bendix? What do you know about Bendix?" His gun hand was trembling. "Turn around right now and walk away, Chapa, or you will be next."

Chapa started to say something, but stopped as he watched Forsythe raise and steady the gun, and aim it at his face.

"Chakowski wasn't supposed to die, you understand that?"

"Sure, I understand."

"We were only planning to leave your reporter friend a little warning. That was all. I'm just an electrician. And that's all I did."

"I believe you."

"But somebody changed something," Forsythe said and looked up toward the house. "Son of a bitch knew how to rig an explosion."

"It wasn't your fault, George."

Forsythe was shaking his head like something was rattling around in there.

"Just get out of here, Chapa, now."

After taking one final look into the man's eyes and seeing nothing but a dark swill of desperation, Chapa turned and walked down the driveway without looking back. He didn't have to look to know Forsythe was still standing there, still pointing the gun at the back of his head.

Chapter 89

Chapa walked down the street and straight to his car, looking back at the house every few steps. The light was still on in an upstairs window, but there was no sign of Forsythe in the front yard or along the driveway.

He got in, started the engine, and drove off, slowing as he passed the house so Forsythe would see him drive by—if he was still watching. Chapa turned left at the first intersection, and then again at the next one, onto the parallel street on the other side of the block, and parked the car.

Chapa had counted the number of houses from 414 Elm Grove to the corner—there were six—and hoped that each had a matching backyard neighbor. The sixth house along this street was a simple brick ranch with a dark green van parked in the driveway and an old red pickup truck along the front curb.

There were lights on in what Chapa assumed was the living room, and more along the back that poured across the driveway, probably through a kitchen window or the landing on the way down to the basement. Chapa got out and approached the house, walking down the sidewalk like he was just another neighbor out for an evening stroll.

Chapa paused when he reached a hedge that ran the

length of the driveway before it disappeared into the darkness past the two-car garage. He looked around and across the street. There were lights on in several nearby homes, but the yards and street were empty.

He turned up the driveway, squeezing past the van, then walked brisk and stayed low. This pavement was smooth and his steps were quiet. The smell of fabric softener spilled out through a steam vent on the side of the house, near a basement window. There were small bushes along the opposite side of the driveway and a basketball hoop above the wide garage door, its net so new it almost glowed.

As Chapa slipped past a side door, he heard a dog bark inside the house. Then again. Now more intense and the animal seemed to be following him toward the back of the house.

When he heard voices coming from inside, Chapa knew the time for coyness was over. He sprinted down the rest of the driveway and into the blackness along the side of the garage.

The dog's barking drifted away into the background, then stopped altogether. Chapa imagined the poor animal being admonished by annoyed owners.

Or perhaps they were about to let the dog out.

Remembering how he'd noticed the fences lining three sides of the yard, Chapa knew he had at least one more obstacle ahead. When he reached the back of the garage, he saw that there were actually two fences pressed against one another.

The near one was a newer, natural wood picket fence standing roughly four feet. Directly behind it was a collection of faded brown splinters that may have once passed for a fence, now held together by twisted, rusted wires.

Apparently the owners of this house had wanted so badly to separate themselves from their neighbors that they'd built a fence against an existing one on the other side. It surprised Chapa that they had not built it much higher.

A series of unruly bushes and tall weeds blocked Chapa's view of the house he was heading for. But one of those bushes also offered a high branch he could grasp to lift himself over both fences. He anchored his foot in the V-shaped elbow between two pickets and searched for stable footing along the older fence. There was none.

Realizing that he'd have to make a leap for it, Chapa placed each foot on pointed picket tips, clutched the branch with both hands, and jumped. The two fences were only separated by six inches or so, but when he heard the branch snap Chapa knew he should've thought twice about this.

He fell to the side, just beyond the second fence, landing on his left shoulder and feeling the bite from an old wound. His trailing leg caught on the wire, the old metal chewing through his jeans and into the flesh of his thigh.

Chapa groaned as he yanked free, taking several rotted slats with him. He rolled into a squat behind the bushes and pressed a hand against his leg, deciding to ignore the ache in his shoulder and back.

Through the branches he could see the unkempt lawn, and the back of the house, but no sign of Forsythe or anyone else. Locating an opening between the bushes, Chapa squeezed through.

The yard was littered with twigs, rocks, and more broken pieces of fencing. As he came around the garage, Chapa saw an awning above a small landing that led to the back door. Through a warped metal screen he saw the door was open.

Needing to get a look inside, Chapa crept toward the house, stepping as lightly as he could manage on a bed of dried twigs and dead leaves. Three cement steps, the bottom one crumbling, led up to the door.

Chapa skipped the first step, but found the second was also is bad shape. He leaned toward the door and listened. A man's voice drifted out from a distant room, perhaps on the second floor.

Then he heard a second man, calmer, no hint of stress in

his voice. But Chapa could not make out what they were saying.

The police should be there in no more than ten or fifteen minutes. But what if Jackson had not taken him seriously?

Chapa knew the cops downtown had zero respect for him. He'd been an irritant, one who occasionally showed them up by revealing a crime that area police had not yet confirmed, or the details of an investigation before they were officially made public.

Would they leave him hanging? The department, yes. But not Tom Jackson. Chapa believed that, at the very least, Jackson would come by and bring a cruiser with him.

But when? How soon?

The voices inside seemed to get a little louder, but Chapa still couldn't make out what they were saying. If he took just a single step inside he might be able to hear everything. That would be good, Chapa thought, he could tell Jackson and his men what to expect when they got there.

The lower floor appeared to be empty, no lights on anywhere, no one to see or hear him enter. And if anyone did come, he could rush out of the house and into the night without being seen.

As he slowly reached for the small round knob to open the screen door, Chapa had another thought, or a rather a series of them in the form of images. He saw Nikki's face, then Erin's, and Mike's.

What the hell am I about to do?

His relationship with Erin was on the ropes because of situations like this, and she didn't know the worst of it yet. Nikki expected her dad to come home for dinner. To be there for her as she grew up, graduated from high school, then college. To walk her down the aisle at her wedding. Mike had not known any other father figure. What kind of example had Chapa been?

These thoughts melded together, then allied with Chapa's growing concern about the wisdom of charging into a house that he was supposed to have been brought to by force. He pulled away from the door, and carefully stepped back down.

The police would be there soon. He'd lean on Tom Jackson to let him follow his men inside. Maybe Jackson would agree, otherwise Chapa would have to find another way in. Regardless, he'd be the only newsman there, and he'd get the story.

He was a father, and man that a woman he loved, a great woman, counted on to be there for her and her child. Running through darkened doorways and into dangerous houses was a job for the police. Chapa would wait until they arrived.

That decision felt right. But Chapa thought about Tim Haas. Could he be in that house? In trouble? Or worse?

A high-pitched moan from somewhere inside the house invaded Chapa's thoughts. So loud it escaped through both an upstairs window as well as the screen door, like stereo. Then another, followed by what sounded like a muffled scream.

Chapa looked around at the ground by his feet and located a piece of broken fencing that was probably as solid as anything he was going to find out here. He picked it up and gripped it tightly in his left palm.

Then he heard another cry, this one even more agonized and primitive than the others. Chapa instinctively reached into his coat pocket and pulled out his press credentials. He draped the badge around his neck as though it would protect him somehow, like a white flag or a Red Cross uniform.

Then he rushed up to the door, swung it open, and slipped inside, without giving it another thought or allowing for even the slightest instant of hesitation.

Chapter 90

The moment he stepped into the dark kitchen, Chapa was assaulted by a parade of pungent odors that reminded him of rotting food, animal shit, and vermin. He thought he heard mice scurrying inside the walls and behind cabinets.

What Chapa did hear was the creaking of floorboards as they seemed to shift, expand, contract slightly with each step. He tried to tread lightly, though it was no use. But he told himself this house probably had so many creaks and squeaks that his footsteps might not stand out over the rest of it.

As Chapa slowly walked through the doorway leading out of the kitchen, and into a narrow hallway, he saw there were two rooms, one along each side. The closest was on the left, its door was closed tight. Chapa gently leaned against it and listened for any sound inside, but all he heard was the shuffling of feet on the second floor.

Chapa slowly placed his hand on the doorknob, tightened his grip, and tried to turn it. But there was no give. The door was locked solid. He thought about whispering Tim Haas' name, in case he was behind the door, but decided against it when he heard a muffled voice coming from upstairs.

The door to the room on the right side of the hallway was

slightly ajar. A hint of moonlight formed a thin line through the open crack. Chapa eased up to the door, cocked his weapon, raising the wooden slat up above his head, ready to strike, then wrapped his fingers around the edge of the door and coaxed it open.

His attention was immediately drawn to the crumpled mass on the floor. He could make out an arm extending from the darkness, and a hand lying open, palm up. Chapa swallowed hard, reached for the light switch and flipped it on.

Any search for Tim Haas was over. The young man Chapa had met just a few days ago now lay sprawled out on the floor. His blood-drenched corpse had been left in a spread-eagle pose—arms and legs extended straight out from the torso, head centered, eyes open.

The look on the dead man's face was one of complete disbelief. As if he had not yet accepted what happened to him—even in death.

It was hard to single out the killing cut. Tim's throat was a tangle of fleshy shards and blood. His shirt was ripped open, and his bare chest had been sliced so many times in every direction it appeared as though the skin had been shredded.

Chapa looked away, then turned the lights off and closed the door. Doing his best to blot out the image of what was once Tim Haas, he continued down the hallway until he reached the stairs.

It was a straight shot up to the second floor, but first Chapa would have to get around the twisted body that was covering much of the bottom three steps. This guy had been stabbed in the gut, the chest, and half his neck had been sliced off. Judging from the jagged bone protruding through his forearm, he had also been pushed down the stairs.

As Chapa began to maneuver around the corpse, he got a good look at the man's face. His expression suggested that, like Tim Haas, he'd never seen it coming. But even more important to Chapa was the fact that he recognized the corpse.

They'd had a standoff outside this same house a few days

ago, during Chapa's first visit. And Chapa wondered now if Cal had been his real name. As the events of the past several hours raced through his mind, Chapa realized that he may have heard this man's last words.

Bring him to the house.

Chapter 91

A carpet runner stretched from the top of the stairs to where the corpse lay at the bottom. Chapa's steps were soft, though he'd never been accused of being light on his feet. As he took each step with care, Chapa couldn't help but look back over his shoulder every few seconds.

A triangle of light covered the upper half of the steps, and Chapa could see the carpeting he was walking on was gray and lavender, badly faded and frayed. His steps became even more cautious now as he leaned into the light. Projected on the wall to his right was the crooked shadow of a railing, bowed and weakened by time and wear, that ran the length of the second-floor hallway.

He heard the sound of two or three men. Only one was talking, the others were making desperate, pained noises.

As Chapa stepped up onto the landing, he looked back down the stairs once more. For some reason he felt compelled to make sure there was still a corpse at the bottom. Though he'd never believed in ghosts or the supernatural, Chapa decided that if a house could truly be haunted, this one was a prime candidate.

The wall facing the steps was bare, except for a single nail protruding from the plaster. There were more nails like that one along the hallway walls. Apparently the current tenants weren't much into art or family photos.

Slipping around the end of the railing, Chapa found he was no more than five feet from the door to the only room in the house that held any signs of activity. He heard the sound of movement from inside the room. There were other sounds too, low pitched and metallic.

Chapa pressed his shoulder against the doorframe, and tried to lean in and get a better look. A man's shadow crossed the only wall Chapa could see. It grew large, then became smaller, before moving out of his line of sight.

Another groan. Then a voice.

"Yes, yes, tell me all about how it hurts." Followed by a whisper, barely audible. "I want to know."

The voice was the same one Chapa had expected to hear, but it sounded different somehow. Too calm, almost free of emotion.

Chapa wanted to get a better look beyond the door before deciding whether to barge in or retreat back down the stairs and wait for the police to arrive. He took a large, calculated step across the width of the doorway, then pivoted and turned his back to the wall.

But he miscalculated, and his shoulders landed against it, making a soft but audible *thud*. Now there was no sound or movement inside the room, and Chapa knew he'd been heard.

He had to act—now.

Electing to go in hard instead of quiet, assuming his presence there was already known, Chapa shoved the door open and rushed in, the wooden fence slat raised above his head.

He'd planned on attacking once he was inside the room. But what he found on the other side of the door scrambled Chapa's senses, as his plans tumbled to the floor in tatters.

Chapter 92

Charles Stoop wasn't talking anymore.

During their conversation, back when the inner workings of Oakton's political and business machine functioned like a carefully crafted instrument, Chapa had wondered what it would take to get this guy to shut up. Now he knew.

Stoop was bleeding from his forehead as well as several other areas of his body. His white shirt was soaked with fresh blood in a way that reminded Chapa of the end of Martin Clarkson's life.

But this setup was far more elaborate than the inside of any windmill. Stoop had been shackled to the wall. His wrists, waist, and ankles held in place by manacles, his bare feet suspended a few inches off the ground.

The plaster was chipped and cracked in those areas where the chains and the bindings were fixed to the wall with long bolts. And Chapa knew Charles Stoop had struggled to free himself. His body convulsing with pain. Until he had no fight left in him.

The wall was adorned with stick figures painted in bright red blood. A few were starting to take on a less glossy, brownish patina. It looked like something out of a chamber of horrors or a French dungeon from the Dark Ages.

Blood was leaking from his forehead, pouring out through a series of jagged cuts, and washing down his face. His fingers and toes were losing blood also, and Chapa saw why. The soft flesh between each of his twenty digits had been sliced.

Stoop's mouth was taped shut, but that was just a formality at this point. He didn't appear to have the strength to speak, or much interest in communicating.

George Forsythe lay on the floor near a window. Eyes wide, he was twitching just a little. Chapa assumed Forsythe was going into shock, judging from the wide bright red gash that extended from his left armpit, up to his shoulder and neck, before continuing its path across his cheek and temple.

The gun he'd pointed at Chapa minutes ago in the driveway had been discarded in a far corner of the floor, a half-dozen feet from Forsythe's outstretched right arm. It may as well have been a half dozen miles, Forsythe didn't look like he had much chance of reaching it.

"Alex Chapa." The voice was calm, flat, like someone reading to himself.

Chapa turned quickly and stared at the man who'd been standing behind the door.

"Are you still going by Greg Vinsky, or have you already moved on from that name?"

He seemed to be looking past Chapa, as though he was waiting for something to happen.

"Your friend isn't coming," Chapa said. "I saw him at the Megamart, he had a run-in with some avocados."

Vinsky smiled, but his eyes revealed no emotion. In one hand he was holding the largest hunting knife Chapa had ever seen. He had a cell phone clipped to one side of his belt, and what appeared to be a holster cradling a large device of some sort or the other.

"Well done, Alex. Yes, *very* well done."

Which part? Chapa thought. *And what the hell happens now?* was Chapa's next thought.

"You're not at all surprised, Alex?"

Chapa's mind was sprinting in several directions at once. Could he reach the gun and fire before Vinsky hacked off one of his arms? What if he rushed him, used the fence slat to take a swipe at the knife? He'd have one shot at it—if he was lucky. And most importantly, how soon would Jackson and his men get there?

"I figured it out some time ago," Chapa lied. "But I wasn't sure until today."

"How? How did you figure it out some time ago?"

"The photo in Martin Clarkson's hand, you put it there." Chapa was playing an angle, figuring Vinsky would be interested in how someone had seen beyond the veneer and into his secret world. Interested enough that it might buy some time. "Everyone thought Clarkson had pulled it out of his wallet as he lay dying. But that's not what happened."

"Oh no, that's not what happened. I brought that photo with me. Took it myself just before Mrs. Clarkson had that terrible accident."

"You like taking pictures of—how did you put it? *Disturbing images?*"

Vinsky grinned as he took a measured step toward Chapa. Straight at him, not favoring one side or the other, narrowing the angles to the door and the gun at the same time.

"Is that all, Alex? The photo?"

"No. There was the dead businessman in Baltimore, the one burned so badly the police had to guess his I.D. You were Roland King then. Who was really in that car?

"Just a former associate. Someone no one would miss."

Chapa nodded. That was what he'd assumed.

"And Jim Chakowski helped. You may have ended his life, but not his work."

Vinsky's empty expression returned.

"Clarkson got to him, and Jim learned a few things he didn't need to know. He became unpredictable, erratic, jittery. Now you look kinda jittery, Alex. Are you jittery?"

Chapa understood now that Vinsky was trying to take stock of how many tracks he'd have to cover.

"Sure, I guess so, considering that one of our community's leaders is bleeding on your wall over there."

"Oh him, no, he's not one of our community's leaders," Vinsky said, then leaned in toward Stoop and casually slashed his rib cage with a single swipe, leaving a six-inch streak of blood across his abdomen.

The flow immediately began running down the side of Stoop's shirt and onto the right leg of his pressed gray slacks. Stoop groaned, but it was a delayed reaction, then Chapa heard him start grinding his teeth.

Vinsky watched with apparent curiosity as Stoop twisted in agony, and for an instant Chapa thought he had an opening. Could he reach the door or maybe take a swing at Vinsky? But his indecision cost Chapa, as Vinsky turned back toward him and all good options were instantly gone.

"His real name, or at least the one I knew him by, was Gilley, and he murdered my mother thirty-two years ago tonight."

On the wall behind Vinsky, Charles Stoop seemed to be trying to shake his head.

"That's why I came to Oakton."

"He's a stickman?"

Vinsky's eyes narrowed and appeared to darken. He stared at Chapa as though trying to see through him.

"You know," Vinsky said, his voice husky, not quite as calm.

"I assumed."

"You could say he's the original stickman."

Chapa pointed to Forsythe, who appeared to be trembling just a bit more than before.

"Is he a stickman, too?"

"George, a stickman, too? In a sense. There's blood on his hands."

Chapa tightened his grip on his makeshift weapon. He'd

been so focused on the three-ring circus of horrors that he'd forgotten he was still holding it in attack position.

"Do you mean the explosion at Chakowski's house?"

"Not just that. George did set up the explosion at Chakowski's house, but I added a little extra *boom*. No, it's something that happened earlier."

Vinsky then looked over toward Forsythe. *Take one step in that direction,* Chapa thought. *Just one.*

"I'm going to tell him about Houston, George. Maybe it'll be in all the papers," Vinsky said, then turned back toward Chapa and took a small step in his direction.

"You see, Alex, there was this strip mall back in Houston where George used to be a big man some time in the last century. Then one day there's an electrical fire, which kills thirteen people. Thirteen people—funny, isn't it? Unlucky number thirteen. Anyway, George had done the electrical contract work, but he's so well connected—"

Vinsky paused, apparently to see if Chapa got the pun. He did, but chose not to react.

"He's so well connected that they manage to blame it on the wiring, or bad luck, or whatever. But in fact, George had hired a couple of untrained workers to do part of the job."

Chapa looked over at Forsythe, who wasn't moving anymore, except for the tears rolling down his battered face.

"He hired some cons. Cheap labor, but not too competent. You might've met one of them on the way up here."

"So you blackmailed George?"

"So I blackmailed George, yes, I guess so."

"And you're going to kill him tonight."

"Yes, tonight. I gave him a charge with my stun gun," Vinsky said, tapping the larger of the two holsters on his belt. "Maybe I'll give him a few more before I bleed him out. Don't know yet. Won't know until the moment."

Chapa realized that Vinsky had calmly and with minimal effort narrowed the distance between them while also cutting off his path to the door.

"So he's the only reason you came here? You came to Oakton to kill Charles Stoop?"

"Yes, Alex, I came to Oakton to kill this monster. Unfortunately I had to eliminate some others. But I did rid this town of a few bits of scum."

Chapa now understood that he'd made a mistake when he first spoke to Greg Vinsky, a few days ago at City Hall. He'd assumed that Vinsky's unusual speech pattern was strictly a trained way of relating to potential customers. It may have been that, but the way he repeated a person's name and how he would regurgitate what had just been said to him also had another purpose. It was his way of feigning empathy—an emotion that probably didn't come easily to Vinsky, if at all. Like a person who phonetically speaks a foreign language that they don't understand.

Chapa decided to try the technique on Vinsky.

"A few bits of scum, sure, but there's a lot more work to do here, Greg. Don't you think?"

Vinsky tilted his head just slightly to one side, like a dog does when he's trying to process what he sees.

"What are you saying?"

"I'm saying that you came here, dealt with some of the scum, eliminated a few stickmen, but there's a lot more work to do." Out of the corner of his eye Chapa saw Forsythe slowly, painfully inching toward the gun, gradually willing his entire body closer to the discarded weapon. He decided to give the wounded man some encouragement. "A man, a real man finishes what he starts."

"You mean here, in this place?"

"Of course."

"I didn't come to save this place. This town can rot in its own perfect hell."

No more than thirty inches separated Forsythe's fingers from the gun. Chapa hoped to God the man was right handed.

"Any more questions, Alex? I didn't want you to die before you had the whole story. You're a quality newsman, and you deserve to get the whole story."

Chapa still had a great many questions, even more now that Vinsky had put it that way. But Forsythe wasn't moving toward the gun anymore, and Vinsky would glance back in that direction soon enough, anyhow. Chapa decided to go on the offensive.

"What do you mean before I die?"

"No, Alex. My exact words were, I didn't want you to die before—"

"I just assumed you wanted to tell me your story before the police get here?"

"Police?"

"Yes, police. I called them earlier, on my way to this house. By the way, do you live here?"

"Live here, this house, no. This is my workplace. My former assistants lived here. When did you call the police, how long ago?"

Vinsky's mind was starting to wander.

"And what about Tim Haas? Did you force him to call me?"

"Tim Haas, ambitious young man, too much so. Yes, he was forced to call you. How long ago did you call the police, Alex?"

Forsythe was inching toward the gun again, but he was still much too far away to reach it.

"Tim must have learned something about you. About who you were. Maybe tried to hold it against you."

Vinsky was looking down, his head jerking a bit from side to side, like he was having a small-scale seizure.

"Yes, Tim Haas let his ambition get the best of him. Learned who I was, tried to hold it against me."

Then, just when Chapa was starting to get a sense of control over the situation, beginning to see a possible out, all the hatred and violence in Vinsky seemed to coalesce, then surge to the surface.

"When did you call the police!" he screamed, and lunged at Chapa in one coordinated instant, thrusting the blade straight at his chest.

Chapa managed to slide to the left, away from the knife, like a matador who momentarily lost sight of how much damage an angry bull can do. He swung the wooden slat at Vinsky's hand. Missed. Then Chapa retreated another defensive step and decided to answer him before he attacked again.

"Twenty minutes ago, maybe a few more."

Vinsky withdrew, straightened his shoulders, and put on his cloak of calm again.

"That's a long time."

You're telling me, Chapa thought.

"That means one of two things, doesn't it, Alex?"

Chapa did not answer, opting instead to remain coiled and ready to defend against the next attack.

"It means that they will either be here soon, or not at all."

"They'll be here. Maybe they're outside now."

Vinsky shook his head, said, "Maybe they're done believing you," and smiled.

He had a point, one that Chapa had fought to avoid thinking about until right now. Jackson should've been there ten minutes ago. To make matters worse, Vinsky knew he had a point. That's why he was so calm again—Vinsky was back in control.

Chapa knew he had to do something to change that.

"I told them who would be here. I gave them your name."

Vinsky's face became like a blank canvas, revealing nothing because there was nothing there. Chapa decided to continue down this road.

"Maybe they're at your house right now. They might've stopped there first to confirm my story."

Damn, that almost made sense. Chapa knew it wasn't the case, but he could sell this.

"I'm thinking that whatever they find there, Greg, will probably result in more cops being sent here."

Vinsky seemed to be processing. Chapa searched for an opening, any opportunity to use the slat to knock the knife out of Vinsky's hand or slam it into the side of his head and make a move to the gun Forsythe was still creeping toward, much too slowly.

"Yes, you would have called the police. You came here looking for Tim Haas, heard Gilley or George and rushed up here." Vinsky sounded as calm as someone analyzing a casual game of chess. "The fact that you brought a weapon, such as it is, suggests you knew there was danger here."

His face at peace, Vinsky nodded at Chapa, who was still looking for that opportunity to strike and was beginning to realize it wasn't coming.

"Only a madman would come here without calling the police," Vinsky added, then took a step back toward Stoop, but not far enough from the door for Chapa to make his move.

Vinsky looked at Stoop, whose brow was covered in blood, fresh over dried, and overflowing like a gutter, and said, "Well then, let's wrap this up."

With a single, decisive step and thrust Vinsky drove his knife into Stoop's neck until its red-tinged tip emerged on the other side. He then yanked it straight forward, slicing through the front of his neck, sending a bloody spray across the room.

Chapa tried to twist away from it, but saw some of Stoop's blood land on his coat, felt tiny warm drops splash on his cheek and forehead. In the moment Chapa spent wiping the blood off his face and onto the right sleeve of his coat, Vinsky shifted his attention.

"Now, George, we both know how this ends," Chapa heard Vinsky say, then turned to look.

Vinsky was standing in place, not advancing toward his

next intended victim. Then Chapa saw why. Forsythe had managed to get his right hand on the weapon and was now pointing it, though with little certainty, at Vinsky's chest.

"Why, George, why would you want to do that?" Vinsky said, sounding like a man who was a seeing a done deal going bad. "Wasn't it you, George, you, who told me too many people had died already? You're responsible for at least one of those deaths. Let me do what I have to, and no one will ever know what you did."

Chapa saw an opening. He gripped the piece of wood with both hands, and cocked it back in a way that would've made Billy Williams proud, then moved in, determined to crush the back of Vinsky's head with one swing.

But he never got the chance.

Chapter 93

Chapa never saw the shot being fired, its sound bouncing off the walls, echoing down the stairway

He did see how Forsythe's entire body strained as he summoned whatever strength he had left just to pull the trigger. And Chapa also witnessed the results.

The bullet blew a hole through Vinsky's right shoulder and came out the backside, before slamming into a wall and biting off a dusty chunk of plaster.

It spun Vinsky around and left him facing Chapa, the knife still clutched in his hand. It happened in an instant. Then time slowed.

But this was not over. A through-and-through wasn't going to stop Vinsky, and it would likely take Forsythe a while to work up to another shot.

Chapa lunged, and swung the splintered and narrow slab of wood, catching Vinsky flush across the side of the face. The impact sent a jolt through Chapa's body, and pain ripped across his back and shoulders.

But instead of falling down or to the side, Vinsky stumbled toward Chapa, thrusting his knife at him, catching him in the ribs.

Chapa heard the blade cut through his suede jacket, then

his shirt, an instant before he felt it slice into his flesh. He recoiled from the slash of pain, then his mind kicked into overdrive.

With a single, force-filled swing Chapa knocked the knife out of Vinsky's hand, sending it flying out of the room, into the dark hallway, and through the railing. He heard it tumble down the stairs.

Chapa felt a sticky warmth against his wounded side, but he didn't let himself dwell on it. No time to bleed.

He struck again, hard, anger replacing fear, driven by a bolt of rage for his daughter, and Jim Chakowski and Warren, and Martin Clarkson and his wife, and all the other families with empty chairs at the table. The fencing snapped in half from the impact of Chapa's next blow against Vinsky's skull.

Vinsky tumbled toward the doorway, then through it. Chapa followed, like they were tethered to one another, catching him in the hallway and jamming the broken end of the board into Vinsky's neck, pushing until he felt it pierce skin.

Chapa had never killed a man, but he was prepared to keep pushing until wood splinters emerged through the other side. But Vinsky grabbed the board, and pulled it away from his neck as blood colored his shirt around the hole in his shoulder.

Seeing a better option, Chapa let go of the board and slammed his fist into Vinsky's wounded shoulder, sending him into the railing.

He saw Vinsky wince, heard him groan with agony, then another sound, a different sound. Chapa heard the sharp *snap*, an instant before the railing gave way and Vinsky fell backwards, beyond Chapa's reach.

There was a loud *crack* as Vinsky crashed into the steps. Chapa rushed to the edge and watched the man tumble. He seemed to bounce a little, slam into another step, then roll and slide the rest of the way, until his fall was finally stopped by the dead body at the bottom of the stairs.

Vinsky lay motionless. His body contorted, limbs appearing to go in different directions at once. A bundle of fury and hatred reduced to a bloody heap of nothing.

But Chapa wasn't feeling at all secure, let alone safe. He needed to make sure Vinsky was as dead as he appeared.

Looking down, Chapa scanned the steps for the knife, but couldn't see it. Maybe it had fallen all the way to the first floor. In which case, it was down there somewhere in the darkness.

Chapa needed a better option. He needed Forsythe's gun.

Taking one last look at Vinsky's body, studying it for movement and seeing none, not even a twitch, Chapa turned and rushed back toward the room. Getting the gun from Forsythe would not take much effort. Chapa was sure of that, having witnessed how the man had strained to reach the weapon and the energy he'd expended just to squeeze off a single shot.

He was wrong. The moment he walked in the room Chapa knew this was going to be anything but easy.

Forsythe was still sprawled on the floor, his life gurgling out through the wounds on his chest and face. But he'd gathered enough strength to hold the gun in both hands, and steady the weapon.

And he was aiming it at Chapa.

Chapter 94

The way Chapa figured it, George Forsythe had been pointing the gun at the doorway when he walked in, ready to shoot whomever entered the room. Set to defend himself against the man he knew as Greg Vinsky.

"It's okay, George," Chapa said, raising his palms just as he had earlier in the driveway. "Vinsky is lying at the bottom of the stairs. He's not moving, I don't suspect he ever will again."

But Forsythe did not lower the weapon.

"Let me have the gun and I'll go downstairs, make sure he's dead, and then call the police again. I'm pretty sure they'll come this time."

Chapa smiled, hoping that would ease the wounded man's nerves. But his smile vanished when he saw Forsythe tighten his grip and narrow one eye to a squint just before he pulled the trigger.

The bullet took out another piece of plaster wall as Chapa dove to floor, rolled, and looked back to the door, expecting to see Vinsky standing there, the target of Forsythe's shot.

But the doorway was empty.

And then Chapa understood. There were to be no survivors. No one who could tell the story of what Vinsky had made Forsythe and the others do. Nothing that could force a grieving family member to alter their impressions of the dead.

George Forsythe was in no way an ally. The next shot took a few specks of dust off the left shoulder of Chapa's jacket.

He wasn't going to let Forsythe get off another. Scrambling to his feet, Chapa arced around the room, and rushed the man as he struggled to change the angle of his arm.

Chapa dove and grabbed the weapon with both hands. Pulling it away took much less effort than he'd expected. And the moment the gun was out of Forsythe's hands his body retreated and he closed his eyes, as though the weapon had been the only thing sustaining him.

Wasting no time, Chapa got to his feet and hurried out the door, into the hallway, and around the fractured railing. He made it down two steps before stopping cold.

Chapa stared down at the bottom of the stairs and into the darkness beyond, and saw only one corpse. Vinsky was gone.

Chapter 95

When the cops later asked him how he could've been so sure, Chapa would only be able to tell them that he just was. He was certain Vinsky wasn't in the house anymore.

Doing his best to ignore the throbbing in his side, paying little attention to the cut along his ribs that screamed at him with each step he took down the stairs, Chapa made it to the first floor. He started for the windows across the front of the house, hoping he might see which direction Vinsky had gone, but stopped when he noticed the blood trail across the wood floor.

The small red drops shone in the darkness, leading him down the hall, toward the kitchen. That's where he lost the trail, but Chapa knew where it led.

He looked around the corner, toward the dark hallway and into the kitchen beyond. The back door was open—had he left it that way? Chapa thought he caught of glimpse of movement in the backyard.

He was about to head in that direction, arms outstretched, his hand clutching the gun, index finger on the trigger, when something crashed into the front door. Chapa froze. And then it happened again, as loud as a canon shot, forcing the door open and nearly knocking off its hinges.

An instant later a half-dozen cops poured into the house.

"Drop the gun!"

"Drop it!"

Chapa did as told. Then, as two officers rushed him, he heard a familiar voice.

"It's okay," Tom Jackson said. "It's Chapa, he's okay."

For a moment, Chapa felt a sense of relief as he watched a uniformed policewoman pick the gun up off the floor. Jackson was silhouetted in the doorway by the light from a nearby streetlamp. It was the most light Chapa had seen in this part of the house, and looking around he could now see that the first floor was empty except for the body at the foot of the stairs.

"Tom, he's out there, Greg Vinsky."

"Greg Vinsky? What about him?"

"It's him—he's responsible for the stickman killings. He ran out the back just a couple of minutes ago." The other cops had stopped what they were doing. "He's wounded."

Jackson ordered three heavily armed officers to go out back and start canvassing the area on foot. Then he told the other two to get back out to their cruiser, radio in for assistance, and begin scanning an eight-block radius.

"We have to get you looked at, Alex," Jackson said, then told one of the other uniformed officers to radio for an ambulance as he searched for the light switch by the battered door. "Let's get some light in here, first."

In an instant of absolute clarity, Chapa saw the future.

"No! Tom! No!"

Chapa rushed the doorway as Jackson flipped the switch. He buried his shoulder into the confused detective's gut as the walls began to emit a sizzling noise.

Driving his body through the doorway, he carried Jackson with him like a linebacker tackling an opponent. They were outside, tumbling down the front steps, and into the yard.

A cop emerged from his cruiser, weapon drawn. Chapa tried to wave him back.

And then the world around them exploded.

Chapter 96

The noise from the blast blocked out all other sounds. It was followed by a too brief silence which was replaced by cries for help, car alarms, and confusion.

Shattered glass, pieces of wood, and broken plaster showered across the front lawn, and covered much of Chapa's body. A section of flooring slammed into his back, and he instinctively rolled to one side an instant before a shard of window glass stabbed the grass he'd been lying on.

It only lasted a few seconds, but the rain of debris seemed to go on much longer.

The air was thick with the smell of fresh smoke and old dust. Chapa stumbled to his feet and saw the cop who had gotten out of his cruiser just before the blast sprawled out on the lawn. There was blood on his face and uniform, but at least he was moving.

Tom Jackson was lying fifteen feet away from Chapa, under a ten-foot section of wall. He was not moving.

Chapa ran over to him. He needed all the strength left in his body to lift one side of the slab. An officer rushed over and grabbed the other end, and together they tossed it aside.

"I think the damn thing broke my arm," Jackson said, grimacing.

Jackson kept his left elbow tucked against his side as he sat up, and he had a few scratches on his face. But otherwise, he seemed okay.

Chapa and the uniformed officer helped Jackson get to his feet.

"Let's get some help in here," Jackson said, back in charge.

Over by a cruiser, a badly shaken officer was already radioing for help. Chapa staggered in that direction, wanting to put some distance between himself and the house.

When he reached the curb, Chapa turned and looked back toward the house, expecting to see a replay of what he'd seen at Jim Chakowski's. This was worse.

Part of the second floor had collapsed into the first, and a portion of the roof along the right side had given way. But the area of the room where Chapa had found Charles Stoop and George Forsythe was still largely intact. Chapa realized that meant Forsythe could still be alive, but he didn't care one way or another.

Chapa's vision began to blur just as his hearing returned to normal. He felt a swell of heat that started in his shoulders, then rushed to his head. Chapa sensed he was falling, a moment before passing out against the curb.

Chapter 97

In his final moments of life, George Forsythe confirmed Chapa's version of events, but not his own direct involvement in the death of Jim Chakowski. That story would be left for Chapa to tell.

Police found three dead bodies at the house before Forsythe increased that number by one. Several of the neighbors had heard the gunshots, but no one saw a man running from the house moments before the police arrived.

Tom Jackson had been delayed at his desk for a few minutes, and made a call for a cruiser to be sent to Elm Grove Street. The car was on its way when a report came in that someone had heard a shot. One cruiser became three and the situation took on a life of its own.

The house had been rigged to blow the moment that the light switch in the front room was flipped on. An investigator determined there was a trip switch near the back door that activated the system. Chapa realized that Vinsky must have set it on his way out.

A team of officers, along with a bomb squad, rushed to Vinsky's residence as soon as they heard Chapa's story. Nothing had been done to the wiring there, but what they found was unlike anything any of them had seen before.

The place was empty, as though no one had lived there for months.

"Even the toilet paper holders were empty and polished clean," an officer Chapa recognized just from knocking around town would tell him at the hospital a couple of hours later.

The only signs of Greg Vinsky were a five-shelf bookcase stuffed with legal pads, each filled with hand-drawn stick figures, and a bulletin board covered in photos. The cops were busy trying to match the folks in the pictures to recent murder cases.

Chapa was being worked on in the same section of the emergency room as Tom Jackson, who had indeed sustained a mild fracture, and a few minor lacerations. When the doctor was done setting his arm, Jackson walked over to Chapa, looked at him, and offered a quick, silent nod. It was the one thanks Chapa would get from his friend, but it was more than enough.

The cut along Chapa's ribs required three dozen stitches, the wound in his leg from his fall over the fence was closed with a strip of suture tape, and the doctor recommended he stay overnight for observation.

"You probably have a mild concussion."

Chapa, however, had no interest in doing that. He wanted to give the cops his statement and then get on with it. He had already phoned Matt Sullivan and told him to hold Page One. He was coming in to write it. He also called Erin and assured her that he was okay. But that did little to keep her from crying.

Except for the throbbing in his side and the subtle ringing in his ears, Chapa felt like a million bucks—give or take a million.

But he knew the hurt would settle in later. It always does.

"Doctor says you were lucky. Just a flesh wound, though I suppose a damned painful one."

"Tell you what, Tom, just for kicks you ought to let some

psycho slice your ribs open sometime and see how lucky you feel."

The immediate efforts to locate Greg Vinsky came up empty, and were quickly expanded into a statewide search. The fact that Vinsky was still out there somewhere made Chapa feel thankful that Agent Sandro was looking out for Erin and the kids.

The Oakton Police Department sent a cruiser to patrol Chapa's house just in case Vinsky headed in that direction. But Chapa could've told them they wouldn't find him there.

After they had patched him up and he'd given a statement to Jackson and another officer, the doctor gave Chapa some painkillers and sent him on his way.

"You should've gotten there sooner, Tom. You missed a hell of a show."

"You shouldn't have gone in the house before we got there."

Jackson was right, and they both knew it, but Chapa heard no conviction in the man's voice.

"Alex, tell me you're going home or over to Erin's to rest for a day or two," Jackson said as he helped Chapa slip back into his bloodstained shirt.

"Hell no. I've got a story to write and three hours till deadline," Chapa said, easing himself off the medical table.

For Chapa, going into the office tonight was not only about being a journalist and doing the job. It was therapy.

"Now where did your guys park my car?"

Chapter 98

Leah Carelli was waiting in Chapa's office when he walked in. She'd turned on the desk lamp, which cast a warm glow across her upper body. She was wearing her hair down, which took ten years off, and a tight white top that drew attention to itself.

"You've looked better," she said and leaned back in his chair, arms stretched upward, hands clasped behind her head, her significant breasts front and center.

"You've looked worse."

That made her smile.

"Listen, Leah, I have no clue what you're doing in my office, and if my head wasn't so scrambled right now I'd probably care about the reason, but I've got a story to write."

Leah stared at him for a moment, a half smile decorating her perfectly made-up face. Then she slowly got out of Chapa's chair and repositioned herself on the edge of his desk.

"Word has gotten out around town about what happened tonight."

"Good, that means more papers sold tomorrow."

She smelled soft and sweet like dessert. Chapa reached over and flipped on the ceiling fan.

"Are you hot, Mr. Chapa?"

He looked at the clock on his desk—just under two hours before tomorrow's *Record* would be put to bed.

"Right now, I'm not anything but on a deadline."

Chapa slipped past her and headed for his chair, but Leah grabbed his arm and spun him around. He winced.

"I'm sorry, honey. I didn't realize you were hurt," she said with a lace of concern in her voice, but did not release his arm. "I just need to know what kind of story you're going to write."

"The truthful, fact-filled kind. Those are the ones I'm good at."

Leah slid closer and her chest brushed against Chapa's.

"I hope, Alex, that you condemn the man and not the system."

The fog in Chapa's head was beginning to clear.

"Meaning?"

"Meaning that things work around here, and I like that. When the dust settles, I could be in a really strong position in this town. I could help you."

"How could you do that?"

"I would be your inside source, and you could tap me any time you wanted."

He felt her warm breath touch his lips.

"Then you want me to fudge the story so that you can move up within a corrupt system?"

Chapa was in no mood for subtleties.

"You don't have to fudge anything, Alex. Just keep the focus where it belongs."

Over the course of his career Chapa had received the sort of threats and offers that seemed to attach themselves to certain kinds of stories. But none had ever been delivered in such an appealing package.

"We could be together again, Alex. This time professionally as well as . . . well, you remember." She smiled, not just with her painted lips this time, but her entire face. Chapa remembered loving that smile.

"I'm in a relationship, Leah."

"So? Lots of people are in relationships."

"I'm in love with this woman. Maybe she'll even marry me."

Leah leaned back, away from Chapa, as though she was trying to get a better look at him.

"Are you still grasping for decency, Alex?"

"Maybe. It's not much of a grasp, I'll give you that. But maybe."

She put a gentle hand on his shoulder. Chapa withdrew a little, but Leah's touch did not hurt. It burned.

"I feel like I'm being held together with sutures right now," he said, leveling his shoulders.

"You know, Alex, every attempt you've ever made at being just another straight-up guy has failed. Your marriage, fatherhood, and as for your career—" Leah surveyed the damage to Chapa's body. "Well, just look at you."

Chapa arched back until her hand slid off his shoulder. But it didn't go far, stopping on his chest.

"Could be I'm getting closer with each failure," he said as her hand slipped inside between two buttons. "Anyway, I want to try again, with Erin, for Erin." He took her by the wrist and eased her hand out of his shirt, squeezed it, then let it drop. "For me. Because it's what I want."

"You going to marry this one?"

"Could happen. If I'm lucky."

Leah shook her head as if she knew something Chapa didn't.

"But you're a tramp, Alex. Always have been. It's one of the reasons I like you so much. Oh, you can clean up good, sit next to this woman at PTA meetings, go meet her family, say nice things about their furniture and manicured lawn."

She placed both hands on Chapa's shoulders, slid closer to him on the desk, until her breasts pressed up against him.

"But you're still a tramp. It's what makes you a good reporter. You're not tethered to anyone or anything. That's why you've survived this long, and when the time comes, which it will, you'll follow your instincts again. Just like you did tonight."

Chapa slipped out of Leah's grasp, dropped into his chair, and laughed.

"You're amused, Alex?"

Chapa shook his head, reached down and turned on his computer.

"No, not really. I just realized why I dumped you, way back when."

She started to say something, less friendly now, but Chapa stopped her.

"Tell you what, Leah, if you want we can continue this dime store seduction bit some other time. Right now, I'm wearing a fresh row of stitches in my side, I'm heavily medicated, and I've got a story to write. So please, go find another friend."

Chapa then began writing his story. He did not look away from his monitor when Leah stood and walked out.

Chapter 99

Ninety minutes later, Chapa sent the story in. He had not spared anyone, and he'd been especially tough on the system that had invited someone like Greg Vinsky in, then shielded him.

Matt Sullivan marched into Chapa's office twenty minutes after the story had been filed. He stood in front of Chapa's desk, and said nothing at first, as though he'd known exactly what he wanted to say but then forgot all of it the moment he walked through the door.

"You've been through a lot, Alex," Sullivan said finally, and let gravity and his weight pull him down into the chair across from the desk.

"A lot of people have been through hell because of the man who called himself Greg Vinsky, and some folks never made it back."

"That's some story you wrote tonight."

"Sure is. Macklin going to let it run?"

"Of course he is. With all the attention that's going to rain on this town the last thing he wants to do is appear complicit in covering anything up."

"Damn, you mean his newspaper might actually get ahead of the story this time?"

Sullivan leaned forward, hands clasped in front between his knees as he looked down at his shoes.

"Matt, do you know why I became a journalist?"

After letting out a heavy sigh, Sullivan answered, "Because your father was one."

"Nope."

Sullivan looked up, curious.

"Because my mother's stories about him convinced me that we are the only shield between regular people and tyranny. Because an independent press is a democracy's best friend, and corruption's worst enemy."

Chapa took stock of the way Sullivan was smirking.

"Did you ever believe that, Matt? I mean, before this became just a job to you, something to preserve at all cost, no compromise too big as long as your name was still at the top of the staff box?"

"That's not fair, Alex."

Chapa eased out of his chair, struggling not to wince from the pain in his side, walked around the desk and sat on a corner.

"You're probably right, it's not. But I hurt like hell, I'm tired, and it would be nice if my newspaper behaved more like a newspaper."

Sullivan nodded, but Chapa understood it wasn't necessarily because they agreed on anything.

"I think you have a choice to make, Alex. This town, your town, will need some rebuilding after all this. You can be an important part of that. You can write the bad with the good, but the goal is to help the people who read our paper feel good about their lives and their community."

Chapa shook his head.

"That's not the goal at all, Matt."

The old chair squealed as Sullivan stood.

"Well, here's how it is. Macklin isn't going to fire you for the same reasons he didn't kill your story."

"Because he can't"

"If you like, sure. But moving on, we're all going to need a shared vision of purpose."

"*A shared vision of purpose?* Are you hearing yourself, Matt?"

"Think about what you want your role to be going forward. It's about the future, now, Alex."

Chapa rubbed his palm across his face and chin as Sullivan's words sank in.

"Matt, Did your mother ever read you the story, *The Emperor's New Clothes*?"

"I think so. You mean the one where the kid is the only person who's willing to tell the truth about the emperor actually being naked? Sure, Alex, I know it."

"Ever wonder how that kid ended up?"

Sullivan's brow curled as he appeared to be giving the question some consideration. Or maybe he was just trying to gauge where Chapa was going with this.

"Not really, Alex. Why, was there a sequel?"

"No. But I'd bet he died alone, broke and forgotten."

"Why do you think that?"

"Because he told folks a truth they didn't want to hear. Because he did the right thing, and made others seem corrupt and foolish in the process."

Sullivan patted him on the arm and Chapa instantly wished he hadn't.

"You're obviously in serious pain. It's time you went home," he said, opening the door and stepping out before turning back to say one more thing. "You're a hell of a reporter, Chapa."

The door closed and Chapa was alone in his office. He sat back down, put his feet up on the desk, and looked at the photos of Nikki on his wall, thinking of all the things he'd planned on doing with her this past week. Chapa stared at the images, moments captured and opportunities lost, for a long time, allowing his thoughts to wander in whatever directions they chose to go. Until they finally started marching back home and coalescing into one, single idea.

Chapa spent ten minutes, maybe less, typing up a letter of resignation for the job he'd held for over fifteen years. He kept it professional, listing *philosophical differences* as his core reason for leaving the *Chicago Record*. But there was much more to it than that.

On his way to the hospital, and even now, he could not stop thinking about his decision to go into that house, knowing that a killer was probably waiting inside. He hadn't been Nikki's father when he did that, he was someone else. Someone who was able to forget those who relied on him just long enough to get himself into trouble.

Was that what Leah had meant? What she'd called his *instincts*?

Reaching down between a bookcase and file cabinet, he pulled out a faded gray satchel. It was a simple two-pocket denim model, all he could afford, maybe even more than, back when he bought it.

Fighting with the zipper until it finally gave, Chapa opened the rectangular bag and laid it on the desk. He then took down all of Nikki's drawings, some were on paper that had yellowed and curled in the five or six years they'd spent on the wall. He placed those in a file folder, which he slipped inside the bag, then did the same with her photos.

Chapa removed all of his notes and address books from his desk, tossed those in the bag. Then his handful of CDs, a half-empty bag of Lemonheads, and a few pens. He coaxed the crooked zipper closed, tucked the satchel under his arm, against the healthy side of his body, and got up.

Looking back at his chair, he saw how his imprint was now a permanent part of the leather backrest. Chapa took off his press pass, and dropped it onto his desk, next to the letter. He thought about all the extra hours he'd spent here, when he could've been home with Carla and Nikki. The late and canceled dates with Erin, and all of the things he'd put off just to get that extra quote or different angle.

Did any of it matter now?

Maybe it was time to revise his instincts—if that was possible. Chapa was willing to find out. He took one last quick look around, turned off his desk lamp, and walked out.

Chapter 100

Three days later

Chapa's mail contained the usual assortment of bills, offers, and junk. But on this day there was something else, too.

The simple white envelope felt thin, like there was nothing inside. He held it up to the sunlight, but couldn't see through, and checked the postmark—*Ortonville, Minnesota.*

Never heard of it, Chapa thought as he tossed the other pieces of mail on a small table by the door.

"It's a beautiful day, let's not waste it," he called toward the top of the stairs.

The envelope had no return address, and for a moment Chapa worried that this might be some sort of threat from a disgruntled reader. Maybe one who saw his work on the Internet. But he shook off that concern—after all, who in Minnesota would want to harm him—and tore open the top of the envelope.

Inside, Chapa found a memo cube–sized piece of paper folded in half. As he unfolded it, a smaller piece fell out and drifted to the floor.

Chapa squatted, picked it up and turned it over. Smiling up at him was a black-and-white photo of Charles Stoop's head. He looked several years younger, but Chapa had no trouble recognizing him. It had been cut out of a magazine.

He dropped the envelope on the table and slowly opened the note. The message had been written using rub-on letters.

It is over.

Chapa doubted that very much. And though the postmark may have been from Ortonville, Minnesota, Chapa knew that by now the man who sent the letter could be in Oak Grove, South Carolina, Oakland, California, or anywhere in between.

"What is that, Daddy?"

Nikki was wearing pink stretch pants, a green sweater with butterflies on the front, and a bright blue pair of those soft shoes with all the holes on top.

"Just another piece of junk mail," he said, tossing it into a drawer before opening the door for Nikki.

He would turn this one over to investigators, there were certainly enough of those around to choose from now. Led by Special Agent Joseph Andrews, the FBI had descended on Oakton over the past couple of days, and begun dissecting the city's politics and deal making, and what role any of it might've played in the area's recent murder epidemic.

Dr. Bendix's plane had been found the morning after Greg Vinsky's disappearance. Andrews sent Agent Sandro and a team out to look for it after he explained to his superiors how he'd helped Chapa survive a crash. When asked why he had failed to inform the Federal Aviation Administration or his boss about the incident, Andrews told them he'd wanted to keep an ongoing investigation into the Oakton murders quiet until he'd gathered enough information.

Andrews took some heat for that decision, but not much. It was the only lie he told, as far as Chapa knew. But knowing the man as well as he did, Chapa understood that single transgression had led to several sleepless nights for his friend.

Chapa was now cooperating with the FBI, having turned all of his and Chakowski's notes over to them, as well as the recording of his conversation with Bendix, along with the doctor's flight log. He owed Andrews a meal or two or more. But their friendship remained solid, like always.

The investigation had turned into a Get Out of Jail Free card for Warren Chakowski, who was now helping the feds determine how his brother's death fit into the puzzle. The charges against Warren had been dropped, in part on Chapa's insistence and his promise to Andrews that in exchange he would never climb into another small plane unless Andrews himself was at the controls.

"You know what, Al, not even then," Andrews said, amending his original demand.

As he drove through Oakton, Chapa realized how different this town looked to him now from the way it had the day he brought Nikki back. The place would never be the same.

Vinsky's killing spree had ended the morning after the explosion, when a body washed up on a small island in the Fox River, just south of downtown Aurora. A group of grade schoolers had seen its feet swaying from side to side with the current as they crossed a bridge on their way to a science museum. A store manager at Lansford's Megamart identified the dead man as the same one who was seen wandering through his store in a daze the night before.

But Chapa was certain that what had come to an end in Chicago's western suburbs would, in time, begin somewhere else. Andrews believed that, too, after nothing could be found to prove who Vinsky actually was or that he'd even existed before arriving in Oakton. The feds were working with authorities in Baltimore to reopen several old murder cases. With Chapa's help, Jan Boll was on the front lines of the reporting on that investigation.

Charles Stoop also proved to be something of a mystery man. Authorities were able to trace Stoop's history back to his previous business in Marion, Iowa, but that was where the trail ended. Connecting him to anyone named Gilley had been a dead end, so far.

After stopping at Blake's Burgers and grabbing a couple of cheeseburgers and orders of fries and drinks to go, Chapa drove to Rocket Park and let Nikki choose their picnic table. The place was empty except for the two of them.

Chapa had counted on that, this being a school day. If there had been other kids her age, Nikki would have wanted to play with them. But Chapa was feeling selfish today, and wanted her to himself.

He would have to drive her to O'Hare the following morning and put her on a plane to Boston.

"Will I get a chance to say goodbye to Erin and Mike again before I leave?" Nikki asked through a mouthful of fries.

"You already did. That's why we stopped there for a moment last night."

She knocked back the mass of food with a big swig of lemonade.

"Is it my fault that you two broke up, Daddy?"

"No. None of what happened is in any way your fault. And we didn't necessarily break up. We've just decided to spend a little time apart so we can sort things out. Adults do that sometimes."

She nodded and took a bite of her burger, but Chapa could almost hear the wheels spinning in his daughter's mind. He had no idea how it would turn out between Erin and him. Except for that brief visit the night before, they had not seen each other or spoken in two days. He already missed the sound of her voice, and had begun noticing the smell of her fragrance in his clothes. It made him feel close to Erin and ache for her at the same time.

"Did you and Mom ever spend time apart to sort things out?"

Chapa took a bite of his sandwich, chewed it slowly to buy himself some time to decide how to best answer.

"Yes, we did."

"It didn't work out too good, did it?"

"You know how it worked out, but I don't think your mom and I were in love with each other anymore by then."

"But you both still loved me?"

"Very much, Nikki," Chapa said reaching across the table and clutching her mustard-smeared hand. "Your mother and I will always love you more than anything in the world."

Nikki smiled and a thin line of catsup curled along her upper lip.

"And you and Erin still love each other, don't you?"

Chapa took a deep breath. The cold air filling his lungs pressed against the wound in his ribs, and he wondered if it would ever fully heal.

"I hope so, Nik. I know how I feel about her."

"That's cool then, cuz she loves you too, so it'll all work out."

She crumpled the napkins and french fries container inside the hamburger wrapper, and ran over to toss it in a waste can.

"C'mon, Dad, let's go up in the rocket," she said, racing toward the giant slide.

Chapa swallowed his last bite, chugged the rest of his soda, and cleaned up the table. Watching Nikki climb to the top, he felt good about the arrangements his attorney had already made for him to visit her around Thanksgiving, then again at Christmastime.

He had not told Nikki anything about quitting the paper. There was no reason to burden a ten-year-old with that kind of problem, and he didn't want it to become the central issue or even a passing topic of discussion during their last days together.

The *Record* had informed him he'd be receiving a severance package. This came as a surprise to Chapa, more so when he saw the amount. Chapa still hadn't decided whether it was a case of guilt or old-fashioned ass-covering, but he was leaning toward the latter.

Zach had been promoted to a staff position, which came as great news to Chapa. They were planning on meeting for lunch some day soon.

Chapa had heard Duane Wormley was heartbroken. First, because his departure could mean Wormley would have to do some hard reporting, and then came the news that he wasn't being promoted.

Chapa's office was left empty and untouched, just like Chakowski's. Two time capsules of a lost industry.

Nikki was waiting for him at the top, her legs resting on the slide.

"Can I come live with you sometime?"

She'd hinted at this twice before in the past day.

"You can visit, Sweetie, but your home is in Boston. That's where your school is, and your mom and Stephen have made a nice life there for you. That's where you should be now."

Two weeks ago Chapa might've answered her question differently, or called his attorney to ask what could be done to make it happen. But a lot had changed in the last two weeks, and Chapa had accepted the fact that his life was no place for a child.

A thick breeze blew across the park, sending a wave of dried leaves from one side to another, depositing several armfuls at the bottom of the slide.

"Check it out, Nik, a soft landing."

"Let's not slide down just yet," she said.

Chapa smiled, nodded.

"How long can we stay up here, Daddy?"

He looked out over the endless blue sky, marred only by a line of clouds drifting away into the distance, put his arm around Nikki and said, "Until someone comes along and makes us go."

ACKNOWLEDGMENTS

All thanks to my super-agent Scott Miller, my talented editor John Scognamiglio, and everyone in the mystery writing community who has offered advice and encouragement, and been so supportive of my work.

Much gratitude to John Sandrolini, who acted as a key technical advisor, along with being a great friend. Joe Konrath for his pitch-perfect advice, generosity, and friendship. Leslie Rocha and J.D. Smith for the time they dedicated to helping me get it right, as well as Todd Fanscali for his great insight. And to Maggie Perez for providing valuable advice.

I owe a debt to the many booksellers who over the past year have kindly opened their doors to the new guy and treated him like a longtime member of the club.

As always, an enormous thank you to my family and friends who have been there every step of the way. And especially to Cheri, Maggie, and Kate, not just for being my biggest fans, but also for putting up with the occasional major disruption to their day-to-day. I couldn't do it without you.